STRANGERS AND PILGRIMS

Maggie Bennett

severn
House

This first world edition published 2010
in Great Britain and in the USA by
SEVERN HOUSE PUBLISHERS LTD of
9–15 High Street, Sutton, Surrey, England, SM1 1DF.
Trade paperback edition first published
in Great Britain and the USA 2011 by
SEVERN HOUSE PUBLISHERS LTD.

British Library Cataloguing in Publication Data

Bennett, Maggie.
  Strangers and pilgrims.
  1. Friars–England–Fiction. 2. Great Britain–History–
  Edward III, 1327-1377–Fiction. 3. Historical fiction.
  I. Title
  823.9'2-dc22

  ISBN-13: 978-0-7278-6927-2   (cased)
  ISBN-13: 978-1-84751-267-3   (trade paper)

Except where actual historical events and characters are being
described for the storyline of this novel, all situations in this
publication are fictitious and any resemblance to living persons
is purely coincidental.

All Severn House titles are printed on acid-free paper.

Severn House Publishers support The Forest Stewardship Council [FSC],
the leading international forest certification organisation. All our titles that
are printed on Greenpeace-approved FSC-certified paper carry the FSC logo.

Mixed Sources
Product group from well-managed
forests and other controlled sources
www.fsc.org Cert no. SA-COC-1565
© 1996 Forest Stewardship Council

Typeset by Palimpsest Book Production Ltd.,
Falkirk, Stirlingshire, Scotland.
Printed and bound in Great Britain by
MPG Books Ltd., Bodmin, Cornwall.

To my Muse

Acknowledgements

Acknowledgements are due to:

As ever, Judith Murdoch, literary agent extraordinary

My sister Jenny and daughter Rosalind for
valuable assistance with research

The staff at Halesworth Library, always helpful and patient

Prologue

September 1340

The screams of agony had ceased, though Master Ralph de Courcy thought the sound of his young wife's unendurable suffering would ring in his ears for the rest of his life. They heard no newly born baby's cry; a heavy silence hung over the whole house. He and Mr Justice Carver had sat up all night, and the first rays of daylight showed through the gap between the curtains. Ralph leaned over the table, his head resting on his folded arms.

The maidservant appeared at the foot of the stairs. 'If ye please, sir, Mistress Carver says to send for the priest,' she said, looking scared.

Carver rose from his chair, his eyes red from lack of sleep, his complexion muddy. 'Call Toby, and send him straightway to the Friary,' he told her. 'It's nearest, and we know they'll send somebody.'

They heard her go into the kitchen where the manservant slept on a wooden cot-bed that folded up by day. He was already awake and dressed; she gave him the order, and the back door slammed shut.

I should have gone, thought Ralph. It would have been right and fitting that I should fetch the Holy Sacrament to her. He glanced at his father-in-law, but Carver did not meet his eye; neither of them dared put their thoughts into words. Ralph stared into space, the deathly silence telling him that all his prayers had gone unanswered.

When Toby returned with the black-robed Dominican, Carver rose to greet him, and pointed to the stairs. He beckoned to Ralph, and spoke quietly.

'Come, Master de Courcy, we shall witness her farewell.' He followed the friar, and Ralph climbed the stairs behind them. The bedroom door was open, and Ralph, who had waited all night to see his wife, now hesitated in fear; Carver beckoned him again, and he entered the room, standing behind the friar. Mistress Carver sat beside her daughter's bed, and the midwife stood on the other side; both women had been weeping. There was no sign of a newly born child, and when Ralph looked upon his wife lying white and still on the bed, he saw that she was dead, and that the child had died within her, unborn. He could hardly suppress a groan, and as if in a terrible dream, he watched and listened as the friar uttered the Latin words of the Sacrament over her, and dipping his forefinger into a little phial of consecrated oil, he touched her forehead and mouth with it. Then they all knelt with hands together while the friar prayed in English for Francesca's soul and that of her unbaptized child; he prayed for the family she left behind, beseeching forgiveness for their sins and time for amendment of life. They all replied 'Amen,' though Ralph scarcely understood what he was saying, so stricken was he with grief and guilt.

His wife Francesca, little Fay, only just past her sixteenth birthday, was dead. He had been honoured – and flattered – when Justice Carver had proposed the marriage. He was eight years older than Fay, and had suggested that the marriage be postponed for a year or two, but Carver had argued that other girls were mothers at fifteen, and when her father asked her if she would like to be wife to Master de Courcy, she had smiled shyly and nodded her assent. Mistress Carver had not entirely approved, and told her husband that Fay was too young, and knew nothing of men, but Carver had insisted that de Courcy should become one of the family, related to them by marriage as well as by profession, for they had been tutor and student. Carver had taken a fatherly interest in the young lawyer, who already took his place on the Common Bench, hearing civil pleas from persons or groups, and settling disputes without fear or favour, to the satisfaction of most of the petitioners. A brilliant career was prophesied for Master de Courcy, who was also blessed with a tall frame, a high forehead, wide blue eyes and curling auburn hair. Carver was happy to have played his part in the rise of this son of an apothecary and had chosen for his son-in-law one who would surely be a good husband.

But now all seemed to be lost. The young wife, the sweet-faced, fair-haired little Fay, their fairy princess, was dead in childbirth, and everything was changed; it was as if Ralph had suddenly come up against a stone wall, and could see nothing beyond it. He heard the low-voiced exchange between Carver and the friar, regarding arrangements for burial of the mother and unborn child.

"Twill be at Our Lady of the Nativity and the Holy Innocents at the end of the Strand,' said Carver. 'And she will remain here until the day of interment.'

It was as if he had no part in the matter, thought Ralph, but without resentment. The Carvers had been her parents for sixteen years, and he had known her barely a year, in which he had wedded her and known her as his lawful wife. She had conceived within a month, and while carrying the child had often felt unwell, with sickness, weariness and pains in various parts of her body. From the moment Mistress Carver had told him of his wife's condition, he had not lain with her again, and her mother had taken over her care. She was so pitifully young, and he had admired her beauty and modesty – and now she was dead because of him. He glanced warily at Mistress Carver who looked briefly back at him with condemnation in her eyes, then lowered her head as if to banish the sight of him.

When the Dominican had left the house of mourning, Ralph felt he had to breathe fresh air. Without uttering a word he left the room and went silently down the stairs. Picking up his black fur-trimmed lawyer's cloak, he threw it around his shoulders, pulling the hood up and forward over his face.

Clear morning light fell upon the city churches' spires and the ecclesiastical palaces that lined the south aspect of the Strand, as far as Charing Cross to the west, and including the magnificent Savoy Palace, with its orchards and terraced gardens sloping down to the river Thames, glittering in the sunshine. Master de Courcy stood looking blankly at the fair city that had become his home, thanks to Justice Carver's patronage, his advising and encouraging, discreetly sending work de Courcy's way.

But now Fay was dead, and it seemed she had taken her husband's career with her. He could not even think about his former ambition, the wealth and prestige that would have been his if life had taken its expected course. What should he do now? Wrapping his cloak against the chill autumnal breeze, he walked towards the Strand and the church of Our Lady of the Nativity and the Holy Innocents. Perhaps he would find spiritual direction there, if he was still able to pray.

One

Facing his father had not been easy for Ralph de Courcy. The apothecary had taken great pride in the meteoric rise of his second son from a nondescript street in Salisbury to become the youngest lawyer on the Common Bench, with a strong probability that he would one day be a judge at the court of the King's Bench, looking into such serious accusations as treason and crimes against the state. And now here he was, proposing to give up his glittering career, declaring that he could not return to his life in the law; and that he intended to enter a monastery and spend his days in prayer, work and obedience to the Rule until death.

'Much as I sympathize with you, Ralph, this would be a great mistake,' de Courcy said. 'Why should the death of your young wife, tragic though it was, end your prospects of a distinguished position in the Judiciary? Nor should it stop you from marrying a second time and siring living children, perhaps a son to follow you into the law.'

'No, Father, I have no desire whatever to marry again – in fact the very thought of it brings back that terrible night of Francesca's death,' Ralph had answered with a slight shudder. 'I caused her such abominable suffering and robbed her of life, hers and the child's. Mistress Carver never wants to set eyes on me again, and I do not blame her. No, don't speak again, Father, for I have made up my mind. I shall present myself at some monastic house away from the world, and ask to be admitted into a community of brothers.'

The apothecary was aghast. 'You, a strong young man of but four and twenty years, with all your knowledge and learning, to shut yourself away from the world, wasting it all on a life of wretched poverty, like a plant starved of sunshine? Besides, it would be against your nature,' he added. 'You're not cut out to be a contemplative, it would be a prison. I can only beg you to reconsider, for your own sake and that of your sorrowing mother.'

Mistress de Courcy echoed her husband's words, but felt keenly for her son's grief. She counselled a time of reflection before making any decision.

'Your eyes are clouded by your grief and regret, my son, and you cannot see clearly,' she said gently, laying her hand over his as they sat on the bench behind the pharmacy. 'Allow yourself a full year to mourn for her, until you regain your rightful mind. By all means take on the duties of a lay brother in some monastic order, but do not take vows or commit yourself in any way during that time. That is what I advise, dear Ralph, for I must agree with your father that you are not fitted for a monastic life.'

Ralph saw that further discussion would be of no use, for he could not convey to his parents his utter desolation of spirit. How could he blame them for not understanding, he reproachfully asked himself, when he could not begin to put into words his miserable uncertainty, even to himself? To become a holy monk, living apart from the world, would surely put an end to further questioning about his future: his thinking would be done for him by his obedience to the Rule. Yet he still agonized over his vocation: did he actually have a call from God? Surely he must have, for he longed for the silence of the cloister in a way that his parents could not understand.

Mistress de Courcy managed to persuade him to visit his elder brother John who had trained with their father and now worked from his own premises in the centre of Salisbury. He aspired to become a surgeon apothecary, and was a respected practitioner of his craft, married to a docile wife who had borne him three children in as many years. Ralph had accordingly visited their fine stone house, and found them willing to advise and entertain the sorrowing widower, extolling the virtues of family life by example rather than argument.

Ralph was not naturally drawn to children, but was unexpectedly touched when his three-year-old niece toddled towards him and held up her arms to be lifted on to his knee, while her younger brother shyly ran to hide his face in his mother's skirt.

John de Courcy laughed out loud when he entered the room and saw his scholarly, black-clad brother nursing the little girl who yawned and closed her eyes.

'Well, here's a sight I never thought to see, Ralph! You with a—' He quickly checked himself, remembering his brother's recent loss; this was no time for mockery. He was also taken aback by Ralph's gaunt appearance and loss of weight.

'Good day to you, John,' said Ralph, smiling. 'My apologies for not rising to greet you, but as you can see I'm otherwise engaged. Your little daughter has fallen asleep.'

John de Courcy nodded and sat down on a cross-legged stool. He had sometimes envied his younger brother's success as a lawyer, while he had followed in their father's footsteps and now pursued a lucrative profession as an apothecary, much in demand. His premises were larger than his father's, and his skills included treating injuries and common ailments, as well as dispensing the herbal medicines he made up from his own garden. He advised on coughs and agues, blocked and loose bowels; he lanced boils and drew teeth, tied wooden splints to broken limbs, and stitched wounds with silk thread. He had built up a reputation for accurate diagnoses, and now attempted to advise his melancholic brother.

'Your wife's death was deeply distressing, Ralph, and your grief is natural,' he said seriously, 'but you won't improve by moping in this idle, unprofitable way – unprofitable in *every* way, for you still need to earn a living. And what's this father tells me about you turning away from the workaday world to become a *monk*?'

'It is true, John. I have no more interest in the world.'

'Good God, Brother, this is folly indeed! You need to rejoin the world, not hide away from it. I can't think of a man less fitted for the monastic life – you'd have to deny your very nature as a man, and your health would suffer. Take my word for it, Brother, the time will come again when you'll need to satisfy those needs which we all share – to find a woman such as I have found, to lie with her in holy wedlock and sire children—'

'No, no, John, say no more, I have lost all interest in women, and would fear to harm – to *kill* another one such as Francesca,' Ralph broke in, almost choking on the words. 'She has taken away all that part of my nature, and I long only for a life of quietness and contemplation. I don't expect you to understand, but my life is changed beyond mending, and I shall never be as I was before. The world means nothing to me.'

'For God's sake, Brother, you speak like an old man. You're young and strong, and women will always be interested in your body, and let's not pretend otherwise. Where's your resolution? Where's your pride? If you only knew how much I once envied you your—'

'Oh, say no more, Brother, for Christ's sake! Take this dear child away from me before I drop her, and let her sleep in a more peaceful place!'

His voice rose, and the child awoke as her mother hurried into the room and took her from her uncle's arms. She gave him a stern look.

'I heard shouting, and wondered what—' she began, but her husband cut her short.

'Hold your tongue, wife, and take the child,' he ordered, and she left the room, kissing and cooing at her little daughter.

The apothecary rose and poured wine for them both from a flagon in a recess of the wall; he handed the cup to his brother, laying a hand on his shoulder as he spoke.

'Here, Ralph, drink this. It will soothe your troubled mind. I should not have spoken as I did, being more used to mending broken heads than hearts.'

Ralph lowered his head, taking a gulp of the wine.

'What you need is not medicine but good counsel,' his brother continued, 'and that will mean consulting a man of God, a man of the church. An abbot, or a priest, perhaps, a man used to hearing confessions and giving absolution. Can you think of any such?'

'There is a bishop who sits on the King's Bench as a lawyer and judge,' replied Ralph. 'He knows me through Justice Carver, and may consent to give me an audience. Thank you, Brother, as much for your understanding as for the wine. I am grateful.'

The great Abbey of St Peter, founded before the Norman Conquest by Edward the Confessor, king and saint, dominated Westminster with all the magnificence of Gothic architecture. Expansion was still in progress when Master de Courcy entered the west door on a cold, blustery day at the end of November, and made his way to the Lady Chapel where he was to meet the learned Bishop of Ebbchester. He knelt down before the icon of the Blessed Virgin Mary and Child, and said an *Ave* to her, begging for direction and guidance. He was still on his knees when the bishop entered, a man in middle age, wearing a lawyer's gown edged and lined with squirrel fur and a scholar's black velvet cap. He stood in silence until Ralph had finished his prayer and opened his eyes; as soon as he saw the bishop standing beside him, he hastily rose to his feet.

'My Lord Bishop,' he murmured, and bowed, kissing the ring on the man's finger.

'Master de Courcy, we have met before as lawyers, and I offer condolence on your recent loss,' came the pleasant reply as the bishop gestured towards a wooden bench that had been placed in the chapel for this meeting. 'Tell me all that is in your heart, my son, your grief for the young wife and child, now at rest in the Father's love, redeemed by the blood of Christ.'

Ralph thought the words held a hint that the time for mourning was due to end. He nodded. 'She and the child are at rest, my Lord Bishop, but I have lost all interest and ambition for worldly advancement,' he began, and he poured out his heart, much as he had done to his parents and brother, but with the added dimension of his Christian faith: his desire to sacrifice his life to God as a holy monk with no other object in life but to pray and work in the company of like-minded brethren.

The Bishop listened in silence, nodding at intervals, frowning or smiling as the torrent of words expressed the grief and guilt that had led Ralph to this desire to renounce the world. When at last he ceased, the two men sat for a while in silence. Then the bishop rose, and beckoned Ralph to accompany him on a walk beneath the open cloisters built around a stone-paved courtyard.

'Wrap your cloak closely round you, Master de Courcy, for the wind is keen. Let us take the Eastern walk first. It is here that the Abbot of this place kneels to wash the feet of a dozen poor men, usually old and frail, on Maundy Thursday, in imitation of our Saviour Christ who washed the feet of His disciples, showing himself to be the servant as well as the Saviour of mankind. That is the example that you will have to follow, de Courcy, if you dedicate your life to His service.'

'That duty I will willingly perform,' answered Ralph promptly.

'Indeed? As willingly as you submit to having your fine head of hair tonsured?' the Bishop continued.

'Yes, my Lord.'

'And to eat vegetables and cheese in place of roasted meats, raw fruit in place of pastry tarts, water in place of wine?'

'Certainly, my Lord.'

'And never to know a full night's sleep, but to attend the eight Divine Offices throughout the day and night?'

'It will be my bounden duty and service, my Lord.'

'For the rest of your life, until released by death, and to be buried in the cemetery of that place?' The Bishop's tone was made more harsh by knowing that he himself would not be able to commit himself to such a life.

'Yes, my Lord.'

'Well, then, Master de Courcy, I recommend that you apply to a monastery such as the Abbey at Netley in Hampshire. It overlooks Southampton Water, and houses an order of Cistercian monks who strictly follow the Benedictine Rule. It was founded just over a hundred years ago, and is dedicated to the Blessed Virgin Mary and Edward the Confessor.

'If you wish, I can recommend you to the Abbot, to be admitted to the community, not as a novice but as a lay brother for a year, working under the monks who have special responsibilities such as bursar, sacristan and infirmarian. As such, you will be excused some of the Daily Offices, and will take voluntary vows for a year, living in subservience to the choir monks, observing the rules of silence and obeying them in all things, speaking only when spoken to. At the end of a year you will be submitted to the scrutiny of the Abbot and his senior monks, who will question you and examine the validity of your calling. If you still then wish to take final vows, and are accepted by the brotherhood, you will be admitted to the Order as a novice for such time as the Abbot sees fit, and then take your lifelong vows as a full choir monk. If not—' The Bishop paused and looked at Ralph intently, eye to eye: 'If not, then you will be released and able to return to the world, free to continue in your profession and to marry. That, my son, is the best counsel I can give you, either to accept or reject.'

'I gladly accept your wise counsel, my Lord, for to tell the truth, it is much the same as my mother gave me, for she hopes to change my mind,' Ralph admitted with a smile. 'And I gratefully accept your offer to commend me to the Abbot – for which I thank you from my heart.'

'May God's blessing go with you, de Courcy,' said the Bishop, adding in Latin, 'Father, Son and Holy Ghost, be with you now and forever. Amen.'

'Amen,' Ralph fervently echoed. At last some progress had been made. No longer racked with uncertainty, he was about to set out on a spiritual quest; light had been shone on his path, and he was determined to follow wherever it led.

It was halfway into December when Ralph made the journey down to Southampton, riding Greyling, the placid mare he had bought two years previously; he intended to make a gift of her to the Abbey on his arrival. Strongly advised not to travel alone in winter weather through dense forest and windy heathland, he returned to London to look around for travelling companions, and found three soldiers who were going that way; one was a sergeant-at-arms, and the other two said they were new recruits, though Ralph suspected they wanted to escape from London, having committed some kind of misdemeanour. Shortly before they set out, a worried-looking woman dressed in black begged de Courcy to allow her and her daughter, a silent girl of about fourteen, to travel with them, and there were no objections; the women rode their own horses, and were able to fit their belongings into the panniers carried by a couple of packhorses hired by Ralph and the sergeant. The mother introduced herself as Dame Crocker, a farmer's widow, and her daughter Margery; she was almost tearfully grateful for the protection of four men on a journey of about eighty miles. As they left London, the conviction came to Ralph it was his first step at the start of a spiritual pilgrimage, travelling with strangers.

The sergeant suggested that they stop at Guildford, about halfway along, and spend a night there; Ralph agreed, knowing that there was a Dominican friary in that town where he could find good lodging.

Little was said on the first day of travel. Ralph and the sergeant rode in front, the women behind them, and the young recruits bringing up the rear; these two muttered to each other, and gave loud guffaws of laughter from time to time, which Ralph found irritating. He suspected that their jokes were coarse and insulting to the women, but the sergeant did not seem to heed them. From time to time Ralph turned round and glared at them, and let it be known that he was a lawyer; he did not reveal the purpose of his journey, and when asked said briefly that he had business in Southampton, which was true enough. By the time darkness was falling over the winter landscape they were all tired, even the recruits, so they rode down into Guildford in silence.

Having invited Dame Crocker and her daughter to come with him to the friary, he was dismayed when the gatekeeper told him that no women were allowed to stay there.

'They can stay over at St Catherine's chapel; there are nuns there who will take them in, but it's a fair way out of the town,' he said. By now it was dark and very cold; Ralph turned to the woman and suggested that she and Margery go up to the Angel Inn where the three soldiers had gone. She was utterly dismayed.

'By my faith, Master de Courcy, I have no wish to lodge my daughter at an inn full of soldiers and riff-raff,' she said. 'Could you – *would* you be so good as to lodge there too, sir? I will pay you in silver for your protection.'

'No, no, Dame Crocker, I will not take money from you. Come, I will escort you both up to the Angel, and lodge there myself.'

The poor widow called down blessings upon his head, and Ralph regretfully left the friary and pointed Greyling up to the inn, now aglow with candle and firelight; the recruits had already made themselves at home, and were seated at a table drinking and entertaining the other travellers, all men. There was a loud laugh as Ralph entered with the two women.

'By God, he's going to make merry tonight!' said one of the recruits with a grin. 'They're all canting rogues, them lawyers – making out he was protecting 'em from the likes of us!'

'He's welcome to 'em,' answered his companion. 'One's been hanging on the tree too long, and the other's as yet unripe!'

Ralph coloured with embarrassment, and called at once for the landlord, demanding a room for the ladies, and one for himself next door to theirs.

'Just as you say, sir,' replied the man with a disagreeably knowing wink, and called a maidservant to take them upstairs and show them two adjacent rooms. Ralph ordered supper to be sent up, and divided the cold meat, bread and cheese between the three of them. He also ordered a bottle of wine to be shared.

'May heaven reward you, Master de Courcy,' said Dame Crocker, and Ralph felt that he had indeed been rewarded, though he passed a restless night, disturbed by loud talk and raucous singing. He told Dame Crocker to lock her door for safety.

On the road the next day, conversation was freer. He learned that the widow's late husband's brother had laid claim to the farmhouse and land rightfully hers, and having no sons to take up her case, she and her daughter were on their way to her parents' home near Southampton, taking their horses and what clothing and valuables that could be packed into panniers. Ralph was appalled at such injustice, and was sorry he was no longer a practising lawyer, and therefore unable to use his legal skill and judgment on her behalf. He could only give her the name of a Southampton lawyer she could consult and who might take up her case.

At mid-afternoon they came to within a mile or so of Southampton, and Ralph first saw Netley Abbey distantly silhouetted against the darkening red sky. He bade farewell to his companions who continued on towards the town, while he rode towards the huge edifice established by Cistercian monks a hundred years previously. It reminded him of the great Abbey of St Peter's at Westminster, where he had talked with the Bishop: it had the same magnificent French-inspired Gothic architecture; the same long windows, dark now in the half-light, though from the Abbey there was a glow behind the row of Norman-arched windows, where Ralph guessed the monks would be at Vespers.

He reined in Greyling, and she stood still as he gazed at the place which was to be his home, a spiritual refuge from the world for the coming year.

'Father in heaven,' he prayed. 'Direct my steps and instruct me how to travel this road.'

Then he patted Greyling's flank, and turned her head towards the Abbey.

Two

1341

When he heard the great abbey bell sound for the Office of None, the grey-haired infirmarian Brother Luke knew that the lay brother working in the herb garden would put his head round the open door to say he was off to attend in the church, though he was not under obligation to do so; and sure enough, Brother Ralph straightened himself up, wiped his arm across his brow and rubbed the dry soil off his hands.

'I'll come straight back, Brother Luke,' he said, and strode off to the church where he joined in the singing of the noonday Office, and gave thanks for the past six months at Netley Abbey, the privilege of working under Brother Luke and the kindred souls he had met, especially Brothers Paulus and Martin. The former was a choir monk and the latter a novice, therefore above him in the hierarchy of the thirty monks and twenty-four lay brothers; close attachments were not encouraged, and his only chance to speak with either of them occurred during the one rest hour of each day.

He gave thanks too that he was able to attend all eight Offices each day, from Matins just after midnight until Compline at six or seven in the evening, without neglecting any of his work, currently in the infirmary. He had completed a three-month stint in the kitchen, preparing the simple vegetable dishes and baking the bread to serve with cheese in the refectory, and had helped in the kitchen garden where the brothers grew their own beans, parsnips and onions, and kept bees to supply them with honey. He had grown leaner, his muscles strengthened by hard labour, and his face tanned by the sun; only the darkened skin beneath his blue eyes betrayed chronic lack of sleep due to attending the night Offices of Matins, Lauds and Prime.

Brother Luke had a cup of fruit cordial waiting for him on his return, and shook his head while Ralph drank it.

'I'm astonished, Brother, at your gentleness towards our sick and infirm old brothers, however difficult they may be, yet you show no mercy towards yourself,' he observed. 'You work your body to the point of exhaustion and starve your brain of sleep. Is it for some penance you have to pay?'

Ralph smiled, for he liked the old infirmarian. 'Yes, in a way, Brother Luke. While I work or pray throughout the day, I have no time to spend on self-pity or self-blame. The rigorous regime of the Abbey suits me well, and keeps old memories at bay.'

'My dear young brother, we can never keep old memories at bay; if we banish them from our waking hours, they will return to intrude upon us in sleep.'

'Not with me, Brother Luke,' replied Ralph. 'When I get up to attend the night Offices, the prayers always remind me of the infinite mercy of God.'

He put down the empty mug, and turned towards the door, but stopped in his tracks as an unfamiliar sound drifted up the hill, upraised voices and horses' hooves, distant at first but coming closer. A group of a dozen or so men and a few women came into view, bearing two litters on which bodies lay, one still and silent, the other groaning. One of the riders drew ahead of the others, and Ralph recognized the mare Greyling that he had given to the Abbey, now being ridden by the Abbot.

'Brother Luke! Where's Brother Luke?' demanded the Abbot, dismounting as the infirmarian hurried forward. 'There's been trouble in the town, Brother, a falling-out between rival stonemasons, and regrettably a fight broke out. You'll know Master Ridout –' he gestured towards one of the litters – 'he's done work for us, and we shall certainly need his services again. He's come for such succour as we can give him, and the benefit of your healing skills. The other's a young lad who got caught up in the affray. He seems to have no parents, so he may also lie here to be mended if God so wills.'

'Even so, Father Abbot,' replied Brother Luke, quickly grasping the situation. 'Get them on to beds,' he ordered the townsmen who carried the litters. 'Brother Ralph, you attend to the boy, and I'll see to Master Ridout. We'll need some help to fetch and carry for us.'

The Abbot sent at once for two more lay brothers from the kitchen, and bid them do exactly as Brother Luke told them.

Master Ridout had cuts and bruises to his face, and his left arm hung uselessly from his shoulder; he groaned loudly, and uttered curses against his assailant, of whom there was no sign. Ralph uttered a prayer under his breath as he turned to the youth, now lying on a straw-filled palliasse, unconscious from a blow on the head, and there was a dagger wound in his belly from which blood oozed; his breathing was shallow, and he was deathly pale.

'Help me remove his tunic – gently, now, be careful,' said Ralph to his hastily summoned assistant. 'Fetch me water and handcloths – and some wool to staunch the blood.' He dipped a pad of clean sheep's wool in cold water and placed it over the wound, holding it in place while he removed dirt and blood from the skin around it, using his other hand.

'How is he?' called Brother Luke over his shoulder as he examined Master Ridout.

'The blood's beginning to clot,' Ralph answered. 'I shall hold the wool over it until the bleeding stops.' If it ever does, he thought grimly. Outside, the Abbot was dismissing the rest of the townspeople, including a young woman who asked to be allowed to see her brother, whose name she said was Nick Geddes.

'We have no women in any part of the Abbey,' he told her firmly. 'When the brothers have attended to him, one of them will come and tell you how he fares.' He returned to the bedside where Ralph watched anxiously as the youth stirred and moaned feebly.

'He has a swelling on the back of his head, Father Abbot, and it will be very sore,' said Ralph, keeping his hand in place over the belly wound, and motioning the lay brother to wring out a handcloth to place over the swelling. 'And he needs to drink water if you can hold a cup to his lips.'

'I'll do it,' said the Abbot. 'Come now, young Nick, you must drink plenty of water – come, do as you're told and take from this cup – ah, good, that's better!'

The bleeding seemed to have stopped, and Ralph slowly lifted his hand from the blood-soaked lump of wool.

'It must stay there, for it's plugging the bleeding,' he said, calling his assistant to bring more wool to place over the first. 'We can secure it with a bandage for a few hours, and keep him lying still – and he must be kept warm, too, he's shivering even in this heat.'

'Ah, Brother Ralph, I see you have a physician's sure touch,' said the Abbot, and turned to the other man. 'How fares Master Ridout, Brother Luke?'

'His left arm is broken, Father, but I think there is not much else amiss,' said the infirmarian, who had gently straightened the man's arm and tied it with bandages to a stout ash walking stick, one of those used by the sick and elderly monks in his care. 'It must be kept still, or it won't heal and won't be strong enough for working with stone.' He raised his voice sufficiently for Ridout to hear, and then went over to look at Nick, who was sighing and licking his dry lips with his equally dry tongue.

'We must offer him water as often as he can take it, for he has lost a fair amount of blood,' Ralph said. 'I'll add a spoonful of honey to each cup, and put it to his lips as often as he can swallow it. I don't know what damage the knife has done in his belly.'

'Thank you, Brother, I will go and tell that to his sister,' said the Abbot. 'And Dame Ridout is also waiting for news of her husband. I release you both from attending Vespers.'

He left the infirmary, and Ralph looked down at the ashen-faced Nick Geddes. 'God save you and grant you further life,' he muttered, for he felt a special interest in this young stranger's fate: it was important to him that Geddes should recover from his near-fatal wound.

The warm weather continued, the heat penetrating even through the thick stone walls of the Abbey; both monks and lay brothers found their woollen habits too warm, though they wore no underclothing. Ralph now slept on a bed in the infirmary, to keep a watch on the two injured men, and slipped out into the velvet blackness of the summer nights for the Office of Matins and into the cool dawn for Prime. Master Ridout groaned and cursed when the pain from his arm woke him up, and young Nick was running a high fever, and mumbling in his delirium. The dagger wound no longer bled, but the site was red and swollen, discharging thick green matter that made Brother Luke shake his head. Ralph constantly held sweetened water to his lips, and re-dressed the wound regularly with honey and clean new wool. The Abbot gave him the Last Rites which seemed to do him good, for he was awake the following morning when Ralph returned from Prime, and was asking for somebody called May.

'May – oh, May, where are you?' he asked, looking up at Ralph who by now knew May to be Nick's older sister who came up each day to ask about her brother. Later that day he went out to the bench seat where she sat by the fragrant herb-garden, and tried to sound encouraging without raising her hopes too high.

'Can I see him, good Brother?' she pleaded. 'If I could but see him, I'd know better than I do from just being told. *Please*, Brother, let me come to his bedside, if only once!'

He could not refuse her, and minutes later she sat beside the bed where Nick lay, pale and still, chalk-white and sunken-eyed. She held his hand and softly whispered his name.

'Nick, dear brother Nick, it's May. Can you hear me?'

Ralph felt a great pity for the girl, for she was scarcely yet a woman, in her modest grey gown and a plain little cap hiding her hair; he doubted that her words would be heard, but the boy suddenly looked up and stared straight into her face: his eyes were fever-bright and his hand gripped hers.

'May,' he said hoarsely through dry lips. 'Don't go and leave me again, May.'

'He's awake and he speaks!' she said through falling tears. 'He lives, Brother! Thanks be to God!'

Hearing a slight rustle, Ralph looked up to see the Abbot standing a few paces behind her, and frowning. He dismissed the girl sternly.

'Leave at once, and do not come within these walls again. You have no business to be here.'

After her speedy departure, the Abbot asked, 'Why did you let her in, Brother?'

'I thought the sight of her would be good for him, Father Abbot,' said Ralph. 'And so it has proved, for he knew her and spoke to her.'

'It must never happen again,' the Abbot said. 'This young man is better, and it is likely that he will live. Thanks are due to you, Brother Ralph, and in God's good time he will be able to step outside the infirmary and see his sister.'

He made the sign of the Cross over Nick, and Ralph held the cup to his lips again. The Abbot nodded.

'Remember that this Abbey is a holy house dedicated to the Virgin Mother of Christ and to King Edward the Confessor. Only men may enter, or there would be temptation.'

Ralph bowed. The reprimand was softened by the Abbot's praise, and Nick's undoubted improvement.

By the end of July Master Ridout had left the infirmary, his arm bandaged to a shorter splint. He thanked the Abbot and the brothers for their care, but had not a word to say to Nick Geddes, now able to walk slowly round his bed, leaning on two sticks. He was pale and languid, but restored to his right mind and willing to eat and drink.

'He'll soon fatten up again,' said Brother Luke. 'I didn't have much hope for him when that wound turned putrid, but it's healing now, thanks to honey by mouth and by application. We owe a lot to our bees – and to Brother Ralph!'

Ralph now found himself acknowledged by monks who had not spoken to him before. It became general knowledge that he was a lawyer and a scholar by comparison with the other lay brothers, most of whom could not read or write and had learned the Latin words of the Mass and Offices by rote. Brother Paulus told him frankly that he was too good to toil at domestic chores, and should put his knowledge of law at the disposal of the Abbey.

'Father Abbot could do with your skills as an arbitrator, Brother.'

'Surely there aren't many disputes among the brothers!'

'None that can't be solved by prayer and admonition, but I mean at the County Court in Southampton where Father Abbot regularly sits in judgment, as at the Ecclesiastic Courts. There'll soon be a session looking into the recent affray when the stone-masons came to fisticuffs – and our friend Master Ridout will use his connection with the Abbey to secure a lucrative acquittal, just mark my words.'

'Do we know the name of his rival – his opponent?' Ralph asked.

'Some poor but honest fellow with a large family to feed, so I've heard. And he's not a stonemason, merely a quarryman, fetching great cartloads of stone from the Cotswold hills. He won't stand a chance against Ridout.'

'But surely Father Abbot will give him a fair hearing?'

'He'll do his best, but Ridout will produce eyewitnesses in his favour, and show off his broken arm – whereas the quarryman's a simple fellow who won't be able to challenge him.'

'But that's unjust!'

'Expediency sometimes takes precedence over justice, in the strict meaning of the words,' said Paulus with a shrug.

Ralph probed Nick Geddes gently to find out what he could remember about the outbreak of violence in the town.

'I didn't seek any part of it, Brother Ralph. All I remember is a gang of men coming at me with clubs and knives,' Nick said wearily. 'Wherever there's a fight, all the vagrants and riff-raff come running to join one side or the other. You might get more from my sister, for she saw what happened.'

That afternoon Ralph missed the Office of None, so as to look out for May Geddes who came up every afternoon to enquire about her brother. He beckoned her to sit on the bench beside him, and questioned her as he had questioned Nick. Her story, told between sobs, matched her brother's, with the addition of her panic when she saw his helpless body on the ground with the knife in his belly; she had thought he was dead.

The lawyer in Ralph wondered if a case could be made to order Nick's attacker to make recompense to him for loss of earnings, but first the man had to be found and identified. A feeling of deep frustration came over him, helpless as he was to aid this young orphaned brother and sister. For the first time he was struck by the precariousness of the lives of the poor, and his lack of action on their behalf.

He would consult the Abbot, he decided, and plead for the brother and sister, that some kind of provision might be made for Nick, an innocent bystander who had nearly lost his life. He braced his shoulders and took several deep breaths before entering the Abbot's parlour, where he received a somewhat unsympathetic response.

'You are asking a great deal, Brother Ralph, and you have got yourself too much entangled with the lives of this young man and his sister. You were seen sitting beside the Geddes girl this afternoon, deep in conversation. This is unbecoming to a man dedicated to serving God according to the Rule of St Benedict.'

Ralph inclined his head respectfully, though he longed to disagree.

'I shall have to acquit Master Ridout in this coming trial, but I shall not pass sentence on his opponent, though it seems he did try to overcharge Master Ridout.'

Ralph inclined his head again, dismayed at hearing this, but the Abbot's next words gave him better hope.

'However, I will call young Mistress Geddes as a witness, and do what I can for Nick, perhaps a weekly payment from his parish funds until he is well enough to work.'

'Thank you, Father Abbot.' Ralph kept his face composed.

'And in return, Brother Ralph, you will promise me not to have any more contact with this pair. The boy will soon be able to leave the infirmary, and will have no further need of your care. You are not to exchange another word with the girl.'

'Very good, Father Abbot.'

'And from tomorrow you will be transferred to the Sacristy and Scriptorium, where you will assist Brother Eustace in the care of the Abbey's vessels, the chalices and candlesticks, besides laundering the vestments and altar linen. In addition, you will wait upon the monks at work on manuscripts, and test your own ability at lettering under the tuition of Brother Paulus. There is always a need for good copyists.'

'Very well, Father.'

'You have done well in the infirmary, Brother Ralph, but you are forbidden to enter it again before the end of the church year. Is that understood?'

'Yes, Father.'

'Good. And I will tell you of my success or otherwise on behalf of the young brother and sister.' He paused and said in a softer tone, 'And as Abbot of this monastery, I carry a certain weight at the County Court. I shall not fail them.'

'Thank you, Father.'

'Go in peace, my son.'

Ralph bowed his head to receive his Superior's blessing, knowing he could only pray for the Geddeses, for he might never again see them or speak to them.

★   ★   ★

It was September again, the first anniversary of Francesca's death, and a year since Ralph de Courcy had given up a promising career in the Judiciary. Looking back, he felt no regrets about the path he had chosen, and he had learned much from the time he had spent in the infirmary, especially since the Abbot had briefly informed him that the Geddes brother and sister were receiving financial help from their parish.

And yet he missed them, just as he missed Brother Luke whom he now saw only in the church or refectory, where silence was the rule, apart from a reading, often by Brother Paulus, from the New Testament and The Lives of the Saints. The rule of silence was also suspended for his tuition sessions with Brother Paulus, a man Ralph considered to be far above himself spiritually, and because the Rule discouraged close attachments, they took to including Brother Martin in their walks and talks during the rest hour, which was how Ralph and Paulus came to hear of the temptations that troubled the novice.

One mellow September afternoon the three of them were strolling in the garden, and Brother Martin brought up the subject of chastity, the excellent state in which they were required to live. The novice seemed on the edge of despair, being unable to rise above his bodily urges.

'I can't put the sin of lechery away from me, no matter how I try,' he told them in mounting agitation. 'I grow weary of fighting against my baser nature when I should be praying and meditating upon my spiritual journey. Day and night I struggle against the Devil's whisperings, and try as I do – and God knows how hard I try – I cannot get free.'

Paulus and Ralph listened with concern to their brother's unconcealed cry for help, and Paulus remarked that Martin had done well in acknowledging the nature of his problem.

'What you feel is common to most men, Brother,' he said, 'and in some of us it is more clamorous than in others. The bodily attraction between men and women is strong – it has to be, because the continuation of humankind depends upon it, but in our monastic life we must renounce it, and for some of us this is a grievous burden to bear. It has to be dealt with rather than suppressed, and its energy harnessed into channels of godliness through fervency in prayer, by hard labour, by fasting—' He stopped speaking, and turned to Ralph. 'What would *you* say to Brother Martin?'

Ralph was sympathetic, but felt he had no comment to make, simply because he did not share the dilemma. His own natural desires for fulfilment with a woman's body had been crushed out of him by the weight of grief and guilt he had suffered at his young wife's death.

Paulus and Martin were awaiting his answer, but the best he could offer was, 'Have you confessed your difficulty to our Father-in-Christ, the Abbot?'

'Yes, I have, and he told me to rid myself of impure thoughts by meditating on the Blessed Virgin Mary, which I cannot do – I dare not even try, lest I commit an even worse blasphemy,' groaned Martin. 'He spoke of mortifying my flesh by wearing a hair shirt for a day, and by spending a whole night in prayer.'

Ralph shuddered at the thought of the remorseless irritation of a hair shirt, and continued, 'St Paul exhorts us to pray without ceasing, but I beg you, Brother, not to be so hard upon yourself. Your particular temptation has been shared by holier men than ourselves, throughout the fourteen centuries since our Saviour's birth and resurrection.'

'Yes, St Benedict himself was tested and troubled as you are,' said Paulus, 'and we're told that he rolled naked in a thornbush to mortify his flesh. And yet he left us the great Benedictine Order and Rule – and that includes chastity.'

Ralph could not hide a smile at the unsaintly picture the words conjured up, but poor Brother Martin covered his face with his hands.

'And how am *I* to keep that cruel vow of chastity, the hardest of vows, when desires come to me in sleep, and I wake up to find . . . oh, God have mercy, Christ have mercy! How do *you* deal, brothers, with that most unruly of members, who seems to have a carnal mind of his own, hardening and rearing like an untamed beast, deaf to commands, disobedient to the counsels of purity – a very devil for intruding on prayer, stealing my thoughts away from holiness, even when I'm kneeling in the Abbey church – how do you keep the sin of *lust* under subjection?'

'Hush, dear Brother, calm yourself, don't attract attention,' said Paulus quickly. 'God in His infinite mercy sees what is in your heart, Brother, and knows your sincere desire to overcome temptation. Let me remind you that a hundred dreams and a hundred fantasies do not add up to one single act of sinning. Brother Ralph and I will pray that you be freed from this demon, and find peace.'

By now they had reached the cloistered courtyard, and Brother Martin tried to express his gratitude. 'God bless you, my Brothers! I will try – with God's help I will try.'

'And you and I too must go our separate ways, Brother Ralph,' said Paulus. 'We must pray for our brother at Vespers.'

Ralph returned to the Sacristy with his thoughts in turmoil. He realized how deeply he had been affected by Brother Martin's distress. How to help him he knew not, but prayed that his brother-in-Christ would be shown a way.

A few days after this encounter, Ralph experienced a sign from heaven, or so it seemed to him. It was at the midday repast, and while the brothers ate in silence, Brother Paulus got up to read aloud from a book on the lives of saints. He had a fine voice both in singing and speaking, and brought the words vividly to life; Ralph suspected that the Abbot had specially instructed Paulus to read the history of blessed St Cecilia, virgin and martyr, and patron saint of music, for the benefit of Brother Martin. He himself quickly became absorbed in the account of this young Roman woman of the second century, a Christian, given in wedlock to a husband, Valerian, whom she persuaded to be baptized a Christian and to share her vow of lifelong virginity, whereupon an angel descended to crown them both with lilies and roses, signifying white for purity, red for love. She went on to convert Valerian's brother, which incurred the wrath of the Roman prefect who ordered the brothers to recant and make sacrifices to Jove. When they refused, they were both beheaded, and Cecilia fearlessly denounced the prefect and confounded his arguments against the Holy Trinity. He sentenced her to a cruel death, and though she lingered in pain for three days, she steadfastly continued to uphold the Faith, praising God with her last breath.

Ralph was struck by the importance placed on virginity, and Cecilia's chaste marriage to Valerian, showing that celibacy could be a joyous gift from God, strong and empowering, not a sacrifice grudgingly offered. He resolved to make Cecilia his own patron

saint, and prayed that his devotion to her and her chaste husband Valerian would lead him into a deeper commitment to the Holy Trinity and to the Abbey.

When November came in with chilly mists and darkening days, Ralph was summoned to attend the Abbot in his parlour, where he received a genial greeting.

'*Deus vobiscum*. Be seated, Brother Ralph. I have an important matter to set before you,' said the Abbot with a smile. 'You have been here almost a year as a valued lay brother, and having consulted among the senior brothers who all recommend you as worthy, I am inviting you to enter on your novitiate now, with a view to taking your final vows this time next year, before Christmas. Do you agree that you are ready to take this step?'

Ralph was slightly taken aback. He had asked to spend a full year as a lay brother, at the end of which time he would review his life, and either leave the Order and return to the world, or enter upon his novitiate for a further year. But if God was calling him now, just a matter of weeks earlier than he'd planned, how could he hesitate?

'I am at the service of God and the Abbey, Father,' he replied, inclining his head.

'Good. A new novice, Brother Carlo, will be joining the Abbey then, and you will therefore be received together, just a month before Christmas. Brother Martin has left us today, and you will replace him.'

'Oh.' Ralph felt keen disappointment on hearing this, but made no comment, though the Abbot noted his brief indrawing of breath.

'Yes, Brother Martin has made his decision, and we must pray for him. Meanwhile I will grant you a week, Brother Ralph, to prepare yourself to accept the invitation that God in His gracious mercy is offering you. You will make your first vows on the Feast of Christ the King, which this year falls on the eve of St Cecilia's day, and the choir monks will sing a specially composed anthem in her honour – and for you.'

Ralph felt his heart leap in his chest. If confirmation were needed, this was surely it!

He bowed his head in acknowledgement. 'I am ready, Father

Abbot. Let me be received on that day, and pray to St Cecilia that I may be worthy of my calling.'

So Brothers Ralph and Carlo made their vows as novices at a High Mass on the Feast of Christ the King, welcomed by the Abbot and all the brothers. Ralph chose to take the name of St Cecilia's husband Valerian, and as Brother Valerian he was henceforth known in the Abbey.

Three

April 1342

Young Dan Widget sprinted round the rear wall of Ebbasterne Hall to the stables, hoping his tardiness would not be commented upon by Ned the groom whose tongue was sword-sharp. On hearing the rattle of shutters being drawn back above him, he looked up and saw the Lady herself leaning out of a high window, her hair hanging down uncombed and unplaited. She gave him a smile, and he stopped in his tracks briefly to bow to her and then run on. In the stableyard he found Ned in no sweet mood.

'Oh, there you are, Widget, not before time. Here's me been playing nursemaid to these brainless monkeys while you feed your face. Get down to those two end stables and muck them out – and move yourself. Save the dung for the bailiff – he can send a man up from the field for it.'

The 'monkeys' were young Mistress Cecily and Master Oswald, both perched up on lively ponies, while little Wulfstan and Ethelreda ran between their older brother and sister, shrieking with excitement.

'Don't know how they expect me to get my day's work done, with you young puppies snapping at me heels,' said Ned with a frown. He looked irritably at Widget. 'Well, get a move on, boy – what are you standing there gawping at?'

Widget had been about to say he'd watch over the children, but thought better of it. He smiled shyly at pretty Cecily, the eldest at sixteen, and made for the stables.

At the window of the best bedchamber Lady Wynstede looked out at the scene before and below her, calling to her husband who still lay in their curtained feather bed.

'Oh, let's go riding, Aelfric! Spring has come again, and everything's fresh and new!' she said eagerly. 'The sky's as blue as

Our Lady's mantle, and the trees are all misted over with green. Isn't this the most beautiful time of the year?'

'And the most hungry,' replied Sir Aelfric, stretching his limbs and yawning. 'Many would praise harvest time above the season of ploughing and sowing.'

'The field's like a great woven tapestry with all those strips,' she said. 'And there are daffodils on either side of the Ebbchester road, as far as I can see!'

'So be it. We'll take breakfast, and then go riding around the estate. Send word to Ned to saddle Chaser and – what steed will you have, Kat? Take Sorrel, she's a good-tempered mare, even you can ride her!'

'I can ride Sorrel as well as you can,' she replied at once, though there was a teasing affection in the look she gave him. At forty-two, Aelfric was still a handsome man, but there were deep frown lines above his nose, and his features were sharpened by the persistent pain in his right thigh from the wound he'd sustained two years previously at the Battle of Sluys. It had been a crushing defeat for the French, but it had nearly cost Wynstede his life. By the time he reached home the wound had stunk and poured with pus; he had no memory of those confused days and nights when he had raved in a sweat-drenched fever, and death had hovered around his bed. His wife Katrine would never forget the moment when after many days he had woken, pale and thin but with cool skin and in his right mind. Relief had flooded through Ebbasterne Hall, and throughout his demesne, for he was liked by his servants and tenants.

A thanksgiving Mass had been held in the Lady Chapel adjacent to the Abbey which overlooked the Hundred of Hyam St Ebba, and Aelfric had knelt before the Crucifix with some difficulty, for his right leg was now shorter than his left, its muscles wasted and weakened. He could walk with a stick and even ride his favourite horse, but would never take part in a battle again, or joust in a tournament as before. King Edward III had rewarded him with a knighthood, turning Kat Wynstede into a Lady and giving their children an enhanced status, and a better outlook for their daughters in the marriage stakes.

Aelfric smiled indulgently at his wife who was now holding out his tunic and shirt to put on. 'We'll cut a pretty picture together on horseback,' he said, knowing that his awkward seat and her riding side-saddle on an ambling mare brought grins from the stable boys. Especially if, as it turned out, the two younger children shared their saddles, Wulfstan with his father and little Ethelreda sitting up proudly in front of her mother.

Down in the stableyard Ned spoke sharply to Dan. 'What are you gawping at now, boy? Get on and move your arse.' Widget quickly wielded the broom and fork.

He'd been watching the family ride down the grassy incline towards the great open field where his father grew leeks, carrots and beans on the two strips he'd been allocated. The Ebbchester road divided the field from the grazing land where the dairy herd contentedly chewed the cud, and above them the oak wood gave shelter and sustenance to the Ebbasterne pigs.

In spite of Ned's ill-temper, Dan Widget smiled over his task at the warm sense of belonging which the day-to-day life at Ebbasterne gave him, not only to the Wynstede family but to all the serving men and maids, the cooks, the blacksmith, the stockmen and stablemen, the peasant farmers who tilled their strips in the open field. After his mother had died, his father had willingly given up Dan, his youngest surviving son, to live at the Hall and be trained as a groom, perhaps one day an esquire to Sir Aelfric. It was a good life for a bright boy who didn't necessarily want to repeat the pattern of his father's and grandsire's lives in their little stone and clay cottages, toiling year in and year out, unlettered and unremembered.

Dan slept on the rush-strewn floor of the main hall, with other young servant boys and the Wynstede dogs; they also shared the space with a few frail old men and women that the Lady had taken in, including Dan's own granddame who wandered in her wits and made messes on the floor which Dan tried to clear up before the house servants complained. Sometimes they were joined by itinerant friars who begged a night's lodging in exchange for preaching a sermon at breakfast, or travelling tinkers hawking their wares; the Lady Katrine was known for her kindness to all comers, and life at the Hall often made Dan think of the beehives at the Abbey where the holy monks sold excellent honey from their little communities of workers, always busily coming and going. And above all, there was young Mistress Cecily, the girl Dan secretly adored.

A tall horse galloped into the stableyard, and Gyfford the county sheriff announced his presence with a loud, 'Halloo!' Ned gestured towards the retreating backs of the Wynstedes. The sheriff remained in the saddle, and gave a brief shrug.

'Shall you go after 'em?' asked the groom.

'No, I can do my business here without your master's assistance,' Gyfford answered irritably, annoyed by the man's failure to address him as *sir*. 'I'll speak with your bailiff, though.'

'He's down in the field,' Ned replied, turning away to the saddlery.

'Then send the boy to fetch him up and be quick about it,' said Gyfford sharply. The groom called out to Dan. 'You're to fetch Bailiff Goode up here to take his orders, Widget, so drop your fork and run.'

Dan hesitated. 'But I—' he began, looking down at his soiled tunic.

Ned nodded. 'Aye, Widget, you stink to heaven, but no matter. Do as the gentleman says.' He then turned his back on Gyfford, grinning to himself at the official's discomfiture, now doubtless wishing he had ridden down to the field.

'Good day to you, Sheriff,' said Will Goode, a stockily built man with a broad, weathered face. 'Pooh! You might've dipped your arms in the bucket first, Widget – sorry about the stink, Sheriff, but it's good for the field. 'Sir Aelfric and his lady—'

'It's you I'll talk with, Goode,' said Gyfford, dismounting. 'Here, take my horse,' he ordered Ned, 'and we can exchange a word in the courtyard.'

Ned grimaced after the two men as they strolled out of earshot, indignant on Sir Aelfric's behalf at what he suspected was some plotting behind his master's back. Ned might bemoan the domestic arrangements at the Hall, but he resented others doing so, especially horse-faced officials who treated him no better than a peasant.

'We came to an agreement with the Abbot over the sheep-shearing, sir,' said Goode. 'And he'll come over to hold the manorial court on Thursday to try these sheep-stealers. I've got them under lock and key.'

'Well done, Bailiff, but I want to have a word with you on another matter,' said Gyfford. 'I'd like to sound out the numbers of able-bodied men on the demesne, young ones mostly, who'd be fit for the King's service.'

'God preserve us, Sheriff, d'you mean there's going to be war with France again?' Goode asked in alarm.

'Has it ever stopped? Ever since Sluys there've been French vessels harassing the south coast like gnats. I have it on authority from Westminster that the King plans to raise a great army to invade Normandy and catch them by surprise. And he'll need good English archers.'

'But we've only a handful of men skilled at archery, Sheriff. The peasants need to work the ground for their very existence, and the craftsmen are occupied with their own livings. They've all got families, and to be blunt, sir, they're not military material. The King had better look to the nobility – like the Castle up yonder.' He gestured in the direction of the imposing Norman keep at the top of the downs, some ten miles away.

'I've already spoken with the Count de Lusignan who keeps a standing hand-picked threescore men trained and armed at the Castle,' said Gyfford with a frown. 'That's Normans for you, always ready and prepared. But it's *you* I'm asking now, to keep your eye open for any promising youngsters. What about that young fellow mucking out the stables? He looks strong enough, and reasonably bright.'

On hearing praise of Normans, the bailiff drew himself up and answered coldly. ''Tis Sir Aelfric you need to talk to. He prides himself on his long Anglo-Saxon history and noble name.'

'Your loyalty is commendable,' said Gyfford with a slight sneer. 'But your master has been a cripple ever since Sluys, and his wife hasn't—'

'Lady Katrine's Christian virtues are well known in Hyam St Ebba and further afield,' Goode cut in. 'She takes good care of Sir Aelfric and the demesne.'

'Hm.' Gyfford had his own views on what he saw as Wynstede's foolishness in marrying Kat Hobbs, a daughter of weavers, though her father wore the livery of the City of London Guild; Wynstede had surely owed it to his status to seek out a sensible woman from the mercantile class, preferably with a good dowry.

'I can see I've been wasting my time with you, Bailiff. Just think on what I've said.'

The bailiff was silent. Young Widget was a favourite, in line to be a groom, perhaps an esquire. Will Goode was horrified to think of him marching with a mixed army of archers and odious foreign mercenaries – for such was the King's private army – and likely to be struck down in the flower of his youth for the sake of the King's dynastic ambition, among riff-raff out for military plunder.

The family made their leisurely way around the boundary of the demesne, Cecily and Oswald riding on ahead of their parents. Lady Wynstede continued to extol the beauty all around them, the fresh new greenness of pasture, the clear blueness of the sky, the sweet music of birdsong.

'This is the time when all is made new again,' she said, her arms clasped around little Ethelreda, her hands on the reins of the docile mare. 'And look at Cecily and Oswald, the very picture of youth and beauty, so full of life! We are blessed indeed, Aelfric, in our children.'

Wynstede winced slightly as a dart of pain shot down his right leg, held close against Chaser's flank; he tightened his hold on Wulfstan who was wanting to hold the reins.

'You're right, Kat, and may it continue to be so. I'm looking at pretty Cecily, for we must start considering her future.'

'Oh, she is but a child!'

'No, she is almost sixteen, Kat, and there are younger girls already made wives and mothers. I've noticed the looks men give her, though she is too innocent to see. Where can we find a worthy husband in Hyam St Ebba?'

'We would need to look farther afield,' replied the lady, who had in fact been having thoughts of her own on the subject. 'Like to the Castle and lands of the de Lusignans. Their son Piers—'

'Piers will look to the aristocracy, as befits the eldest of a Count. We might hope for a younger son at most,' replied Wynstede, 'but I have no taste for seeing Cecily marooned up there in the Castle, where I doubt we would be much welcomed. No, Kat, my opinion is that we should look to the mercantile class, the men of the future – the wool merchants. The best cloth calls for many skills, as we know – carding, spinning, weaving, fulling, dyeing – and such an enterprise can no longer be controlled by the Guilds.' Wynstede's face was thoughtful as he spoke of the changing face of cloth manufacture, for it was a field that he would have chosen if his health had permitted. 'Men with vision and a little money are investing in conveying the wool from craftsman to craftsman, village to town and town to port, finding the best markets – men like that Master Blagge who came over to see the Abbot not long ago, and no doubt struck a mutual bargain, paying a good price for raw wool and turning it into broadcloth to sell to markets all over Europe. Yes, Kat, it might be worth sounding out Master Blagge and enquiring about his sons!'

'But isn't he an unlettered man with no Latin or poetry?' she asked.

Wynstede chuckled. 'He may not be a scholar, but he can certainly add up! And you can be sure that his sons have had some instruction in how to court a young lady. Yes, I think we may count on Master Blagge to welcome the condescension of Sir Aelfric and Lady Katrine.'

She looked at him sharply. It was sometimes difficult to know whether he was serious or making gentle fun of her.

Young Oswald dug his knees into the pony's flanks, to urge him into a gallop. Cecily was getting too far ahead of him, her dark-brown hair streaming from beneath the simple circlet she wore around her head, signifying her maidenhood. Two years younger than his sister, Oswald was already proficient in fencing and archery, learning how to use the longbow, the formidable weapon of war that made England feared in battle. Even at Sluys, fought at sea between ships, the murderous arrows had flown from the English decks to the French and Flemish vessels and mown down their opponents with their useless swords and daggers. Oswald's sharp ears had lately picked up talk between his father's menservants, that the King was planning another invasion into French territory to lay claim to lands he considered belonged to the English crown; the boy dreamed of fighting alongside the King's son Prince Edward, about the same age as himself and already known for his strength and skill: life could be so full of adventure and brave deeds, and a young lad such as Oswald gave little thought to the darker side of warfare, the wholesale slaughter and the sort of lifelong injury that had ruined his father's health.

Cecily's spirits rose to greet the spring morning; like her mother she rejoiced at beholding the signs of the awakening earth all around her; it touched upon deep, unnamed desires stirring in her young body, now turning from girlhood to curving womanhood. When her monthly flux had commenced, her mother told her that it meant she was ready to bear a child – though not until she was married to a husband, and her hair plaited and hidden under a silver net and headdress such as Lady Wynstede wore. This was as intriguing as it was bewildering, for to Cecily there seemed no connection between the secret flow of blood and the face of a handsome prince who would come speedily to save her – from what? A villainous brigand who would seize her round the waist and drag her away to – what? Some grievous damage to her woman's body, some dreadful violation . . .

Cecily gave a little shiver and spurred the pony towards the Ebbchester road; would her prince come riding down such a highway to rescue her from the brigand? She pictured him slaying her tormentor with one blow from his shining sword, and then he would lift her up in his arms and place her on his fine, strong mount, leaping up behind her and taking her away to his own fair castle. There he would look upon her with love in his wide blue eyes, and she would be his beloved Lady, willingly bound to him for as long as they lived, and beyond . . .

Cecily's dark eyes softened as she pictured such perfect happiness and what the future might hold for her; a thought of Dan Widget suddenly came to her mind, the stable boy whose honest eyes had looked into her own with such shy adoration that she had smiled back at him, and Ned the groom had sharply despatched him back to his menial task. Was that how her prince would look at her?

When the invitation had arrived at the Blagges' newly built house, the master had been away on business in Europe, so his scrivener had opened it and sent apologies for postponing a reply. Ten days later, Master Blagge landed at Dover, and proceeded to his Hampshire home. He was intrigued by what the scrivener read out to him.

'No mention o' the golden fleece, then,' he noted, referring to the wool which had made him rich. 'So there must be some other reason for it.'

"'Tis a friendly overture, Jack, and we should accept with grace,' said his wife, a plain-faced woman of about fifty. She was neatly dressed in a grey wool gown and a neat white cap with a band passing under her chin. Her husband's tunic was of the same material with intricate embroidery at the neck and hem which, like the fur edge to his cape, proclaimed a successful merchant. Born into a humble cottage industry of spinners and weavers, he was not ashamed of having risen in the world by his own initiative and hard work; he had married a thrifty woman who had quietly supported him without any pretence of social graces, yet their sons had been sent to the Ebbchester grammar school, and their daughters taught to read, write and play on the lute and flute. Jack Blagge was proud to be a self-made man who had chosen a wife from the serving class and taught her obedience.

When the Blagge family and their children were received at the front entrance of Ebbasterne Hall by Sir Aelfric and Lady Wynstede, Blagge saw and understood at once the reason for the summons. The eldest daughter, Cecily, was as sweetly charming as she was beautiful, and was therefore in need of a wealthy husband. Beauty and status were offered in return for gold: a fair deal.

Cordial introductions were made, and mead and honey cakes were brought in for the guests; milk and watered fruit cordial was available for the younger children.

Mistress Blagge presented their sixteen-year-old twins Edgar and Maud, and Janet aged nine.

'My eldest son is married and lives in Ebbchester,' Blagge told his hosts. 'And our eldest daughter was married only this year to a lawyer's clerk in London.'

Congratulations were offered on hearing this happy news, and Aelfric thought he heard the underlying meaning in the words: that the Blagges were doing very well in the marriage stakes. Shy little Janet was immediately taken in charge by Ethelreda and Wulfstan who proudly took her to see their new litter of puppies. Cecily and Oswald were quietly instructed by their mother to take the twins to the stables and show them the ponies.

'Let our guests mount them if they would like to, and make sure that Ned's standing by,' she told them, then turned her attention to Mistress Blagge, who seemed a little overawed by Ebbasterne

Hall; Katrine smiled and questioned her in a friendly way about the two recent weddings in her family.

The four young people made their way to the stables, and Cecily, like her mother, attempted to put their guests at ease by asking about their interests. Edgar Blagge, tall and rather awkward, left it to his sister Maud to do the talking to this confident sister and brother. He hesitated when pretty Cecily asked if he liked horses.

'Yes, I have a quiet brown mare I use for riding when my father sends me on a business errand . . . er . . . Mistress Cecily.'

'But don't you like to go for a good gallop over the downs?'

'Er, not very often, no.'

'Don't you practise archery?' asked Oswald.

'No, I haven't learned that art.'

'But don't you know that the King's gathering a great army to invade Normandy? His own son Edward is already skilled at archery and wears a hauberk, though but the same age as ourselves,' persisted Oswald.

'My father doesn't speak much of such things,' answered Edgar, feeling that he was being mocked. 'His business takes him to cities such as Paris and Milan, where English broadcloth is much in demand.'

'Heavens, Oswald, Edgar and Maud are here to be entertained, not questioned as in a manorial court!' Cecily cut in. 'You must pardon my brother who dreams of warlike adventures, though not yet old enough to ride a destrier. Come, would you like to mount our ponies? We'll lead you down to the meadow and up to the woods.'

With Ned's help, the twins mounted the ponies, and led by their young hosts, the talk continued, Oswald enthusing about the day when he would don full armour and enter the lists to joust at a Castle tournament.

'The whole art of jousting is in the timing – to rush your opponent with a blunted lance and give him such a knock as to unseat him and send him sprawling to the ground,' he explained.

'Or be knocked off your own mount first, and break your neck,' murmured Edgar, at which Cecily laughed delightedly, and Edgar shot her a grateful look. Oswald shrugged, having decided that the Blagge fellow was a milksop.

★   ★   ★

Sir Aelfric, sharing a flagon of wine with Master Blagge, was coming to a favourable conclusion about Edgar, more into books than weapons. Everything his father said about him was to his credit, and the only objection was his youth, which suited Cecily's father who had no wish to part with his daughter so soon. The next four or five years would see the young man's shoulders broaden, and he had a good business head. Sir Aelfric decided to speak directly.

'Master Blagge, would you and your lady wife agree to a formal arrangement between your son and my daughter? A betrothal, agreeing that in four years' time, when they will have reached the age of twenty, that a marriage should take place between them? There's plenty of time to work out the details. What do you say?'

Jack Blagge hesitated, though only for a moment. 'You're very open with me, Sir Aelfric. I presume that you've already spoken of this with Lady Wynstede?'

'As you must have spoken with Mistress Blagge.'

Actually Blagge had not spoken with his wife because he had not expected such a direct proposition on his arrival at Ebbasterne Hall that day.

'Er . . . yes, Mrs Blagge is in complete agreement, sire.'

'Good. We shall have a contract drawn up without further delay. I'll have my attorney see to it for us.'

The knight and the merchant shook hands, and so the matter was satisfactorily concluded without any involvement of the two young people chiefly concerned.

'And how do you like Master Edgar, Cecily?' asked Kat Wynstede after their guests had departed.

'He's rather quiet and serious, Mother, but he gave a clever answer to Oswald's boasting!' replied Cecily with a smile, quite unaware of any hidden meaning behind the question.

'And how do you like Mistress Cecily, Edgar?' Jack Blagge asked the prospective bridegroom as they journeyed home.

'She's very pretty, and talked a lot with us,' replied the boy. 'I don't much care for her brother, though.'

Four

1342

February the light-giver, thought Brother Valerian on the last day of that month, standing with his fellow novice, Brother Carlo, in the Abbey church at the Office of Prime. Snowdrops were nodding their virginal heads in the churchyard, and soon there would be daffodils. Valerian felt a lightening of his heart, reflecting the lightening of the sky. He glanced at Carlo, to find that the young novice, for he was only nineteen, was gazing at him with shining eyes. He had more than once told Valerian that he had never known such happiness as now, devoting his life to God's service every hour of the day, seven days a week and month by month. He had all the rapturous dedication of a young man swept off his feet by first love, and Valerian prayed that it might not grow dim with time; he almost envied Carlo's innocent devotion, and to avoid becoming too close to his fellow novice, he sought the company of Brother Paulus during the rest hour, or some other older and more experienced brother with whom he could talk as an equal. He had in fact confided in Paulus that he was embarrassed by Carlo's attachment to him, not being able to live up to such hero worship, and Paulus, with his usual sympathetic understanding, advised that he should only converse with Carlo on general spiritual matters, and to direct him to the Abbot for sacramental Confession about anything personal.

As spring advanced, so did contact with the town. Merchants arrived to buy wool from the monastery, and wagons trundled up to the Abbey with supplies of salt, flour, oil of olives and such foods as the monks were unable to produce themselves; also special requirements like parchment and the various coloured inks and costly gold and silver leaf for the illuminated manuscripts, so prized by Cathedral libraries. The Abbot rode Greyling on his journeys to Ecclesiastic Courts and meetings with Bishops and high-ranking clergy in London and Ebbchester, and knowing of Valerian's legal background, he had begun to confide in him.

'Judging can be a difficult and delicate business, Brother Valerian,' he said. 'You get an honest peasant fellow complaining that his hovel has been pulled down because the local landowner wants to expand a field. I may sympathize, but I can't find against the landowner, and all I can hope is to have a quiet word with him, and suggest that more compensation should be offered to the fellow. Then you get a wretched child who's stolen a bun, and the parent is fined – but the son of a well-to-do craftsman who kills the pet cat of a field labourer's child can't be brought up before a judge, and in any case, I couldn't find in favour of a landless peasant and his cat. Some cases are brought simply to obtain revenge for an injury, real or imagined, that took place years ago. It isn't easy.'

'Surely, Father Abbot, all judgments must be made in the light of truth, and given without fear or favour,' observed Valerian.

'Ah, Brother, it can be difficult to discern the truth, and one must not be misled by liking or disliking the participants – or trusting them,' replied the Abbot with a wry smile, which did not satisfy Valerian, who mentioned the matter to Brother Paulus.

'The Abbot has to modify his judgments with a certain measure of worldly wisdom,' replied Paulus. 'To favour the poor man above his betters would undermine the community. A judge must decide what would be the greatest good for the greatest number, and that may mean a little deviation from the letter of the law – can't you see that?'

Such was Valerian's respect for Paulus' opinion that he said no more, but he was not persuaded. He had lately been aware of a vague restlessness within himself, and put it down to a lack of the enthusiasm he saw in Brother Carlo.

He looked back to those weeks in the previous year, when he had worked in the infirmary at a crucial time, and had known for certain that he was doing God's will in the service of others; he wished he could recapture that happiness, but knew that he had no right to wish for anything except to do the will of God. The blessed St Cecilia and her husband Valerian had faced death without flinching, so surely he should ask for nothing more than to be a holy and obedient monk, like Brother Paulus.

And so as the months passed by, he applied himself to follow the daily round of Offices, improving his skill at copying manuscripts with elaborate decoration; working in the garden, gathering herbs to use and preserve; he learned how to shear a sheep and remove a honeycomb from a beehive. He filled his life with labour, and prayed to draw nearer to God.

But at the end of the summer, his second at the Abbey, he received a shock that turned his world upside-down and shattered his hopes of holiness. Brother Luke suddenly collapsed in the Abbey at the noonday Office of Sext, and was carried by his brothers to the infirmary.

The Abbot urgently beckoned Valerian to take charge of the old monk, dismissing all the others; his voice betrayed his anxiety.

'What do you think afflicts him, Brother Valerian? Could it possibly be the plague? There have been one or two cases in the town.'

This possibility had already occurred to Valerian, and he told the Abbot that they should assume it was the plague until proved otherwise; the contagion could spread throughout the brotherhood.

'He must be kept completely apart from the other brothers, Father Abbot,' he said with unconscious authority. 'The infirmary must be emptied of its two occupants and declared out of bounds. I will stay to take care of him, but let nobody else come near.'

'But Brother Valerian, the danger to yourself—'

'I fear no danger, Father. If indeed it be the plague and I fall victim to it, I accept God's will that it should be so. Bless us both in Christ's name, and may God preserve you and all the brothers.'

An old blind brother, who had been in the infirmary for some time, was removed to a room within the Abbey, and a brother with a twisted ankle was carried to his dormitory cell. Every precaution was taken to prevent the spread of infection. The door connecting the infirmary with the kitchen was locked, and food was brought round and left on the step of the outer door, for Valerian to take in. The Abbot visited each day, standing on the outer doorstep, and special prayers were offered up at every Office.

For three days Brother Luke continued with a high fever, tossing and turning on his straw mattress and muttering in delirium. Valerian washed him and attended to his intimate needs, sponging his sweating flesh with tepid water and coaxing him to drink watered wine. He mixed a soothing sedative of powdered valerian roots in warm milk, and gently held it to the old man's lips at night. All the time he looked for the signs of the plague, the black spots, the swollen glands in the neck, armpit and groin, the flux of blood from the bowel. To his great relief they did not appear, and on the third day Brother Luke's breathing became softer and more regular; his fever had gone, though it left him weak, and he had regained his wits.

Valerian notified the Abbot that the crisis had passed, their prayers had been answered, and their brother was out of danger. There was great relief and rejoicing, and prayers of thanksgiving were offered up in the Abbey.

That night he gave Luke another valerian posset, and lay down on his palliasse, where he soon fell fast asleep, being very tired after three disturbed nights.

He awoke suddenly, to find a half-moon risen in a velvet-black sky. Not a sound was to be heard, and Brother Luke still slept soundly. So why was he suddenly so wide awake? As he sat up and listened, he heard a rustling sound, then creeping footsteps and whispering voices. Who on earth could it be at this hour? Thieves? Horses had been stolen from the Abbey stables in the past, and Valerian could not ignore the possibility; he rose, stepped into his sandals and pulled his habit around him. Yes, there was somebody outside. His heart began to thump, for he was seized by a terrible suspicion, something he could hardly name, but he had to investigate, and as he drew back the bolt of the outer door, he was silently praying, 'Oh, let it be thieves, horse thieves – anything else but—'

Out in the warm night air, he crept along the infirmary wall, led by the low voices, and stopped by the little wood-shed where Brother Luke kept the special small kindling sticks he used to heat water for his infusions. The door was shut, but had no lock on it, and Valerian froze in his tracks at the sounds coming from behind it. There were sighs and giggles, a woman's voice squealed '*Oooh!*' and a man's voice muttered, 'Keep still, can't you – I'm nearly there—'

Valerian felt suddenly sick, and his heart seemed to miss a beat, for he understood the sound, and knew the voice, yet knew that he had to see to be sure. Behind the door the man's voice continued brokenly, 'I'm there, that's it – Christ! – it's a storm, a storm – aah!' As his words gave way to an incoherent groaning, Valerian put his hand on the latch, and heard the woman hiss, 'Ssh, listen, there's somebody out there – stop, stop!'

The man's voice answered, deep and drowsy. 'No, sweetheart, they'll all be sleeping in their lonely cells, dreaming they've got a girl like you in their arms – no, don't move, stay close for a few minutes more—'

Valerian lifted the latch and pulled the door open to its fullest extent. A shaft of pale moonlight revealed two figures lying on the bundles of kindling sticks, the woman's legs spread wide, the man lying between them. He looked up at Valerian.

'Death and damnation,' he muttered. 'I'm discovered, and I wish it was by anybody else but you, Brother.' Valerian stared in silence as Paulus got to his feet and pulled his habit around him, speaking sharply to the woman. 'Get up and get going, back to the town with you, and be quick!'

She needed no second bidding, and pulling down her skirt she ran off, her feet pattering on the grass. Paulus turned to Valerian. 'Well, Brother, what are you going to do? At this moment I think I would almost welcome the plague.'

Valerian could think of nothing to say; what *was* there to say? He turned away, but Paulus put out a hand and gripped his arm. 'What are you going to do about my sin, Brother Valerian? My yielding to temptation? Tell the Abbot? Have me shamed in front of them all? Well? What will you do?'

'Nothing,' answered Ralph heavily. 'It is *your* duty to confess to God through Father Abbot's mediation. I shall say nothing.'

'May God reward you, Brother Valerian! I'll strive to regain chastity – and humility, for I couldn't bear to leave the Abbey.' He released Valerian's arm, and his voice choked with emotion. 'Blessings on you, good Brother, let me kiss your hand – praise be to God, I won't have to leave the Abbey!'

'No, Brother Paulus,' said Valerian, drawing back his hand. 'But I will.'

'I am grieved beyond words, Brother Valerian. I had such hopes of you. I saw you as an ornament to the monastic life, a leader of men, an interpreter of the scriptures, a future Abbot, even the

founder of a new Cistercian house—' He spread out his hands.
'I cannot believe it, my son!'

'I too am grieved, Father, yet it must be so,' he answered firmly.
'My life here has become a sham, and I must leave the Abbey
today.'

'*Today*? And leave behind those who have loved you and looked
up to you, though you are but a novice as yet? Brother Paulus,
Brother Luke? Our young Brother Carlo? I beg you to reconsider,
my son, for the love they bear you, and for my sake, too, do not
leave us!'

'I must go, Father.'

'In God's name, *where* will you go? How will you live?'

'I must earn my bread by whatever means come my way, whatever
honest work I can find – a scrivener maybe, a clerk – or a field
hand, a street sweeper, whatever God leads me to do. Only I cannot
stay here as a holy brother; it would be a mockery.'

The Abbot shifted slightly on his chair and looked into Valerian's
deep-blue eyes, which did not flinch. 'Have you a confession to
make, my son, for I can hear it now, and give you Absolution,'
he said quietly. 'Know that God is able to forgive all sins, however
black, however wicked, of a repentant sinner. Come, my son, avail
yourself of this holy Sacrament.'

Valerian shook his head. 'I cannot do so, Father, for it would
involve another.'

'Ah.' The Abbot's eyes lit up with what he thought was the
truth. 'That is indeed a grievous sin, and cries to heaven for mercy,
yet this is not the first time that a holy brother has been tempted
by the devil to succumb to fleshly lust, and sadly it will not be
the last. You may confess, my son Valerian, and be forgiven at
once by God's mercy. All is not lost!'

'I do not fully understand you, Father Abbot. What must I
confess?'

The Abbot looked stern. 'You know what I mean, and you
need not doubt God's power to forgive, shameful though it is to
lead a younger brother into temptation. I have seen the looks
passed between you and Brother Carlo.'

'Brother *Carlo*? He had nothing to do with it, Father. He is a
young, dedicated novice with a clear conscience, and—' Valerian
stopped speaking as the full import of the Abbot's words dawned

upon him, and he blushed a deep, angry red. 'God is my witness, I have never committed the sin of Sodom with that young monk, or with any man. Let me exonerate him – and me – from blame, and may he find a better mentor than I.'

'Then – a woman?' persisted the Abbot tentatively.

'*No.* My malady is to do with the spiritual life, Father, and I can no longer follow it with honesty. Pray give me leave to go, or I must leave without your blessing, for I cannot stay.' Valerian turned as if to quit the room, but the Abbot rose from his chair and held out his right hand as if trying to rescue a drowning man.

'Brother Valerian! *Ralph!* Tell me what troubles you, and receive pardon and peace!'

But Valerian made for the door. 'That is for another to tell you, Father, not I. May he receive this pardon and peace, for he has robbed me of mine.'

And he walked out of the Abbey on that September day, in his monk's robe and with no money or possessions. He left Greyling in the stables, not wanting her to share his hardship, or be sold to some hard-eyed horse dealer.

He had walked the length and breadth of Southampton and stood at the docks where ships lay at anchor with their sails furled, and their crews ashore. He had eaten nothing, but one or two of the townspeople, seeing his habit and thinking him to be a friar, gave him a few pence, for to give alms to a holy man was thought to bring good luck. His thoughts were in turmoil; he still shuddered to recall the sense of betrayal that had shattered his strivings towards holiness. Paulus will never know the injury he has done me, he thought bitterly. He allowed me to look upon him as a mentor, and advised me concerning Brother Carlo, and he dared to advise poor Brother Martin who was at least honest about his temptation. And all the time he was secretly fornicating with a woman of the town, with no thought for *her* salvation. Such cynicism, such hypocrisy!

He looked back to his brief marriage to Francesca; he had been nervous and she fearful, but their actions had been lawful, not to be compared with the unworthy dalliance he had witnessed. He felt himself to be an outcast, bearing another man's guilt.

Meanwhile his belly was empty and dusk was falling. He was used to fasting, and the meagre fare of the brothers had become habitual, but his body now longed for food and rest in equal measure. And where would he lay his head tonight? Rounding a corner of a narrow street, he came upon a booth where a woman was selling hot mutton pies; the scent of cooked meat and onions made Valerian's nostrils twitch, and his belly gurgled. A group of five seafaring men eagerly gathered round the booth, and a swarthy fellow with a red scarf tied round his bushy black hair bought a pie which he cut into six slices with a knife from his belt.

'Look what he's done!' jeered the others. 'He's cut an extra slice for himself!'

'No, I ain't, it's for that poor monk standin' there watchin' us,' was the reply. 'And I want him to bless my next voyage. Ho, there, good Brother, d'ye want a bite of our pie?'

Valerian nodded gratefully, and took the slice straight from the fellow's grimy hand.

'Give us a blessin', Brother, and ye're welcome to a sip o' wine!' said one of them, taking out a leather flask and offering it to him. They bowed their heads, and he made the sign of the Cross over them, reciting the blessing of the Trinity, then hastily moved away to hide his emotion. Rough as their manners were, they had shown him kindness and asked for his blessing upon them; they had treated him like a *brother*.

Where would he go now? His best plan would surely be to get out of the town and look for a hay barn or cow byre where he could spend the night and pray for direction. He trudged northwards into darkening fields, and eventually he saw a solidly built stone farmhouse with a lighted window and a barn nearby. He walked up to the door, knocked on it, and it was opened by a pleasant-faced middle-aged woman who stared for a moment, then smiled in deference to his monk's habit.

'Good evening to you, er, Brother,' she said. 'What brings you to our door at this hour?'

'I beg your mercy, good mistress, I . . . I wish only to sleep in your barn tonight.' His voice faded to a whisper, and his knees weakened. The woman called out, 'Come here, husband, there's a man swooning on the doorstep!'

A stocky, bearded man appeared, and Valerian was half-led, half-carried into a room where a table was spread with the remains of supper. A young man and woman came to help lay him down on a wooden settle; the woman poured water from a jug into a pewter mug.

'Drink this, good Brother, and rest yourself awhile. How came you to be wandering abroad at this hour?'

Valerian took a gulp of the water, and raised his eyes to the man and his wife; something about her face tugged at his memory. When he spoke, his voice was thin and weak.

'I thank you, good people. I have nowhere to rest my head, and beg to sleep in your barn tonight.' As he spoke, he became aware of the woman's questioning look.

'Good Brother, we have met before,' she said, then clapped her hands together in recognition. ''Tis Master de Courcy!' she exclaimed. 'You remember me telling you, Dillwyn, of the lawyer who was so kind to Margery and me when we fled from London, two years ago, nearly! Oh, good master – good Friar, you are welcome to stay under our roof – isn't that so, Dillwyn?'

'If he's the man you remember, wife, then as Christians we're bound to give meat and drink to the stranger,' answered her husband. He looked intently at Valerian. 'Is this true, friend? Are you indeed he who helped my wife and daughter when they were in need?'

Valerian looked at the woman as realization dawned.

'Dame Crocker,' he whispered, at which she turned triumphantly to her husband. 'You see, Dillwyn? He is the very same.' To Valerian she said, 'I am Mistress Dillwyn now, for I married this good man last year, and my daughter Margery is now happily betrothed to Dillwyn's son. God must have sent you to this house, good Brother.'

And Valerian always firmly believed that He had.

Five

At first Valerian gratefully accepted the hospitality of the honest Dillwyns, but after a few days of rest and reflection he realized that his austere monastic poverty was now an embarrassment, for with no means of repaying his kind hosts, he was a beggar in their house. When he accompanied the family to Sunday Mass at their parish church, he prayed once again for guidance in his pilgrimage.

The church of St Boniface was a good example of the stonemason's and woodcarver's art. Brightly painted statues of the Virgin and Child and St Boniface stood in opposite alcoves, and above the altar was a stained-glass window depicting Christ in Majesty; above the west entrance was a depiction of the Last Judgement where the souls of men were weighed and either escorted above to live with the angels and saints, or pitchforked below where Satan and his grinning devils awaited them.

After the prayers were read in Latin by a thin-faced clerk who frequently had to stop for a bout of painful coughing, the congregation joined in saying the Paternoster, learned by rote, after which they sat down and listened to the clerk preaching on the story of Joseph and his brothers. In spite of coughing fits that left him breathless, the man was a powerful preacher, enthralling his listeners up to the happy conclusion where Joseph forgives his brothers, the emphasis being on the need for forgiveness if we are to have our own sins forgiven. Valerian thought the homily was as entertaining as it was admonitory, exactly suited to a rustic congregation which could neither read nor write. Everybody then went up to receive the Sacrament of the Body and Blood, and as he took it, an idea entered Valerian's head as to what his next step should be.

On the way out he noticed carrots and onions left in the porch, bowls of eggs and cheese wrapped in cloth. Master Dillwyn added a loaf of his wife's bread, and Valerian assumed that it was some kind of collection to be distributed among the poor of the parish, and remarked on it to Mistress Dillwyn.

'Well, yes, in a way it is, Master de Courcy,' she said. 'Poor Master Hotham who led us in prayer today gets paid very little for doing Father Berringer's duties – he's the proper parish priest, but away most of the time. Master Hotham is a good man, but he isn't at all well, as you can see, and with another winter coming on –' she gave a shrug – 'we give him of our bounty.'

'Well, he's surely got enough to fill his pantry for this week and the next,' said Valerian with a smile, and got the impression that there was more to the story of Master Hotham than she was telling. He had no right to question her, for she was showing him great kindness in return for his small service two years previously, when he had given her the name of a Southampton lawyer to whom she might apply for justice against her stepson who had claimed her home; but the lawyer had refused to take on a case concerning a property too far away for him to deal with.

'But it all worked out right in the end, because it was at this lawyer's house that I met Master Dillwyn who was there to settle some dispute with a neighbour at the time. We got to talking about our circumstances, how we were both widowed, and he said he needed a woman to keep house for him and his son Hugh. We were soon married, and you've seen how it is with Margery and Hugh, and it's all thanks to you, Master de Courcy!'

Valerian smiled; the idea that had come to him at Communion was taking shape in his head, and the next morning he went to call on Master Hotham.

First he introduced himself as Ralph de Courcy, now known as Brother Valerian. He explained that the contemplative life of the Abbey was not for him, and he had left before taking final vows. He now wished to serve God and his fellow men in the world.

'I see you are in sole charge here at St Boniface, sire, and wonder if you could make use of my services as an assistant to you for a few weeks, until I see my way clearly ahead? I do not need payment, only a roof over my head and to share your table.'

Master Hotham looked at him, a question in his sunken eyes. 'It is as if my prayer is answered, Brother,' he said carefully. 'But have you been told of my history?'

'Mistress Dillwyn told me that you are not well, sire, and if

I could relieve you of some of your duties, you could rest each day and improve your health,' Valerian replied. 'And it would be a favour to me.'

'I have little chance to rest, Brother, and if you could come and take on some of the parish duties, I would be greatly in your debt. But—'

'Then let it be settled, sire, to our mutual benefit,' said Valerian eagerly, but the other man coughed and held up his hand.

'Wait, you have not heard all. I would be a doctor of divinity now, or at least have a parish of my own, but due to a past misdemeanour, I may never aspire to be anything but an unbeneficed clerk. Did not Mistress Dillwyn speak to you of this?'

'She said nothing, sire, and you have no need to explain anything to me.'

Master Hotham heaved a sigh, and lowered himself on to a wooden seat. 'At the outset of entering upon holy orders, I got a young woman with child, to my shame. As you know, the clergy are not allowed to marry, although there are some who live in quiet concubinage, and the Church sometimes turns a blind eye, especially if the man does his work well. This was the course advised by my Bishop at the time, but I could not consent to it, because I loved her. I had dishonoured her, and she had a right to expect her honour to be restored by marriage. So we were married, and she lives in a little cottage on the edge of the wood you can see from here – she and our three children.'

'Ah,' breathed Valerian, understanding why the gifts of food were left in the Church porch. 'And so you stayed in the Church?'

'Yes, thanks to the intervention of Father Berringer whose living this is, though he is often away in London or at Oxford. He asked the Bishop to let him take me on as a mass-priest, to carry out clerical duties on his behalf. It was allowed, provided that my wife does not live with me at the priest's house. My parishioners are kind and forgiving, and my loved ones do not go short of food, but I am not well, Brother. I fear I have a wasting disease consuming my lungs and robbing me of strength. I spit blood and am so tired, so weary at heart . . .' His voice tailed off into silence.

'Say no more, Master Hotham, for I have come to help you,' said Valerian, moved by the man's integrity, and his loyalty to his wife – in contrast to the behaviour of Paulus. 'If it is convenient to you, I will commence my parish duties here today.' He held out his hand. 'If I am an answer to your prayers, sire, you are surely an answer to mine.'

'And do you think my Enoch is getting better, Master de Courcy?' asked Mistress Hotham, her eyes beseeching him to give a hopeful answer. Valerian was standing on the doorstep of her cramped little cottage, while the eldest child, a boy of about ten, also awaited his reply. Two little girls stood behind them, staring wide-eyed at the stranger.

'He's about the same, Mistress, and it will take some time before he can celebrate Mass again.' Valerian despised himself for misleading her, but could not bring himself to destroy her hopes by speaking the plain truth, and in front of the children. When he had moved into the priest's house and taken over the parish duties, Enoch Hotham had gratefully let go of them, and now only solemnized marriages. Towards the end of October Enoch took to his bed, and Mistress Hotham and the children spent more and more time in the priest's house; she cooked for them all, making good use of the produce donated by the congregation.

Hotham's racking cough and resulting breathlessness disturbed his nights and took away his appetite for his wife's mutton broth and onion soup. Valerian gave him sips of mulled wine sweetened with honey, and sent a message by the Hotham boy to Brother Luke at the Abbey, begging for honey from the hives and hyssop from the herb garden to make a hot infusion; back came a whole honeycomb and valerian roots with the hyssop, to make a sedative syrup and clear the lungs. With them came a message from Brother Luke, asking that no thanks were to be sent to the Abbey, by which Valerian guessed that Brother Luke was the sole donor of the goods, and the less said about them the better.

His days were filled with parish duties, keeping church accounts and visiting homes where there was sickness or trouble of any kind, often aggravated by poverty; he had to judge which were truly deserving cases to be allotted money from parish funds. At first he discussed such matters with Hotham, but by mid-November the sick man was unable to concentrate his mind on them, and was losing mental and physical strength, to the extent that his wife could no longer deceive herself, and whispered tearfully to Valerian, 'He's dying, isn't he, Master de Courcy?'

'Yes, good Mistress, the end is near, and you must trust in God to help you and your dear children,' he answered gently. 'You may stay at his side whenever you wish, and this house is open to you and yours.'

In fact Hotham lingered until Christmas Day, and there was little cheer in the priest's house, though at church Valerian preached the angels' message of peace on earth and goodwill to mankind, emphasizing the poverty of the Holy Family when the Saviour of mankind was born in a stable. He took the three children with him to church, leaving Mistress Hotham with her husband, and when they returned with Mistress Dillwyn who came to offer help, Enoch's spirit had departed. Mistress Dillwyn was willing to take the children to her own home, and Valerian knelt beside the bed with Mistress Hotham to pray for the repose of her husband's soul and for herself and her orphaned children.

As the early dusk was falling, there was a sudden commotion in the yard outside as two horsemen arrived, dismounted and knocked loudly at the door. Valerian went to answer, and was confronted by a solidly built man in a black cloak who announced himself as Father Berringer; the other was his manservant.

'I intended to be here for the Mass of the Nativity, but I got delayed at Oxford, and—' he began, but stopped short at the sight of Valerian. 'Good heavens, man, who are you? And what's *she* doing here? I have to speak with Master Hotham – where is he?'

Valerian could hardly manage to be civil. 'I presume that you are the absent rector of this parish,' he replied, and before the man could rebuke him, went on, 'If you have come to see Master Hotham, you are too late.'

'What? How dare you address me thus! Where is he? And what is this woman doing in my house?' blustered Berringer. 'What has been going on in my absence?'

'Come with me,' said Valerian shortly, 'and I'll take you to him.' He led the angry priest up the wooden staircase and into the room where the body of Enoch Hotham lay, covered with a white sheet pulled up to the chin, so the face was visible; the eyes were closed, and the expression peaceful.

Father Berringer turned quite pale with shock, and crossed himself. 'Good God in heaven!' He put his hand to his throat. 'Sweet Jesus, have mercy – *dead?*'

'Yes, he died today at noon,' said Valerian Master de Courcy. 'His wife was at his side, and I was taking the Mass of the Nativity at St Boniface. Their children are at the Dillwyns' farm.'

At hearing this, Berringer gave him a sharp sideways glance. 'So the fact of his marriage was known to you?'

'It has been known to his parishioners for some time,' answered Valerian drily. 'And thanks to their charity, the family has not starved, considering the miserable stipend that he was paid. I have acted as his unpaid assistant for nearly three months, when he became too ill to continue. Priests from other parishes have pre-consecrated the Bread and Wine, and solemnized marriages.'

Berringer's bluster had evaporated, and he asked, 'Why wasn't I told of this?'

'Begging your pardon, sire, we didn't know where you were – London or Oxford or wherever.'

'And where are you from? And why did you come here?'

'I was a novice monk at the Abbey, but left before taking final vows. I believe it was the guidance of the Holy Spirit that led me here, by a series of chance meetings. I am willing to stay on here as an unbeneficed clerk until a replacement for Master Hotham can be found, otherwise I can leave tomorrow.'

'No, no, there's no need to leave just yet,' said Berringer hastily. 'It would be helpful if you can stay as my assistant until I have consulted with the Bishop. Meanwhile thanks are due to you, and you will receive payment for the time you have worked here.'

'I had rather you paid Mistress Hotham any monies due to me,' said Valerian. 'And that the family be properly housed and fed now that their breadwinner has gone.'

'Yes, of course – certainly, Master ... er ... I shall see that she is supported from parish funds.' Berringer coughed. 'Merciful heavens! This has been a most unfortunate business.'

Valerian did not contradict him.

As it turned out, Father Berringer's thanks took the form of recommending to the Bishop that Valerian be enabled to study with a view to becoming a parish priest, having proved himself worthy by his care of the parish of St Boniface. Berringer had connections at Oxford, and used his influence to direct Valerian to that revered University.

'If you want to advance as a priest of the Church, de Courcy, you need a degree in theology, and be able to read the Bible in Hebrew and Greek. You obviously have a talent for dealing with people of different stations, so take my advice, accept payment for your services here, and apply to St Saviour's College at Oxford, where I was once a student, and I will recommend you. You could teach Law and Latin in exchange for your board and lodging.'

For Valerian this was a clear direction from the Almighty, and early in the new year of 1343, he set out on his academic career. The very word *Oxford* to him meant the Promised Land, where he would learn from some of the nation's wisest men. St Saviour's College rose before him, an architectural masterpiece, founded some fifty years ago, and already regarded as having equal eminence with Merton, Balliol and Oriel, founded in the last century – or so said Master Jeremy Byrd, a fellow undergraduate who welcomed Valerian through the imposing portals, across a courtyard and up a twisty wooden staircase to his room on the second floor.

'Most of the students live in lodgings down in the town,' explained Jeremy, 'but you're also a tutor, so you'll live in College with the Friars, and eat with them in hall.'

Valerian was impressed, even excited by everything he saw, and pleased above all that his tutors would be mainly Franciscan Friars, for St Saviour's was also a conventual lodging for their Order, teaching and studying theology, Latin, Greek and Hebrew, mathematics, astronomy and astrology. *This* is where God will guide and direct me, he believed, through these scholars of the holy Scriptures.

He settled easily and happily into College life, proud to be a scholar at this great powerhouse of learning. As a tutor of civil and canon law at the age of twenty-seven, he commanded the respect of his students; and as a student himself, some six or eight years older than the rest, his eagerness quickly brought him to the attention of Dr de Witt, the revered Master of St Saviour's; he it was who introduced Valerian to the scientific discoveries of Archimedes, the mathematical laws of Pythagoras, and the geometric precision of Euclid, all interrelated in their philosophies, the absolute truths of the natural world, not opinions or arguments but constant and irrefutable facts. Great theologists like St Thomas Aquinas and St Anselm explained the relationship of these natural laws to scriptural teaching, how they emanated from the mind of God when He created the world.

As soon as Valerian had a fair grasp of Hebrew, he read for the first time the books of the prophets, their chronicling of Jewish history, their warnings of God's wrath upon the disobedient, and His mercy towards the repentant. Every minute of his day was filled, yet he still found time to discuss theological points with young Master Byrd, for here there were no silences to be observed. Jeremy freely admitted that he intended to use his degree as a way to gain preferment in the church: to become a Bishop or hold some high office at Court or in a great house as chaplain to a noble family and their household.

'That way I shall have greater power to do good than if I were a mere priest in some poor rural parish,' he told Valerian with a confident smile. 'I shall make the very best use of the talents I've been given – and I predict that you will go even farther!'

But Valerian had been studying the life of St Francis, his insistence on poverty and his mission to nurse the sick – and he still felt drawn to the work of a parish priest with a mission to all, rich and poor, men and women, old and young; but when he tried to put this to Jeremy, all he got was an affectionate laugh.

'Don't tell me that's your whole ambition, de Courcy, or I shall not believe you! Imagine wasting your gift for preaching on a congregation of bumpkins, hearing their stammering confessions, smelling the stink of them, baptising, marrying and burying the poor wretches! Heaven knows there are plenty of plodding clerks to take on the burden of parishes, but *you* have a duty to use the talents you've been given, not to bury them. As a Bishop *and* a lawyer, I see you taking your place on the King's Bench, a man to be revered – Bishop de Courcy of Oxford, remembered by his statue on a plinth in the courtyard of St Saviour's College, and his beautifully illustrated sermons in the library!'

He laughed again at his friend's puzzled frown, but Valerian decided to consult Dr de Witt, and an opportunity arose the next day, at the end of a session with the doctor on the use of the magnifying glass, invented by a former fellow of the University, Roger Bacon.

'A Franciscan friar, de Courcy, with an amazing brain,' said the doctor. 'He was a radical thinker in his religious beliefs.' He paused and shook his head slightly. 'Though his views were dismissed and discredited, as being contrary to the teachings of the church.'

'In what way, Dr de Witt?' asked Valerian.

The doctor lowered his voice and looked around them before replying. 'Bacon taught that God was accessible to all who sought Him, without need of intercession. He went against all contemporary religious practices, even questioning the authority of the Pope. He said all men may come to Christ when He calls them – if they believe He has called them.'

De Witt hesitated, seeing a gleam of recognition in de Courcy's deep-blue eyes. 'And Bacon was twice imprisoned for *heresy*,' he warned. 'Take my advice, de Courcy, and stay with the accepted theology as taught by the scholars.'

There seemed to be nothing more to be said, and Valerian bowed to the venerable doctor, whilst neither convinced nor contented with what he had been told. It was just as well that he taught Law and Latin, and not theology, he thought, for he realized that he was unsure about his own standpoint, and inclined to embrace the radical Christianity of Bacon. But to discuss such *heresies* with his students could put them all at risk.

From then on Valerian became less willing to take part in theoretical argument and counter-argument such as delighted Jeremy Byrd and his friends; he grew dissatisfied with a dry intellectualism that seemed to have little to do with the God of the Prophets and Psalms, or with the lives of such dedicated men as St Francis of Assisi who had lived and worked among the poor – and his own patron Saint Cecilia who had faced martyrdom rather than deny her Lord, proclaiming her love of her Saviour right up to the moment of her painful death. Gradually over the passing weeks and months Valerian came to realize that Oxford, for all its architectural magnificence and rarefied atmosphere of scholarship, was not the shining light he had once thought, nor the place where the Christ of the Gospels was to be found.

The final disillusionment came on a hot July morning, as he sat on a bench in the main courtyard, translating the Prophets from Hebrew to English; he had reached the Book of the prophet Micah, and warmed to the man's natural simplicity and common sense. Nearby a group of students had gathered in the sunshine to debate the nature of angels, their size, weight, velocity and ability to appear and disappear.

'You've missed the whole point of their existence as heavenly beings,' declared a supercilious student who revelled in such discussions. 'They have not bodies as we have, occupying space, but are airy spirits that pass between earth and sky – so ten thousand of them may throng together on the point of a needle, and then vanish to the four corners of the earth in an instant.'

A burst of loud agreement and even louder disagreement greeted this, and Byrd called out to Valerian, 'And what does our learned lawyer friend have to say about these heavenly beings? Come, Master de Courcy, we don't hear much from you these days – *speak!*'

Valerian put down the transcript he was engaged upon, and looked down at the words he had just translated.

'My friends, we would all do well to heed the words of the prophet Micah,' he said. 'Listen. "*He hath shewed thee, O man, what is good; and what doth the Lord require of thee, but to do justly, and to love mercy, and to walk humbly with thy God?*"'

For a few moments there was silence, as if they had been rebuked, and they began to drift away in twos and threes. Valerian rose, went up to his room on the second floor and knelt down beside his narrow wooden bed. His prayer was one of thanksgiving, for he saw the prophet's words as a moment of enlightenment. It was as if his time as a lay brother and then as a novice at Netley Abbey, his months as an unbeneficed priest at St Boniface and his present experience both as a tutor and undergraduate of Oxford University had all been part of a necessary spiritual journey, and now he saw clearly what he must do when he received his theology degree in September. He would become a follower of St Francis, a Franciscan friar under vows of poverty, chastity and obedience, with no convent or college to shelter him; he would live his life as a mendicant, a solitary pilgrim, working or begging his way from place to place, preaching and doing any honest work that came his way, farmhand or scribe. He would trust in God to supply all his needs, though knowing that there would be times when he'd be hungry and cold. And he would dedicate his life to his patron saint, Cecilia.

★　　★　　★

Valerian gained his degree as summer passed into autumn, and at once set out on his journeys as a mendicant Friar. Winter came in with icy winds and sleet, short daylight hours and scarcity of food for men and beasts. He trod the open road in bad weather as in good, often surprised by the kindness of strangers. Not many nights did he have to spend in haybarns or stables, for there was usually a kitchen floor to sleep on, or the rush-strewn hall in a great house, beside the embers of the fire. As a holy Friar, he was generally respected, and ladies of noble families gave him their menfolks' cast-off shirts and breeches to wear under his grey woollen habit. His parents and brother were horrified by his chosen way of life, but he was generally welcomed under the roofs of rich and poor, especially when there was sickness of some kind. His remedies were simple and obtainable; sick people were to be allowed to rest, keep warm and drink as much water as could be obtained. High fevers responded well to sponging with a towel dipped in tepid water, and hot, wet towels were applied to boils. When the sufferer was beyond human aid, Valerian murmured words of comfort and administered the Last Rites in an atmosphere of peace and calm. On leaving a great house, he was usually given victuals to take on his journey, and he would stop at some poor cottage and hand the food to tired, overworked mothers of children, who thanked him and blessed his name – Good Friar Valerian.

After what seemed an interminable winter the spring came again, and the life of mendicants became easier. Valerian had never before rejoiced as much as he did that spring, turning into a particularly warm summer.

His reputation as a lawyer grew, and he was invited to sit on County or Manorial Courts to help solve difficult cases – 'to do justly' – and he usually tried to bring about a compromise that satisfied both parties to a greater or lesser extent. It was while he was assisting at an Ecclesiastic Court in Guildford that he received an invitation from an Abbot at a place called Hyam St Ebba in north Hampshire. He gathered that it was a tricky case, involving the young son of a nobleman who had seduced the previously respectable daughter of a pig-farmer and got her with child. He had denied the charge, and refused to admit his guilt, let alone marry her as her angry father demanded. The Abbot whose name was Athelstan was on good terms with the man's father, Count

Robert de Lusignan, and felt that he could not act as judge in such circumstances. A disinterested lawyer was needed, and Friar Valerian's name had come to the Abbot's ears, so on a bright June day Valerian set out on a borrowed horse to Hyam St Ebba.

He was met and welcomed into St Ebba's Abbey, where he and Athelstan sat down to consider the facts in the case. First he asked to interview separately the defendant, Charles de Lusignan, then the heavily pregnant girl and her aggrieved father who demanded that his daughter's honour be restored by marriage.

Having weighed up the conflicting evidence, Valerian asked Charles if he would care to settle out of court in exchange for a hundred gold sovereigns, fifty for the girl and fifty for a good-natured farm worker who was willing to marry her and call the child his own.

The offer was eventually reduced to sixty sovereigns, thirty each to the girl and her hastily wedded husband, and a successful compromise was reached, with no public loss of face to Charles, though his own father would no doubt have something to say.

'Well done, Friar Valerian!' beamed the Abbot, 'and don't leave us yet. We've been invited to a great Tournament at Castle de Lusignan, which will be fine sport, especially as there'll be emissaries from the King, looking for good military material for an army he's raising against France. There's always an excellent table, too,' he added with a gleam in his eye, 'and good French wine. I'm taking one or two of the brothers with me, and you're very welcome to come too.'

Valerian had never witnessed a tournament, and accepted the offer; later he always looked back on that day as being foreordained.

Six

June 1344

Field and forest lay bathed in bright midsummer sunshine, and a cloudless blue sky augured well for the Tournament. Traders and followers had been assembling at the Castle lists since dawn, sellers of sweetmeats, itinerant street musicians with bagpipes, flutes and tabors, jugglers and tumblers; a swarthy man led a tired, red-eyed bear on a chain, and two monkeys, dressed as a lady and gentleman, sat on their owner's shoulders, ready to perform their antics as a quarrelling husband and wife, to the laughter of the gathering crowd.

Excitement rose as the noble guests of the de Lusignans began to arrive. Some came in horse-drawn carriages, some on horseback, while others came by water, for the Castle was built above the point where the river Dene met the Bourne nine miles up from the Bourne estuary. A jetty had been built for river boats to tie up, and ladies in their finery were helped on to the landing stage and escorted up to where the lists had been constructed on the broad greensward just below the Castle whose huge round tower dominated the country for miles around.

Castle de Lusignan was one of the first Norman fortresses built by the Conqueror after his victory at Hastings nearly three hundred years ago. The thick stone walls enclosed an inner and outer bailey; in the first the family and retainers could walk and talk undisturbed, while in the outer bailey a standing army, some three or fourscore strong, were kept in training, ready at a moment's notice to come to the defence of King and country under Count Robert de Lusignan, upon whose ancestor the Castle had been bestowed for his services at the Conquest. It was being said that this great Tournament was to be a testing-ground for knights and Englishmen of all ranks and stations to show their prowess; the King had sent emissaries to scour the southern towns and villages for good military material to join his army for the planned invasion of France. The King's own son who would one day be Edward IV, had been created Prince of Wales in the previous year, and although as yet only fourteen years old, would be accompanying his father on this great military adventure, an example to English youth everywhere.

Count Robert de Lusignan and his sons Piers and Charles were to compete in today's Tournament, to be followed by knights of the shire and then any able-bodied man who wanted to try his luck in the lists would be lent a lance, shield and helmet. Halfway through the day's jousting an hour at noonday was to be set aside for the 'Little Tourney' where the likes of Oswald Wynstede and Warren Gyfford, mounted on their own ponies and palfreys, could charge full-tilt against a man-sized bag of straw tied to a post halfway down the field, and equipped with a helmet and shield. The youths would endeavour to knock the shield aside and pierce the bag with their lance, which would count as a victory; to topple the straw man's helmet would also earn some points.

Sir Aelfric and Lady Wynstede, with Oswald and Cecily, dismounted in the courtyard, and having been formally welcomed by the Countess Hélène de Lusignan, they were invited to take their places with their hosts on the front row of tiered benches under an awning, to watch the procession preceding the Tournament. Cecily sat next to the de Lusignan daughters Marie and Alys, who exclaimed gleefully when the richly dressed 'King-of-Arms' appeared, bearing the banners of some of the knights taking part, but Cecily remained silent, as if she had no interest in the proceedings. Her mother, seated on her other side, was troubled for her, and only too well aware of the reason. Cecily had lost much of her former vivacity in the last two years following her betrothal to Edgar Blagge. Her parents had been disappointed, but hoped that in time she would come to realize her good fortune. Edgar was an unobjectionable young man with a good business head that would enable him to keep her in comfort, and not too far from her family at Ebbasterne Hall; he had no bad habits like idling his time away with other young fellows who would lead him into excessive drinking and too-early experiences with women.

'He's very pleased to have you for a wife, Cecily, and he'll devote his time to making you happy,' Lady Wynstede had assured her. 'Your father and I are delighted with the match. You do realize, dear, that a girl in your position can't expect to choose a husband for herself, because there are so many practical matters to be considered.'

'But father married *you* without the agreement of *his* parents, Mother, and you have been happy together, in spite of all their objections,' Cecily had bluntly replied, and her mother had bitten her lip, unable to deny the fact.

'Your father was very insistent, and a man can stand up to objections better than a woman can,' she said. It was true that her own marriage had been a love-match that caused a scandal at the time. The de Lusignans would not recognize a tradesman's daughter as a neighbour, and the young Wynstedes had been ostracized. But time had gone by, Wynstede's service to the King had earned him a knighthood, and their children had grown up as healthy and as handsome as any born into nobility. Time had blurred the past, and young Mistress Cecily's beauty was famed throughout the county. Master Edgar Blagge was openly envied by young men who had not his need to work for his living.

'It isn't as if you have another preference, dear, and you will come to love Edgar as your husband in time, especially when . . . er, when you bear his first child. That's something every mother knows, and I can't describe the joy it brings. You'll find it out for yourself one day, I promise you.'

Cecily remained silent. By now she knew in theory what happened between a man and a woman in the marriage-bed, and Edgar Blagge, with all his advantages, was far from her ideal of the handsome, adoring prince she had envisioned; that dream was over, and she had discovered the difference between imagination and reality. She had no desire to bear Edgar Blagge's child, and was not sorry for his absence today, for he had no interest in such pursuits, while her brother Oswald could hardly wait to take his turn in the Little Tourney and show off his prowess to his father and mother.

Cecily sighed. In another two years' time her abundant dark hair would be gathered into a net and hidden from sight under a headdress, to indicate her status as a married woman; and not only my hair will be netted, she thought miserably: I'll be like one of those poor wild birds caught and imprisoned by the birdcage sellers among the crowd.

The procession began, and the 'King-of-Arms' was followed by the trumpeters, half a dozen of them in pairs, announcing the arrival of the knights. They wore blue and red tunics, belted at the waist, black hose and black velvet hats with upturned brims. Next came the judges, older men who had distinguished themselves in the field in past years, and Cecily roused herself to sit up as her father appeared in the flowing red gown of a judge, with a flat black hat decorated with an ostrich plume. He bowed to the ladies sitting on the front bench, and had a special smile for his daughter whose solemn little face smote him to the heart. He made up his mind to have a word with young Blagge, and encourage more meetings between the pair; if Cecily still could not accept and at least *like* her intended husband, he would declare the betrothal void, no matter what the consequences.

Then came the procession of the competing knights on their destriers, strong horses trained for battle and to carry the weight of a knight in armour with his lance and shield; the lances were blunted, for in this warlike sport the aim was not to kill one's opponent but to unseat him. Cheers rang out as the Count led his sons on finely groomed stallions, their helmets and chain mail hauberks gleaming in the sun. The hauberks were made of hundreds of metal circles linked together by tiny rivets and worn over a padded gambeson to prevent chafing; a light tunic embroidered with a cross or simple heraldic device was worn over the hauberk, and metal elbow-cops and knee-cops protected the joints.

The Count's helmet was the bascinet type, an inverted metal basin over the head, with a visor to shield the face and a chain mail tippet to fasten on to the hauberk. He directed his destrier to the ladies in the front row of spectators, where he lifted his visor and gallantly bowed to the Countess, and to the delight of the crowd his horse also lowered its head before her. The lady wore a magnificent particoloured gown in scarlet and white, with huge sleeves edged with fine embroidery. Her hair was plaited and wound in a circle on each side of her head, secured with gold netting and topped by a fine silk veil and jewelled coronet. Cecily noted that Marie wore her fair hair in plaits around her head, and Alys wore hers loose on her shoulders; as she looked at them a dark-browed knight approached the Lady Marie and bowed before her. She blushed becomingly and held out a red ribbon which he took and tied to his lance: it was a sign that he was competing in her honour, as his chosen lady.

'That's Sir Gilbert Benoît who's asked our father for Marie's hand,' whispered Alys, and Cecily's eyebrows rose with interest.

'Has he?' she whispered back, watching Marie's sparkling eyes as her knight rode away to join the rest. 'And does she love him?'

'Oh, yes, she has vowed to have none other, or go into a nunnery,' came the smiling reply.

'Look, there's the Abbot with some of the brothers,' Lady Wynstede remarked as the crowd surged in closer to the edge of the field. Cecily followed her mother's glance in the direction of the Abbot and his companions; two of them wore the black robes of Benedictines, but one was a grey-robed Franciscan friar with a length of rope for a belt and worn leather sandals on his feet. Cecily eyed them thoughtfully, silently wondering about their celibate lives, untroubled by the need to marry and sire children on a woman who might not love them. Would she be happier as a nun living with other women in a house of God, dedicated to a life of work and prayer? The thought had already occurred to her as an alternative to marrying Edgar, but she doubted she was sufficiently pious to spend her whole life in such a way.

Her thoughts were interrupted by a loud fanfare of trumpets. The Tournament was about to begin, and Count de Lusignan was taking his place at one end of the field to face a challenging Flemish knight at the other. With visors down, shields held on their left hands and lances in their right, they waited for the signal to advance.

They were off! Horses and riders sped on each side of a palisade, a low wooden fence, to meet each other halfway down the field. Lances smashed into shields, horses reared and whinnied, being used to the sport, and both men had to hang on to their bridles for dear life and dig in their knees to keep their seats. Neither was unhorsed, and neither lost his lance: a roar went up from the crowd as they turned their destriers round and made for the opposite ends of the field for their second encounter. The Countess and her daughters sat in rigid silence, scarcely able to breathe in fear for the Count's safety. He was renowned for his jousting, but the Fleming had been reckoned as a formidable challenger to start the Tournament.

Down the field they galloped again at full tilt, and this time the Count's lance splintered against his opponent's shield. A muted cheer went up from the crowd when both knights were seen to be still in the saddle. A third attempt would be allowed, but no more, and the winner would be the knight awarded most points by the judges.

For the third time the destriers' hooves thundered down the field, the Count's voice raised in a warlike yell of 'De Lusignan! De Lusignan!' His new lance crashed against the opponent's shield as both mounts reared and bucked; the Fleming's horse, wild-eyed and distracted by the shout, reared again and brought his hooves down on the fence which collapsed beneath his weight, leaving the two riders regarding each other at close range through the eye-slits in their visors. Neither was an outright winner, but the challenger gained the most points for breaking the Count's lance. There was muted applause and heartfelt sighs of relief.

It was an inauspicious start to the morning, but there was plenty of excitement to follow when Piers was unseated and slithered to the ground hanging on to his bridle, landing on his feet. His younger brother Charles overthrew his opponent, a cavalryman from his father's standby army. Bruises were sustained by all riders and horses, but so far there were no serious injuries.

The Tournament continued, with a win for Sir Gilbert Benoît, which drew smiles of relief and pride from the Lady Marie. The sun rose higher, and the crowd grew ever more excitable until at noon a halt was called, and the field prepared for the Little Tourney. This was Cecily's only real interest – and apprehension – of the day, for her brother Oswald was almost beside himself with impatience to show off his prowess to his parents and sister. The spectators were now joined by two more ladies, Mistress Blagge and Mistress Maud who were accompanied by their groom. Lady Wynstede introduced the newcomers to the Countess who graciously made space for them in the second row, behind the Wynstede ladies and apparently too close to old Lady de Lusignan who glared at them and put her walking stick on the bench between them and herself.

'Perhaps you had better go and sit beside your future mother and sister-in-law, Cecily,' whispered Kat Wynstede. 'They have shown great courtesy by coming all this way.'

Cecily obediently rose and did as she was told, seating herself between the Blagge ladies and the walking stick.

Refreshments were now served to the gentry in two pavilions, circular tents in which trestles had been laid with plates of cold mutton from a whole sheep that had been roasted the day before, cheese and bread fresh from the castle kitchens. Flagons of spiced mead were on a separate trestle, and jugs of the root beer that was brewed in large quantities. The Abbot and his monks were invited into the pavilions, and mixed easily with the company, but the grey-robed Franciscan politely declined and vanished into the crowd. Oswald was almost too excited to eat, though his groom, Dan Widget, was more than ready to join others of his kind in a tent set aside for the menservants. Dan had been Oswald's groom for the past half-year, and had proved capable of dealing with refractory horses and his young master's contrary moods.

Seats were resumed by the spectators to watch the Little Tourney. The straw man was tied to a post halfway down the field, and armed with a shield and helmet. There were half a dozen young competitors, headed by a nephew of the Countess, to be followed by Oswald Wynstede and Warren Gyfford. Three other youths had come from a distance to pit their skill against the proud confidence of these three, now mounted on their horses and waiting for the signal to begin. They wore helmets in case of a fall, and they carried blunted lances, but no shield or hauberk was needed to defend them from a straw warrior.

A fanfare sounded, and the first horse was spurred into action; the Countess's nephew held his lance aloft before aiming it downwards on to the shield of the straw man, which it barely grazed. Cheers, jeers and sympathetic groans rose from the onlookers, and Cecily took hold of Maud Blagge's hand as Oswald took up his position in readiness for the signal; off he sped on his lively steed, aiming his lance at the shield with strong enough impact to shift it a couple of inches, but not enough to pierce the sack of straw beneath it. He turned his horse and struck again, meeting the edge of the shield but not displacing it. More shouts went up, and the ladies clapped his efforts, though he had to give way to the next entrant, young Master Gyfford, who managed to knock the helmet off the silent opponent, but failed to displace his shield. Uncomplimentary epithets were hurled at them by the crowd, but silence fell when it was Oswald's turn again, and his mother and sister held their breath.

It all happened in a moment: the horse galloped down the field with Oswald carrying the lance horizontally before fiercely thrusting it under the right side of the straw man's shield, where it pierced the sack, scoring a victory for Oswald; but whether it was his warlike yell or some disturbance in the crowd, his horse shied, reared up and threw off his rider backwards. The horrified onlookers saw Oswald's hands clawing at the mane as his feet left the stirrups and he landed with a heavy thud on his backside; he lay where he had fallen, stunned by the shock. Lady Wynstede screamed, and Cecily jumped up from her seat to run with her mother to the scene, while Sir Aelfric in his judge's gown limped behind them. Dan Widget had streaked across the field and was at his young master's side as they all drew near.

'He's dead, he's dead!' wailed Kat Wynstede, and her husband put his arm around her, also fearing the worst, while Cecily knelt beside her brother, uttering a prayer under her breath.

A calm, quiet voice broke in. 'Is his heart beating? Does he yet draw breath?' asked the Franciscan friar who had suddenly appeared among them. Cecily at once moved aside to give him room to kneel down and put his hand under Oswald's tunic in the region of his heart; he then leaned over the lifeless form and put his ear directly on the chest. He listened and nodded. 'His heart beats and he breathes,' he informed them quietly. 'He has been stunned by the force of the fall.' He blew a sharp breath on to Oswald's nose and mouth, and then another.

'Open your eyes, young man,' he said. 'Open your eyes and see your mother and father.'

The boy's eyelids began to flutter, and a long-drawn-out groan announced the return of consciousness.

'Blessed be Christ, he's alive!' cried Kat Wynstede, and flinging herself down beside her son, she attempted to take hold of his head, to cradle him in her arms.

'Hush, lady, let me have care of him,' said the friar. 'I need to test for broken bones. Turn over, young man, and lift yourself on to your hands and knees. Come on, I'll help you.'

With a groan the youth managed to assume this position while his mother wept and her husband and daughter tried to pacify her.

'Good, I do not think there are bones broken,' said the friar. 'The force of the fall has shaken his spine right up to his head, and that's why he swooned.' Realizing that the distracted lady was not listening, he turned to Cecily.

'Let him be taken home and put to bed in a quiet room, mistress,' he said.

'Listen to the friar, Cecily, and do as he bids,' said Sir Aelfric, and she turned her head and looked straight into the man's wide blue eyes. He seemed to be gazing at her in wonder, as if he could read all her thoughts, and for a moment the world seemed to stand still. Then he recollected himself, and rose to his feet.

'Take care of your mother, mistress,' he said in a voice that shook slightly. 'She needs you to comfort her.'

'Aye, good Friar, I will,' she answered, and inclined her head towards him. When she looked up, he had gone.

He had taken the opportunity to disappear quickly into the crowd and away from the tiltyard. He stumbled down the steep grassy slope to the place where the rivers Dene and Bourne met, and a willow tree stood on the bank. He leaned against it, his heart thudding in his chest and his breath coming in short gasps. He had fled because he could not trust himself to stay: he was unnerved by the sight of the girl's lovely face, the sound of her clear voice. She was Cecilia! – his patron saint, his guardian angel, exactly as he had pictured her, sweet and virginal, with soft, dark eyes that had looked into his as if she too recognized him, though surely they had never met. Was he having a vision? Or an illusion? No, she was his Cecilia, breathing, speaking, *living* in the world of the present time, not in a distant past.

'I thank Thee, Lord, for revealing her to me,' he whispered against the bark of the tree. A great amazement swept over him as he remembered her face, the sadness in her eyes – and at the same time he was aware of a lightening of his spirit, the lifting of a four-year burden that had hung over him, a grey fog of grief and guilt. His beautiful young wife Francesca, that reproachful ghost, cruelly robbed of life with her unborn child, had flown away into eternity. She had let him go, and now he could truly rejoin the land of the living. He was free.

But when would he look upon Cecilia again? Would he ever? Yes, he felt sure that he would, though he did not know her family's name, nor where she lived.

Oswald groaned loudly again and blinked at the faces around him. Sir Aelfric issued hasty orders to Widget to fetch a litter to carry his son from the field, and while Dan sped off on his errand, he looked round for the friar.

'We must thank the holy brother,' he said. 'Which way did he go, Cecily? He was talking to you – can you see him? Wake up, girl!'

She blinked and tried to collect her thoughts. 'He . . . he just disappeared into the crowd, father,' she answered, and obeying the order she had been given, knelt beside her mother to murmur comforting words while two menservants arrived to carry the groaning Oswald to the wagon in which the Blagge ladies had arrived, now put at the Wynstedes' disposal.

'He'll be all right after he has rested, Mother. You heard what the friar said, he has been badly bruised, but not broken. He'll be better by tomorrow, you'll see.'

Oswald was placed in the wagon, with his mother and Cecily on each side of him, accompanied by Mistress Blagge. Mistress Maud was willing to ride on Cecily's mount with Sir Aelfric at her side, and Widget was in charge of the other horses.

And so the party arrived back at Ebbasterne Hall in very different circumstances from when they had set out, but relieved beyond words that Oswald's fall had not been fatal.

'My poor boy, he must go straight to bed in towels steeped in witch hazel,' ordered his mother as he was carried up the stone stairs to his room.

Little Ethelreda and Wulfstan came running into the hall, their eyes wide with fear. 'What's happened, Mama? Is Oswald dead?' cried Ethelreda.

Cecily smiled. 'Hush! No, no, little sister. Our brother fell off his horse, but thanks be to God, he has nothing worse than aches and pains, so you must be very quiet and not disturb him, there's good children.'

In the room she shared with Ethelreda, now sleeping, Cecily stood and looked out of the window at the darkened countryside of a summer night. She saw again the grey-robed friar who had suddenly appeared and reassured them that Oswald was not fatally injured. And then he had turned to her and his wide blue eyes had looked straight into hers as if he knew her thoughts and felt a tender compassion for her. In the dark room, silent except for her little sister's soft breathing, she smiled and clasped her hands together in a prayer of thanks.

For surely, his was the face of her imagined knight, the prince she had seen in her lost dreams, alive and real! From somewhere deep within her being, Cecily discovered new strength, new courage to face whatever Fate had in store: it was as if God Himself had sent the holy friar to her.

Seven

1344

A week after the Tournament Abbot Athelstan received a cordial invitation from Sir Aelfric and Lady Wynstede, requesting the honour of his presence at their table on the following day, and if possible to bring with him the Franciscan friar who had attended Oswald at the time of his fall. At receiving the Abbot's prompt acceptance, Sir Aelfric called to his wife.

'And he *will* bring the friar with him; his name's Valerian, like the plant, and next week he'll be leaving the Abbey, so we're just in time to thank him, Kat.'

Lady Wynstede was delighted. 'How pleased he will be to see Oswald doing so well!' she enthused, looking fondly at her elder son, though Oswald was less enthusiastic at being reminded of his very public accident. His mother's preoccupation with him made her less observant of her husband's increasing pallor and tiredness, and though Aelfric did not complain, he secretly worried about the future for his family.

For Cecily, the news from the Abbey caused her heart to leap: *she would see him again*, he who had filled her dreams, waking and sleeping, from the day she had looked into his eyes and recognized her prince, her noble knight! But her second thought was one almost of dread. Would he be as she remembered? What would he say to her, if anything, and would she be able to reply sensibly, without blushing or stammering? Worst of all, would he be able to read her foolish thoughts? It seemed that her father sometimes could, for two days previously he had asked her if she felt happier about her betrothal to Edgar Blagge. She'd told him that she was content to agree to the arrangement made for her, for there was no reason not to be, and her mother constantly assured her of the rightness of the match. As she spoke she noticed that her father looked paler than usual.

'Are you not well, Father?' she asked anxiously, and was surprised by his reaction.

'My little girl – my Cecily,' he replied with unusual emotion, embracing her and holding her close. 'Edgar Blagge is a very fortunate young man, and I hope he knows it, and it's true that you could do far worse, my Cecily, but if you weren't happy—'

'Dear Father, I've put away the dreams I once had, and I've learned to accept reality,' she'd assured him, though in fact she thought constantly of the holy friar who had so disturbed her recent dreams, thoughts which must remain secret, never to be mentioned. But oh, if *he* were Edgar! She would not want to wait two years, but would gladly wed this very day! But *he* was a holy friar, under lifelong vows, and not for her or any other woman.

The next day dawned fine and clear, a continuation of the warm summer weather. Lady Wynstede had sent word to the Blagge household, inviting them to come to the Hall and meet the Abbot and his visitor. Master Blagge and his son were away on business, but the ladies accepted, including Janet, now eleven.

When the Abbot and the friar arrived at Ebbasterne Hall, they were cordially greeted in the courtyard by the Wynstede family, and introductions were made. Sir Aelfric was soon deep in conversation with the Abbot about the rumours of an invasion of France; it was known that King Edward III's intention was to build up a strong army, well trained and disciplined.

'It won't be this year, but will almost certainly be next,' said Sir Aelfric. 'Robert de Lusignan's sons Piers and Charles will surely go—'

'But Oswald is far too young,' interposed Lady Wynstede, at which the young man referred to looked rebellious, and stayed with the men rather than join the ladies, especially when Lady Wynstede suggested a walk in the demesne with the Blagge ladies, herself and Cecily and the three children accompanied by the dogs, running in all directions, with a great deal of laughing, shouting and barking. While the two elder ladies talked, Mistress Maud Blagge was happy to watch the children, cheerfully joining in their games; Cecily followed her mother and future mother-in-law at a distance, her head lowered, silent as a nun, occupied with her own turbulent thoughts as they passed through the empty stableyard.

When she heard footsteps behind her, she knew at once that

they were *his,* and waited for him to draw close to her. She'd thought he was with the men, but here he was beside her, the grey habit tied with a rope around his lean frame, his abundant reddish-brown hair down to his shoulders with a tonsure shaved over the crown. She glanced at his profile, then quickly looked away, but he had felt her eyes upon him, and turned to look directly at her. Their footsteps slowed and came to a stop. The sound of laughter and barking faded away like distant birdsong as they stood in the yard. Oh, let this moment of time stand still, she thought, here beside him, not speaking, not breaking the spell – but when she saw again those piercing blue eyes, she caught her breath, because *yes!* It was true, he was indeed the knight of her dreams. When he held out a hand to her, she took it and it was as if they knew each other's thoughts.

'You are sad, Mistress Cecily,' he said gently, and she felt no need to pretend with him, but answered at once, truthfully.

'It's because I'm promised in marriage to Master Edgar Blagge, Friar, the son of that lady talking with my mother.'

'Ah, I understand,' he answered, keeping hold of her hand. 'And when is this marriage to take place?'

'In two years' time, Friar, unless there is war, which might make it earlier,' she said, clasping his hand as if he were saving her from drowning.

'And your parents give their unreserved consent?'

'Yes, they look kindly on the match, Friar. Master Blagge is wealthy, and we are not. My own feelings are dismissed as whims and fancies, and I must obey, as all girls must obey in these matters.' There was a pause, followed by silence for a minute, and then she added, revealing her heart, 'And you are a holy friar, consecrated to God and St Francis.'

Her words fell between them, a shared knowledge, the thoughts that reflected his own.

'To God and St Francis and St Cecilia,' he answered. 'I must go wherever God directs me – but whatever fortune or misfortune I meet, you will be forever in my heart, Mistress Cecily.' He spoke like a man taking a solemn, lifelong vow, and added quietly but clearly, 'I have sworn devotion to St Cecilia, and you and she are one and the same to me.'

'And you will be forever in *my* heart, Friar Valerian, and in my prayers.'

Taking her hand in both of his, he raised it to his lips. 'I give thanks, Mistress Cecily, that whatever life holds for us, however far apart we may be, our hearts will be together.'

She answered with equal intensity, 'Yes, I know, Friar Valerian, always together.' And she too raised his hand to her lips, sealing the words with a kiss.

It was time to rejoin the others, and as they left the yard, Dan Widget's eyes followed them, for he had been behind a stable door and had heard much of what had been said. His honest heart ached for Mistress Cecily, for he too loved her, and with no better hope than the friar, seeing she was bound to Master Edgar Blagge.

'We shall meet just one more time before I travel on, Cecily,' said Valerian. 'I'm staying at the Abbey until Monday, and will be concelebrating Holy Communion on Sunday with Abbot Athelstan.'

She nodded. 'To receive the Body and Blood from your hands will be great joy to me.'

He kissed her hand again reverently before they walked on, exalting over their shared, sacred secret: Valerian and Cecily. Cecilia and Valerian.

On the following Sunday morning, Lady Wynstede led Cecily and her two younger children to the Abbey for the morning Mass. Sir Aelfric had said he would prefer to rest in bed after a disturbed night, and Oswald still could not sit down comfortably for any length of time. Kat had not chided her husband, for she was alarmed by his pallor and reproached herself for not noticing earlier how thin he had become, how constantly tired. She mentioned this to Cecily who admitted that she too was worried about her father, but tried to convince herself and her mother that their fears were ungrounded.

When the Bread and Wine had been consecrated by the Abbot, Friar Valerian and a grey-haired brother stepped forward to receive the Sacrament from his hands. They then faced the congregation, who, shriven of their sins, filed forward one by one to receive the Bread from the friar and the Wine from the black-robed monk. Cecily caught her breath as she drew near to the chancel steps, and privately whispered a prayer of humility: *Lord, I am not worthy that Thou shouldest come under my roof* – then stepped forward to stand before the friar. His giving and her receiving of the Blessed Sacrament was of such solemnity that she trembled at the sacred moment of Communion; but once received, she was filled with thankfulness, rejoicing as she returned to her place, strengthened and consoled. Now she accepted her duty, resigned to marrying Edgar and bearing his children, for God had sent her this lifelong blessing, chaste and holy, to light her way along the path of obedience to parents and husband. Her prince, her noble knight had come to her after all, in the guise of a man of God who loved her and would never have a wife to supplant her in his heart.

That summer continued hot, and the cornfields turned from green to golden. From Castle de Lusignan came news of another tournament to be held in September, three months after the previous one. In spite of Lady Wynstede's misgivings and in direct defiance of her wishes, Oswald was determined to enter the lists of the Little Tourney again with Charles de Lusignan and Warren Gyfford. A great deal of practising in bowmanship took place on the uneven grassy slope to the south of Ebbasterne Hall, and young Wulfstan narrowly escaped being hit by an arrow, thanks to Oswald's clumsiness with the longbow.

'Get out of the way, you little fool! Whoever let you out needs a thrashing – or a ducking!' Oswald roared, sending the boy crying to his elder sister who strode down to where the youths were practising.

'Don't you *dare* to speak to your little brother like that!' she shouted to Oswald who reddened with embarrassment at being thus rebuked in front of Charles and Warren. 'It's just as well you're such a bad shot. Imagine if you'd—' She broke off, chilled by the very thought of such a calamity, and stalked off back to the manor, leaving Oswald to face the grins of his two companions.

'Is Oswald still playing at jousting with those other boys?' asked Kat, frowning.

'I think all three of them are finding it more difficult than they bargained for,' replied Cecily, neatly avoiding a direct answer, knowing her mother's anxiety about her son. Life wasn't easy these days; the servants were growing slack and disrespectful, and both she and her mother worried about Sir Aelfric's health. Heaven only knew what would happen if – but it was foolish to worry over what might not happen. Even so, she suppressed a shiver.

Unable to talk frankly with her anxious mother, she found herself confiding in her future sister-in-law. Maud was a shy but friendly girl, happy to join in children's games, but quiet like her mother in company. She readily listened to Cecily's fears about her father's health, and sympathized accordingly.

But it was the unexpected that happened. On a mild September morning, just two days before the Tournament, a messenger rode into the inner courtyard, dismounted and told Dan Widget that he must speak to Sir Aelfric and Lady Wynstede at once. Cecily, who had seen his arrival, came out and recognized him as a manservant of the Blagges. He bowed to her, but repeated that he had been told to speak first to her parents. She obediently led him up two flights of stairs to her parents' room, where Aelfric lay dozing in bed, and Katrine, fully dressed, was sitting on the side of it. As soon as Cecily mentioned that the man was from the Blagge household, Kat rose at once, filled with alarm, for such a sudden intrusion could only mean bad news.

'What in God's name has happened?' she asked as the man bowed to them.

'Your – my news is bad, Madam,' faltered the man, 'and my master's grief is great, for his good wife lies dead in their bed. He found her cold beside him when he awoke.'

'Good God, what trouble has befallen!' cried Katrine, and Cecily went to her mother's side and placed a hand on her arm. 'Hush, Mother, let him speak.'

The messenger could only affirm what he had said and give what few details he had. Quiet, unassuming Mrs Blagge who had shown no signs of illness nor made any complaint, had died peacefully in her sleep. She had been sixty years old, a good length of contented life. Cecily's first thought was of Maud, her friend, and her second thought was of Edgar, her future husband, the brother and sister so suddenly robbed of their mother.

'Oh, poor Master Blagge!' wailed Katrine, shaking her head. 'Is this true? I cannot take it in. Oh, what a tragedy! Whatever can we do to help the family?'

Aelfric looked grave, but kept his feelings to himself, letting his wife express hers. *His* first thought was for his daughter Cecily, and what changes this might make to her life, losing a kindly mother-in-law, a potential good friend. His heart sank within him, for he knew that his own time was short and he feared for the future of his loved ones.

The messenger was sent back to the stricken household with condolences, and Lady Wynstede and Cecily prepared themselves to visit the Blagge family immediately.

'The house will be in disarray after such a shock, and poor Maud will have to take over her mother's duties,' said Katrine. 'She'll have to give orders to the servants, and see that food is prepared and served. Perhaps I'll be able to advise her. Let us take some provisions with us – there'll be a newly baked loaf in the oven, and a round of cheese from the dairy – and there's plenty of fruit – oh, I simply cannot believe it!'

On their arrival at Blagge House, Maud ran out to meet them as Cecily dismounted, holding out her arms to her friend. 'Cecily! I knew you'd come to us, as soon as you heard.'

'Oh, my poor Maud.' The girls embraced, and Maud bowed to Lady Wynstede.

'Edgar's in the study with my father. There are so many things to be done at a time like this. She . . . she will be buried in the Abbey cemetery, and the sexton is coming to make the arrangements. Oh, Cecily, it is so hard to bear – gone without farewell or blessing, and I can't believe that I shall never see her again,' Maud said in a burst of sobs, hitherto restrained.

'All our lives are a journey, dearest Maud, and your mother was a virtuous woman who has gone to meet her Lord and Saviour in the heavenly courts,' Cecily said, her own eyes filling with tears, and leaving out any distressing reference to purgatory.

A maidservant brought in a tray with wine and water in pewter cups, and a plate of sweet pastries. Maud sent her to Master Blagge's study, to tell him they had visitors, and about ten minutes later Edgar appeared, looking pale but composed. He bowed to the ladies.

'You are very kind,' he said awkwardly. 'But my father is unable to receive visitors.'

'Of course we understand, Edgar, and I too must ask your pardon for Sir Aelfric's absence due to . . . er, feeling unwell,' said Katrine.

'But Cecily and I are here to offer our sympathy in your great loss, dear Edgar, for you are already dear to us.' She gave Cecily a nod, to indicate that she should speak, but Cecily, still holding Maud's hand, was silent.

'You are very kind,' Edgar repeated. 'My sister is much comforted by Cecily.'

'Please tell your father that we share your sorrow at the loss of Mistress Blagge,' said the lady. 'And we will not intrude longer on your grief. If there is any help we can give—' She nodded to Cecily to add her own condolences.

'Of course, we are so very sorry,' Cecily said at last in a low tone, looking from Maud to Edgar, and back to Maud. There seemed to be nothing more to say, and the mother and daughter therefore took their leave and returned to the gate where Dan stood patiently waiting with the horses, his face suitably grave.

Kat Wynstede felt at a loss as to what to say to her daughter. Edgar had been civil enough but his manner so restrained as to be chilling compared to her own courting days with handsome young Aelfric, when she had run into his eager arms at every meeting. After a little reflection, she reined in Sorrel so as to be beside her daughter and out of earshot of Dan, following behind them.

'All men are different, Cecily, and Edgar is not a man to show his feelings in public, and especially at a time like this. When you are married, and share his bed, you will no doubt be surprised at how changed he will be, how he'll show his love for you. It isn't easy to describe in words the closeness, the—' She stopped speaking, unable to find the right words. There was a brief silence, and then Cecily spoke.

'Don't worry, Mother. I shall be happy to wed Edgar. I am resolved to do my duty and bear his children, and ask for nothing more.'

Words failed Kat Wynstede, for her daughter sounded as unemotional as her intended husband. It suddenly struck her that Cecily had been different for the past two months, not overly happy or unhappy, but with a sort of quiet contentment that radiated from within. She saw a little smile playing upon her daughter's lips, and finally spoke again.

'Your father and I will be happy if you are happy, Cecily dear.'

Cecily did not reply, but inside her head she was continuing
the little speech she had just made.

*I ask for nothing more − nothing more than knowing that Friar
Valerian loves me in a much deeper way, and says prayers for me every
day, as I do for him.*

The crowds of pedlars, street entertainers and spectators that gathered
around Castle de Lusignan on the day of the Tournament exceeded
even the numbers at the June event. Sir Aelfric sent for his barber
to trim his beard, and made an effort to dress himself grandly
enough to accompany his wife who wore a low-cut green velvet
gown and her hair plaited and gathered into a silver net, encircled
by a chaplet of silver interlocking discs. The Countess invited them
to sit with herself and her daughters Marie and Alys, and confided
to Katrine that a wedding was to take place early next year between
Lady Marie and Sir Gilbert Benoît. The ceremony was to be in
the Lusignans' family chapel, followed by a great feast in the Castle
with noble guests from all over the county. The Wynstede family
would be invited, which Katrine was gratified to hear, and said as
much to her husband. 'It's a great condescension on Lady Hélène's
part, Aelfric.'

He nodded, noting that the de Lusignans now extended their
patronage to the weaver's daughter they had once shunned. It
was a sign of the changing times, he thought, like the new
generation of farm workers who weren't content to slave on their
lord's land for no payment other than some of the produce and
the lease of a humble little cottage on the lord's demesne. He'd
recently had a long and disturbing interview with his bailiff Goode
who was finding much discontent and downright insolence among
the workers, and had tentatively suggested that Sir Aelfric come
out and speak to the men with the authority that a bailiff lacked.
'They wouldn't dare defy *you*, sire.' But Aelfric no longer felt
strong enough to make the effort, and Oswald was as yet only a
lad of sixteen. How would his wife and Will Goode manage the
estate without him? The very thought of his beloved Kat in such
circumstances filled him with dismay, and his thoughts turned to
Cecily, as they so often did. Edgar Blagge would be a careful,
reliable husband who would ensure her security, and old Master
Blagge, having gained a daughter-in-law, would surely look after

the interests of her bereaved family. Cecily had said she was content to marry Edgar, and whatever shortcomings he might have as a husband, Cecily would be compensated in due time by the birth of children. Aelfric prayed that he might live to see her made a mother.

The sound of trumpets announcing the start of the Tournament roused him from his uneasy thoughts, and he sat up and put on a good face for his wife's sake.

For many months to come, the story of that second Tournament at Castle de Lusignan would be spoken of and marvelled over. There were triumphs and disappointments during the morning, and Sir Gilbert Benoît acquitted himself well, wearing Lady Marie's red ribbon, much to her pride as he bowed before her.

More spectators than usual gathered to watch the Little Tourney during the midday refreshments, for word had gone round that Oswald Wynstede was competing again after his disastrous fall three months previously. So there were gasps of amazement when on the first attempt, seated on Chaser, he succeeded in knocking down the straw man and thrusting the lance under the hauberk in the region where his heart would have been. He emerged as the out-and-out champion of the Little Tourney, and bowed deeply to his parents before he left the field in a blaze of glory and many predictions that he would be a great soldier of the King when the time came. Lady Wynstede could have wept with relief, and Sir Aelfric too was gratified and pleased by his son's prowess, for surely such a strong, brave young man would be able to take his father's place as head of the family . . .

Oswald did not have long to enjoy his success, for on the following day his father collapsed at table, and was carried to his room where he was waited on by a conscience-stricken wife who blamed herself for persuading him to attend the Tournament. She and Cecily took turns at nursing him day and night, with help from an older female servant. The apothecary was sent for, and brought medicinal roots to be ground to powder, and leaves to be boiled and strained to give as a concoction to ease pain, induce sleep, quicken the appetite and open the bowel. Every effort was made to keep him comfortable, and Ethelreda and Wulfstan were allowed in to see him for a short while each day; his little daughter sang him simple songs in her sweet child's voice, which comforted him, though his eyes filled with tears as she sang.

Ebbasterne Hall was hushed; the servants walked on tiptoe and spoke in whispers in the vicinity of the sickbed. Kat Wynstede prayed earnestly for his life to be spared a little longer, but when he began to sink into the final sleep, Dan Widget was sent up to the Abbey to ask for a brother to come and administer the Last Rites. Oswald and the children were summoned when Abbot Athelstan himself came to perform this Sacrament, anointing Aelfric's forehead and mouth with holy oil and uttering the words of the Absolution. They all joined in saying the Paternoster, and Cecily clearly saw in her mind the figure of Friar Valerian, his right hand held up in blessing upon the dying man. She closed her eyes as the soul of Aelfric Wynstede departed, and held her mother's hand as Kat wept silently at the bedside. After an hour had passed, Cecily and one of the women servants washed the body and put on the white shroud. She was calm and composed as she performed this last office for her much-loved father; she knew that she had been upheld by the blessing of the holy friar, and his closeness brought her peace and renewed determination to do her duty.

Eight

1345

Everybody agreed that it was no good time for a wedding but rumours of war with France had caused the Count and his lady to bring the day forward, for Sir Gilbert Benoît would certainly accompany the king on his invasion; another consideration was the approach of Lent, with its fasting and abstentions, so the wedding was fixed for Shrove Tuesday.

At Ebbasterne Hall there was indecision: should Lady Wynstede and her family accept the invitation, five months after the passing of Sir Aelfric? Kat was only now beginning to recover from her bitter loss, and did not really want to attend, though the new Sir Oswald was eager to go, having become friendly with Piers and Charles, and determined to go to war as soon as the king decreed it. Ethelreda and Wulfstan wanted to see a wedding, and Cecily thought her mother would benefit by meeting old friends and neighbours on a happy occasion.

'What I shall do without you, Cecily, I really don't know!' her mother constantly sighed, and Cecily tried to reassure her that her own wedding to Edgar Blagge would not take place for another year at least. It was Cecily rather than her mother and brother who consulted with Will Goode about the running of the estate, and she feared that they would not be able to keep all the house servants. Aelfric had always been rather vague about managing money, and his widow was not used to making economies.

'We shall all need new clothes if we go to the wedding,' she said, and Cecily gently tried to tell her that it was unnecessary.

'Dear Mother, new clothes are a luxury we can't afford, and we have gowns, cloaks, gloves and shoes a-plenty, all perfectly good enough. And who's going to be looking at *us* at such a grand wedding?'

'The people of Hyam St Ebba look up to us, and they mourn

with us for your dear father,' Kat answered sharply. 'What would *he* say if he saw us shamed before those Normans?'

In the event, Kat, Cecily, Oswald and Ethelreda, dressed in their best, went to the wedding, leaving Wulfstan, who was coughing and sneezing, at home with the woman who had been nursemaid to all four children over the years. They travelled in an open horse-drawn wagon, with Dan Widget as both escort and driver. Now a well-grown young man of twenty, he was even more devoted to the family, and protective of the ladies. He understood only too well how his Lady felt about losing Cecily to matrimony, and their present impoverishment. He would willingly have worked for nothing but his board, sleeping on the reed-strewn floor of the hall by the dying embers of the fire. His old grandmother had died the previous winter, and had never lacked food or warmth, thanks to the Lady's generosity.

Even in summer sunshine Castle de Lusignan had a forbidding aspect, standing on a rocky eminence above the river Dene; it had been built nearly three hundred years ago, when a nobleman's dwelling needed to be a fortress as well as a home. A thick-walled tower crowned with battlements presented an impregnable front, a position from which arrows and stones could be rained down on invaders, and boiling oil poured over them. Now with a grey sky above and a grey winter landscape around it, combined with a bitter north-east wind carrying flakes of snow, the Castle looked grimmer than ever, but once inside the great hall, the guests were treated to a blaze of light and colour; a roaring fire burned in a hearth wide enough to roast a whole ox on a spit, and candles set on the trestle tables and torches in sconces along the walls illuminated the brilliant woven tapestries hung up to keep out the draughts; the contrast with the grim exterior could not have been greater. A spiral stairway set in an angle of the wall led up to the family chapel where the ceremony was to take place in the presence of close relatives of the bride and her betrothed, and they would then join their guests for the wedding feast, sitting at the top table on a raised dais at one end of the hall.

Three trestle tables, each laid for twenty places, stood at right angles to the top table. Many of the guests wore rich, embroidered gowns and tunics, fur-lined cloaks and velvet jackets, much to little Ethelreda's wonder. There were a few gaps where some guests living at a distance had been unable to face the journey in winter weather, but it was a large assembly which rose to its feet when a fanfare of trumpets heralded the new husband and wife as they descended the spiral stairs, followed by the Count and Countess de Lusignan, old Lady de Lusignan, Piers, Charles, and Lady Alys. Sir Gilbert seemed to have no relatives; his mother was dead, and his father had fallen at one of the many battles against the Scots. Abbot Athelstan followed them, having performed the marriage ceremony, and took pride of place at the top table, sitting between the newly married pair.

The Wynstedes were placed halfway down one of the three tables, Cecily between her mother and Ethelreda; Oswald sat the other side of Lady Wynstede, next to an eager young man who was looking forward to fighting the French, so they soon struck up a friendship. The three Wynstede ladies were quite awed by such magnificence, and the dishes set out on the tables: roast beef, game pies, creamy cheese and new-baked bread with sweet pastries. Mulled wine, mead and ale flowed from flagons and jugs into brimming pewter mugs. After the Abbot had risen to ask a blessing upon the fare, the feast commenced. Cecily stole a glance at the newlyweds: it was said to be a love match, and Lady Marie was radiant, looking up at her husband with love and pride. Sir Gilbert was about ten years older, stern and dark-browed. He was in a genial frame of mind today, but there was an hauteur, an imperious set of his mouth that showed he was used to being obeyed, and hinted that he might be cruel if thwarted. He and his new wife were to return to his family home at Stratfield, and Cecily wondered how Marie must feel at the prospect of sharing his bed that night: would he be kind and patient with his young wife? It was said that he wanted to get a child on her before he left to join the King. Cecily tried to imagine herself in Marie's place, but found her thoughts turning, as they so often did, to Friar Valerian: she warmed her heart at the steady flame of their mutual love, even when parted by time and distance – and suddenly she caught a sharp glance in her direction from Sir Gilbert and lowered her eyes at once, ashamed to be caught staring.

'Isn't he *old*, Cecily?' piped up Ethelreda, referring to Sir Gilbert. 'And when he stands up, he's no taller than the Lady Marie!'

'Hush, *hush*, Sister, you must not say things like that in company!' said Cecily hastily. 'And he's not so old, he only seems so because you are still very young.' She could hear Oswald on the other side of their mother, speculating eagerly on the likelihood of war before the year was out, and wished that her brother would take more interest in the Ebbasterne estate, but at swaggering seventeen he seemed born to be a soldier, and it was useless to try to persuade him otherwise. Since he had become *Sir* Oswald after his father's death, he had not shown any greater awareness of his responsibilities, and Cecily could not get used to his new title, inherited from such a worthy father. She thanked heaven for bailiff Goode and grooms Ned and Dan – the latter would be having his dinner somewhere in the castle with the other servants, including those who like himself had accompanied their masters' families. Dear Dan, such a comfort, so loyal . . .

Before February was out, another change was sprung on Cecily. Master Blagge the elder rode up to Ebbasterne Hall to speak with Lady Wynstede. He was shown into the room that had been Sir Aelfric's study, and soon came to the point.

'I'm a plain man, Lady, and it seems to me that we need no longer delay in marrying Edgar and Cecily. If there's going to be war, it's better that our families be joined. My home is without a mistress, and although Maud does her best, I have other plans for her future.' He gave Katrine a knowing look. 'What say you?'

She hesitated, feeling somewhat affronted. This man clearly expected her daughter to keep house for him and his family after the marriage.

'I . . . er . . . what about Edgar?' she asked. 'Does *he* agree to marrying so soon?'

'Of course he does, he always agrees with his father,' Blagge replied briskly. 'Come, Lady Wynstede, you'll find me generous, and the marriage will benefit all of us. I shan't expect a dowry, in fact all the expenses will fall on me. No need for a grand wedding like the de Lusignans, and I'll be damned if I ask any of them to our table. What say you?'

'I . . . I don't know what Cecily will say,' said Katrine helplessly.

'Then find out – send for her and ask her! She's a sensible girl, and not likely to object to an arrangement that's all in her favour, and her family's too. I'll speak to her myself if you like. Edgar's not much for making pretty speeches.'

'No, Master Blagge, I shall speak to my daughter myself, at a time convenient to us,' said Katrine in a firm and dignified manner. She was recovering her composure, and considered that Blagge had overstepped the bounds of courtesy, as if addressing a weaver's daughter rather than the widow of a knight. She would make him wait for an answer.

'My husband agreed to a four-year betrothal, when both young people will be twenty years old,' she said, 'and as his widow, I have to keep to his wishes. Perhaps we may talk again in a month's time.'

In vain did Blagge protest and try to convince her that circumstances had changed since the betrothal had been agreed upon; she remained implacable, and he had difficulty in restraining his impatience. However, he assured the lady that he would give her as long as she liked, and took his leave.

The outcome of this visit was inevitable, for both Cecily and her mother saw the undoubted advantage of an earlier marriage and the security it would bring, to have a wealthy cloth merchant as a close relative. Cecily turned pale when her mother told her what Blagge had said, but she called upon the reserves of courage that the holy friar had brought to her, the God-given strength to follow the path of duty, and she gave her consent, at which Kat Wynstede had burst into tears, and once again Cecily had to comfort her. Master Blagge was sent for and thanked for his offer, now accepted.

'You've made a right decision, Lady Wynstede and Mistress Cecily,' he told them with a respectful bow, for he had realized the need for sensitivity in dealing with such matters. 'I'll see Abbot Athelstan and arrange a time for the wedding to take place in the Lady Chapel of the Abbey.' He smiled and added, 'Leave Edgar to me,' which was hardly encouraging to the bride and her mother.

The wedding was fixed for a morning in mid-April, a time of spring daffodils and burgeoning trees. The birds were singing as Cecily walked with her mother and brother to the Abbey, and Edgar rode with his father and two sisters Maud and Janet. His married brother and sister were also present, and Ethelreda and

Wulfstan were in attendance on their sister who wore a white, long-sleeved gown trimmed with white ermine at the neck, wrists and hem, a wedding gift from Edgar's father. They all took their seats in the Lady Chapel before Abbot Athelstan; the marriage vows were made clearly, and a ring was put on the third finger of Cecily's left hand. Prayers were said for their future happiness, they were exhorted to remain faithful to each other to their lives' end, and a prayer was made that they would be blessed with children; Kat Wynstede echoed this with all her heart, for it was now her greatest hope that Cecily would soon be made a happy mother.

The wedding feast was held at Ebbasterne Hall, and the servants bowed to the newly wedded couple when they arrived with their families to take their places in the hall, smaller than at Castle de Lusignan, and not half as grand, but warm and welcoming. One long table sufficed to seat them all, with the Abbot seated between the new husband and wife in the middle, and their families placed on each side to the end. Dan Widget bowed to the couple, and reserved a smile for Cecily, for she had asked if she might take her mare Daisy to Blagge House with Dan her groom, who would sleep above the stable with two other male servants. Oswald had not been willing to give his groom over to his sister, but Ned had found a substitute, Brack, a youth from a poor Hyam St Ebba family who was eager to be trained under Ned's watchful eye. So I shall have two friendly faces at Blagge House, thought the new Mistress Blagge, my sister-in-law Maud and Dan.

Abbot Athelstan had seen the looks that passed across the sweet face of the new Mistress Blagge, and secretly thought of Friar Valerian whose confession he had heard during the friar's visit to the Abbey the previous summer. When he, Athelstan, had given Absolution, he had gently advised the friar to keep away from Hyam St Ebba for the good of his soul, and to meditate daily on the gifts of the Holy Spirit; and yes, if the friar found comfort in praying to St Cecilia, virgin and martyr, he might do so, asking her for the gift of purity of heart.

Cecily Blagge, having vowed to be a faithful wife to Edgar, now also resolved to be obedient to his wishes, honouring his rights over her and willingly yielding up her virginity.

And so it was on that night in Blagge House, in a room specially prepared as a bridal chamber, she lay on her back as her mother had told her, and tried to respond to his tentative kiss and cautiously exploring hands. She realized that he was as nervous as she was, and whispered to him in the dark what her mother had advised her to say.

'I'm your wife, and I . . . I welcome you, Edgar.' As she spoke the words, she felt her body soften and her limbs relax as she lay beside him, and Edgar, conscious of his own arousal, and invited by her words to proceed, raised himself up, then carefully lowered his body over hers. Slowly, trembling a little, she separated her legs and drew up her knees on either side of him. She felt his hardness and gave a brief, sharp cry as he entered her, a stab of pain that her mother had warned her to expect, and she put her arms around him as he moved within her, his breathing coming in short gasps, quicker and quicker, thrusting deeper and deeper, until with a wordless groan like a man in pain, he reached a climax, as beneath him she received his seed. Then came a quietening, a calming like a storm subsiding – and a sense of achievement at having done her duty and pleased her husband. Edgar kissed her and spoke her name, and then turned on to his side, soon falling asleep.

For a while Cecily lay pondering on what had happened on this her wedding night. She had honoured him, and he had been kind. All the prayers had been answered, not only hers and her mother's, but also the prayers of Friar Valerian. She sighed, smiling in the darkness, and then she too slept.

Life at Blagge House was very different from Ebbasterne. The house was much smaller, and was as Maud told her, 'a man's house,' ruled by Blagge senior who wished everything to continue exactly as in the life of its former mistress. Maud, already a friend, was helpful in initiating Cecily into the domestic routine, and twelve-year-old Janet had to accept her, but only because she had no choice; Cecily sympathized with her, for surely any girl would resent an intruder in her mother's place, but Janet remained sad-faced and unresponsive.

There was a cook, Edda, who needed no instruction, for she kept to her old ways 'as when Mistress Blagge was here.' Two housemaids, Bet and Mab, tended to ask questions of Mistress Maud rather than Mistress Blagge; and above all, it was the atmosphere that was different, for whereas at Ebbasterne there was always somebody talking or singing, children playing, and dogs allowed to roam all over the house, here there was silence for much of the time, and the one dog lived in a kennel outside, in the care of the servants. In the afternoons Cecily and Maud did their embroidery in a south-facing room, and their talk sometimes turned to laughter; Cecily never admitted to loneliness, but conjured up the beloved face of Friar Valerian, and remembering their mutual love, felt no longer alone.

Once or twice a week she rode up to the Hall on Daisy, with Dan walking beside them. Those were her happiest days, when she was greeted with joy by her mother and young brother and sister, and the servants were all smiles. Dan would go off to the stable to see Ned and the horses, Chaser and Sorrel, and hear the latest news.

'Oswald wants to join the Earl of Derby. He's the King's cousin, and he's raised an army to attack France,' said Kat Wynstede doubtfully. 'Of course I don't want him to go.'

'It's not out-and-out war, Mother,' explained Oswald, 'it's just an opening shot. The Earl wants to win back some of the King's possessions in Gascony, and Sir Thomas Dagworth is sailing to Brittany to overrun the French garrison there – just skirmishes before the main action led by the King, but the de Lusignans and I want to be in at the beginning.'

'Sir Benoît will be joining the King, so why can't you wait until then?' asked Katrine.

'We don't know when that will be, Mother,' he replied. 'There are rumours everywhere about when he'll embark, and where he'll land, but nobody knows.'

Kat remarked to Cecily that Sir Gilbert and Lady Benoît were talking of moving out of their present home in Stratfield to one nearer to Hyam St Ebba.

'I'm sure he wants to be nearer to Castle de Lusignan,' she said, 'especially if the Lady Marie—' She stopped and gave her daughter a significant look. 'Just as any young wife needs to be with her mother at a time when—'

Cecily did not reply, because she wanted to be sure of her own news. She had not had her monthly flux since her wedding, and had been feeling a little strange lately, but of course the great change in her life could explain that.

On their way back, Cecily passed on to Dan the news of Sir Benoît looking for a home nearer to the Castle, but he stared straight ahead, with no expression of interest. She smiled.

'Don't you care to hear news of our neighbours, Dan?'

He shook his head. 'I'm sorry, Mistress, I was thinking about something else – different breeds o' horses, and that.' He smiled apologetically to hide his real thoughts, the rumours he had picked up from the bailiff and the groom.

One May morning Edgar took his leave of her, having been despatched into Kent on business for his father; there was a possibility that he would sail to the Netherlands.

'You will look after my sisters, I know, Cecily, and I'm glad you are a good friend to Maud. She may not live in Blagge House for much longer, because father is arranging a marriage for her.'

Cecily's heart sank. 'Oh, Edgar! Does she know?'

'Not yet. He wants to get it settled first. Don't say anything to her.'

'No, but—' Her first thought was of how she would miss her sister-in-law, and when Edgar had ridden away, she walked thoughtfully back to the house. Her father-in-law called to her from his counting-house, and met her at the door. He was frowning.

'Yes, Father?' she said, for so she had been told to address him.

'I must remind you that you are my son's wife, Cecily, and that this is your home now, not Ebbasterne. You are far too fond of dashing off to see your mother, like any half-grown, half-witted girl, and God knows what tittle-tattling goes on.'

She stared at him in utter disbelief. 'I *never* gossip, and never say anything but good about Edgar and your household,' she said. 'And he'll tell you I am an obedient wife.'

'You say well, but your actions tell another story. In future you may not visit Ebbasterne Hall without Edgar's permission, or if he is away, then mine.'

Cecily continued to stare, open-mouthed.

'And another thing – you are far too free with the servants, chattering to them as if they were equals, and especially that Widget fellow. He thinks too much of himself, and no wonder, the time you spend talking and laughing with him, like any common maidservant.'

Cecily felt her heart pounding, and a hot flush coloured her face and neck. Now she realized how spoiled she had been as a child growing up in the easy-going atmosphere of Ebbasterne Hall. From now on she would have to learn to be truly subservient, not only to her husband, but also his father – and if she was going to lose Maud, she could hardly bear the thought of losing Dan too, her faithful groom. She said no more, but bowed her head briefly to Blagge and went upstairs to the room she shared with Edgar. She could face no one in her present distress, not even Maud. Sitting on the side of the bed, Cecily wondered how long Edgar would be away; heaven only knew when she would see him again, and Blagge had taken advantage of his son's absence to show himself in his true colours. She burned with anger and resentment against the man she had formerly looked upon as an ambitious merchant with a sharp eye for a bargain, including making prudent marriages for his children. She saw his aims more clearly now: a knight's daughter for Edgar had been a good move, even if costly, but having gained her, he now revealed himself as a bullying domestic tyrant, contemptuous of the very class of minor gentry which he courted – families like the Wynstedes.

What could she do? She longed to see her mother, but he had forbidden her to visit Ebbasterne Hall without permission, and had threatened to dismiss Dan if she continued to be 'over familiar' with him. And it seemed that she was also to lose Maud, her only friend in this gloomy, hostile house. With such a prospect before her, she did not dare to defy Blagge, for if he carried out his threats, her life would be intolerable. Even if Edgar were here, she doubted that he would defy his father, for even though she had proved herself to be a docile wife who carried out her conjugal duties and had shown a willingness to learn to be mistress of Blagge House, Edgar did not really understand her, and his dutiful attachment to her was not the sort that would champion her cause in such a case. She could only submit to the restrictions placed upon her if she wanted to keep the few freedoms she still had.

What could she do? she asked herself again. Her mother would be looking out for her, and Cecily thought of sending Dan up to the Hall with a note, but that would entail going to the stables, and she felt Blagge's eyes always upon her, waiting for an opportunity to reprimand her and curtail her movements further. She was trapped like a wild bird in a cage.

She laid herself upon the bed, listening to the rapid beating of her heart. She closed her eyes, and took some slow, deep breaths; Friar Valerian would advise her to pray, so she got off the bed, and knelt beside it.

'Hear me, most merciful Father, and help me,' she whispered. 'Show me what I should do, and grant me the strength to do it, O Lord. Help me, Lord, and comfort me. In the name of Thy Son and my Saviour, Jesus Christ, Amen.'

She remained kneeling and as she repeated the words, she gradually became aware of a calmness, a consoling presence in the room, sent like an angel of the Lord. She felt a featherlight touch upon her forehead, like a hand giving a blessing. She drew in her breath and exhaled slowly. *Friar Valerian.* She felt the touch again, soft as a butterfly's wing, but now upon her belly.

And then the presence left her, but did not leave her uncomforted. She stood up and placed her hand upon her belly where she had felt the touch, and instantly knew that she and Edgar had conceived a child. The knowledge drove every other thought from her mind; she was to be the mother of a son or daughter, and her heart overflowed with thankfulness.

Thanks be to God and his holy friar who prayed for her daily! Let Blagge hold her captive and use his power to forbid and to threaten her, for now she too had a weapon, something too important to be ignored and set aside. And she would use it.

Cecily said nothing of her news straight away, but waited until the four of them were seated at supper that evening. Their father's taciturnity had a subduing effect on Maud and Janet, and Cecily's silence was unusual, as she generally led the conversation about little domestic events, and lately news of the king and his son Prince Edward who was to accompany his father on the invasion of France, though only fifteen years old.

'Where do you get hold of all these rumours and hearsay?' Blagge had asked her, chewing on his cold meat and crust of bread.

'From my brother Sir Oswald, who intends to fight alongside the king with his friends the de Lusignan brothers,' she had answered, at which Blagge gave a sceptical grunt. 'Huh!'

But this evening not a word was said; they ate in silence until the wine was poured; it was mixed with water for Janet, and Cecily held up her hand and shook her head when Blagge went to pour her wine.

'Not for me, Father, I shall drink only water.'

'Why, what's the matter?' he asked ungraciously, remembering his reprimand that morning, and thinking her refusal due to a sulky mood.

Cecily looked him straight in the eyes, then turned to smile at Maud and Janet. 'For a very good reason, Father. I am going to bear Edgar a child.'

There were gasps around the table, Maud gave a happy squeal of surprise, and Janet looked at her sister-in-law with a new respect.

'*What?* God's teeth and bones, why didn't you say so before? How long have you known this?' Blagge asked, looking distinctly taken aback, and not a little embarrassed.

'I've only been certain today,' replied Cecily. 'I have suspected it, but now I am sure.'

'Oh, Cecily, how wonderful,' Maud said excitedly. 'What will Edgar say when he comes home again and hears the news?'

'You had better speak with Dame . . . er, what's her name? . . . the Hyam St Ebba midwife,' Blagge said gruffly. 'She came to my wife when Janet was born.'

'I have no need of a midwife yet, Father, not until next year. What I *do* need is to see and consult with my mother, as all young wives do.' Again she looked steadily into Blagge's eyes. 'I shall go to see her tomorrow.'

She waited for his objection, but none came. She had caught him off guard, and knew that this child of Edgar's was far too precious for him to risk doing it harm by upsetting the mother, tiresome girl though he thought her.

'Oh, dearest Cecily, I'm so happy for you!' exclaimed Maud. 'We must take very good care of you now, mustn't we, Janet? What happiness to have a little baby in the house! Aren't you pleased, Father? This will be your grandchild.'

'Yes, of course – Edgar is to be a father,' replied Blagge, as if hardly able to take it in.

Cecily smiled round the table, but said nothing more. She had let fly her arrow, and it had found its mark.

The rejoicings at Ebbasterne Hall soon made the news common knowledge in Hyam St Ebba, and Blagge found himself congratulated by men he would never have dreamed of confiding in about such matters; there were good-natured jokes about his son's strength and prowess, to get his pretty young wife with child so soon after the April wedding. His manner towards Cecily mellowed, and she was allowed to visit her mother every week. When Edgar returned in September to be met with the news, he became almost obsessive about Cecily's health, and vowed that he would not leave home again until after the child was born, which Lady Wynstede reckoned would be in January. Cecily now saw her husband in a different light, for his concern for her and the baby took precedence over the business, and he invited his mother- and brother-in-law to take dinner at Blagge House one evening in October. Cecily was delighted, and old Blagge prudently joined in the rejoicing at his daughter-in-law's enhanced status; he had to admit, if only to himself, that she had become radiantly beautiful since she had conceived a child. So for the time being at least, he would play the good grandfather.

As they talked around the table Lady Wynstede remarked to her daughter that the de Lusignans had become rather aloof lately.

'Lady Hélène didn't send us an invitation to the Tournament this year, though Oswald competed in it, and did very well,' she said. 'I took Ethelreda and Wulfstan to see him joust, but we were spectators only, not guests of the family.'

Oswald made no comment, because he too had felt a coolness in the de Lusignan brothers' attitude, and put it down to the fact that he had outshone them in the Tournament.

'Lady Marie Benoît carries the same happy burden as yourself, Cecily, though I didn't go over to congratulate her and Sir Gilbert as I once would have done,' said Katrine with a sigh. 'I thought them uncivil, but that's the way of the world – there's not much reason to keep company with a widow of small means.'

Cecily privately suspected that the de Lusignans looked down upon the successful but unlearned cloth merchant to whom the Wynstedes were now related. Blagge clearly thought the same, for he now gave his opinion.

'That family's friendship is no great loss, Lady, so take no notice.'

'Oh, it's no matter to me, Master Blagge,' she replied, and changed the subject, but Cecily remembered Ethelreda's embarrassing remarks about Sir Gilbert at his wedding, and how disdainfully he had looked at herself. She agreed with her own mother and, for once, her father-in-law, that they need not mind being cold shouldered by a family not related to them.

But then came the dark November day when a messenger from Ebbchester rode into the courtyard of Ebbasterne Hall with a letter for Lady Wynstede: he had been sent by Humphrey d'Aincourt, he said, an Ebbchester lawyer acting on behalf of Sir Gilbert Benoît, the rightful owner of Ebbasterne Hall. He sent a maidservant to fetch Lady Katrine Wynstede, so that he could put the important letter straight into her own hands: it was from Attorney d'Aincourt, he told her, who wished to visit Lady Wynstede at an early date to discuss the matter. The messenger said he had been told to wait for her reply, but he had to return without it, for on reading the letter with Ethelreda's help, Kat Wynstede had fainted.

Nine

Sir Oswald Wynstede could only stare and utter imprecations against Sir Gilbert Benoît when his mother, pale and tearful, told him of the letter and the peremptory demand for her to name an early date for a visit from one of Ebbchester's most prestigious lawyers, regarding the ownership of Ebbasterne Hall, home of the Wynstede family for as long as anybody in Hyam St Ebba could remember. This, Oswald realized, explained the de Lusignans' recent strange behaviour: it was sheer embarrassment, knowing that their new son-in-law was out to claim Ebbasterne Hall, and evict Lady Wynstede and her family, so soon after the death of her husband who might have been able to contest the claim.

'Let me call on Cecily, Mother – she might be able to obtain some assistance from the Blagges.'

'*No!* I will not worry Cecily with this matter, being near to her time, and having the care of her own household,' declared Kat Wynstede firmly. 'And it is by no means certain that old Master Blagge would be able to help us, not being a learned man, hardly able to read. I can't see him or Edgar standing up at the next court sessions to defend our family's right to call the Hall our own. No, Oswald, the one person I can think of as likely to take our side is Abbot Athelstan. He holds the ecclesiastic courts at the Abbey, and used to come here sometimes to act for your dear father when he was not well enough to judge at the manorial court. Go to him, Oswald, and tell him of our trouble.'

He had to obey his mother's order, and without much enthusiasm he saddled Chaser and rode up to the Abbey. When he was cordially asked his business, he showed the letter and waited in silence while Abbot Athelstan read it, looking extremely grave. Oswald feared he would refuse their request, but eventually he spoke.

'This is shameful, Sir Oswald, and I have no idea where Benoît gets his information, but it will need a very clever lawyer to argue with d'Aincourt, and I have not that expertise. I know of only one who could meet him on his own ground. Do you remember Friar Valerian?'

Oswald nodded, for he had every reason to remember the friar. 'Yes, he visited our home a while back, when father was alive. But how could a friar help?'

'Ah, he was not only a friar, but a practising lawyer in London before a crisis occurred in his life that made him give up his seat on the Bench of Common Pleas and dedicate his life to the service of God. I had cause to admire his legal skill when he stayed at the Abbey some time ago, and settled a domestic matter that had come before me. Unfortunately he's a mendicant friar and travels from place to place, so cannot be easily found – but he may be in Southampton where many of the military are assembled in preparation for the invasion of France. It's possible that he intends to accompany the king on this venture. Have you a manservant who could ride to Southampton and seek him?'

'It would be like searching for a needle in a haystack, Father Abbot,' said Oswald gloomily.

'Perhaps not so difficult, for if he *is* there, he's no plodding mendicant begging his bread. He has remarkable powers of healing, and is known as Good Friar Valerian, so he'll stand out from the crowd.'

'I'll seat my sister's groom on a good horse, and send him to search for the friar,' said Oswald. 'My mother fears she won't stand a chance against a man like d'Aincourt.'

'Tell her I'll visit her at once,' said Athelstan promptly. 'And *I* will decide a time when she can receive Humphrey d'Aincourt, and *I* shall be there beside her when he comes, to tell him there can be no hearing until I have called upon my lawyer to represent her, and that won't be until after Christmas, when, God willing, we shall have found Friar Valerian!'

It was the third day of Dan Widget's sojourn in Southampton, a town full of soldiers and sailors thronging the streets, inns and houses of ill repute. He was tired, cold and had used up the shillings Lady Wynstede had given him in a purse which he wore under his clothes, on a belt round his waist; it had been spent on meagre portions of bread and cheese, and stabling for Chaser. His enquiries about a holy friar had brought only head-shakings, and a derisive, 'We ain't got no holy friars down this way, stranger!' Priests at the two churches he had visited had never heard of Friar Valerian, though there had been a monk, he was told, a Brother Ralph who had lived up at Netley Abbey who'd had unusual powers of healing and treating the sick and injured. Nobody knew where he was now, and Dan was near to despair. He *must* find the friar, for the sake of his Lady and her family, especially sweet Mistress Blagge, now almost due to have a child. Did she still keep Friar Valerian in her secret heart? And would he be willing to come to her family's aid? Dan had known for weeks that Sir Gilbert Benoît had his eye on Ebbasterne Hall, for very little news escaped the grapevine of servants' gossip, and Dan feared that the business with the Ebbchester lawyer would be signed and sealed before the friar could be found.

With a heavy heart he trudged into a grassy courtyard, not big enough or grand enough to be called a field, and almost collided with a workman, followed by his apprentice carrying his master's tools.

'It be hard goin' this time o' year, friend,' remarked the man in sympathy for Dan's woebegone appearance. 'Lookin' for work, are ye?'

Dan shook his head. 'No, Master. I be looking for a friar, a holy man o' God with the gift o' healing, supposed to have come here from Hyam St Ebba.'

'What's his name?' asked the apprentice. 'Did he work at the Abbey some years back? Was he tall, with reddish-brown hair down to his shoulders, and clever?'

Dan was immediately alert. 'Yes, that sounds like him – Friar Valerian he's called.'

'I think I may know him,' said the apprentice eagerly. 'He brought me back from the jaws o' death, only he was called Brother Ralph.'

'Where can I find him?' asked Dan. 'It's very important that I find him. Where is he?'

'Try Dillwyn's farm in the parish of St Boniface,' the young man said. 'He was visitin' there when we had the floorboards up, lookin' for woodworm, though we didn't find any. D'ye remember, Master? If he's not there, they may know where.'

'Thanks, friend, I'll go there straight away,' said Dan, seeing a glimmer of hope at last. The apprentice called after him.

'If you find him, tell him who sent ye – Nick Geddes, apprentice carpenter!'

'I'll tell him, Master Geddes! Thank you!'

With renewed heart Dan followed their directions and found the farmhouse, some way out of the town and about a mile from the church of St Boniface. His knock at the door was answered by a plump, pleasant-faced woman, and her face lit up with a smile as soon as she heard his enquiry. She called out over her shoulder, 'Friar Valerian! There's a young man here looking for you!'

And the next thing Dan saw was the friar himself who seized his shoulder and demanded, 'What's happened, Dan? Is there trouble? Is it Mistress Blagge? Tell me, for God's sake!'

Within an hour of reading the letter Dan gave him, the two of them were on their way to Hyam St Ebba, where they were greeted joyfully by Abbot Athelstan.

'Thank God, Friar Valerian – I knew you'd come if he found you – welcome!' he beamed, holding out his hand; Valerian bowed and kissed the ring on his third finger.

Turning to Dan, the Abbot told him to let Lady Wynstede know that Friar Valerian had arrived and that they would both call on her the following morning.

'Sir Oswald should also be present as master of Ebbasterne Hall. And you must take supper with us in the refectory,' he added to Valerian, 'after which I'll go over such details as we have before you meet the Lady tomorrow. Attorney Humphrey d'Aincourt has a hard reputation for getting what his client wants, by whatever means.'

Valerian bowed. 'I shall be glad to take him on, Father Abbot, by all honest means available.'

When they were later seated at a table in the Abbot's private room, Valerian carefully studied the letter addressed to Lady Wynstede, from d'Aincourt.

'The worst of it is that Sir Aelfric never made a Will,' said the Abbot. 'I have some records kept by my predecessors at this Abbey, but they will be of small use, I fear. There was indeed a widowed Dame Benoît living at the Hall at the turn of the century, and we have here the wedding of her daughter Merle in 1297 to a country lawyer called Wynstede. We have a document giving the birth of their son, Aelfric in 1300, he whom we now mourn. The widow's husband died young, and she lived on here with her daughter and son-in-law for several years. Our Sir Aelfric's mother was therefore a Benoît, but there was no title until he was knighted by the king in 1340 for his valour at the battle of Sluys.'

'Did his grandfather – this Benoît who died young – did he leave a will?' asked Valerian.

'Not that we know of, not here at the Abbey.'

'Are there records at Castle de Lusignan?'

'Nothing that we can access – Sir Gilbert being their son-in-law!'

'Or at Stratfield, the home of the present Sir Gilbert and Lady Benoît?'

The Abbot shook his head. Valerian sat silently considering the information before him, stroking his short beard and frowning.

'I thank you, Father Abbot, for inviting me to look at this case, and for offering me board with the brothers. We will meet with her Ladyship tomorrow.'

There was a short pause, and Athelstan said quietly, 'Mistress Cecily Blagge knows nothing of this. Her mother has forbidden that she be troubled with it at this time when she is approaching her . . . her confinement.'

'Yes, Father Abbot, so I was told by young Widget on our way here. I think her Ladyship is quite right.'

'At least not until this case has been won or lost,' said the Abbot with a sigh. 'As things are, it doesn't look promising.'

'Don't be dismayed about it, Father,' said Valerian with a half smile. 'I shall need to go up to London and revisit the Inns of Court where many manuscripts are kept of the peerage and so on. And there is the parish church at Stratfield, with its records. If d'Aincourt believes he can outwit me, he may have to think again.'

'Well said, my son,' said Athelstan. 'And now let's go to Vespers, and pray about it.'

* * *

The friar bowed to Lady Wynstede, and enquired cordially about her family.

'Well, Sir Oswald here is waiting for the king to invade France, though he knows I don't wish it,' she said, giving her son a reproachful look. 'Ethelreda is a little lady of ten summers, and is a great comfort to me, as is Wulfstan, growing up fast.'

'And Mistress Blagge?' asked the Abbot, knowing that Valerian would hesitate to ask.

'Oh, my poor Cecily, she knows nothing of all this trouble; I won't allow it to be mentioned, not before she gives birth to her first child.'

'Ah.' Valerian felt his heart leap, but gave his full attention to the matter in hand. 'It will be an honour to defend your right to Ebbasterne Hall, Lady Wynstede.'

The four of them sat down at a long table to study the Abbot's scanty documents.

'First of all, Lady Wynstede, have you any records of your family's history at Ebbasterne Hall?'

'No, good Friar, my husband seldom spoke of it.' Kat Wynstede shook her head sadly. 'I know that his mother was a Benoît, and his father was Ernulf Wynstede. There were those who said he'd married beneath him when he married me, a weaver's daughter.' Tears came to her eyes as she went on, 'But it was a love-match, and we had four beautiful children, so in spite of all the gossip and jibes, we were happy!'

'Even so, Lady Wynstede, and I'll do everything in my power to settle this matter in your favour, and as a friar under a vow of poverty, I take no fee,' he added, smiling.

'Bless you, holy Friar, I know I can trust you!' cried Kat, her eyes overflowing again. Valerian bowed and kissed her hand, but Abbot Athelstan kept his thoughts to himself. Had he done right to send for this lawyer friar? He could see no easy answer to Benoît's claim, especially if backed by the wiliest attorney in Ebbchester, for not even the learned Friar Valerian could contradict such evidence as there was.

December came in with fogs and chilly mists. Cecily's back ached, and the baby's sudden kicks were disconcerting when she lay quietly on the bed she shared with her husband. Edgar had proved himself to be attentive to her comfort, although they had little in common to talk about, apart from the approaching birth of their child. She was ever more thankful for Maud, now patiently sewing clothes for the awaited new arrival – dear Maud! The two sisters-in-law had grown closer over the months, and Cecily felt that she could not love a sister more.

When Oswald asked her if he might borrow Dan to ride Chaser on an errand, she warned her brother that he was on no account to indulge in any 'practice' warfare in a way that might put Dan or the horse in danger, and when he politely assured her that there would be no threat of danger to Dan or the horse, and that he deeply appreciated her consent, it was so unlike her usually haughty brother, that she now worried for a different reason: was something being kept from her? When she tried to pray, she saw only Friar Valerian in her mind's eye, as clearly as if he was in the room with her. Was he thinking of her? Heaven knew she thought of him, night and day, and she pictured their thoughts winging to and fro between them like birds. He was a holy friar dedicated to God, and she was a married woman soon to give birth to a child, yet the very whisper of his name comforted her, and her love for him transcended all other attachments.

A letter was written to Attorney d'Aincourt, signed by Lady Wynstede and Friar Valerian, informing him that the friar, formerly Ralph de Courcy of the Court of Common Pleas, was to defend the Lady's ownership of Ebbasterne Hall and its demesne. Due to the friar's need to go to the Inns of Court in London to research his case, he formally requested more time to prepare his defence, and named the first week of January as being convenient to Lady Wynstede and himself, adding that Abbot Athelstan had graciously consented to hold the hearing at the Ecclesiastical Court at the Abbey.

A messenger was sent the next morning to Ebbchester with the letter, and he returned in the December dusk with a sarcastic reply from d'Aincourt, who said that if the learned friar wished to distress Lady Wynstede further by postponing the hearing until after Christmas, let it be so, the conclusion would be the same. And d'Aincourt had no intention of appearing before Abbot Athelstan; the hearing, when it took place, would be at Ebbchester County

Court. Before that, he had no wish whatever to parley with the friar.

'Don't be intimidated by all the bluster,' Valerian told Katrine and Oswald. 'It's only because he's now on the defensive. He won't be favouring you with a visit before I return.'

'Thank God!' said Kat Wynstede as he bent over her hand to kiss it and take leave of her. Abbot Athelstan said a prayer as Valerian rode away on Chaser to travel the London road, no easy journey in a bitter wind along muddy pathways and stony heathland, amid bare trees and early pitch-black darkness. On his arrival in London he called at a Franciscan friary and begged to stay under their roof and share their table for three days. He was readily received among them, and invited to attend the Offices in their little chapel when he was not out gathering material for his defence of Lady Wynstede: he knew that this would be his trial as well as hers.

It felt strange to see this great city again after more than four years, and to find nothing much changed at Lincoln's Inn where he had studied law in those far-off days. He studied endless cases of disputations over the ownership of land and property, fields, farmland, rights of way, churches and churchyards. There were many laws about inheritance: primogeniture, where an estate was passed down to the eldest surviving son, however unfit he might be; or the entailment of an estate to a male cousin or nephew of the same family name, when there were only daughters whose name would change on marriage, ending the line. He assumed that Attorney d'Aincourt would use this latter argument to defend Sir Benoît's claim to the Hall.

Immersed in these manuscripts, he was seen by a black-clad judge in a scarlet-lined cloak who stopped, turned round and stood regarding this friar so intent on his work.

'De Courcy?' he asked, at which Valerian turned round to face his former father-in-law, Justice Carver. He immediately stood up.

'Yes, sire,' he said quietly. 'I was once de Courcy, and now am Friar Valerian, and am here to prepare for defending a case in Hyam St Ebba.'

'You have clients, then?'

'No, sire, I'm a Franciscan friar under vows of poverty, chastity and obedience, and I was asked to take this case by Abbot Athelstan of the monastery there. It is for a widow whose right to her family home is being challenged.'

'Ah, property – it's at the root of so many disputes,' replied the Judge. 'But how are you? It's five years, isn't it? My wife and I thought you'd be married again, and raising up a family, but I see you've dedicated your life elsewhere. I shall tell her that we were wrong, and that you haven't taken another wife. She will be pleased to hear it.'

Valerian inclined his head. 'Even so, sire,' he said in a low voice. 'No other wife.'

They shook hands, and Carver asked if he might know the outline of this case that had brought the friar to the archives of Lincoln's Inn. When he had heard the details, omitting the names of the disputants, he asked what the friar had learned from the archives in this place.

'It sounds as if this knight, whoever he is, may be claiming the widow's estate under an entailment, by which a male relative with the family name can inherit in place of a daughter,' answered Valerian. 'He dwells at Stratfield House in a small village about twenty miles north of Hyam St Ebba. I have not yet seen his home, though I shall need to.'

'Yes, indeed, you need to leave no stone unturned if you're to get the better of Humphrey d'Aincourt! When you've got what you need here, go straight to Stratfield, and ask to see the parish records in the church. Lay low, of course, don't let yourself be seen by this knight or his kin. There may be something they're keeping quiet about, and anything you can find might be of use at the hearing.'

'Thank you, Father-in-law,' said Valerian quietly, holding out his hand which the judge shook warmly. 'Please convey my regards to Mistress Carver.'

'I'll give her the news of you, Friar, and may God go with you.' They exchanged a brief bow before the judge departed for home, leaving Valerian rejoicing that Francesca's father had shown him warmth and goodwill. And it was true that he had taken no other wife.

The parish church at Stratfield was dimly seen through a snow blizzard, and Valerian dismounted, leading Chaser as he plodded his way through the whirling flakes to the door of a low brick house that shared the churchyard. It had to be the priest's house, and he knocked twice, praying that somebody would be at home, for his head was aching and he felt chilled to the marrow of his bones. To his relief, the door was partly opened by an ill-favoured man who gave him a suspicious look.

'We don't entertain beggars,' he growled when Valerian tried to explain his presence on such a night.

A voice called out, 'Who is it, Sam?' at which Valerian raised his voice and answered, 'I'm a Franciscan friar, and I come in peace. Let me in, for the love of Christ.'

On his master's orders, the manservant called Sam opened the door to let the traveller in, and he stumbled into a study where a scholarly man with bright, observant eyes and curly hair down to his shoulders sat by a fire, drinking mulled wine; a mug was fetched for Valerian, and he thankfully gulped the warming, spicy-sweet liquid. He was invited to take off his cloak, and dry it on a wooden frame by the fire. Steam rose up from it, and Valerian remembered Chaser tethered outside.

'Have you stabling for my horse, sire? He's come a long way, and is weary.'

'Like his rider, I suppose. Very well. Sam, will you put this guest's horse in the barn? Not in with my Duchess, or he might do her mischief. Now, Friar, my name's Peter Owedith, and I'm the priest of this parish. Who are you, and what brings you here in such weather?'

Valerian gave his name, but when he asked if he might see the parish records, the priest was wary. 'Parish records? Yes, I have a few, but there are gaps. And first you'll have to tell me why I should show them to a stranger.'

Valerian shivered, and drew nearer to the fire, realizing how tired he was, how cold and empty. He must be careful here, he thought; this priest might be closely connected to Sir Gilbert and the Benoît family of Stratfield House.

'Are the Benoîts your parishioners, sire?'

'I would say so, yes. Do you know them well?'

Valerian searched for the right words. His headache was almost unbearable, and he shivered violently. Finally he managed to murmur, 'Not as well as I know the Wynstedes of Hyam St Ebba.'

'Ah.' Peter's eyes were humorous. 'I think I may know your direction, Friar; it's about some dispute over property, am I right?' Valerian nodded. 'But as parish priest to the Benoîts, I'm not free to say anything more.'

'More – more than what, sire?' As he stumbled over the words, there was a buzzing noise in his ears, and the room seemed to whirl around his head. He heard the priest's urgent summons, as if from a distance.

'Sam! Come quickly, this man must be put to bed. No, no, he must go in mine, the guest room's too cold, and he has a fever.'

And that was all Valerian knew for the next three days, sweating and shivering by turns, calling upon St Cecilia to intercede for him. Father Owedith wiped the sweat from his face, and offered him warm water and wine, reciting the Paternoster and Ave Maria, in which Valerian feebly tried to join.

Then came a morning when his head was clear and he remembered where he was. Peter Owedith was standing beside the bed, smiling.

'Good morning, Friar! Welcome back to the land of the living. You've been away talking with St Cecilia, so she must have preserved you from death, and now it's nearly time for the Feast of the Nativity. You must be hungry, you've had nothing but wine and water. Now, can you remember why you came here, and what you want of me?'

'Yes – oh, yes, this is Stratfield, and I must see the records,' said Valerian, remembering his errand. The priest sat on the bed and shook his head. 'I have a fair idea of what you seek, Friar, but it's not for me to disclose the family matters of my parishioners. However, when you are strong enough, I can point you in the direction of one who may be able to help you more than I can, if you show him proper respect. But first you must regain your strength.'

It was a full week before Valerian was able to put on his cloak and the boots lent him by the priest, to walk with Sam to a ramshackle thatched dwelling where an old scrivener called Sylvanus lived.

'There y'are,' said Sam. 'Don't reckon ye'll get much out o' Master Sylvanus, he's as mad as a monk in his cups.'

Valerian had to knock three times before a bent, bearded old man came to the door and peered at him. 'A friar, eh? What business are ye after?'

'I am indeed a friar, Master Sylvanus, and a lawyer. I believe you hold some Stratfield parish records in safe keeping?'

'Who sent ye here? Was it them Benoîts o' Stratfield House?'

'No, sire, I'm no friend of theirs. I am defending a widow against their demands on her house,' replied Valerian, deciding to deal straightforwardly with this old man, as Peter had advised.

'Oh, ah. Ye can come in and have a look at what I got. Which part d'ye want?'

'The turn of the century, sire, the births and deaths of the Benoît family, if you please,' said Valerian following the old man into a smoky little room with a fire burning on an open hearth and a strong smell of dogs; a scrawny wolfhound stretched out on a hearthrug.

'Sit there, Friar. I'll fetch 'em for ye.'

He disappeared into another room, and returned with a sheaf of manuscripts, which he spread on the table, clearing it of the remains of his breakfast.

'There y'are, birth o' Gilbert Benoît, 1311, that's the one who lives here now with his new wife.'

'Ah, yes,' nodded Valerian. 'Sir Gilbert Benoît, the one who's after Ebbasterne.'

'That's the one, born to Joanna Benoît, daughter o' the Benoîts who lived at Stratfield House then, and cousin o' the Benoîts who lived at Ebbasterne Hall. It was said she died giving birth to the boy, and her husband was killed at the Battle o' Bannockburn three years later, when the Scots defeated King Edward II. So the poor babe was an orphan twice over.'

Valerian frowned, aware of something unexplained. 'Is there no record of his father?'

'Not of a funeral, seeing as his body lay on the field o' Bannockburn – and they said he'd changed his name to Benoît so as to match it with hers.'

Valerian was bewildered, hardly able to take in this new information, and it was some minutes before he saw the possible significance of it.

'This could be useful to me, Master Sylvanus. May I make a copy of it?'

'What for?' asked the old man with a glint in his rheumy eyes.

Valerian hesitated, trying to marshal his thoughts together. 'I . . . I'm acting as lawyer for my Lady Wynstede of Ebbasterne Hall, and to prove that it's rightfully hers.'

'Ah!' A grim smile spread over the old man's deeply furrowed face. 'Then maybe ye'd better look at these other pieces o' paper I got.'

He placed on the table copies of the records of the Wynstede family, which Valerian had seen at the Abbey, the marriage of Merle Benoît to Ernulf Wynstede in 1297, and the birth of their son Aelfric in 1300.

'Old Dame Benoît outlived her husband for many years, and lived at the Hall with her daughter Merle and son-in-law,' he continued. 'She left a letter I've kept safe all these years, where she says she bequeaths Ebbasterne Hall and its demesne to Aelfric and whatever issue he may have. So I don't see how this 'Sir Benoît' thinks he can lay claim to the Hall. Here it is – I was her scrivener for years, right up to her death, and it's in my handwriting.'

Valerian picked up the yellowing letter. 'Take care with it, Friar, or it'll fall to bits else,' warned Sylvanus.

By now Valerian's head was clearing, and he stood silently contemplating the evidence on the table, hardly able to trust himself to speak.

'Is all this any good to ye, Friar?' asked the old man.

'It's all I need, and more, good scrivener, and may God and all the saints reward you for keeping these documents,' said Valerian with emotion.

'Hail, bright St Cecilia, for thine intercession,' he whispered.

Ten

1346

Riding back to Hyam St Ebba, Valerian at first basked in a glow of triumph over the success of his quest, and the way that he had been led to Sylvanus, the source of information that would prove Lady Wynstede's legal right of ownership. He anticipated the lady's relief and joy, and Abbot Athelstan's congratulations. Yet as he rode on he was aware of a nameless unease, a presage of trouble that he could not explain; he put it down to weakness after his illness, but in spite of his efforts to throw it off, it settled over his spirit like a grey fog.

'Blessed St Cecilia, intercede for me,' he prayed as Chaser covered the twenty-mile journey. 'Grant me the necessary strength of body and mind.' It was late afternoon when he descended to the valley where Ebbasterne Hall lay halfway between the Abbey and the town; and as he entered the Abbey's demesne, his apprehension persisted.

Although there was relief in the Abbot's reception, there were no smiles of welcome.

'You have been away for nearly three weeks, Friar Valerian, with no message. We have prayed for you daily, fearing that you had been robbed and were lying in some ditch with your throat cut, or succumbed to some fatal fever – perhaps the plague! Thank heaven you're safely returned to us at last, but I've had to ask for a postponement of the court hearing, which did not please Attorney d'Aincourt.'

There was reproach in the words, and Valerian asked for pardon. 'I have indeed been laid low by a fever, Father Abbot, but you see I've recovered and have good news for Lady Wynstede and her family. I carry with me proof that Gilbert Benoît has no entitlement to Ebbasterne Hall. May I take this news to her before nightfall? She will be—'

'Hush, Friar, say no more,' said the Abbot, cutting him short.

'Lady Wynstede is at Blagge House, comforting her daughter in the travail of childbirth.'

'O merciful heaven, so soon?' gasped Valerian, instantly alert. 'Surely it wasn't to be for another month yet!'

'You forget how long you've been away, Friar; we are well into January, and Mistress Blagge's pains came upon her three days ago.'

'O my God, sweet Cecily, what sorrow is this?' groaned Valerian, remembering his uneasy thoughts on his journey from Stratfield. 'Let me go to her, let me speak to her!'

'Hush, Friar, this is highly unseemly. Mistress Blagge is a married woman, bearing her husband's child. I forbid you to intrude on such women's matters—'

'No, I must go to her – I *will* go,' Valerian almost shouted, all other considerations set aside by this alarming news.

'Be quiet and listen to me, my son,' the Abbot began, but at that moment there was a knock on the door, and a grave-faced brother appeared. He glanced quickly at Valerian.

'Forgive me, Father Abbot, but a message has come from the Blagge household, requesting that a brother be sent at once to the bedside of Mistress Blagge, to administer the Last Rites, for she is close to death.' The last words were uttered in a whisper, but Valerian heard him, and turned deathly pale. A memory rose within his head, a terrible vision of another bedside, another young mother dying with her unborn child. He waited no longer, but ran from the Abbot's cell and out of the monastery. The messenger, Dan Widget, stood waiting outside the main entrance. He was distraught.

'Oh, come to her now, Friar, she's leaving us and needs a sight o' ye before she goes!' he begged, weeping as he spoke. 'Here, get on your horse and make haste!'

Valerian grabbed the bridle and vaulted up on to the back of Chaser, who had been tethered to a post at the door. Dan remounted his own steed, but before they rode away, a brother came to the door and called to Valerian:

'Father Abbot says you'll need this, Friar – here, take it,' – and held out a small silver phial; it contained consecrated oil for anointing the sick. Valerian seized it and he and Dan set their horses at a gallop, down to the town together.

At Blagge House Dan was dismissed to the stables, and Valerian spoke to the Blagge father and son who were waiting in the parlour, away from the scene of women's business upstairs. No man but a holy priest or friar was allowed into a birthchamber, and then only when the mother or child appeared likely to die. A weary, red-eyed Edgar Blagge told him that the child had been born within the last hour, and was a living girl, but the mother had since lost an enormous amount of blood, due to weakness following the hard and prolonged effort of giving birth, and had fainted.

Valerian hurried up the stairs to the birthchamber and knocked at the door, saying, 'It's Friar Valerian,' then quietly lifted the latch and entered; he would never forget the scene that met his eyes. On the bed lay Cecily, wax-pale and still, her eyes closed. The sweating midwife, a stout, red-faced woman with greying hair, had a hand between Cecily's legs, striving to staunch the bleeding with a torn sheet rolled into a ball and thrust into the birth passage. Kat Wynstede sat weeping, and beside her Maud sat holding a mewing bundle on her lap, wrapped in a bloodstained towel.

Valerian's first thought was that his beloved Cecily was dead. He stood at the foot of the bed, and silently prayed for help, to know what he should say and do. He began by crossing himself and reciting the ancient introit, 'In the Name of the Father, and of the Son, and of the Holy Ghost, Amen.' His voice was firm in spite of his inner turmoil, and the three women briefly looked up at him; Kat shook her head and wept afresh, the midwife and Maud nodded acknowledgement of his presence.

'God grant that ye be not too late, Friar – her life's flowing away in the blood.'

'She's gone, Friar Valerian,' wailed Kat. 'She's left us mourning, and this poor child is motherless. Lord, what sorrow I've seen since Aelfric died!'

He moved to the side of the bed opposite the midwife, and touched the cold forehead. 'Into thy hands, O Lord, I commend the soul of thy handmaid Cecily,' he said quietly, and repeated the introit to the Trinity. He took the phial from an inside pocket of his robe, dipped a forefinger in it and leaning over the still form, touched her forehead, then her mouth with the holy oil. He put his mouth to her ear and whispered a fervent plea, *Don't leave me, my love, my Cecily!* – then made the sign of the Cross over her, and prayed aloud.

'God the Almighty Father, have mercy on us; sweet Jesus Christ our Saviour and Son of the Father, take pity on us; Holy Spirit, save us. Blessed St Cecilia, intercede for us.'

There was absolute silence in the room. Kat Wynstede held back her sobs, and even the newborn baby in her aunt's arms ceased her pitiful mewing; then slowly, before their incredulous eyes they saw Cecily's eyelids flutter and open; she stared unseeingly around the room until her gaze came to rest on the man beside her. She drew a deep breath, and a beautiful smile of recognition transformed her pale face like a ray of sunlight. Her white lips parted, and she murmured clearly, 'Valerian! O, good Friar Valerian!' For a timeless moment they looked into each other's eyes; then she lifted her right hand, which he took and raised to his lips. There was no need of words to convey the love between them.

'Thanks be to God, she sees and speaks,' breathed the midwife, and looking below the sheet covering Cecily's secret parts, she added, 'And the bleeding's stopped. She lives! O praise God for a miracle!' To Cecily she said, 'Ye've come back to us, my dove, don't worry, ye've got a little daughter. If ever I did see a soul brought back from the jaws of death . . .'

Kat Wynstede's sobs turned to exclamations of joy. 'Oh, Cecily, my daughter, I never thought to see you awaken – O bless the Lord and His holy Friar for bringing you back!'

She attempted to kneel before him, but he turned to Maud and gently taking the baby from her arms, asked her for clean water in a basin. Holding the infant carefully, he uttered the words of baptism, dipped his forefinger in the water and made the sign of the Cross on her tiny forehead. 'Has she a name?' he asked, but nobody answered so he named her Katrine, after her grandmother. Then he tenderly handed her into her mother's arms for a few moments, while the three women watched in awe.

'Give Mistress Blagge water with a little wine to drink, and fresh milk,' he said. 'Keep her warm and comfortable, for she must rest. Let there be no disturbance, no noise or upset of any kind. I will tell her husband that he may come up and see her and the baby for a short while only.'

Descending the stairs, his knees felt suddenly weak, and he clutched at the wooden handrail. The emotion he had so far kept in check now overcame him; tears spilled from his eyes and down his face, and he knew that he could not stand before Cecily's husband. Seeing young Janet sitting halfway down, he hastily wiped his eyes and told her that Mistress Cecily was recovering, and her baby girl had been baptized Katrine.

'I must return to the Abbey now,' he muttered. 'Pray go and tell your brother that he may see his wife for a short while, but not to tire her after the ordeal she has been through. You're a good girl – thank you.'

And with that he hurried away, avoiding the room where the Blagge father and son were waiting, and left by a back door. Outside he found Dan Widget waiting in fear for news, and told him that Mistress Blagge had revived and was going to live.

'Thanks be to God, Friar,' said Dan, and without another word the two of them embraced, the friar and the groom, sharing their thankfulness that the woman they both loved had been spared.

Abbot Athelstan was worried on two counts, and neither concerned him directly. Both centred on Friar Valerian, a man of exceptional spiritual gifts, yet Athelstan felt obliged to warn him against temptation in the strongest terms.

First was the problem of the Benoîts and their claim to ownership of Ebbasterne Hall. When the Abbot had first been told of Lady Wynstede's case, he had been more than happy to seek out Friar Valerian and ask him as a lawyer to defend the lady and her children. Now he questioned the wisdom of this choice, because he had come to realize the depth of the friar's love for his client's daughter Mistress Blagge, who, it was said, he had rescued from death. This could not be allowed to continue; the friar must not enmesh himself any further in this unlawful attachment; it was not fair to the young wife and mother to have Valerian so near at hand. How much was she involved, the Abbot wondered: did she know of the friar's secret passion for her, and if so, did she return it? Athelstan shuddered at the possibility, for it could lead to betrayal of her marriage vows and the ruin of Valerian's vocation, with irredeemable disgrace to them both. And was the friar's legal skill and knowledge a match for the wily attorney who dealt regularly with cases like this? When Athelstan had sent a message to d'Aincourt suggesting a day in February for the court hearing, a haughty reply had been sent back, dismissing the suggestion because of Master d'Aincourt's many other commitments, and naming a date in March which would have to do, and no later under any circumstances. Smarting under this discourtesy, Athelstan would have liked to send Valerian away from Hyam St Ebba and Mistress Blagge, but this was no time to dispense with his services, for if the outcome was victory for the Benoîts, the widow would be evicted from her home, to face unthinkable hardship.

Gradually Mistress Blagge recovered her strength; her mind was not only on the painful soreness of her woman's parts, stretched and torn by the baby's journey out of the womb, nor her weakness from the heavy loss of blood; she still re-lived her experience of being called back to life.

It had been no dream. Her mother affirmed that the friar had indeed visited her to administer the Last Rites of the church, and that she had revived at his touch, and life had returned to her: her mother, sister-in-law and the midwife had seen it with their own eyes.

When Edgar entered the birthchamber and saw her awake and smiling, he was almost overcome with relief – and there in the wooden cradle was his baby daughter, no longer mewing but crying lustily. The ordeal was over, and Cecily gladly held up her face for her husband to kiss.

Later she heard that her father-in-law had wanted to give money to the friar.

'But of course it was refused, and we haven't seen him since,' said Kat. 'Oh, Cecily, we are indebted to that man of God for more reasons than one!' And she burst into tears.

'Dear Mother, don't cry, but give thanks for dear little Kitty,' said Cecily. 'My baby that Friar Valerian baptized and named Katrine! – that's the name I was going to call a girl. A boy would have been John, after Edgar's father – but why are you crying?'

'Oh, Daughter, you don't know the half of what we've had to endure from that accursed knight, Sir Gilbert Benoît!' wept Kat. 'I wouldn't let them tell you while you were carrying the baby, and I would shield you from it now, but you'll have to know sometime.'

And bit by bit the story came out, to Cecily's shock and anger, and she chided her mother for not telling her before.

'I couldn't bear to worry you, Cecily, and I wouldn't be telling you now if I was sure that we would win the case,' sobbed Kat. 'But Sir Benoît has found a very clever attorney in Ebbchester, a man they say who always finds in his client's favour, right or wrong, and I think the Abbot has his doubts also. Oh, Cecily, what will become of us if we lose our home? We shall be homeless and begging for our bread!'

'Hush, dear Mother, don't be dismayed,' said Cecily, remembering that she had not liked what she'd seen of Sir Gilbert Benoît. 'You say that Friar Valerian is acting for you against this Ebbchester lawyer? Then we have no need to fear, because he is sure to win. Don't worry, dear Mother, you have got the very best of advocates.'

'How can you be so sure?' asked Kat, and Cecily replied firmly, 'I just *know* he'll rescue us, Mother, so be comforted.' Even so, it was distressing to see her mother's tears, and to think of her worrying all these weeks without Cecily's knowledge; she prayed earnestly that Friar Valerian would prove more than a match for the wily Humphrey d'Aincourt.

Ebbchester was a busy, prosperous Cathedral city, with a busy marketplace and buttery where livestock and produce were sold throughout the year. The Court House was a handsome building with ecclesiastic features, part stone, part Flemish brick. Beyond its imposing entrance there were two courtrooms, the smaller used for petty misdemeanours, where cases were judged by local Justices of the Peace; the quarterly assizes were held in the main court for serious crimes where the County Sheriff might act as judge, or a local abbot or prior in cases such as blasphemy, adultery and fornication; and where no agreement could be reached, a judge was sent from the Court of Common Pleas to preside, and a jury was sworn in.

It was to this place that Sir Gilbert arrived on a windy, chilly March day, with Attorney d'Aincourt in his black robe with white collar and bands, and a tasselled black velvet cap. Sir Oswald Wynstede also took his place in court, representing his mother, accompanied by the Franciscan friar in his grey habit tied with a rope around his waist. He smiled at his young companion, pointing out the judge and jury, telling him not to judge by appearances.

Sir Gilbert Benoît's advocate had produced an impressive number of documents, laid on a long table beneath the judge's bench. Both sides having sworn to tell the truth, Attorney Humphrey d'Aincourt was invited to put his client's case before the Court for examination. He first asked for their indulgence while he retraced the histories of the Benoît families, for there had been two branches at the turn of the century; they were distant cousins, one branch living at Ebbasterne Hall, and the other at Stratfield House. Both had suffered the losses of several children, and Merle Benoît had been the last surviving issue at Ebbasterne Hall. In 1297 she had married a country lawyer, one Ernulf Wynstede – d'Aincourt sneered at this point – and their son Aelfric had been born in 1300. The Benoît line had therefore ended here, and Aelfric had married Katrine Hobbs, a weaver's daughter of Hyam St Ebba (another sneer), and their four children were Wynstedes; the eldest daughter was married to a cloth merchant named Blagge.

D'Aincourt paused to let these facts be absorbed, for there were murmurings around the Court, mainly of surprise; it was not generally known that a Benoît had lived at Ebbasterne Hall at any time. Bidden by the judge to proceed, the advocate continued with a history of the Benoîts of Stratfield House. A Sir Walter and Lady Benoît had lived there for several years, and their daughter Joanna had sadly been their only surviving issue. She had married a gentleman called Nigel Fitzherbert who had taken on his wife's illustrious name of Benoît. Their only son, Gilbert, his client represented here today, had been born in 1311, and his mother had tragically died giving him birth. There was a brief pause, when all eyes turned to look at Sir Gilbert. To add further sorrow, said d'Aincourt, his father had been slain at Bannockburn whilst fighting for King Edward II against the marauding Scots, so Gilbert became an orphan twice over, to be brought up by his grandparents. On Sir Walter's death his hereditary title had passed down to his grandson, and now that same grandson was married to the Lady Marie de Lusignan, and had a little son. For his son's sake Sir Gilbert was now claiming his legitimate

property after being excluded from his rights for so long, and
the jury were invited to look at handwritten copies of the records
held at Stratfield parish church for confirmation of names and
dates of Benoît births, marriages and deaths. Sir Gilbert Benoît
was then asked to verify all that his advocate had told the Court,
and this he did in a quiet, subdued voice, betraying his emotion
at hearing again the sad history of his parents.

Friar Valerian, formerly Master Ralph de Courcy, attorney-at-
law, was then asked if he wanted to ask any questions of d'Aincourt,
and he replied that he needed time to examine the parish records
set out by his opponent. He was granted the rest of the day, and
the court was adjourned, to reassemble on the morrow.

After due examination of the records, Valerian and Sir Oswald
stayed overnight at an Ebbchester inn where they could stable their
horses, and Oswald was glum as they sat at supper. 'The evidence
that man produced was convincing enough, and written down for
all to see – whoever can read,' he muttered.

'Don't be talked into defeat by his persuasive tongue, Oswald,'
Valerian said lightly. 'I too have evidence to produce when I'm
called upon to stand up in Court.'

'There's nothing to dispute anything he said this morning.'

'Maybe so, but I have another document up my sleeve,' replied
Valerian, thinking of the letter that old Dame Benoît had left to
her daughter Merle and son-in-law Wynstede, stating her clear
wish that the Hall should remain in the hands of their son Aelfric.
He smiled grimly to himself as he thought of d'Aincourt's fury
when he saw that irrefutable evidence.

When the Court reconvened the following morning, Valerian
was asked if he had duly examined the parish records, and he
replied that he had, though he was fairly sure that part of the
Stratfield records had been forged. He then told the Court that
Peter Owedith, the priest of that parish, had directed him to a
Master Sylvanus who had been scrivener to Dame Benoît of
Ebbasterne Hall, and had produced the same Stratfield records
as those shown in Court the previous day, except that there
were gaps, like the marriage of Joanna Benoît – though Gilbert's
birth was shown – and no record of her death in childbirth,
nor of her husband's death at Bannockburn. Valerian now laid
his own documents on the table, to be examined by the judge,

jury and d'Aincourt, who angrily declared them to be a forgery, deliberately casting a slur on Sir Gilbert's parents. On questioning, the friar spoke calmly.

'It is certain that *one* of these is a forgery, my lord,' he said, addressing the judge. 'I ask you to believe that I obtained them from an impeccable source.' He did not want to have old Sylvanus hauled before the court to testify to their validity, but knew it might be necessary.

'Regarding the history of the Benoît branch at Ebbasterne Hall,' he continued, I have here a letter, undoubtedly genuine, written by Sir Aelfric's grandmother, the dowager Dame Benoît of Ebbasterne Hall, in which she bequeaths the Hall and all the land pertaining to it, to her daughter Merle and son-in-law Ernulf Wynstede.' And he placed the yellowing parchment on the table. There were murmurings around the Court, and d'Aincourt leaped to his feet.

'*That's* a forgery, if ever there was!' he shouted. 'I demand to know from whence this fake letter has come – and who actually wrote it. Name your source, Friar!'

Valerian's heart sank, for this meant he would have to produce the old scrivener in person, which he was reluctant to do. Sylvanus was both eccentric and unpredictable, and he might refuse to appear, or be disbelieved if he did.

'In any case, forgery or not, this letter cannot override the evidence of the parish records and the law governing the inheritance of property,' d'Aincourt went on. 'Whatever the old dame's wishes were, they are of no relevance in the face of hard facts, and this property was entailed upon the Benoîts of Stratfield, after the name died out at Ebbasterne.'

There were louder murmurings, and the judge called the Court to order, saying he would adjourn the hearing until the Tuesday of the following week, to give both parties the opportunity to delve more deeply into the records, and decide which were forgeries. D'Aincourt and Sir Benoît were furious, but had to restrain themselves from arguing with the judge's decision, thus laying themselves open to the charge of contempt of court.

Valerian now saw the possibility of losing the case, though he had noted a certain uneasiness on Benoît's face when the letter was produced; he had clearly had no idea of its existence, or of the rival 'parish records' that his opponent had produced.

Valerian and Sir Oswald had little to say as they rode back to
Hyam St Ebba, the friar to the Abbey and Oswald to the Hall
he had always believed was his home. Lady Wynstede wept when
she heard her son's account of what had happened, and said she
would be willing to appear in Court herself to defend her right
to her family's home.

'I'll face that villain Sir Benoît myself, and call upon all present
to pity my situation, so soon after losing my poor husband,' she
sobbed, and Oswald was at his wit's end.

And then an idea came to him as a last hope: Cecily. He knew
that their mother had told her of Sir Benoît's claim, and Cecily
had said that Friar Valerian would surely win their case; he now
believed that his sister should be made aware of the dire straits
they were in, now that she was recovered and back to being mistress
of Blagge House. Without telling his mother, he mounted Chaser
again and though dusk was falling, he rode down to the town. It
was just possible that Cecily might get some advice from old Blagge.

On his arrival the family were seated at supper, and Oswald
sent a message through the maid Bet that he wanted to see Mistress
Blagge. Blagge sent back an order to Oswald to join them at their
table and say what he had to say, so taking a few deep breaths,
he did as he was told. Cecily was shocked and horrified at hearing
of the turn of events, and old Blagge's face registered his rage at
not being told of the situation earlier. Cecily tried to explain that
her mother had not wanted to worry her while she was carrying
a child, and since she'd been delivered, she had been sure that
Friar Valerian would win her mother's case. This cut no ice with
Blagge.

'Why didn't Lady Wynstede come to me at once?' he roared,
banging his fist on the table. 'D'ye think it means nothing to me
that my son's family be disgraced by yours? By God, you Wynstedes
are fools! Why wasn't I told? Were *you* told, Edgar?'

'No, Father, but I can understand why – how—'

'Don't argue with me, boy!' said his father, rising from the table
and knocking over a jug of ale. 'Get that Friar what's-his-name
to come to see me at once – *at once*, d'ye hear me, not tomorrow,
tonight – no, wait a minute, I'll take Chaser and ride up to the
Abbey to see the man and the Abbot, whatever the hour, and tell
them how I feel – *betrayed*!'

'But Father, he's the friar who saved Cecily's life,' Maud said timidly, but he took no notice of her, and within half an hour was riding furiously up to the Abbey, leaving Edgar and Maud to comfort Cecily as well as they could, and Oswald to walk slowly home.

A sound of angry voices and accusations disturbed the silence of the Abbey, and the brothers came quickly to the scene. Old Master Blagge had burst into the sacred precincts, pushing aside the brother at the gate, and demanding that the Abbot call Friar Valerian.

'What can a chanting fool of a monk know of the world's ways, the crookery of lawyers?' he shouted. 'Bring me this friar, and ask him why in God's name wasn't I told!'

'Hush your noise, blaspheming scoundrel!' retorted Athelstan, also raising his voice. 'How dare you trespass in these hallowed walls? I'll have you thrown out – come, Brothers, and seize him! Out with him!'

A brief scuffle ensued as three brothers struggled with the furious man, and received cuffs round their ears and kicks on their legs; this was the scene that met Friar Valerian when he came to see what was happening. As soon as he recognized Blagge, he intervened.

'Wait! Stop, my lord Abbot, and hear this man out. I know him.' Turning to the intruder, he said calmly, 'You are Master Blagge, sire, are you not?'

At the sight of his grave face and sound of his voice, the brothers drew back, and the Abbot, hearing the name *Blagge*, held up a restraining hand.

'Take him into my parlour, Friar, and let him speak with you there.'

Valerian bowed and beckoned the angry, red-faced man to follow him into the parlour where he closed the door and indicated a seat on the bench which ran round three walls.

'Good evening, Master Blagge. Peace be with you.'

The merchant looked him up and down suspiciously. 'You're the man who revived my son's wife, then? You didn't stay long. My son would have rewarded you well.'

'I needed no thanks, sire.'

'And now ye're supposed to be defending Lady Wynstede against the rascal who threatens to take Ebbasterne Hall from her?'

Valerian inclined his head in affirmation.

'Then why in the name of Christ didn't you tell me of this? Why should she confide in you, and not in me? By what the boy Oswald says, ye've lost out already!'

'Not yet, Master Blagge. Attorney d'Aincourt has produced records that seem to indicate that Sir Gilbert Benoît may have some justification in claiming Ebbasterne Hall as his true family home, but—'

'Family home be damned! The Benoît man's a liar and a nobody who wants to get his paws on a better dwelling than what he's got!' Blagge broke in angrily. 'So he waited till that poor, sickly Aelfric was out of the way, and Oswald still too young to thrash him! But I know something about the Benoîts o' Stratfield. What's he saying now, then?'

Valerian hesitated. Was this uncouth man of business to be trusted with Lady Wynstede's private griefs? He was after all father to Cecily's husband, and perhaps should be heard rather than rejected, if only for her sake.

'Come on, come *on*, man, Friar or what-not, are ye going to tell me or not?' demanded Blagge. 'Remember, it'll be *my* disgrace as well as the Wynstedes if this case is lost, seeing that my son's connected to 'em by marriage. Make up your mind!'

Valerian nodded, for he now felt that this man had been sent to him for a purpose.

'Very well, sire, let us be seated together and I will explain the whole matter. Will you take some wine?'

'No,' was the ungracious reply. 'I want to keep a clear head. I'll have a sip o' water.'

Beginning with the history of the Benoît family at the turn of the century when a Benoît had lived in both Ebbasterne Hall and Stratfield House, Valerian revealed what was known – or alleged – about both branches, and the fact that the last member of each had been a woman. Merle Benoît had married a Wynstede, and Joanna Benoît had married a Nigel Fitzherbert who had added his wife's name to his own and fathered a son, Gilbert. Sadly Joanna had died in childbirth, and Nigel Fitzherbert Benoît had been slain at Bannockburn.

'Huh!' snorted Blagge. 'And so our Gilbert so-called Benoît has wormed his way in with those high-nosed de Lusignans, and got Humphrey d'Aincourt to stand up and spout this stuff at Ebbchester Assizes. And you listened to it all without asking any questions?'

Valerian shrugged and nodded; by now he dared to hope that this man with a grudge against the de Lusignans might furnish him with more tangible evidence against Benoît.

'Is there anything you can add to this history, Master Blagge?' he tentatively asked.

But a change had come over the elder Blagge. The fury had subsided, and a look that was almost regretful passed over his blunt features. He turned away from Valerian and chewed his bottom lip in silence for a few moments; then he looked up again.

'Ye say ye've spoken with the old scrivener at Stratfield? Did ye pay him anything?'

'Certainly not! I don't deal in bribes, and I'm as sure as I can be that Master Sylvanus is an honest man, and that his records are true, incomplete though they be. He's an old man, and I wouldn't like to drag him before the courtroom to give evidence, but I may have to.'

Blagge nodded, and looked sharply at the friar. 'So, if I were to ask payment for whatever I could tell the court – to call Benoît's bluff and win the case, you'd refuse to pay me, then?' he ventured with a cunning smile. Valerian steadily returned his look.

'I have already told you, sire, that I do not deal in bribes, and if your evidence – your solemn word costs money, I have to reject it.'

'Very high and mighty of you,' said Blagge. 'When does the hearing recommence?'

'Next week. Tuesday. I am sorry that you have been driven to thoughts of perjury, and I have to bid you good day,' said Valerian with cold politeness, repelled by the thought of Cecily having to live under this man's roof; and so their interview was ended.

'Has the man any knowledge that can help our case?' asked Athelstan eagerly.

'No, my lord Abbot. I am going into the church. It will soon be time for Compline.'

There was nothing more to be said.

★　★　★

For all his outward composure, Valerian could find no peace of mind. However much he prayed and turned over ideas in his head, he always came back to the thought that he had failed to defend Lady Wynstede against the claims of a heartless, grasping man, and that his beloved Cecily would share her mother's humiliation, and the fate of her brothers and little sister, turned out of their home and robbed of their inheritance. And how would he, a penniless friar, be able to help them? He groaned aloud as he knelt alone in the Abbey church.

He decided to ride over to Stratfield and talk with Sylvanus again, so set out in the afternoon of Sunday, hoping to beg the old scrivener to testify in court; but when he reached the tumbledown cottage, he learned to his utter dismay that Sylvanus was at death's door, attended by Peter Owedith who was administering the Last Rites. Valerian knelt beside the deathbed and joined in praying for the old man's soul. His last hope gone, he confided in Peter who suggested that he should return to London and the Inns of Court, to study again the relevant laws about inheritance, and try to discover a last glimmer of hope; he could consult his father-in-law, Justice Carver – but time was short, and he was due at Ebbchester Court in two days; Master d'Aincourt would never agree to another postponement, and Valerian had to face losing the case; there was no alternative.

On his return to the Abbey he found Sir Oswald waiting for him, with the news that Lady Wynstede was insisting on appearing in court to put her case before the judge, and call on the assembled company to pity her in her distress. Valerian did not attempt to try to change her mind, for it was just possible that she might succeed in moving the hearts of those who saw her and heard her impassioned pleas.

The court reassembled at mid-morning on the Tuesday, and Valerian resumed his position as advocate for the defence. The clerk of the court leaned over to whisper in his ear that Lady Wynstede had been shown to the bench behind the jury where witnesses sat, and added that there was a gentleman sitting beside her, who had introduced himself as a witness on her behalf, likewise another lady. Valerian turned his eyes towards the man, and his heart gave a leap as he recognized Master Blagge senior.

Next to him on his other side sat a woman soberly clad and with a black veil concealing her face. Valerian's heart began to race: what trickery was old Blagge up to?

The judge asked Master Humphrey d'Aincourt to summarize the evidence he had collected in support of his client's claim to Ebbasterne Hall, and Sir Gilbert gave a magnanimous smile around the court when the lawyer stated that his client intended to show every courtesy to Lady Wynstede and her children, and to give them a year's grace to stay in the Hall before they would be requested to leave. Nobody challenged the attorney's evidence, and the judge then called on Friar Valerian to make his own client's position clear.

The clerk of the court quickly whispered to Valerian that he would call Master Blagge next, described as a respected cloth merchant of Hyam St Ebba, and to a collective buzz of surprised murmurs this witness rose to swear to tell the truth.

The court fell silent when the judge addressed the man, asking clearly what Master Blagge had to say to the Court. Blagge answered with words that the legal world of Ebbchester would remember for a very long time.

'I regret having to distress the lady I've brought with me today,' he said, 'but for the sake of justice she must stand up and be named. Take off your veil, Mistress Benoît, and behold again your son!'

Murmurs turned to gasps as the lady stood and revealed herself as a woman in middle life, wearing a nun's black habit. Her features bore the mark of a sad life – and something else, a strong resemblance to the man who sat beside d'Aincourt.

'Ask her name, Friar Valerian,' said Blagge. 'Ask her when her son was born and why she had to leave Stratfield in a hurry, and leave her baby boy to be brought up by his grandparents. Ask her who his father was, and where he went – and ask her where *she's* lived all these years. Come, Mistress Joanna Benoît, tell the court!'

But the woman gazed upon Sir Gilbert Benoît, and burst into bitter tears. Valerian, filled with pity for her, tried more gently to repeat the questions Blagge had asked.

'What is your name, Sister?'

'Sister Magdalene,' she whispered, and when the judge told her to speak up, 'Sister Magdalene, your honour.'

'And where do you live?'

'At Lacock Abbey in Wiltshire, sire. I'm a lay sister there.'

'And how long have you lived there as a sister?'

'For thirty-three years, sire.'

'And what was your name before you entered the Abbey?'

'I . . . I was Joanna Benoît of Stratfield House,' she faltered.

'And did you marry a gentleman by the name of Nigel Fitzherbert who fathered your child?' demanded Blagge, and was reproved for interrupting.

'No, sire, I did not. I never married, and there was no such man as Nigel Fitzherbert.'

More gasps greeted this admission, and the judge asked for silence in court, as the witness's voice was so low. Valerian tried to reassure her, and asked her to continue her account of the long-ago events.

'After my baby was born, my parents sent me away to Lacock Abbey to become a nun, and gave out that I had died in childbirth and my baby's father was away fighting the Scots. Later they said he'd been killed there.'

'And was your son Gilbert Benoît, whom now you see here in this courtroom?'

'Yes, he is my son, my lost son,' she repeated, and broke into anguished sobs. Permission was granted for Valerian to question John Blagge.

'What do you know of Sister Magdalene – Mistress Benoît?'

'Ye could call me her half-brother, seeing that it was my elder brother who got her with child,' muttered Blagge, and another gasp ran through the courtroom.

'And was this, er . . . this elder brother called Blagge?'

'Yes, he was a tailor's apprentice who was packed off to Yorkshire and given money to stay away from Stratfield. I heard that he married somebody else, and I broke with him – don't know where he is now.' Blagge was looking flushed. 'It's hard for me to dredge up old family scandals, but I'm connected to Lady Wynstede through my son's marriage to her daughter, and I won't see her turned out of her home by *that* bastard—'

'Watch your language in Court, Master Blagge,' interrupted the judge.

'Why?' demanded Blagge, unabashed. 'I've shown up Gilbert

Benoît to be my brother's bastard with no right to a knighthood, let alone somebody else's property!'

When the hubbub had died down, a white-faced Gilbert Benoît, clearly shaken by the sight of his mother, but not moved to go to her side, was questioned by both advocates, and lamely testified that he'd always believed she was dead, and that his father had died in battle.

The jury lost no time in upholding Lady Wynstede's claim, and Benoît was dismissed, to the fury of his attorney who blamed his client for bringing false evidence.

While Friar Valerian was being surrounded, praised and thanked by Sir Oswald and his mother, he silently offered up a prayer of thanks to God and the blessed St Cecilia.

Eleven

1346

The reverberations from what came to be known as the Ebbasterne Hall affair spread far beyond Hyam St Ebba, a subject for discussion in the taverns of Ebbchester as well as in legal circles; the story of how a celebrated attorney had been outwitted by a sandalled mendicant friar in a worn grey habit, gave rise to amusement in some quarters and caused resentment in others. Valerian's first reaction was one of relief, for he had earned the tearful gratitude of Lady Wynstede and Sir Oswald, and knew that Mistress Blagge would share their thankfulness; but he also knew he would have lost the case without old Master Blagge and his dramatic revelation, and it put him under obligation to the man, which he found irksome.

'Mark you, Friar, it was a close-run thing,' chortled Blagge, rubbing his hands together. 'The old Abbess wasn't at all happy about me taking Sister . . . er . . . whatever she calls herself these days, Joanna Benoît, away for a couple o' days, but I dropped a few gold sovereigns into her coffers, and said it was for the benefit of Joanna's son who needed her to come to his aid – hah! That's a good tale, eh, Friar? And didn't ye see d'Aincourt's face? He wouldn't listen to another word from Benoît, though mind you, he'll have charged the man a fortune! And it's a good kick up the arse for them de Lusignans, finding out their son-in-law's a fraudster, and a baseborn one at that!'

Only for Cecily's and her family's sake could Valerian stay civil to this uncouth man who cared nothing for Sister Magdalene's heartbreak; only Lady Wynstede had gone to her side and thanked her fervently for coming to the Court. The lay sister wanted only to return to the silent peace of Lacock Abbey, and gratefully accepted the Lady's offer of a groom to escort her back to Wiltshire.

★   ★   ★

To celebrate the legal victory, Lady Wynstede gave a feast at the Hall, to which she invited everybody who had shared her recent sufferings. The guest list included Abbot Athelstan and Friar Valerian, as well as the Blagge family and several other families of Hyam St Ebba who had wished her well. It was to take place in mid-April, and Kat Wynstede wondered whether to ask the de Lusignans, but was persuaded against it by Sir Oswald, who said that they would either send a cold refusal, or if they accepted, old Blagge would say something offensive to alienate them again.

'I shall need you to assist me, Cecily,' her mother said. 'You must leave little Kitty with her nurse for the day, and come up to the Hall. We'll have a goodly table to set before our guests, and you will help entertain them. And how glad we shall be to see that good Friar Valerian again, he who saved your life and saved our home! We shall be forever in his debt.'

Cecily's mind was in that state of dreamy detachment that comes to a new mother, that mysterious bond with her baby who depended entirely upon her – for the sweet warm milk on which Kitty thrived, and the maternal devotion that kept her safe, clean and comfortable. Nevertheless, when her mother mentioned Friar Valerian, Cecily's heart gave a leap. She had not seen him since that day three months ago when he had come to the birthchamber and revived her, putting her newly baptized baby into her arms.

'He brought you back when you were about to leave us, and restored you to your child,' her mother had told her solemnly, and Cecily knew this to be true. And now he was to be an honoured guest at her mother's table; he would smile and speak to her, asking about little Katrine, and she would shyly look into his blue eyes again – her prince, her shining knight, no girlish dream but flesh and blood, not in armour but in the robe of a holy friar who had taken the name of St Cecilia's chaste husband.

It was time for Friar Valerian to move on, and Abbot Athelstan threw out some hints that he should do so soon. He did not allow the friar to administer the Bread at Holy Communion in the Abbey, so as to avoid close contact between him and Mistress Blagge. When they received Lady Wynstede's invitation, Valerian said he would go to the celebration and leave the Abbey the following day.

'Do you really think you should attend this feast, Friar?' asked the Abbot, unknowingly interrupting Valerian's private thoughts: it would be his last opportunity to see Cecily for a long time, perhaps years, which made it all the more reason that he should accept.

But the Abbot had his doubts, and strongly advised the friar to leave before the feast, to escape from temptation. Valerian tried to assure him that his love for Mistress Blagge was no earthly passion, but entirely spiritual, a closeness of souls and not of bodies.

'That's as may be, but you must take care not to be alone with Mistress Blagge at any time,' the Abbot told him seriously. 'Keep with the other guests, make sure there is always a family member or a servant present in the room if you encounter her.'

'I won't need any such restraint, Father Abbot, for I'd die rather than dishonour her.'

'You say well, Friar,' said the Abbot, but remembering the time of Mistress Blagge's confinement, he was not entirely convinced. 'Answer me this one question, my son, and forgive me for asking it: if the chance – if the opportunity arose that you were able to embrace her in your arms, to kiss her—'

'No, never, Father Abbot!' Valerian interrupted. 'If such a situation accidentally arose, I would give her a blessing and assure her of my prayers for her – and her husband and child.'

'Very well, Valerian, but remember that God sees the hearts of all men – and women. You may keep your thoughts from me and from everybody else, but not from Him.'

Valerian nodded and gave a brief bow to his superior, repeating his intention to leave the Abbey and resume his travels on the very next day after the feast.

Alone in his guest's cell, he reflected that God, who sees the secrets of all hearts, knew the nature of his love for Cecily, and that to hold her in his arms would be happiness past all imagining; but his love for her was great enough to distance himself from her. To pray daily for her and her husband and child would always be his duty and his joy.

★ ★ ★

The day of the feast dawned fine and clear. Cecily rose early and fed her baby before passing her over to the nurse for the day. She was worried about Maud who looked unhappy and anxious, and said she would rather not go to the celebration.

'Oh, Maud, whatever's the matter? There's something troubling you, isn't there?'

'I'm sorry, Cecily, I'm just being silly. Please forgive me.' And she burst into tears.

'What is it, dear Sister? You can tell me, you know how much I care about you. Tell me,' Cecily begged, taking Maud's hand in her own.

'I can't — Father says I'm not to tell anyone yet.'

At hearing this, Cecily at once guessed the reason for Maud's distress. 'Is it that Father has found a husband for you? He's been talking about it for some time, but oh, Maud, dear, are you betrothed?'

'Yes, to a Master August Keepence. He's a grain merchant, the same age as Father, and lives at Waldham,' wept Maud. 'He's the owner of a windmill, and Father says he has made plenty of money, so he's a good catch. His wife's been dead for seven years, and he says he's ready to take another wife — oh, Cecily, I must marry the man, and I don't love him! And Waldham is so far away — whatever shall I do?'

Cecily held her sister-in-law in her arms, wanting to comfort her; she weighed her words carefully.

'Listen to me, Maud. You know how much I love dear little Kitty, your niece, and you've said you envy me, for being a mother? Well, Maud, it's true, being a mother is the greatest happiness a woman can have, and when you hold your own child in your arms, you'll know it's worth all the begetting and the birthing. Come on now, put a brave face on, and come with me to the Hall!'

It was indeed a happy gathering, and a busy time for Cecily and her mother. In the great hall two long tables had been set up on trestles, and spread with loaves baked in the kitchen from early morning, with a variety of cold meats, mutton, pork and poultry, with pastries and pies; fruit was scarce at this time of year, but there were quinces preserved in sugar, and onions in vinegar.

Wine and ale flowed freely, and it was remarked that Lady Wynstede was looking more like her former self as she welcomed her guests; Master Blagge senior was early on the scene, but Edgar was away in Kent, having some business of his father's to attend to. The Abbot and friar were greeted with much enthusiasm, though Valerian deliberately looked away from the young mother he loved, and winced as he heard her father recount the story of how he had upheld Lady Wynstede's claim to the fine Hall in which they now stood, and got the better of Humphrey d'Aincourt.

'Thinks himself so clever, but I was cleverer still, eh, Lady Wynstede?'

'More cunning, certainly!' said Oswald with a laugh in which Blagge joined.

'Hey, does anybody know how so-called Sir Gilbert fared with the Lusignans?'

'Last seen heading for Portsmouth,' said somebody, and 'Gone to join Lord Derby's army in Gascony,' said somebody else.

'Ah, I suppose he reckons to cover his name with glory, and get a real knighthood from the king!' chuckled Blagge. 'I'll guess that young wife of his regrets she ever said yes!'

Cecily felt for the Lady Marie, and hoped that her baby son was a comfort to her; she thought of her own baby, how Kitty would be missing her mother's milk which Cecily had in abundance, her breasts by now full and aching.

Old Blagge gave a shout. 'Everybody gather round, I've got an announcement to make. Silence in court!' he joked, just as if he were the host, thought Cecily, and feared that Maud was about to be embarrassed. She was not mistaken.

'Where's Maud? Where's that dutiful daughter o' mine?' shouted Blagge, his face flushed with drink. 'Come up here, girl, and show yeself – hah! Come and meet your husband – hey, where's he hopped off to? Don't be shy, man!' He whistled for the bridegroom to be, as if for a dog. 'That's better – ladies and gentlemen, meet Master August Keepence, grain merchant of Waldham and my future son-in-law. Give me your hand, August – now yours, Maud, that's right, link them together, and we'll all drink a toast to the happy couple!'

Cecily lowered her eyes in embarrassment for her sister-in-law. Master Keepence was at least fifty, of heavy build and round belly;

his hair was thinning, and though his eyes were smiling now, he gave the unmistakable impression of a hard-headed business man.

'Looks more like Master *Keepmoneybags,* rather than just *pence,'* mused Oswald. There were further remarks bordering on ribaldry, and Cecily could stand it no longer. She had to intervene in some way, but how? Then an idea occurred to her: her breasts were sore and heavy, and showed a wet patch on her bodice. Should she call out to Maud that she needed her help to return to Blagge House? Jack Blagge would be furious at the interruption in the middle of his announcement, but what else could she do?

Then she felt a sense of being watched, of wide blue eyes upon her, and spun round to meet Friar Valerian's questioning look. She involuntarily looked towards the scene of Maud's humiliation in front of the company, and then looked back at the friar who nodded, understanding her wordless message. He strode purposefully towards the Blagge father and daughter, and said pleasantly, 'Good Master Blagge, if it pleases you to pardon my intrusion at this point, sire, I must beg a favour of you.'

'Eh?' Blagge frowned as the friar stood before him. If it had been any other man, he would have been angrily dismissed.

Cecily looked down at the wet patch in dismay. Good heavens, the friar must have noticed it, she thought as Valerian continued, 'My respects to Master Keepence, but I must beg for the assistance of Mistress Maud.' Thanking heaven that for Cecily's sake he had remained civil to this man, he went on, 'Mistress Cecily Blagge has to leave us to attend to your pretty granddaughter, sire, who has need of her mother.'

Before Blagge could answer, Maud shook off Keepence's hand and rushed to Cecily's side. 'Dearest Sister, let me take you home,' she implored. 'Little Kitty will be wanting her mother's milk!'

Blagge and Keepence stared in astonishment at this unexpected commotion; Keepence shrugged and remarked gallantly that men have to give way to women in these matters, and that if Maud was needed by her sister-in-law, so be it. Blagge muttered that it was unusual, unfitting, in fact, for a friar to interest himself in women's matters. Full breasts overflowing with mother's milk were subjects best avoided by men, especially holy men. He gestured to Keepence to pick up his pewter mug and down the contents. Women!

Lady Wynstede was by now at her daughter's side. 'My poor Cecily, I should have noticed that you needed to feed little Kitty! – but how kind of Maud to offer to take you home. I'll ask for Dan Widget to go with you.'

'That won't be necessary, Lady Wynstede,' said a quiet voice close at hand, and she turned to see Friar Valerian. 'I will accompany the ladies, and see them safely down to Blagge House.' He smiled and bent down to whisper in the lady's ear, 'Remember that I was there in the birthchamber.'

'Oh, yes, good Friar, indeed you *were!*' she cried, clasping his hand. 'You baptized the child, and have every right to see how she has progressed – and with Mistress Maud present – oh, Maud, you've been dragged away from your newly betrothed husband-to-be, and I really ought to go instead of you.'

Maud hastily assured her that she was more than willing to go with Cecily, and in ten minutes' time the trio left for Blagge House, watched by Abbot Athelstan as they went down the grassy incline, the ladies on horseback, the friar walking between them.

'How kind of Friar Valerian to leave the feast to escort them home!' Lady Wynstede said to him. 'He worked a miracle, you know, when he saved my daughter's life and baptized the baby. No doubt he'll be glad to see little Katrine again.'

'No doubt,' replied the Abbot.

On their arrival at Blagge House, the nurse thankfully handed the howling, hungry baby to her mother, and Cecily sat down in the nursery and eagerly offered her right breast, at which the baby sucked vigorously and the nurse held a cup under the left breast to receive the milk that dripped from it. Oh, the relief and deep emotional satisfaction of nourishing her child! It did not matter that Friar Valerian had noticed her overflowing breasts; the fact that he had intervened to rescue her and Maud from wretched embarrassment was all that mattered.

Maud showed the friar into the parlour and offered him a glass of wine. After about twenty minutes, she returned and beckoned to him.

'Mistress Blagge and Katrine are ready to see you now, Friar,' she said, and as he followed her to the nursery, she added hastily in a low tone, 'I'm in your debt, too, Friar; you rescued me from . . . from my father and Master Keepence.'

'Don't thank me, Mistress Maud, I was happy to be of service to two ladies at one stroke!' he said with a smile. 'I will pray for you. And please, you must stay with us now.'

As soon as he approached Cecily, she handed him the baby to hold, and he sat beside her with the satisfied bundle in his arms. With Maud fondly looking on, his world had become all peace and calm. The light of a warm April evening streamed through the west-facing window, and he imagined St Cecilia looking down on them bathed in its gentle glow while her namesake sat beside him, living and warm, a bountiful mother. For a while time seemed to stand still, and they sat in blessed silence; nevertheless time marches relentlessly on, and when he handed the baby to Maud and asked her to stay in the room, he turned to Cecily and took her right hand in his.

'I have to leave the Abbey tomorrow, Mistress Cecily.'

'So leaving *me,* good Friar,' she said sadly.

'No, not really. I shall not see you for . . . for as long as God wants me to serve Him elsewhere,' he replied. 'But you know I am always with you in spirit, every day and hour.'

'Do you know where you'll be going?' she asked.

He hesitated for just a moment, and then replied, 'I shall go abroad – to France with the king's army, as a chaplain; there has been a long delay, but by midsummer I believe the invasion will take place. Abbot Athelstan has heard from the Abbot of Netley Abbey that a fleet of ships is assembling along the Solent. Merchant vessels in the Port of London have been taken over for transporting men and horses across the Narrow Sea.'

'Oh, Valerian, what shall I do?' she cried, forgetting convention. 'What *can* I do?'

'You can pray for me, Cecily, and I shall be strengthened by your prayers.'

He raised her hand to his lips as she answered, 'Oh I shall, I *shall* be with you, Valerian.' She briefly held his hand against her face and returned the kiss. Maud saw and understood that they were of one heart and mind, with no need for passionate avowals of love.

'I must return to the Hall, Cecily. The Abbot will be expecting me,' he said, thinking to himself that he had not disobeyed the older man's advice: there had always been a third person present. Dear Maud, he thought, may her husband treat her well. He rose.

'It's time, Cecily.'

She nodded. 'Give us your blessing, Friar, before you leave us.'

He stretched his hand out over them both and the baby, and making the sign of the Cross, he invoked the blessing of the Trinity upon 'you and yours for ever. Amen.'

Then he left, for the everyday world awaited him.

As spring advanced into summer, and little Kitty learned to hold up her head and smile at her loving mother and aunt, the only cloud on the horizon at Blagge House was the inexorable approach of Maud's wedding to Master Keepence. Waldham being some twenty-five miles south-west of Hyam St Ebba, and Keepence constantly occupied with his business, it was not considered necessary for him to visit his bride-to-be again before she became his wife. A date in mid-June was fixed, and the ceremony in the Lady Chapel of the Abbey was to take place early in the day, followed by a wedding breakfast at Blagge House before the newly married couple set out for Mill House, Maud's new home in Waldham. Lady Wynstede had offered Ebbasterne Hall for the breakfast, but Blagge senior had declined.

'We don't want a lot of fuss,' he said. 'It's August Keepence's second marriage, and Maud'll put on a face more suited to a funeral, so the sooner it's over the better.'

Cecily was surprised when her father-in-law came to ask her for a favour.

'My wife isn't here to tell her daughter about her duties as a wife,' he said bluntly, 'so I'll leave it to you to have a quiet word with her about women's matters. August has had experience, and so have you, and seeing that women talk more easily to each other about these things, I'll trust you to prepare her.'

August Keepence had indeed been married before, and had a grown-up family and several grandchildren; he had told Blagge that he had no objection to siring one or two more, and Cecily made this the most important point in her serious woman-to-woman talk.

'Just think of the happiness you will feel, when you hold your own little one in your arms, dearest Maud,' she said, knowing how much she would miss her friend, as close as any sister; privately she prayed that Maud would have an early conception, for the only real comfort she could offer was to reassert the joy of motherhood.

Pondering on what little she knew of Master Keepence, she realized anew how fortunate she was in having Maud's twin brother Edgar for a husband. Her brother Oswald thought him extremely dull but Edgar was a steady man, no drinker, no womanizer, and honest in his business dealings; he would not have sat with the baby in his arms as Valerian had, but men on the whole did not appreciate very young babies; she hoped that Master Keepence would enjoy becoming a father again.

Meanwhile there were the practicalities of the wedding; Blagge restricted the guest list to family only, apart from Abbot Athelstan who was to marry the couple; Edgar, Cecily and Janet, Lady Wynstede, Sir Oswald, Ethelreda and Wulfstan. Two days beforehand, Oswald suddenly left to join the king's army, saying that there was nothing to interest him in a Blagge wedding.

'Of all the times to desert me, Cecily,' wailed poor Kat Wynstede. 'I shan't have another minute's peace with my dear boy away, risking his life in this wicked war. He's taken Dan Widget with him, and I just hope that Dan will look after him and not let him run any unnecessary risks!'

Cecily thought it selfish of her brother to take the groom, and was sorry that she had not had a chance to say farewell to faithful Dan.

The wedding took place on a beautiful midsummer morning, and the Blagge family rose with the dawn chorus to get ready for the early ceremony. Cecily and the maids prepared the table in the parlour, and Edda was busy in the kitchen baking bread. Cecily then helped Maud to dress in a gown of green velvet with a lighter green overskirt. She wore a circlet of gold upon her head, below which her hair flowed out over her shoulders and down to her waist, signifying her virginity.

'As soon as the marriage ceremony's over, I shall braid your hair and wind the plaits into two coils, one on each side of your head, and gathered into a gold net,' Cecily said, thinking that Master Keepence was very lucky, for in spite of her pallor, Maud looked lovely.

He arrived promptly on horseback, accompanied by a groom whose horse drew a wagon in which sat a frosty-faced personal maidservant to wait upon the bride, and which would carry her belongings when she left for her new home. The groom also led a fine chestnut mare, Clover, a gift for the bride, on which she would ride back with her husband, wearing his other presents, a pearl necklace and a gold ring. Master Blagge senior was well pleased by this show of generosity to his quiet, pale-faced daughter, and told her she was very lucky. The guests from Ebbasterne Hall arrived, Lady Wynstede still grieving over Oswald, and at the Abbey they were met by the Abbot and two of the brothers, who led them into the Lady Chapel and showed them to their places.

And so the couple were joined in holy matrimony, with blessings upon their union, and prayers for the marriage to be fruitful. Tears came to Cecily's eyes, for Maud and for her mother, grieving over Oswald.

On their return to Blagge House, the newly married pair rode side by side at the head of the little procession, followed by Cecily and her father-in-law; Edgar and Lady Wynstede came next, with Janet, Ethelreda and Wulfstan behind them; last came the two Keepence servants, the groom and the maid whose name was Meribel.

Edda, Bet and Mab awaited them with the wedding breakfast, and toasts were drunk to the happy pair; Maud clung to Cecily who whispered encouragement.

'Remember, Maud, how we have prayed for children. God grant that you will be carrying a child before the year is out.'

Well before midday the wedding party was on the road to a new home and a new life for the new Mistress Keepence. Cecily waved and watched until they were out of sight, then went to the nursery to hug little Kitty who was her great comfort and consolation. Her mother had asked her to go back with her to Ebbasterne Hall for the afternoon, riding in the wagon with Kitty. Ethelreda wanted to see and hold the baby, and Lady Wynstede could not help but smile at the little aunt's admiration of her baby niece.

'Oh, Cecily, be thankful that she's a girl and can't go off to fight in a war!'

When Cecily returned to Blagge House she found that Edgar had left for Ebbchester to visit the home of a couple newly recruited to Blagge's roll of home workers; the wife carded and spun the raw wool that the husband wove, and Jack Blagge had told Edgar to make a surprise inspection.

'If she's up to keeping him supplied, and if he can keep ahead of what we want, I'll keep 'em on, if not . . .' He gave a shrug, and Cecily thought what a slavedriver he was, sending his son off on a business errand on the very day of his daughter's wedding. Before retiring she went to thank Edda and the maidservants for their service, and all the good fare they had provided, now in the process of being eaten up as leftovers. She was touched when Edda commiserated with her over the loss of her good friend Mistress Maud, now married to 'that old man – er, sorry, Master Keepence.'

''Tis good we've still got our dear little Kitty,' said Mab, wiping her eyes on the corner of her apron, and Cecily was warmed at hearing her child called *ours*; it meant that she was accepted into the household, with the full status once held by her predecessor.

Cecily looked into the parlour where Jack Blagge sat dozing, an empty wineskin beside him on the table. She tiptoed away without a 'goodnight', and went up to the nursery where the baby slept with her nurse, and gave a last breastfeed before going to her room. She took off the daisy-patterned gown she had worn all day, and unplaited her hair. She washed her face and hands, put on her nightgown and knelt beside the matrimonial bed to say her prayers and ask a blessing on Maud – what was happening at this hour? Was Keepence gentle? – and for a safe passage for Valerian whenever he embarked for France; then she thankfully laid down on her side of the bed; it had been a very long day.

When she suddenly awoke with a start, it was dark, with a faint gleam of moonlight through the curtained window. Was that a creak on the stairs leading to her room? Could it be Edgar, returning late from Ebbchester? She sat bolt upright, listening intently, and heard another creak, followed by heavy footsteps in the corridor, accompanied by a belch and some muttering. The hairs at the nape of her neck pricked: it could only be her father-in-law who had been drinking for much of the evening, and he was coming to her door. She leapt out of bed to turn the key in the lock, but it

was too late; it was already clicking open, and Jack Blagge stumbled
into the room, cursing when he nearly tripped on the rug beside
the bed. He reeked of sour wine, but was not too drunk to grab
Cecily roughly round the waist.

'Come on now, pretty Cecily, ye deserve better than that cold
fish I caught for you – hah! Many's the time I've wanted to roll
ye over, God knows—' He pushed her down on the bed, and
when she tried to cry out, he clamped a huge hand over her
mouth. She could hardly draw breath, let alone cry for help.

'Be a good girl, dear, this is your lucky night,' he said with a
hoarse laugh that sent shivers down her spine. 'First of all, I'm going
to give ye a good spanking, not before time, and then ye'll get such
a ride-a-cock-horse as ye've never had – aah! No use hitting me,
lady, nor kicking me – aah, damn you, vixen!' he shouted as she
sunk her teeth into the ball of his thumb. For a moment he took
his hand from her mouth, and she screamed, '*Help! Help me!*'

'Hey, don't wake the maids and make them jealous!' He clamped
his hand over her mouth again, but her resistance was strong, and
as he tried to climb over her she raised her right leg and pushed
the knee into his groin. He gave a howl of pain.

'Damn ye, little bitch,' he panted, his foul breath in her face,
and again she bit his hand, this time on the forefinger; he took
it away, and she cried out, '*Help! Help me, Friar Valerian! Valerian!*'

Blagge heaved himself up, cursing. 'Friar Valerian, eh? That
canting monk, it's no good calling him now – he ain't here, but
I am!'

She screamed again, and he slapped her face. 'Shut up! Ye think
ye've got the better o' me, but I'll show ye! I'll tell Edgar ye
came to my room, wearing nothing but your beauty – hah! I
wonder what your lady mother'll say to *that*, seeing as she owes
me for saving her precious Ebbasterne Hall – not the holy monk,
but *me*.' He was standing up, and Cecily curled her body into a
ball, like a hedgehog under attack.

'Get out,' she said through gritted teeth.

'Don't worry, I'm going, you little fool, and if ye tell a word
o' this, it'll be the worse for ye.' He stumbled out of the room,
nearly tripping over the rug again.

As soon as he'd gone, she got up and locked the door. She was
trembling from head to foot. Was this what life was going to be

like, here at Blagge House, without Maud and with Edgar often away? How in God's name would she be able to bear it?

But gradually she stopped shaking, and calmer thoughts prevailed. She had successfully defended herself, and he had not ravished her. And if he could threaten her, she could threaten, too. He had told her to keep her mouth shut: very well, she would – as long as he too kept silent. If she spoke out, her mother would believe her, and she suspected that Edgar probably would also. And so would the Abbot. It would be the scandal of Hyam St Ebba. Her heartbeat gradually slowed, and she said a prayer of thanks for her deliverance. It was as if Friar Valerian had come to her rescue when she called upon him.

And so life at Blagge House went on as usual, and midsummer passed into July. Neither Jack Blagge nor Cecily spoke of their encounter on the night following Maud's wedding. She behaved as if nothing untoward had happened, and he tried to do likewise, though on one occasion when they had disagreed over some trifling domestic matter, he had looked defiantly at her; she had stared back at him unafraid, until he shrugged and looked away.

She made a point of chatting happily with Edgar, to show their mutual marital trust; Jack saw that in the event of a showdown, her word might possibly be believed against his. Stupid creature, he thought, throwing a good offer back in his face and turning him into a fool. Devil take her, he thought, I should never have gone to her room, especially after emptying that wineskin – oh, damn the little witch to hell!

It seemed much longer than four years since Valerian had abruptly left the Cistercian Abbey at Netley, and now, sitting in the Abbot's parlour he felt like a traveller re-visiting a once-familiar place after a long time away. On arriving at Southampton, he found it heaving with men-at-arms, archers, horses, wagons and bristly faced boatmen; every available lodging was packed full, and he had sent a message to the Abbot by a carter carrying provisions, asking if he might visit before he embarked for France. He had received a courteous reply inviting him to be a guest at the Abbey until the invading force under King Edward set sail.

'There are many contradictory rumours going round about the King's choice of time, and where he plans to land his forces,' he told the Abbot. 'It makes for discontent among the men, not knowing when and where they are to be deployed.'

'Ah, but neither do the French,' replied the Abbot. 'It's the King's way to keep them guessing where to send their troops to meet the invasion, so they have to disperse their fleet along an extended coastline. Southampton seems the likeliest point of departure, but there are men at Dover and Hastings getting impatient with waiting, and therefore a thorough nuisance to the citizenry. Our infirmary is already occupied by the consequences of town brawls, made worse by this heat. I wish you a peaceful crossing, Friar, and not only for the weather! – but I suppose you meet all sorts in your travels, good and bad.'

Valerian smiled. 'On the whole I'm well received, Father Abbot, for we are supposed to bring good luck to households who sustain us!'

'Your modesty becomes you, Friar. Your skill at dosing the sick and healing of wounds has spread far and wide.'

'And ridding a dwelling of fleas, Father Abbot, don't forget that!' said Valerian in amusement. 'Tell me, does good Brother Luke still tend the sick and injured?'

'Ah, yes. Our beloved infirmarian is never happier than when he's brewing comfrey tea and applying woundwort to cuts and abrasions. He's actually looking forward to the return of the wounded, that's if ships can be found to ferry them back across the Narrow Sea. There's talk of many thousands setting sail, and the ships will be horribly overcrowded, not to mention the poor, wretched horses.' He lowered his voice to add, 'But it's cheaper to commandeer merchant vessels, empty their cargoes and use them as troopships, rather than build new ones. Even fishing boats have been seized from their owners. But come, Friar Valerian, how does the mendicant life compare with the monastic? You are thinner, but no doubt strong in muscle – Brother Luke will approve of you!'

'And how fare the other brothers I knew, Father Abbot?' asked Valerian in a carefully casual tone; 'Such as Brother Carlo?'

'He's our youngest choir monk, and a joy to us all,' said the Abbot warmly. 'He'll be pleased to see you, as will Brother Eustace and Brother Paulus. You'll meet them at supper in the refectory, though the rule of silence must be kept. Tomorrow at the hour of recreation you'll be able to speak with them and answer their questions. Meanwhile, it is a great satisfaction to me, Friar Valerian, that God has led you to serve him in this way.'

No mention was made of the circumstances in which Valerian had left the Abbey, and when he met the brothers again, he was greeted eagerly; Brother Paulus made no mention of their parting, and Valerian assumed that he had either made his confession to the Abbot and been absolved, or that his sin was known only to God – and himself, Valerian.

After spending two nights at the Abbey the long wait ended, and Valerian was called as a chaplain to the King's army when it at last put to sea in a wide variety of ships, from merchant vessels, galleys and painted barges to flat-bottomed cogs; it was in one of these that Valerian sailed, not from Southampton but Portchester, moving in a seemingly never-ending convoy from Portsmouth Harbour into a calm Narrow Sea on the twelfth of July.

The *Te Deum* was sung as they left harbour, and Valerian added his own special prayer: *Hail, bright Cecilia, hear my plea, and watch over her whom I love more than life. Bless her husband and child, and keep her safe from all who would do her harm, whether foes abroad or close at hand. Amen.*

Twelve

By the time little Kitty was six months old, daily life at Ebbasterne Hall and Blagge House had settled into the usual seasonal routine. Kat Wynstede fretted daily for Oswald away at the war, and everybody missed Dan Widget; Ned the groom resented the way Dan had been obliged to accompany that young fool Oswald into danger, quite forgetting how he, Ned, used to shout at Dan and call him stupid. And at Blagge House Cecily noticed that Mab, the younger of the two maidservants, also waited anxiously for news of the good-natured, hard-working young man. On her part she missed Maud keenly, and resolved to make a friend of Janet, now thirteen years old. Maud had told her how Janet had sat on the stairs, waiting in fear for what news Friar Valerian would bring to her – and how she had rejoiced at the glad tidings of the survival of both mother and child. Her former resentment of her sister-in-law was replaced by sisterly affection, and she loved to help look after baby Kitty and watch her progress from week to week. Cecily treasured the friendship that blossomed between herself and Edgar's younger sister, and they drew ever closer as the weeks went by with no news from across the Narrow Sea.

And there had been other changes of heart in Hyam St Ebba. Count de Lusignan and his sons had gone to join the King's army in Gascony; Gilbert Benoît had left in April, leaving Mistress Benoît, no longer Lady, and their little son Henri with her parents. As Kat Wynstede pondered the situation of them all, she decided that the estrangement between the Castle and the Hall was unnecessary and ridiculous. Both she and the Countess had menfolk away at the war, and they should be comforting each other. After all, it had not been the de Lusignans but their disgraced son-in-law who had caused the rift. She wrote a note with the aid of Ethelreda who had learned her letters, saying that she wanted them to be friends and show mutual sympathy at this difficult time. Three days passed with no reply, and Kat felt rudely rebuffed – until a note arrived from the Countess, thanking Lady Wynstede for her offer of friendship, most gladly accepted. Kat found out later that old Lady de Lusignan had dismissed her note as impudent, considering the difference in their social standing, and had forbidden Hélène to reply. This had released a long pent-up rebellion in Hélène's heart, and a furious quarrel with her mother-in-law had ensued, which resulted in a healing of the breach between the two families. Old Master Blagge was scornful, but he was beginning to realize that he no longer wielded absolute authority in his home.

One evening when Cecily and Janet sat out of doors in the fading light of a hot summer's day, Cecily was conscious of a great wave of happiness washing over her, and her thoughts flew to Friar Valerian, wherever he was at this moment. She knew that there was a real possibility that he might not return, but die in the service of the King, his body returning to earth in a foreign field; but now at this blessed moment she felt his presence near, his love streaming towards her across the miles, his prayers protecting her and Kitty. She sighed for sheer happiness at the deep peace which enfolded them both together. Valerian!

'Why are you smiling, Cecily?' asked Janet who had been watching her face. 'You look so happy!'

'I *am* happy, Janet dear; it's such a lovely evening,' she replied.

Valerian rubbed his eyes and stretched his limbs; although used to sleeping in hay barns and cow byres, even in the open under the stars, he could not remember such utter discomfort as the seasickness he'd experienced on the voyage, followed by the night spent on open heath at the tip of the Cherbourg peninsular, with a sizeable number of the King's army of invasion. He was thankful that the voyage had been no longer, for rumours had hinted at somewhere on the Gascony coast as the place of landing, which would have meant further rolling and dipping in the Bay of Biscay. He ran his tongue around his dry lips, and knew that his breath must be foul. Aching in every muscle he looked around at the encampment where some men still snored, though one or two were lighting fires on which to cook corn gruel, with chunks of bread and ale. On the boat there had been a young Dominican friar who said he was a chaplain to the king's army, but Valerian had been too ill to answer; each time he'd opened his mouth, bile rose up in his throat, green and bitter. Now here was the black-robed friar again, holding out his hand and hauling Valerian to his feet.

'These men are breakfasting without saying a grace,' he said.'Come, Brother Friar, we'll stand together and lead them in prayer.'

Valerian was ashamed of his feebleness, and forced a smile. 'Thank you, er—'

'Friar Gawain I'm called, and I've come from London in answer to God's call,' the young man said briskly. 'The souls of these men are in our care, to be admonished and encouraged as necessary, and all to be given in love.'

Valerian felt somewhat admonished himself, and called a number of the men together, to start the day with the Lord's blessing. After Gawain had said grace, Valerian prayed aloud, asking for protection and strength in the battles that lay ahead. The men stood in rows with bowed heads, and Valerian felt somewhat restored; he uttered his own silent, private request as the men were dismissed and lined up in columns.

Save us and help us, Lord, and do thou, blessed St Cecilia, comfort her I have left behind, who prays for me.

A column of men was quickly formed, for they were eager to be on the march towards Caen. Foot-soldiers were at the front, watched by a mounted escort; then came the bowmen and men-at-arms, with the lancers and mounted knights and their squires, and then the King himself, surrounded by his own knights-at-arms. At the rear, rumbling noisily along behind the column came a line of horse-drawn carts carrying armour, longbows, tents and provisions, the latter consisting of bread, water and salt beef. A message was passed from the back of the column that the King wanted them to *chevauchée* through Normandy; they were not to harm the people unless attacked by them, but the military would be allowed to help themselves to a reasonable amount of food and necessities for an army on the march; no armour need be worn, for reprisals were not expected from a farming community unprepared for the invasion.

'We shall have to wear a hauberk over our habits when we go into battle,' Friar Gawain told Valerian, referring to the chain mail tunics made up of small interlocking rings riveted together. 'And a helmet of some kind.'

Valerian raised an eyebrow, having not thought of a holy man wearing armour. 'Why? We won't be fighting, will we?'

'You can't expect to give spiritual aid in the middle of a battle if you're not in the thick of it, Friar,' replied Gawain. He laughed shortly. '*We* shall need protection against enemy arrows just as much as any of the men and horses.'

The column began to move, the two friars marching in the middle, behind the bowmen; after an hour they came to the head of a green valley, and Valerian stood looking down at the idyllic rural scene spread out below them. He saw fields of ripe corn and barley, peaceful pastures where sheep and cows grazed, and horses drew cartloads of hay to barns beside farmhouses with their stables; fat chickens and ducks scratched in the yards, and pigs rooted happily in orchards full of ripening fruit.

And within another hour everything was changed. A charging army fell upon its peace and plenty: horses were taken from the fields and orchards were plundered, chickens had their necks wrung to augment the men's rations, and cheese and butter were taken from the dairies. Women and children ran screaming with terror into their houses, holding their weeping children close to their breasts, and in vain did the householders beg for mercy; the *chevauchée* was relentless, acting like strong wine on the soldiery who began to eye the younger women with appraisal.

'Don't stop to force the girls,' said the same officer with a sly grin. 'There'll be more willing ones at Caen!'

The pillaging continued before Valerian's horrified gaze, and tears came to his eyes in pity for these simple country people and for his own helplessness, the incredulous shock at witnessing the behaviour of his countrymen. When Friar Gawain spoke to him, he neither heard nor answered, and the friar spoke again, more loudly.

'It's a pity, I know, Friar Valerian, but the men can rightfully claim the spoils of war, and the French would do just the same to us if they were invading our own country. You heard the order from the King, forbidding us to lay a hand on any of the people—'

At that moment a loud, prolonged scream echoed across the valley. It was the wife of a farmer who'd been knifed in retaliation for some act of defiance, and his body now lay blood-bespattered in his own farmyard; a great wail went up from the women who had gathered round him.

Valerian could not in conscience ignore them, and broke from the ranks to go to them, holding up his arms to show that he had no weapons. They shrank back from him as he knelt beside the dead man, and reaching into an inside pocket of his habit, he drew forth a small bottle containing consecrated holy oil which he applied to the man's forehead and mouth, then over his heart where the knife had stabbed through the ribcage. He gently closed the staring eyes and made the sign of the Cross, speaking in Latin. Rising to his feet he looked towards the group of women and children huddled together in a corner of the yard, but did not raise his hand in blessing, for to do so would appear hypocritical in the extreme; instead he bowed low towards them and let them see his tears.

The army continued to march towards Caen, leaving ruin and devastation in its wake, and when they came in sight of that town, they saw that the inhabitants had been warned of their approach. It was a dark time for Valerian, for he was treated with contempt by the soldiers, and found himself unable to pray, except for asking forgiveness for his presence here with a marauding army of barbarians, for he could not see this English invasion in any other light. It seemed futile and cynical to pray for these innocent country people while he was marching along with their enemies, and he could only say, *Lord, have mercy upon me, a sinner* as the army rampaged on. He felt unfit to approach St Cecilia, that holy virgin and martyr who had herself died a cruel death on the order of a Roman governor, and as for his own beloved Cecily, a wife and mother, he could not bear to think of the horror she would feel at his present degradation. He was impervious to Friar Gawain's attempts to give a rational explanation as to why the 'spoils of war' were legitimate plunder in enemy territory.

'This land of Normandy is ours by right and ancient tradition,' Gawain argued. 'It belongs to the English crown, as does Aquitaine and Gascony. We're here to win back the King's own dominions, and inevitably there will be some plunder, and some bloodshed.'

'But these simple country folk have done nothing wrong!' protested Valerian. 'They've been robbed of their possessions and driven out of their homes. It *cannot* be the will of God – more likely the work of the devil!'

'Ah, Friar Valerian,' answered the younger man, turning down the corners of his mouth. 'King Philip's men will use ours in just such a merciless way when we meet them in battle, as you'll see for yourself. And our men here are glad of our presence with them, for we can hear their confessions and absolve them.'

'So that they may go and be just as cruel and greedy again before a day has passed!' retorted Valerian. 'No, Friar Gawain, the only reason I don't desert and go to find a boat to carry me back to England is the hope that I can bring a small crumb of comfort to these poor families by offering the Body and Blood of Christ to them and their households, and anointing them with the Last Rites when they fall foul of some brute's knife – I don't hear confessions, for it is I who should confess, not them – oh, it's abominable!'

'I respect your sentiments, Friar Valerian, but I have to believe that God has called us to support our King and succour his soldiers when they inadvertently give way to wrongdoing,' said Gawain, though he looked uncomfortable, and Valerian turned away, seeing argument to be useless. Young Friar Gawain had become hardened to the sight of suffering, and deaf to the voice of conscience; the two men found no pleasure in each other's company.

The citizens of Caen were desperate to defend their homes. They had gone up to the rooftops with stones, bricks and iron bars, anything that could be thrown down on the heads of the invaders, and within half a day they had killed or injured two or three hundred of King Edward's men, to the fury of the King himself, arriving on the scene with his son, the sixteen-year-old Prince of Wales, and the Earls of Northampton and Arundel with reinforcements recalled from fighting in Gascony. The King immediately ordered that the entire population of the town be put to the sword, a decree that shocked some of his knights, and one of them knelt before the king to ask that this savage order be repealed. Friar Valerian also threw himself down on his knees with the same fervent prayer, not caring who saw him, and there was general relief when the king apparently relented, insofar as the order was withdrawn, but he then ordered the burghers of Caen to surrender their town to the English. When they refused, the resulting sacking lasted three days, in which many French and English lost their lives. Valerian stood by helplessly, giving succour to the people when he could; when he saw a frantic, grief-stricken widow with her two daughters dragging the body of her husband off the street, he stepped forward, holding up his hands to show he was unarmed, and invoking the Trinity. His only desire was to bring some spiritual comfort to them, but the woman turned on him in fury, her face full of hatred.

'*Va t'en, va t'en, diable anglais! Moi, je crache au ton visage!*' And fitting action to words, she spat violently into his face. A spray of spittle hit his left eye, and he felt the slimy moisture run down his face.

'*Je crache aux tous les anglais! Va t'en!*' she cried, and a group of soldiers standing nearby guffawed with laughter at seeing their all-too-holy friar 'getting it in his gob' in return for his overture of peace; but Valerian did not even wipe his face, so ashamed was he of belonging to an army that could provoke such hate.

The King took command of the now augmented army, marching eastwards. Valerian continued to march with them but not of them, unable to eat or sleep beside such butchers, as they seemed to him. He became an object of scorn and ridicule among them, and could have wished himself among the dead of Caen, for it was as if God Himself had forsaken him for the company he kept. He could not remember ever feeling such despair.

But then on the evening when they reached the river Seine, and stopped to camp overnight, he walked some way apart from the soldiery, and lay down at the foot of a green knoll about two hundred yards from the men. Resting his aching limbs in the tall grass, he closed his eyes; dusk was falling over a golden summer landscape, and the air was very still, but then a light breeze blew across his face, an angel's breath, sweet and refreshing; a great peace came over him, bringing comfort to his spirit and strength to his body. Pain and hunger were forgotten as he was enfolded by an unseen presence.

'Cecilia!' he whispered. 'My saint, my Cecily.' He smiled, clasping his hands together, oblivious of his surroundings, the raucous laughter of the men eating their supper of purloined fresh meat.

Hail, bright Cecilia!
And so for a blessed moment they were united.

In the crucial days that followed the successful crossing of the river Seine, over a bridge hastily repaired by the king's carpenters, and their arrival at the banks of the river Somme where again the bridges had been broken, Valerian was able to distance himself from the grossness all around him and be true to his conscience in humility. He was able to pray again, even in the most unpropitious circumstances, for those around him, the Englishmen who had become hardened into brutality, the French citizens caught up in a cruel war they hardly understood. He tried to follow the example of Christ, and when faced by the taunts of the soldiers and the curses of the people, he was able to forgive them instantly, and his pitying look sometimes had the effect of silencing them.

Unable to cross the Somme by a bridge, and beset by rumours of French cavalrymen leaving Paris in pursuit of them, the King led them northwards towards the sea, where the river became tidal, and where there was a wide, sandy-bottomed ford which became just passable at low tide. Here fortune favoured them, for the tide was out, and the men were ordered to cross with their horses and wagons, as speedily as possible. They had no choice but to obey, and Valerian found himself in a scene of confusion, knee-deep in the eddying water, shouting encouragement and offering his arm to men struggling and fearing to sink in the treacherous sand, for there were places where a gap appeared in the river bed and the water suddenly became much deeper. Some men and horses failed to reach the opposite bank, and a wagon loaded with armoury had to be abandoned, its wheels embedded in the sandy floor churned up by the crossing. Valerian had his own doubts about reaching the far bank in safety, and committed his spirit and those of his companions into the Lord's hands; yet even as he muttered the words in the chaos all around him, he heard a familiar voice close at hand.

'Good Friar, help my master, for pity's sake! His horse is sinking, and I can't shift him − help us, good Friar, for the love of − oh, *Friar Valerian*, thank God!'

At hearing this desperate plea, Valerian's heart seemed to miss a beat, for he knew that breathless voice: *Dan Widget*. Turning back amid men and horses struggling in the water, he saw Dan hanging on to the bridle of a big horse across which the apparently lifeless body of Sir Oswald Wynstede had been thrown. Straightway his sinews filled with renewed strength: resolution powered him to new and tremendous efforts.

'All right, Dan, keep hold of the bridle, and I'll pull him off the horse and on to my shoulders – you tug on the horse, and I'll carry Mistress Cecily's brother.'

Amid struggles and shouted oaths, the main body of the King's army got across the Somme before the tide turned and the water swirled back, making it impossible for French pursuers to follow. Valerian and Dan fell thankfully on to the grass of the river bank, and Valerian let fall his burden; Oswald stirred and groaned, and Dan hastened to reassure him.

'We're safe ashore, Master, we've met Friar Valerian!' he gasped. 'He's saved us!'

'My m–mother said the friar saved us all,' mumbled Oswald in slow, slurred tones, and gave a loud belch.

It transpired that Sir Oswald and his groom had been in Gascony since June, but after the English landing in Normandy, the King had put the Earl of Derby in charge, and ordered the main body of his troops to turn north and join him with the Earls of Northampton and Arundel to face King Philip's army at Abbeville; Oswald and Dan had been in those reinforcements, while the de Lusignans had remained in Gascony.

And now here they were, a stone's throw from Abbeville where King Philip was preparing a much larger and better provisioned army to confront the exhausted men under King Edward's command.

Oswald groaned, rose to his feet and stood, eyes closed, leaning against his horse.

'Has he been injured?' asked Valerian, and Dan quietly explained that his master had succumbed to sickness brought on by the fighting in Gascony. 'He found it all much worse than he'd expected, Friar, but I hope a few days' rest will restore him.'

But there was to be no rest. The King ordered the men to assemble and prepare for battle. He led them to a commanding position backed by the forest of Crécy-en-Ponthieu, and looking down into a valley. It was by now late afternoon, and the King divided them into three columns; the right flank under the command of the sixteen-year-old Prince of Wales and the Earl of Arundel, the left under the Earl of Northampton, while the King himself was in charge of the centre column, a short way behind the line. The bowmen were placed in the middle of each column, armed with their huge longbows and two dozen arrows in quivers worn over their shoulders. Valerian had always thought the longbows unwieldy compared to the traditional crossbows of the French, lighter and surely easier to carry and aim. He watched Dan help Oswald to put on his armour, and donned a hauberk of chain mail over his habit.

'I'll have to leave you here, Dan – look after him, and may we meet again after the battle, by God's grace.' He made the sign of the Cross over them and went to join Friar Gawain to lead the troops in a prayer for victory, after which he was ordered to take his place in the right-hand column and stay near to the young prince who sat proudly astride his warhorse, wearing the black armour for which he was to become known.

It was Saturday, the twenty-sixth day of August as the English army waited in a strange, breathless silence, the sun setting behind the forest to their rear.

When King Philip rode out of Abbeville with an army made up largely of French and Genoese crossbowmen, they greatly outnumbered the English, who were ordered to stand where they were and not to fire before the signal was given.

A line of Genoese crossbowmen began to advance towards the English, but were halted by a short, violent thunderstorm, which both armies hoped was a good augury for them and a bad one for the other side. When they began to advance again, almost to within a hundred and fifty yards of the English, King Edward gave the order to his bowmen to fire.

Valerian's jaw dropped as a great cloud of arrows filled the air and fell upon the Genoese archers who had the setting sun in their eyes; as the wounded fell, another arrow-storm quickly followed, darkening the sky and driving the archers back into the advancing French cavalry who rode them down. King Philip quickly lost all control of events, as each attack by the French broke against the incessant rain of murderous arrows from the

English longbows. They pierced the riders' helmets and armour, maddening the horses who began to rear and trample over the fallen; the bodies of men and horses piled on top of each other in hideous confusion. Valerian saw to his consternation that the Prince of Wales had been unhorsed and lay on the ground while his standard-bearer hacked at his opponents until the Prince got up and remounted his horse; Valerian could only admire the boy's courage and tenacity, and hoped that he would survive to be another King Edward.

The slaughter continued until nightfall, by which time many of the French knights had been quietly slipping away, leaving their dead and wounded lying on the field in the darkness which finally put a stop to the killing. King Philip succeeded in escaping with a small party to rally the remnants of his army; the English lost only a few hundred men, but because of the darkness they did not realize the extent of the casualties they had inflicted on the French. When dawn broke on the following morning, the countryside was blanketed in a thick white mist and soaked in the blood of some fifteen thousand men.

In the desolate aftermath of victory, Valerian went looking for Oswald and Dan, who might for all he knew, be among the dead. He found a group of battle-weary men, some of them wounded, camping by the banks of the Somme. They were eating a meagre breakfast of bread and water, and called out to him to join them.

'No, friends, I'm looking for a young knight called Wynstede and his groom.' He gave a description of them and said they had been with the troops that had come up from Gascony.

'They were English and came from a Hampshire town, Hyam St Ebba,' he told them, but they mostly looked blank. There seemed to be no point in further questioning, and Valerian returned to the battle-field to search for any wounded who had survived the night.

It was a terrible place of dead men and horses; some of the poor beasts were still twitching in their death-throes. Wounded men that had lain untended overnight had mostly died by morning, and lay in their own blood, the deadly arrow still embedded in their flesh. A few had managed to cling to life, and to these Valerian gave what comfort he could, anointing them with holy oil, giving absolution, whatever their nation, and commending their souls to God. There were one or two other men, both French and English, searching the field and bearing a litter to carry away any man still living.

As Valerian knelt beside a dying Frenchman, hardly more than a boy, and crushed under a horse, a shadow passed over him, and he looked up to see a thickset man with a bandaged head, limping with a stick; he wore a black cloak with a hood.

'I can wish you good morning, Friar, seeing that there are many enemies of the King lying here,' he said, 'and so few of our own countrymen.'

'It's hardly a good morning in such a place of death,' Valerian said gravely. 'And it will be worse when the sun comes up and the flies start humming. The smell of blood is sickening enough already.'

'So perish all the King's enemies,' said the stranger. 'And so you are here to look for comrades-in-arms, Friar? And perhaps the odd leather belt or two, and jewelled dagger?'

Valerian stiffened. 'I am no plunderer,' he said, disgusted at the man's suspicions. 'I do but comfort any left alive, and say a prayer for their souls.'

'Ah, a good Friar indeed,' said the man with an unpleasant undertone that made Valerian look up sharply. 'And the wit to turn your good deeds to advantage!'

'You, sire, are fortunate to have escaped with your life, and should spend your time in prayer and thanksgiving,' said Valerian, wishing this man would go away.

'And so should you, good Friar, giving thanks for your looks, your quick brain, and a flowery tongue to please the ladies!'

Valerian straightened himself up. 'I don't know your reason for speaking to me thus, stranger, and if you have nothing better to say, please leave me alone with these poor men who cannot answer.'

'Oh, do not be so unkind, good Friar! I have merely come to answer your questions concerning the whereabouts of a noble knight, Oswald Wynstede.'

Instantly Valerian was alert. 'I'm searching for that very knight, stranger, and if you can tell me where he may be found, alive or dead, I shall be in your debt.'

'Ah, good Friar, we seem to be of one mind. But may I first ask *you* a question?'

'By all means, sire, ask me whatever you wish, and I will try to answer truthfully.'

'How soon did you start bedding the widow Wynstede after her husband's death?'

In an instant Valerian's eyes were opened, and he saw and recognized Gilbert Benoît. He stared for a moment into the man's insolent eyes; silence would be taken as an admission of guilt, and though he cared not much what was said about himself – he had got used to taunts during his sojourn in King Edward's army – he could not stay silent about a slur on Lady Wynstede's honour, she who was mother to Cecily.

'I see that the dismissal of your unlawful claim to Ebbasterne Hall has much embittered you, Master Benoît,' he said quietly, but with ice in his blue eyes. 'God knows the lady's innocence, whatever lies are spoken of her by evil men. I have no more to say to you.'

He turned back to the body of the young man crushed under the weight of a fallen horse, but Benoît threw aside his stick and shouted, his face livid with rage and hate.

'Curse you for a canting, psalm-chanting lecher! You filthy so-called monk, get ready for hell!'

Valerian saw the flash of a dagger aimed at his neck, but as he jerked his head round, the blade sunk into his right cheek, and he felt the stinging point of it in his flesh, drawing a deep cut from the corner of his eye to the side of his mouth. The movement was the work of a moment, and Valerian thought he was to die in this field of blood, one more carcass to rot on Crecy's soil. He heard Benoît's voice upraised in a furious stream of obscenities, which abruptly turned to a wordless roar as an arrowhead was thrust between his shoulders. He swayed, threw up his arms and fell backwards, hitting the ground and writhing horribly. Not Valerian but Gilbert Benoît now lay dying, a bubbling groan in his throat. Valerian's right cheek was streaming with blood and dripping down his chest. He gasped and thought that he too would fall, but an arm was put around him, and he half collapsed against the body of a sturdy young man, and heard a familiar voice.

'God's bones, Friar, you must get a bandage on that cut! I came out looking for you, and saw the two o' you talking – and thought it was trouble, and right I was, so I came up behind him with an arrow that'd already killed one man, and . . . and now you'll have to absolve me, for it's killed another.'

Valerian leaned heavily against him, fighting against the faintness which threatened to overwhelm him. His breath came in short gasps, and he could not speak. All he knew was that he had narrowly escaped death in this dreadful place.

Thanks be to God, and to Dan Widget, surely sent to him by the blessed St Cecilia, just in time.

It was on a morning in September that the news came. Cecily was bathing her baby in her wooden tub, and Janet Blagge was helping.

'Look at the way she holds up her head and kicks out with her little legs!' said Janet, admiringly. 'Yes, sweetheart, I'm your big sister! Oh, wouldn't my sister Maud love to see her in her bathtub, Cecily! Do you think she'll come to visit us soon?'

'I don't know, dear, Waldham's a fair way off, and Master Keepence sounds to be very busy,' sighed Cecily who had gathered that Maud's husband was constantly occupied with his mill and the marketing of the flour, much as her father-in-law's time was taken up with the wool trade. 'Now I'll pour in some more hot water – so take hold of her, Janet, and lift her out for a moment—'

Kitty gave an indignant yell at being taken from her bath, but smiled when Janet lowered her into the warmer water, where she splashed and gurgled happily.

Downstairs there was a knock at the door.

'That'll be somebody to see your father,' said Cecily. 'Bet can answer and show him into the parlour.'

But the next thing they heard was a cry of surprise and delight. Doors were being opened, and male and female voices upraised. Bet came running up the stairs.

'Mistress Cecily! Mistress Cecily! Dan Widget's here, back from France!'

Cecily drew in a sharp breath, and her face paled. Janet saw her trembling hands, and said quickly, 'I'll take care of Kitty. I'll dry her and dress her and put wool between her legs – you go to see Dan and hear his news, Cecily.'

Cecily rose and wiped her hands; she hung on to the rail as

she went downstairs and found her father-in-law, the cook and maids clustered round a tired-looking Dan in the hallway. Mab's eyes were wide and shining at the sight of him.

'Thank heaven you are safe, Dan,' Cecily said faintly. 'And what of my brother?'

'I've taken Sir Oswald to the Hall, to his mother, Mistress Blagge. She's giving thanks for his safe return, and wants you to see him.' He glanced at Jack Blagge who frowned.

'Mistress Blagge is occupied with her child, so her brother will have to wait,' he said irritably. 'And how goes the war, Widget?'

'It's been bloody, but a victory for the King, Master Blagge. Sir Piers and Sir Charles Lusignan are staying—'

'Don't mention that family to me. What about the, er, Friar – he who went off to France after the lawsuit?'

Dan drew a breath and answered, 'He has a knife wound on his face, sire.' Without looking at her, he was aware of Cecily's fear.

Oh, my God, his face – his eyes, his beautiful eyes.

'The wound will heal, and leave but a battle scar, sire.' Dan's words were addressed to old Master Blagge, but his message was for Cecily. 'His eyes are spared, and he would not be persuaded to come home with us. He's staying with the King's army, on the march to Calais.'

Thanks be to God, O merciful heavens.

Blagge gave a non-committal grunt. 'Well, give Widget some refreshment, and then he may go back to Ebbasterne Hall, with our compliments to Lady Wynstede and Sir Oswald. And now we can all go back to work,' he added with a pointed look at the maidservants, and turning on his heel, returned to his counting-house.

Somehow Cecily managed to smile and not to faint; there was no opportunity for her to speak to Dan alone, and after he'd politely declined refreshment, she returned to the nursery where she told Janet that Dan's news sounded good; at least there had been no recorded deaths among the men from Hyam St Ebba.

As soon as she could seize the opportunity, Cecily rode up to Ebbasterne Hall, and was met by her mother whose emotions were in turmoil.

'The fighting was far worse than Oswald expected, and he was overcome by the dreadful sights and sounds – and smells of war,' she said. 'He couldn't continue to serve in the army, and Widget found a boat to bring the pair of them back over the Narrow Sea.'

'Why, what's the matter with him, Mother? Has he any injuries?'

'Not on his body, but his head has been hurt inside, Cecily. According to Dan Widget he's been drinking too much, and needed to come home. He'll be restored to health here at Ebbasterne Hall, and you'll be able to help me make him see sense.'

'I understand, Mother – at least I think I do. We are much in debt to Dan Widget for his care of Oswald; it can't have been easy. And Friar Valerian is wounded in the face, but Dan says it will heal, and he's staying out there with the King's army. God has been good, and we must trust in Him to spare the good Friar as He has spared my brother.' Her voice broke, and she could say no more. She held out her arms and Kat Wynstede enfolded her in a motherly embrace.

'Dearest Cecily, how selfish I've been,' said Kat, reproaching herself for her daily moping over Oswald. 'I should've known how much you too were missing your dear brother!'

Thirteen

1346

News of the King's victory at Crécy filtered through to England, the main source being from men who, like Sir Oswald Wynstede, had returned from France. The majority of the survivors had been persuaded to stay with the King and accompany him to the gates of Calais, an important port he was determined to take and add to his other dominions in France.

Stories of the battle at Crécy and its aftermath were spread by word of mouth, and lost nothing in the telling.

'Did you hear the young Prince of Wales fell off his horse and broke his neck?' it was whispered among the servants at Ebbasterne Hall. 'And his squire lifted him up and put him back on the horse, and straightway his neck was mended! It was a miracle!'

At Blagge House there were similar hair-raising stories. Bet and Mab told Edda the cook and Kitty's nurse that the armies of the King had come to a wide, rushing river which they were unable to cross.

'But then the waters parted to let 'em through, like when the Israelites passed over the Red Sea – and when they were all across, the waters came together again in a mighty roar, and drowned the French coming after 'em, just as the Egyptians drowned, horse and rider, all that time ago!' they repeated in awestruck tones.

Cecily longed for more news of Friar Valerian, and whether his face wound was healing. She consoled herself by praying for him at the beginning and ending of each day, and there were times when she sensed his presence near her, as if his thoughts and prayers had winged to her across the Narrow Sea.

Meanwhile, as summer gave way to autumn there was plenty to occupy her; little Kitty was being gradually weaned from her mother's milk and taking softened bread sweetened with honey from the Abbey bees. Cecily felt able to leave her more often in the charge of her nurse and half-sister Janet, while she visited

Ebbasterne Hall to help her mother with Oswald. Katrine
Wynstede, overjoyed at the return of her son, soon found to her
utter dismay that he was no longer the proud, self-confident youth
who had gone to France; he was subject to abrupt changes of
mood, and sometimes used extremely coarse oaths and blasphemies
in front of herself and the maidservants. He would sit drinking
wine all the evening, fall fast asleep in his chair and have to be
carried up to his room by a manservant and laid on his wooden-
framed bed where he snored in a stupor, unaware of his full
bladder which emptied into the bed, soaking the feather-filled
mattress. The shame of this was so distressing to his mother that
Cecily decided he needed a firm hand, and she would see that
he got it; she ordered Dan to be his private manservant, permitted
to deny him access to strong drink, and to encourage or reprimand
him as necessary.

'He needs to learn his obligations,' she said. 'For too long he's
had his own way, and now it's time for him to face facts. You're the
best person to take charge of him, Dan, and guide him into the
right paths.'

Dan was not sure of his ability to guide Sir Oswald anywhere,
but for Mistress Cecily he was willing to do his best to take his
young master in hand.

When the Countess and her unmarried daughter Alys asked
if they might come over to Ebbasterne Hall to see Sir Oswald,
Kat Wynstede instantly invited them. They hoped that Oswald
might supply them with some information as to Count Robert
and the brothers Piers and Charles.

'I just hope that Oswald will receive them courteously,' Kat
confided to Cecily, 'and not say anything untoward.'

Cecily reassured her mother that she and Dan would smarten
Oswald for the visit of their noble neighbours, and they brushed
his hair, put a clean shirt on him and sat him on a chair in the
room which had been Sir Aelfric's study. In vain did he beg them
for a mug of ale; all he was allowed was fruit cordial, as served
to the ladies.

It felt strange to Kat Wynstede to see the Countess de Lusignan
and Lady Alys in Ebbasterne Hall for the first time, in the very
room where Sir Aelfric had discussed estate matters with Will
Goode and the manorial court with Sheriff Gyfford. Cecily sat

quietly in the background, and nodded to Oswald to stand and bow to their visitors.

'Good afternoon, Sir Oswald,' the Countess Hélène began. 'How very thankful we are to see you safely back from France.'

'Yes, my Lady,' said Oswald uncomfortably. 'There was much danger out there, so much killing, such sights—'

'Yes, it must be dreadful, and I . . . I've come to ask if you saw anything – anything at all of my husband and my sons. Can you recall seeing them or hearing about them at any time?' Her voice, like her eyes, was full of pleading, and Kat Wynstede's heart ached for her, a wife and mother fearful that she might already be a widow. There was a long silence, and Cecily tried to prompt her brother into answering.

'Did you see the Count or his sons, Oswald?' she asked slowly and clearly.

'I saw them when I was in Gascony, but then we were ordered up to meet the King's army at Caen, and that's where we met with Friar Valerian, and he helped us to cross the Somme – and then it was the battle, dead men, dead horses—'

'By *we* you mean yourself and Dan Widget, do you?' asked Cecily. 'Dan Widget is Oswald's groom,' she added to the Countess.

'And were my husband and sons in this battle?' asked the Countess tremulously.

'No, I don't think so, they stayed in Gascony with the Earl of Derby.'

'Are you *sure* that you saw the Count and his sons, Oswald?' asked Cecily, as confused as the de Lusignan ladies by his uncertainty.

'I think I saw them, but I didn't say anything to them – nor with that other rogue who tried to claim Ebbasterne Hall,' Oswald replied with a flash of his former arrogance. 'He came up to join the King's army at the Somme, but we didn't see him in the battle, nor afterwards, the baseborn liar!'

Cecily met her mother's eye. This was hardly the way to refer to the Countess's son-in-law, and the Lady Alys gasped. Oswald's face was pale and sweating.

'I can't remember any more,' he muttered, leaning back and closing his eyes. 'Mother, let me have a mug of wine, I can't remember anything, it was – oh, God, it was *hell*.'

The Countess rose. 'Would it be possible for me to see Sir Oswald's groom, Katrine? He might be able to remember more.'

Poor Kat, afraid that her son was about to break down and weep, told Cecily to show the Countess and Lady Alys into the solarium, and to send for Dan Widget.

Dan proved to be a better witness, but had little real information to impart.

'Yes, my Lady, I *did* see the Count and his sons in Gascony, but they stayed there, and Sir Oswald and I came up to meet the King's army at Caen.'

'And did you also see—' The Countess hesitated. 'Did you see Gilbert Benoît?'

'No, my Lady, I didn't,' Dan lied promptly, having no wish to answer questions about a man he knew to be dead in horrific circumstances. He had made his Confession to the Abbot, and been absolved, and there he wanted to leave the matter.

'So you can't give me any of the latest news about Count Robert and our sons?' she asked in a voice that shook.

'No, my Lady, only to say that the Count and his sons have as good a chance of coming home as any other soldier in the King's army. They'll likely be at the gates of Calais now, laying siege to it, under the King's command.'

'And how long will that take, Widget?'

'My Lady, I don't know. It depends on how long the people of Calais can hold out without food.'

'Lord have mercy on us, what a fearful thing is war!' cried the Countess, and nobody contradicted her.

That evening at supper in Blagge House, Edgar avoided asking questions about Cecily's visit to Ebbasterne Hall. His father had no such qualms.

'Well, how did you find your brother today?'

Cecily had been expecting the enquiry, and answered in a matter-of-fact tone. 'Thank you, Father, he is making slow progress.'

'Where exactly is he wounded?' At hearing this, Edgar glanced quickly at Janet. Cecily had confided in them both, and they now waited to see how she would answer.

'He has a head wound, Father,' she said, 'and gets bad headaches and attacks of giddiness. My mother hopes that with rest and quiet, and proper food, he will recover.'

'Huh. At least he's still got his arms and legs.' There was a short silence, and then he continued curiously, 'Does he say much about the war, and the victory at Crécy?'

'No, Father, his memory about the war is very uncertain, and he couldn't give much news to the Countess de Lusignan when she visited him today, trying to find out where her husband is at present, and their sons – whether they're alive or dead.'

'*What?* D'ye mean your mother opened the door to *that* family after the way they treated her when their bastard son-in-law was trying to rob her of her home? Hah! I wouldn't have let 'em over the threshold.'

Silence reigned for a while, then he spoke again. 'Well? What *did* your brother have to say to 'em, then? *Had* he seen 'em?'

'Only at a distance, Father. They didn't speak.'

'Let it stay that way, then.' Old Blagge's contempt for the de Lusignan family was undiminished, and he resented their contact with Lady Wynstede and Cecily. He'd have a quiet word with Edgar and tell him to make haste and get Cecily with child again, to keep her away from Wynstedes and de Lusignans, as bad as each other in his opinion.

As the weeks went by, Sir Oswald slowly began to recover his self-respect, and with Dan's help he drank less, leading his mother to hope that he would take more interest in the estate, where money was always a problem. Cecily knew that her father-in-law's discreet weekly contributions helped her mother to maintain Ebbasterne Hall and its staff, which annoyingly put Cecily under further obligation to him. When she suggested that she might visit the homes of the tenants on the Ebbasterne Hall estate – the wives and children of the men who farmed their 'strips' in the great open field – old Blagge would have none of it, and said she would bring fleas and fevers home to her baby daughter. He told her she should take up needlework as Maud had done, and make tapestries for the walls of Blagge House, cushions for the wooden chairs and bench seats, and embroidered shirts for Edgar and himself – and to teach Janet the housewifely arts. The mention of Maud increased Cecily's longing to see her, for they had heard nothing of her for weeks, and Cecily wondered if she might visit the Keepences' house at Waldham; she asked Edgar if he would escort her there before winter set in, but when he mentioned it to his father, the old man at once dismissed the idea.

'No, Edgar hasn't got time to go trotting round the country on women's errands,' he snorted, and when she asked if Dan Widget might accompany her, she was told to wait until she was invited. 'August Keepence is a busy man, and won't want to listen to women's talk,' old Blagge said impatiently. 'Why can't you be content to stay at home with your husband as a married woman should, and look after your child?'

The virtuous tone in which Jack Blagge reminded her of her duties as a wife and mother was almost too much to bear in silence. Maud was his daughter, after all, and had he forgotten what had happened on the night following her wedding? Ever since then Cecily had bolted her door when Edgar was away, and wished that Edgar was not so much under his father's thumb; this fact was soon brought home to her in a particularly humiliating way.

Her husband had always been courteous at those times in the privacy of their bedroom when he turned towards her to take her as his lawful wife, entering her to deposit his seed before they settled down to sleep. In recent weeks this had happened more frequently than usual, and on one occasion when she felt very tired, she remonstrated with him.

'Edgar, this is the third time this week, and we should be sleeping. Am I not an obedient wife, willing to do my duty to you? Why are you demanding so much of me?'

Edgar rolled off her and lay on his back, regaining his breath after his exertions.

'I have no complaint to make about your willingness, Cecily, and I'm sorry if you find me too demanding,' he said earnestly. 'But my father has urged me to get another child, and he wants a son. It would be convenient if we could give him a grandson next year, and a brother for little Kitty. Don't you want that, too?'

Cecily was too angry to reply, so deeply did she resent Edgar's father's intervention in such a deeply intimate matter. She pictured the old man regarding her as time went by, looking out for signs that Edgar had been successful, and it made her feel used, an object with no purpose but to supply a grandson for Jack Blagge.

News came from France that King Edward had reached the gates of Calais in the first week of September, and had announced his intention of staying there, his armies forming an impassable ring round the town until its citizens yielded it up to him. Lady Wynstede shuddered.

'Think of the women and children starving there,' she lamented. 'Imagine a mother unable to feed her starving child!' She felt for the Countess who lived in fear from day to day, for news of her husband and sons.

October came in with its early frosts and whirling leaves, and Cecily desperately longed for news of Friar Valerian. Lately there had been fewer of those moments of closeness to him that she had felt in the past year: did it mean – oh, God forbid that it meant he was dead! – if so, she would have no comfort anywhere, for she would be a mournful mother to little Kitty.

And then one morning she saw a brother from the Abbey, on horseback, stopping and dismounting at the gate of Blagge House. Her heart fluttered: what news was this? The monk looked around him as if to see if anybody was about, and then came to the back door and knocked. Edda was in the kitchen, but Cecily flew past her to open the door.

'Good morrow, Brother!'

'Good morrow, Mistress . . . er . . . Blagge?'

'Yes, I am Mistress Blagge. Do you come with news from the Abbot?' Her voice trembled as she spoke.

'Yes, Mistress. I bring a letter for you.' He put his hand in an inside pocket of his habit, and drew forth a folded sheet of parchment, sealed with wax. He held it out to her, and she hardly dared to hope: but *yes*, it was a letter for her, from Friar Valerian! He had sent it to the Abbey, and the good Abbot Athelstan had sent it on to her. O heaven be praised!

Yet her fingers trembled as she looked at it, almost afraid to break the seal. She thanked the brother, then ran upstairs to her room and bolted the door; sitting on her side of the matrimonial bed, she broke open the seal.

Greetings to Mistress Blagge, peace be upon you and within your walls.

I send this letter by the captain of a ship bound for Southampton in the hope that it will reach Hyam St Ebba and the Abbot, and from him to you. The King is laying siege to Calais, and says he will not move his army but will stay all through the winter until the citizens yield. I remain here as chaplain as long as my services are needed.

I have news of two deaths. I deeply regret to tell that Sir Piers de Lusignan was slain in single combat with a foot-soldier. His father and brother are here at the gates of Calais. The other death is of Gilbert Benoît, who fell at the battle of Crécy. I trust that Abbot Athelstan will carry this sorrowful news to Castle de Lusignan, and I beg that you and your mother will give what comfort you can.

I pray for you and for all your family, that God will comfort you and preserve you all, your husband Master Blagge, your daughter Katrine, your mother and your brothers and sister. From me this day with love in Christ's Name, Fr Valerian.

With tears of joy spilling from her eyes, Cecily laid the letter to her lips, and then against her heart: he was alive, and praying for her, God be blessed forever! Though it was a time to mourn for the fallen, she could not help but rejoice that he, her beloved Friar Valerian was alive and had sent his blessing and his love to *her*, Mistress Blagge, his Cecilia! She fell on her knees to give thanks, and begged forgiveness for her own happiness at such a time. She decided to go straight to the Abbot to show him the letter.

Abbot Athelstan was troubled in his conscience. Friar Valerian had sent him news of the deaths of Piers de Lusignan and Gilbert Benoît – though the Abbot knew already about the latter, from Dan Widget's confession. The Friar had also sent a sealed letter to be passed on to Mistress Blagge, a married woman. What should he, the Abbot, do with this letter? After much deliberation he sent it to her as Valerian had asked, and prayed that he had done right.

And so he had, for he was visited by Mistress Blagge on the very day she received the letter. She was conducted to a small waiting room with a carved wooden figure of the Virgin and Child in a niche in the wall, and two bench seats. When the Abbot appeared and held out his hand, she kissed the ring on his finger.

'Good morrow, my lord Abbot,' she said. 'I thank you for sending me the letter from Friar Valerian. Do you know the sad news it contains?'

'Yes indeed, Mistress Blagge – the deaths of young Piers de Lusignan, and Gilbert Benoît – and I shall have to go to the Castle and tell of it,' he said heavily.

'He asks that my mother and I will visit them also, to give what comfort we can,' she answered solemnly. 'See, here is what he says, look—'

She unrolled the sheet of parchment and spread it before him. He secretly reproached himself, for here was no lovesick troubadour, but a pious man of God imparting sad news and assuring her of his prayers for all her family.

'Ah, yes, Mistress,' he said. 'I shall be thankful for the presence of your mother and yourself as I take such doleful news, for you will give such comfort as only women can. May God give us the right words to say – and let us both pray for the safety of Friar Valerian.'

'Oh, I *do*, my lord Abbot, every morning and night,' she assured him, and after she left, he begged God's pardon for ever doubting her innocence.

Jack Blagge absolutely forbade Cecily to accompany her mother to Castle de Lusignan, and Edgar would not go against his father's express orders.

'It would only cause a cloud over the house that would affect us all, Cecily,' he said, pleading with her to yield gracefully. 'Show him that you are the obedient wife and mother you can be. After all, my father did win your mother's lawsuit against Benoît, and surely she can take your condolences to the Castle and speak on your behalf as well as her own.'

'But Edgar, what about *your* duties to me as my husband?' she retorted. 'Have you no authority at all in your own home, that you can place your father's wishes against mine?'

'Cecily, you know the Church's teaching on wives' obedience to their husbands – and my father is the master in this house. I must ask you – no, order you – *not* to go to the Castle, and there's an end of the matter.'

Cecily would have disobeyed both husband and father-in-law, but knew that to make an open enemy of old Blagge would serve no good purpose to anybody, including little Kitty; and so she reluctantly gave way, and told her mother she must visit the Castle alone.

But Cecily did not yield entirely to her father-in-law. If she was not allowed to visit the Castle, she *would* go to visit her sister-in-law at Waldham, with Dan Widget as her escort. Oswald had by now sufficiently improved to be left without his jailer, as he called Dan, for a couple of days. Let old Blagge bawl and bluster, she thought; on this she would stand firm.

'Maud is your own daughter, Father, and my sister-in-law. I want to see her, and I will not be forbidden.' She uttered these words with a very significant look, and old Blagge could not meet her eyes; he stomped away to his counting-house with a muttered oath about the treachery of women.

Lady Wynstede's account of her visit to the castle was heartrending. 'I expected to see the Countess burst into floods of tears, but that long moan she gave was terrible to hear,' she told Cecily. 'Her daughters sat one on each side of her, and the Abbot read a psalm from a prayer book, but I don't think they heard a word of what he read. I felt like an intruder, but poor Hélène beckoned me forward, and I knelt before her, thinking of how I'd feel if it had been Oswald. Lady Alys was crying, and I shed tears, too, but Lady Marie just sat quietly holding her mother's hand, both of them so white and dry-eyed.' Tears came to Katrine's eyes as she remembered the scene, and Cecily's heart ached.

'Oh, Mother, I'm so sorry I wasn't there for you. Did she not speak at all?'

'She said something about the world coming to an end, and I said something about life going on, but then the Abbot had to tell Lady Marie her news.'

'Oh, whatever did he say?' asked Cecily. 'How *could* he say it, after that first shock?'

'I can't remember his exact words, but he told Lady Marie

that her husband was dead, that she was a widow and little Henri an orphan. He prayed that God would give them the strength they needed.'

'Oh, my God! What did she say?' Cecily asked, almost fearful of the reply.

'It was strange. She faced the Abbot, looking straight into his eyes, and then she said, "Thank you, my lord Abbot – and you, Lady Wynstede. I ask your prayers for the souls of my brother and for the father of my child. I will tell my grandmother of these losses." I wondered how she could stay so calm. It must have been the shock. Oh, what a dreadful thing is war!'

Cecily shook her head sadly, but suspected that the Lady Marie had been released from a joyless, burdensome marriage.

Fourteen

1346

By mid-October, just as Cecily was ready to visit Maud at Waldham, she realized that she was with child again. She decided not to tell Edgar or her mother because of the anxiety it would cause, and the opposition there would be to her travelling so far on horseback in such a condition, with no other guard but Dan. Edgar said at first that he would accompany her, but his father dismissed this, reminding him of important business to attend to in London, and adding that the groom Widget had proved his mettle in France. Dan was to ride Chaser, while Cecily rode on Daisy, the good-tempered palfrey. They took water-flasks and bread, cheese and cold mutton to sustain them on the twenty-five mile journey which they hoped to complete in about four or five hours, stopping for rest and refreshment on the journey, and returning two days later.

They set out on a clear, chilly autumn day, leaving Kitty in the care of her nurse and a great deal of advice from Lady Wynstede. Edgar kissed her and said he wished he was going with her, and old Blagge gave her a grudging farewell, eased somewhat by a bag containing five gold sovereigns to wear under her clothes, 'next to your skin,' he ordered. One alone rejoiced at her stubborn insistence on making this journey, and that was Dan Widget, hardly able to believe his luck, to be the guardian and protector of his Mistress Cecily; he slipped a sharp knife into the scabbard on his belt. Kat Wynstede spread a large sheepskin blanket over Daisy's back for Cecily's comfort, but as soon as they were on the Ebbchester road Cecily dismounted, rolled up the blanket and tied it with a leather strap, telling Dan to sling it across Chaser's wide rump.

'I don't need it, Dan,' she said, 'so it can be a gift for Maud. Oh, how I'm longing to see her and to know if she is well! We should be there well before dusk.'

Dan wouldn't have minded if the journey were twice as long; he was in a state of near-perfect happiness, for at twenty-one, he had not outgrown his first love. Young Mab, the maidservant at Blagge House, had been giving him some sidelong smiles, and he thought her pretty, but not to be compared with this beautiful woman he had loved at first sight, though he guessed what, or rather who she would want to talk about, and how he would answer.

Sure enough: 'Dan, I want you to tell me how you met with Friar Valerian in France, and how he looked when you left him – tell me everything, Dan!'

He smiled and said he would try, going back to when he'd met the Friar at the Somme, when they had both helped Sir Oswald and his horse to cross the river.

'Sir Oswald had been so shocked by what he'd seen of war—' he began, but she cut him short. 'It's Friar Valerian I want to hear about – tell me the truth about how he was knifed in the face.' She shuddered as she spoke, and Dan was not sure how best to tell her whilst concealing the dreadful fact that he had killed a man.

'It was the day after the battle of Crécy, Mistress,' he said carefully; 'a very misty morning, and the field was a terrible sight, all those bodies of men and horses, you couldn't avoid treading on them. We hadn't seen Friar Valerian since the previous day, and it seems that he went out into this . . . this field, to look for us, hoping not to find us there among the dead. And he was seen by somebody, Mistress, a man who wished him no good.'

'What do you mean, Dan? What man?'

'I mean Gilbert Benoît, Mistress.'

'Oh, my God, Dan, what happened? Did that wicked man try to kill Valerian?'

Dan hesitated, bracing himself to tell a lie. 'I wasn't there to see, Mistress Cecily, but an archer, a big, burly man, told me that he'd seen Benoît raising a knife at the Friar, and he came up behind Benoît and plunged an arrow into his back. Then this soldier, this archer, he dragged the Friar back to the camp, bleeding from the knife wound on his face, and in a swoon. And that's where I met them.'

'Oh, what a dreadful thing is war!' cried Cecily, echoing her mother and Lady Hélène. 'So this soldier, whoever he was, killed Benoît?'

'It was either the Friar or Benoît, Mistress Cecily. I took care o' the Friar and found an army physician to staunch his wound. And I took a horse who'd lost its owner, poor beast, to get us down to the shore, and a boatman to take us over the Narrow Sea, I mean Sir Oswald and me. I did my best to persuade the Friar to come home with us, but he said he'd stay there with the King's army, marching off to besiege Calais.'

'Oh, if I had only known! If only I could meet that archer and reward him! He must have been an angel sent from God!' cried Cecily, to which Dan could make no answer.

They rode on in silence for a while, each occupied with their own thoughts, and made good progress over wide, open heathland; Cecily was aware of a sense of freedom, a lightening of her spirits as she left Blagge House and its master behind her, for although she missed little Kitty, she knew that the child was in safe hands. When their way descended towards a large manor house and farm near a village on the edge of thick forest, they skirted the brown fields of the demesne, and a huddle of wattle-and-daub dwellings which housed the peasants and their families who served the lord of that Manor. Cecily remarked that there was a forlorn air about them, and Dan agreed.

'They're not all as lucky as we who serve Ebbasterne Hall, Mistress Cecily,' he said with a shake of his head. 'Your father treated his people well, almost like part of his family, and your mother's been the same, always good to the workers on the demesne. You remember how she took in my poor old granddame, though she was crazed and the servants complained about her, but I guess that here she'd have been left to die o' cold in one o' these little shacks. A lot of old people die in the winter, and half the children, especially in cold weather.'

'But that's disgraceful!' cried Cecily. 'Why don't they move to some better landlord?'

'It's not easy for a man with a family, Mistress Cecily, and it's against the law to leave a demesne without permission. Some o' them can't even marry off their daughters without his lordship's say-so. And they're not supposed to take rabbits or boar from the forest, let alone deer, 'cause it's the King's hunting ground – even if their children are going hungry.'

'Heavens above, Dan! Are there no laws to prevent such injustice?'

Dan shook his head. 'There's one law for the rich and another for the poor, Mistress Cecily, and some peasants are treated the same as sheep and cattle, as if they'd got no feeling for pain.' His forehead clouded over as he continued, 'But some say a day'll come when they won't stand it any longer, and they'll find a leader and rise up against them that keeps 'em down – though to speak the truth, Mistress, I can't see it happening. How can peasants unite when they can't read or write or make contact with other shires? Most o' them find it safer to put up with their lot, and make the most o' the holy-days o' the Church when there's a bit o' feasting and mirth – and praying for an early death to his lordship!'

He turned to smile at her. 'I'm sorry, Mistress Cecily, I've no business saying all this, when I should be giving thanks for her Ladyship's kindness. And even old Master Blagge treats his servants well enough.'

Cecily privately wondered what Dan would say if she told him of old Master Blagge's behaviour when drunk, or of his forbidding her to visit families on the Ebbasterne estate, in case she brought back infections to her baby daughter. She decided to change the subject, and with a smile she ventured a more personal question.

'Don't you ever want to marry and have children of your own, Dan?'

He shook his head. 'I haven't given much thought to it, Mistress Cecily.'

'But I know a certain young woman who has eyes for you alone, Dan,' she teased. 'And she's a good girl, and pretty too – you must know who I mean, my maidservant Mab. Couldn't you be kind and take a little notice of her?'

'Oh, no, Mistress Cecily, I . . . I'd far rather stay as I am,' he stammered, blushing so painfully that she said no more, though he pursued his own thoughts. *As if I could look at Mab or any other girl, as long as I've got the privilege of* this *lady's company; and though he knew full well where her heart lay, this journey gave him the opportunity to serve her.*

'Let's stop here for a while, and take some refreshment,' she said, and they dismounted on the edge of the forest. Dan tactfully suggested that she go a little way into the trees for a moment of privacy; and that he would do the same when she returned. Having relieved herself, she returned to guard the horses, grateful for his thoughtfulness. While she waited she took a hunk of bread out of the basket he carried, with a slice of creamy cheese cut from the round, and started to eat.

Suddenly she heard shouting and several heavy footsteps from the wood.

'Hey, lads, here's a bit o' luck – horses! And only a slip of a girl with 'em!'

'Quick, grab 'em, Wal – we can get down to the sea by nightfall!'

Cecily's heart lurched. They sounded like outlaws, men who would do them harm. She stood still and listened in fear as they emerged from the trees. Dan's voice broke in with a shout as loud as theirs.

'Leave our horses alone! I'm escorting a lady to Waldham.'

'Runnin' away with 'er, more like. Come on, Seth, get 'old of 'em – you and me can ride together on the big 'un, and let Tom 'ave the palfrey!'

'She's a comely dame!' said the one called Tom, just as rapid footsteps trampled through fallen leaves, and Dan appeared.

'Don't you dare lay a finger on her!' he shouted, his face flushed. 'She's on the way to Waldham to visit her sister, and I'm her groom.'

'Ah, very likely. What says the lady?'asked the one called Wal.

"Tis true, I'm going to Waldham, and my groom is protecting me on the journey,' said Cecily, trembling and feeling suddenly sick.

'Give over bandyin' words, and take the 'orses!' urged Tom, the black-browed eldest of the trio. 'Damn' lucky chance we found 'em, we can gallop down to the coast in no time. Come on, don't stand around parleyin', get into the saddle and get orf afore 'is lordship sends 'is soldiers arter us!'

'Please, please, gentlemen, I pray you, I beg of you,' pleaded Cecily. 'Don't leave us here without our horses – we have much ground to cover yet.'

'So 'ave we, lady,' said the swarthy Tom. 'We're makin' a bid for freedom, gettin' away from that pig, that son of a whore who's kept us slavin' on 'is bloody manor – we're settin' oursel's free!'

Cecily saw that these men were just the sort that she and Dan had been talking about, peasants forced to work for a bad master, who had become rebellious and were running away. They surely deserved sympathy, but stealing their horses was a different matter.

'Take but the big horse and leave us the mare,' she begged. 'I wish you no harm, and hope that you escape from the landlord, but show us mercy, for the love of God!'

'Sorry, lady, we don't wish yer no 'arm, neither, but we need the 'orses – ye can keep yer rolled-up carpet!'

'Wait – let's take some vittles with us – give me that loaf an' the meat,' said Tom. 'Come on, Wal, get up on that big beast – come on, let's *go,* for Christ's sake!'

And digging heels into Chaser's flanks, Wal and Seth galloped off, with Tom following on Daisy. Cecily and her groom were left stranded in an out-of-the-way spot on a chilly autumnal day without horses, food or any means of finding help, and no defence but Dan's sharp knife in its scabbard.

'A fine guard I've been to ye, Mistress Cecily,' he said mournfully. 'I'd go for help, only I can't leave ye, we're miles from anywhere. If ye can but walk part o' the way to the next village, about ten or fifteen miles, and I carry the stuff, we might just get there by sundown – oh, Mistress Cecily, can ye manage it?' There was pleading in his voice, for he dreaded the dark and all its dangers.

She longed to agree to his proposal, but her knees buckled beneath her, and she sank down to the ground while the woods, sky and Dan Widget whirled around her head. Tears came to her eyes, and a terrible thought came into her head. *Miscarriage.*

'I'm sorry, Dan, I can't . . .'

'Are you ill, Mistress Cecily? Don't worry, I'll stay here while ye rest,' said Dan, kneeling down beside her. 'Are ye in pain? Just tell me, dear Mistress.'

'I am with child, Dan, about two months,' she confessed in a low voice. 'I didn't tell anybody before we set out, for fear of not being allowed to visit Maud.' In her weakness and nausea she began to weep silently. 'I fear I may miscarry,' she whispered, putting a hand on her belly as if to protect the new life growing within.

He gave a gasp of surprise and shock; then a great wave of tenderness for her swept over him.

'Don't worry, dear Mistress Cecily, I'm here with ye. Look, I've got a drop of water left, they didn't take it – have a sip o' that. And if ye can but rise, I'll carry ye somewhere ye can rest under the trees. Don't be afraid, I'm here with ye, and I'll take care o' ye, whatever happens. If ye miscarry, ye must tell me what to do, only trust me.'

Somehow she got to her knees, and he hauled her up into his arms, carrying her a few yards into the wood, progressing along the path from which the outlaws had appeared. He came to a clearing, and there, like an answer to prayer, was a rough wooden shack which the outlaws had used, and which would give them shelter for a few hours.

'You lie down here, Mistress Cecily, and rest while I go back for the blanket,' he said, taking off his cloak and putting it down for her to lie on. He went back to the path and quickly returned with the sheepskin, holding it up with a smile.

'See, your mother's kindness was meant for this! Ye can wrap it around ye.'

So gently did he settle her down in the shack, that she let herself be soothed to sleep, and woke after about an hour. 'Valerian!' she said, holding out a hand to Dan who took it in both of his.

'How are you now, Mistress Cecily? You've had a good sleep.'

'I feel much better, Dan – but your hands are so cold, and you're shivering without your cloak – how selfish I've been! Here, take your cloak and put it around you!'

'I have an idea by which we may both rest and be warm, Mistress Cecily,' he said tentatively, not wanting to alarm her, but realizing that they would have to stay in this cold wood overnight. 'If we both lie on it, we can wrap the sheepskin around us, and lie back-to-back. Would ye mind if—'

'Oh, Dan, of course – why didn't I think of that while you were shivering with cold? Yes, that's what we'll do.'

And so they did, lying back-to-back in the sheepskin's warm embrace, while the hours went by until dawn. Cecily's dreams were confusing, and mostly included Friar Valerian watching over them, guarding them from danger; Dan Widget hardly slept at all, but simply gloried in the sensation of feeling her back close against his, like a comforting warm fire; he rejoiced at being granted this privilege of lying beside her, keeping her warm, keeping her safe. He had heard her say the Friar's name when she first woke up, and he knew where her heart lay; but just for now, just for these few glorious hours of the night, she was under his protection, and his alone.

She awoke refreshed and hopeful, and the fear of miscarriage had receded. They finished the water, but were by now very hungry, and he wanted to continue their journey on foot to the next village if she felt able. So they set out together, he carrying the sheepskin over his left shoulder, and supporting her with his right arm. He hardly dared hope to reach a village or a hospitable farmhouse by midday, but fortune favoured them; a horse-drawn farm cart passed beside them, going in the same direction, and a bearded farmer called out to ask where they were going, as he was heading for a farm at a place called Buck's Horn Oak, and could take them with him.

Cecily climbed into the cart with almost tearful thanks, and Dan told how their horses had been stolen by a trio of villains, who had then ridden off; he did not say the direction they had taken, because he wanted to give them a chance of escaping a bad landowner. He knew that he would remember until his dying day the night he had spent wrapped in a sheepskin with her, and felt he owed them a favour. At Buck's Horn Oak Cecily drew out the bag of five gold coins that old Blagge had given her; she used one to pay the farmer for rescuing them, one to buy bread and cheese and replenish their water-bottle at the farmhouse where the cart stopped, and three to hire two horses on which to ride the rest of the way to Waldham.

Waldham had been a settlement since Saxon times, and stood on the river Walde which formed the county boundary. It had developed over time into a town, and its main road was now a busy thoroughfare, largely due to the milling and selling of grain; it was dominated by the windmill with its whirling vanes and Mill House, built in stone on the lines of a manor house. In the chilly afternoon light Cecily thought it a cumbersome building, a larger version of Blagge House with an unwelcoming air, matched by the woman who met them in the small entrance hall. Cecily recognized her as she who had been brought to Maud's wedding to be her personal maidservant.

'We were expecting you yesterday, Mistress Blagge,' she said, and nodded to a waiting manservant to take Dan to his quarters. 'And see that their horses are fed and stabled,' she added before turning to Cecily again. 'I will show you to your room, Mistress Blagge, and send for some refreshment from the kitchen.'

'But Mistress Keepence, where is *she*?' demanded Cecily sharply. 'I have come a long way and faced great danger, to see my sister-in-law.'

'I'm afraid that Mistress Keepence is not well, Mistress Blagge,' answered the woman. 'I am keeping her confined to her bed, and you may see her in the morning.'

'I will certainly *not* wait until morning,' returned Cecily with spirit. 'Pray lead me to my sister at once. If she is unwell, I need to know exactly how she is. Take me to her.'

The woman who had clearly been used to acting as housekeeper in place of the lady of the house, stared back at Cecily for a moment, and then tossed her head and led her into a wide passage off which a staircase ran up to a floor above. Cecily followed close behind her, and was ushered into a master bedroom; there in the matrimonial bed lay Maud Keepence, and Cecily gasped with shock at the sight of her. Rake-thin, with closed, sunken eyes, her body scarcely showed beneath the bedcovers; one transparent hand lay on the sheet, every bone visible, almost skeletal. A jug of water and a mug stood on a small table beside the bed.

'She's asleep,' whispered the woman, putting a finger to her lips, 'and I hope she is not about to be disturbed. She needs to rest.'

Cecily stared at this shadow of the woman she had known, her husband's sister who had become as close as her own. For a moment words deserted her, so shocked was she at the sight of this dear friend who was so clearly dying.

'Why was not a message sent to her father?' she whispered. 'How long has she been in this state? Has an apothecary been called to see her?'

'Master Keepence sent for a wise-woman who cares for women in childbed and prepares the dead for burial. She came and found Mistress Keepence with child—'

'Surely not!' interrupted Cecily in a low voice. 'How could she be, wasted as she is?'

'It's what Dame Lightfoot said,' came the answer, 'and she said that Mistress Keepence has the mother's malady, in which her stomach throws back every scrap of food she eats. The dame said that if . . . if she reaches three months the sickness might stop, and the child will start to grow.'

This long speech, though spoken softly, awoke Maud who opened dull eyes and muttered, 'Meribel, are you there?'

'Yes, my mistress, I'm here to take care o' you,' answered the maidservant in a voice that combined kindness towards her charge with resentment against this visitor who had come to cause trouble. 'Will you try to take a little sip of water now?' She moved towards the side of the bed and picked up the mug, holding it to the invalid's thin lips; but Maud had seen Cecily, and her eyes brightened in recognition.

'Cecily – oh, Cecily, is it really you?' she asked weakly. 'Or am I dreaming again?'

Cecily moved towards the bedside. 'Step aside, please,' she ordered Meribel. 'I wish to speak with my sister.' Reluctantly the woman stepped back, and Cecily took Maud's thin hand between her own.

'Maud,' she said quietly, her eyes filling with tears which she blinked away. 'Yes, dear Sister, it is I, Cecily, your friend, come to take care of you, and get you well again.' For in that moment Cecily knew she could not return to Hyam St Ebba, leaving Maud almost certainly dying. Her thoughts flew on ahead: Dan must return and tell Edgar and old Jack Blagge of Maud's sickness and let Lady Wynstede know that she would be staying at Mill House until Maud recovered. Or until . . . but she could not name such a possibility, even to herself.

'Master Keepence isn't going to be much pleased if I'm not allowed to look after his wife in her time of need,' Meribel said defiantly. 'He gave me orders to stay with her until the sickness stops, as Dame Lightfoot says it will. He won't like it if—'

'I will speak with Master Keepence,' said Cecily who would have spoken with more force had it not been for Maud lying there helplessly. 'And you can take this water-jug and mug away, for from now on I will allow no hands but my own to touch her food or draw water for her to drink.'

Meribel flushed darkly with anger, but as it turned out, the mill owner welcomed Cecily's presence, and confessed to her that he had hoped against hope that the wise-woman Lightfoot had been right, and that Maud's excessive sickness was due to her being in the early months of carrying a child. He had not wanted Maud's family to know before she recovered, when they could share her happy expectations without going through the anxiety that he was now enduring. Meribel had been lady's maid to his first wife, and he trusted in her experience and good common sense; but if Mistress Blagge was able and willing to supplant Meribel in the care of his new wife, he cared not whose feelings might be hurt. He would do anything, pay anything to see Maud well again, and growing big with his child.

Cecily took on her new duties straight away, and Dan was sent back to Hyam St Ebba with the hired horses, carrying messages for Blagge House and Ebbasterne Hall. She missed Dan's reassuring presence in this strange house, but she soon realized that Meribel's concern for her sister-in-law was genuine, and decided that it would be better to treat her as an ally.

'I intend to find out the cause of Mistress Maud's sickness,' she told the woman. 'And you will do me the greatest service by continuing to run the household, Meribel.'

She asked Master Keepence to send for the wise-woman again, to ask her opinion and why she thought Maud was with child. When Dame Lightfoot arrived she was shocked at the invalid's appearance.

'She be worse than when I saw her last week,' she admitted, and doubted her earlier assertion that Maud was with child. 'Many a woman's sick in her first few weeks, but it usually stops by the third month, and then her belly starts to grow, but I never saw one to puke like this. I see death awaitin' her if no cure can be found soon. Be ye giving her milk or cordial? A little wine and water? Mutton broth or corn gruel?'

Cecily tried everything to settle Maud's rebellious stomach, but only a very little water and fruit juice was taken; all other offers were immediately vomited, and Maud's haggard face wrinkled in disgust at the very sight of food. Master Keepence was anxious about her, though he did not curtail his occupation with the mill and granaries; he told Cecily that he felt useless at his wife's bedside, so left her in the care of her female attendants.

Three days later, Edgar Blagge arrived on a newly purchased horse to replace Chaser, and bringing with him the maidservant Mab from Blagge House on another, to give assistance with the nursing. Cecily gave her the task of night-sitter, to attend to any of Mistress Maud's needs, and to call on Cecily in the room next door if anything untoward happened. Edgar shook his head sadly at his sister's appearance; she hardly seemed to know him as she lay looking up with dull, half-closed eyes.

October passed into November, and winter set in with bitterly cold winds. Maud showed no improvement, and Cecily, Meribel and Mab faced the prospect of a wretched Christmas at Mill House, each of them secretly thinking that Maud would no longer be with them by then. Cecily began to be aware of her own growing child, and reckoned that by the New Year she would have reached the three-month mark, but still she told no one; she felt well, and all their cares and hopes were centred upon Maud.

And then came the night when the tide turned. As Mab was dozing in a chair by the bedside she was wakened by the rustle of bedclothes and a low moan. Maud was trying to sit up, but was too weak to raise her head from the pillow.

'Cecily,' she whispered. 'Cecily, are you there? Get me a drink, I'm so dry.'

Instantly Mab was on her feet. It was the very darkest hour of the night, but a candle flickered on a shelf, and Mab brought it to the bedside. Maud groaned again that she was 'dry,' and said, 'water – I need water.' Mab offered her the cup of water, and she drank greedily, emptying it and asking for food.

'Bread, Cecily, bring me bread,' she pleaded, and Mab went to call Cecily who hurried into the room in her nightgown, shaking herself awake.

'Cecily's here,' she said. 'What do you want, dearest Sister?'

'Drink – bread – meat, anything,' said Maud, looking up at the two anxious faces.

'I'm thirsty – thirsty and so hungry, Cecily.'

Surely, this was a miracle! Mab was despatched to the kitchen to light a fire from the glowing embers in the hearth, and to fetch bread from the pantry.

'Call for Meribel, too,' ordered Cecily, and for the next half-hour of that dark November night the three women watched in wonder as Maud ate ravenously; it was like seeing her brought back from the very jaws of death; she would have taken more, but Cecily said she must not overfill her stomach after so long a fast. In her heart she could not quite believe what was happening. Would it last? Should she start giving thanks to God? And then, as had happened before, she gradually became aware of a presence, like a warm current of air that blew softly over herself and Maud, now sleeping peacefully. A dark shadow had gone out of the room, out of the house. Death had been defeated, and had taken himself away. Cecily opened her eyes, and smiled for the first time in days: peace and thanksgiving filled her heart.

'Thanks be to God and the blessed Saint Cecilia,' she said silently. 'Peace be with Valerian, O Lord, and bring him safely home. Amen.'

The reason for Maud's sudden recovery was soon explained. Having eaten a good breakfast with her thankful husband at her side, she became restless and clutched at her belly.

'Help me to the close-stool! I must ease my bowels!' she cried, and Meribel dragged the close-stool from the corner of the room to the bedside, while Cecily pulled back the bedcovers and put out her hand to give support; but Maud gave a groan and fell back on the bed, instinctively spreading her legs apart. Bloodstained water gushed forth, followed by a tiny, unformed human being, scarcely three inches long, encapsuled in what seemed like a transparent skin. And it was dead.

Dead. Maud had conceived, but the child had caused her great sickness, and its death had been her cure. Cecily's eyes filled with tears: did her own unformed child look like this? How could she ever tell Maud that she was with child for the second time, after all that her sister-in-law had suffered?

Fifteen

The winds of March whined around the stone walls of Blagge House, as if searching for crevices to send draughts whipping through. Lady Wynstede shivered. 'This house is much colder than Ebbasterne Hall,' she said, wrapping her wool blanket more closely around her.

'Ah, but the days are getting longer and the daffodils are in bloom,' Cecily reminded her with a smile. 'Do you remember Father saying that March comes in like a lion, and goes out like a lamb?'

'If only this wicked war would end,' sighed Katrine, stabbing her needle into the next stitch. 'Poor Lady de Lusignan lives from day to day, wondering whether the Count and Sir Charles are alive or dead.'

As I wonder about Valerian, thought Cecily. News from France was scarce; Abbot Athelstan had told them that he'd heard the siege of Calais was still holding on after six months; the King had got his men to build themselves wooden huts around the besieged port, to provide shelter for them during the winter, and small ships arrived regularly with fresh victuals; but no vessels had been able to get through the blockade to bring food for the citizens of Calais who would soon have to choose between captivity and starvation.

'What wickedness!' exclaimed Kat. 'Imagine a poor mother, half-starved herself, and unable to give her children a crust of bread! It's a blot on the escutcheon of England's honour – King Edward must be cruel and heartless.'

'Hush, Mother, the king is famed as a leader of men and a formidable opponent in battle,' said Cecily quickly. 'The fact that Friar Valerian has stayed with his army testifies to its rightness, serving under a king who faces the same dangers as his men.'

Kat Wynstede pursed her lips and shook her head slightly. 'By what Oswald says, Crécy was a bloody battle, a frightful slaughter of men and horses, as indeed were the battles in Gascony. He was sickened by the sight of—'

'Oswald was more sickened by drink than by the misfortunes of war,' Cecily broke in. 'If it hadn't been for Dan Widget and the help of Friar Valerian, he'd have drowned in the river Somme, most likely. It's time my brother grew up into a man, and took more of his duties on his shoulders.'

Kat sighed. 'He's only nineteen – and he *is* trying to run the Ebbasterne demesne with Will Goode.'

They sat in silence for a while, their needles busy with small garments for the expected baby, due about the beginning of June, Cecily surmised. She had been much blamed for her visit to Maud: old Jack Blagge had scolded her for keeping her condition secret before her journey to Waldham, thus putting his expected grandson at risk, for he was certain that this child would be a boy. His daughter's miscarriage sounded like a blessing rather than a disappointment, he said, and Maud had plenty of years left to have children. Lady Wynstede had wept, reproaching her daughter for concealing the fact that she carried a second child.

Cecily's thoughts now were with Maud, her sister-in-law and dearest friend, cooped up all winter in that gloomy house. It was now more than three months since the tragedy that had happened so close to Christmas, and she wondered if Maud had conceived again, now that the days were lengthening and winter giving way to spring. She wanted to invite Maud to stay a little while at Blagge House; it would be a change of surroundings for her. She knew Master Keepence's real concern for his young wife, and was fairly sure that he would be willing to let her go on a visit to her childhood home. She mentioned this to her mother.

'But my dear, here you are with child again, and with Kitty to care for,' objected Kat. 'You need to be taking care of yourself for the next three months, not entertaining a guest!'

'But Maud and I are as close as any sisters,' returned Cecily, a little impatient at her mother's constant fretting. 'Janet is a great help, though she is but fourteen, and little Kitty is devoted to her, as much as to any nurse – but Maud is my dearest friend, and nearly died. I have a duty towards her.'

'And so have you a duty to your husband and child, not to

mention your mother and your father-in-law,' retorted Kat. 'Edgar and his father were very upset when you insisted on staying at Mill House until nearly Christmas, and then when Edgar and Dan Widget came to fetch you and Mab, I've heard you seemed reluctant to leave. I was deeply hurt, Cecily, that you'd put Maud Keepence's wishes before mine.'

'That simply isn't true, Mother. Maud's wish was that I would stay with her until after Christmas.' And so I would have done, too, she thought, if she had not recovered so well.

They sat there with their sewing until dusk began to fall, each with her own thoughts, until Kat Wynstede rose and folded up her needlework.

'I must be getting back to the Hall, to find out what Ethelreda and Wulfstan have learned today from Brother Matthias,' she said. Now approaching fifty and with grey hair, Lady Wynstede often looked old and tired. Ethelreda and Wulfstan were growing fast, and were inclined to run wild, though they were now able to read and write tolerably well, thanks to Brother Matthias who came from the Abbey on two days a week to teach them.

Having seen her mother ride away into the dusk with Widget, Cecily felt the baby kick, and placed a hand reverently on her belly, marvelling anew the miracle by which Edgar's careful and respectful intimacy had resulted in the making of another human being, another soul to make the journey through life if by God's grace it survived infancy. Her thoughts turned again to Maud, and that evening at supper with the Blagge father and son and young Janet, she casually suggested that if Master Keepence would agree, Maud might benefit from a visit to her childhood home, to reacquaint herself with family and friends; Edgar glanced at his father, and old Blagge shrugged and said that he placed no restriction on his daughter, though he thought seeing Cecily with a young child and big with another might make her envious and discontented. If *he* were August Keepence, he wouldn't let her go gallivanting round the country like any silly girl with no husband to please.

'Thank you, Father,' said Cecily dutifully, and an invitation was sent forthwith to the Mill House; by the end of March Maud was at Blagge House, escorted there by one of Master Keepence's menservants, and accompanied by Meribel. There were kisses and embraces when the visitors arrived, though Cecily was careful to continue to treat Meribel as an equal, and introduced her to the servants as one who was to be obeyed; fortunately Mab had already met her, and was used to her imperious ways.

Edgar welcomed his sister warmly, remembering how close he had come to losing her, but old Jack Blagge tactlessly asked her if August Keepence had planted a seed before she left Mill House. Little Kitty went straight to Maud, which touched Cecily, for Maud showed no sign of envy, only of affection for her little half-sister.

As soon as the two sisters-in-law had a chance to sit down together and talk freely, Maud whispered in Cecily's ear that Jack Blagge's coarsely expressed question about an implanted seed had not been so untimely after all.

'It's been seven weeks since my last flux,' she confided, 'and I've felt slightly sick some mornings, though nothing as bad as before – so I'm hoping that it may be so. I haven't said anything yet, not even to Meribel – but oh! Cecily, if only *I* could have a dear child like Kitty, I'd not ask anything more from—'

Her words were stifled in a close, joyous embrace from Cecily, and they agreed that Maud should not tell anyone else until she was sure.

'And you must stay here until you *are* sure, dearest Maud, and make your husband happy when you return!'

'Yes, poor August was so wretchedly anxious when I was ill,' said Maud. 'That was why he was willing to let me come here, hoping that I'd benefit from the change. Now I hope to have really happy news for him when we meet again!'

'So, you're content with him, Maud? He's kind to you, is he?' Cecily asked carefully, and Maud paused for a moment before she answered.

'I think I'm as happy with him as you are with my brother,' she said slowly. 'We are fortunate in our husbands, considering that they were chosen for us.' She paused and looked meaningfully at her sister-in-law. 'But I have no Friar Valerian in my life.'

'How did you know that, Maud?'

'Don't you remember that evening when my father announced my betrothal to August, and you were overflowing with milk and the Friar asked me to go with you to our house? He came with us, and we sat in the parlour with little Kitty – and he told you he was going to France with the King's army. I was there, and I saw the way you looked at each other – and dearest Cecily, I envied you, and not just for little Kitty.'

There was silence for a minute, and Cecily felt her child give a kick, as if to remind her of her duties as a wife and mother; but she needed no reminding, and answered calmly.

'Yes, Maud, you are right, but this is no earthly love; he is a consecrated friar under vows as I am under vows to your brother. Yet he is my lodestar, and my love for him – and his for me – is something apart from the earthly bonds of matrimony, and doesn't contradict them – in fact it reinforces them, because it is entirely spiritual. My marriage vows are lifelong, as long as Edgar and I both live – but *this* . . . this communion of souls is for eternity.'

Maud listened and believed that she understood.

Halfway into April there was news from Castle de Lusignan: the Countess joyfully announced that her husband and Sir Charles had returned from France, thin and war-weary, with minor wounds that were healing slowly; but they were *home,* and safe, so there was muted rejoicing at the Castle and a thanksgiving Mass at the Abbey, where prayers were said for the repose of the soul of Sir Piers whose heirdom now passed to his brother Charles.

The Wynstedes were invited to the Mass and the supper which followed at the Castle, and Katrine Wynstede was happy to accept, taking Ethelreda and Wulfstan with her. Reluctantly, Cecily and Maud stayed away because of Jack Blagge's animosity towards the de Lusignans, and to deliberately flout his wishes would be foolhardy and cause unnecessary tensions at Blagge House. They were, however, eager to hear from Katrine all about the ceremonies at the Abbey and feast at the Castle, where the Count and his son Charles were settling back into their lives and beginning to look like their former selves; but there was a shadow over their lives, a loss that could never be replaced. The Countess became a closer friend of Lady Wynstede, and even old Lady Lusignan, the Count's mother, turned a more favourable eye on the widow and her children. Oswald continued to improve, and because he could not boast of his exploits during the war, he too became more acceptable at the Castle.

April turned to a showery June, and Maud became certain that she was again with child; although she wanted to tell her husband, she decided to wait until Cecily was delivered, and quite soon came a morning when Cecily began to feel the first pangs of travail. Lady Wynstede was summoned, and the midwife; Maud Keepence was also at the bedside, and Meribel could hardly get a look in, but Cecily's travail progressed well and without unforeseen dilemmas; by evening she was delivered of a son whose lusty yells resounded through Blagge House, gladdening the hearts of his father and grandfather who waited below. Cecily, relieved of the excruciating pain of the final half-hour before delivery, was embraced by her mother and sister-in-law, and Maud held her newborn nephew with tears of joy and anticipation for when her own child would be born.

'We shall call him Aelfric, after my father,' said Cecily. 'Kitty is named for her grandmother, so he will be little Aelfric.'

However, when the menfolk were allowed into the birthchamber, Jack Blagge strode in ahead of his son – just as if *he* were the father of the child, thought Cecily – and said that the boy would be called John, after himself. Nobody dared oppose him, but Cecily decided he would be called John Aelfric at his christening, and that she would call him Aelfric.

Maud then returned to Waldham with Meribel, escorted by a manservant sent by Master Keepence. Cecily greatly missed her confidante, the one friend who knew and understood her love for Valerian.

At the beginning of July while Cecily sat suckling Aelfric John, she heard a messenger on horseback arrive in the yard. She rose, and holding the baby, went out into the passage just as Jack Blagge emerged from his counting-house and strode to answer the door. She quickly withdrew, heard a brief exchange of words and a clink of money, then a low muttering as Blagge tried to decipher the message.

'Edgar!' he called, and then remembered that his son was out in the town. 'Cecily! Come and tell me what this scrawl's supposed to be saying!'

She trembled as she entered his inner sanctum, still holding the baby. Blagge held out his arms to take him from her.

'Come, little man, come to your old grandsire!' he said in a more tender tone than he ever used to other members of his family. 'Read this through, will ye, Cecily? I can't make head or tail of it – here, take it.'

She reached out a hand to take the sheet of paper, feeling slightly faint as she did so, and sat down to read it. It was in an unfamiliar hand, and at first the scribbled words swam before her eyes without meaning.

'*Such bitter disappointment, such sorrow – unexpected – the midwife – so sorry – why this should have happened—*'

Then the words rearranged themselves, and the meaning became all too clear. Cecily closed her eyes and groaned aloud. 'Maud has lost the baby, Father. She's had another miscarriage.'

'Devil take it!' he exclaimed. 'Are you sure? Has she written it herself?'

'No, Meribel has written it for her. Oh, poor Maud! What shall we do? I will go to her, and—'

'No, you will not,' retorted her father-in-law. 'What would happen to my grandson without his mother's milk? Die, quite likely. I absolutely forbid it. When did it happen, then?'

'This was written two days ago. Oh, Maud, my poor friend!' Cecily could not contain her tears.

'No good carrying on like that, girl, Maud's got years ahead o' her yet, and we must wait for better news another time. Ah, don't cry, little man, don't cry! At least we've got you, haven't we? Take the messenger to the kitchen, Cecily, and tell Edda to give him some refreshment. And write an answer straight away, so he can take it back. I'll put a few gold coins in with it. Poor August, he must be feeling cheated.'

When Edgar returned he showed more sympathy, but there was little comfort that he could offer.

'Has your mother been told yet?' he asked, and when she silently shook her head, he said he would take her and the baby to Ebbasterne Hall, so that she could share her sad news with her mother. 'Ask Janet to look after Kitty until you return,' he said. 'Both my sisters are close to you, and for that my father and I are thankful, Cecily; Father thinks a lot of you, although he may not show it.'

Dear Edgar, thought Cecily, he's been taught by his father not to show emotion, and can't unlearn it now, but I'll take up his offer to go to Ebbasterne Hall.

When they arrived there, they were greeted by an excited Kat Wynstede.

'Ah, Cecily, so you've already heard! I had half a mind to send you word, but now—'

'Yes, Mother, it's the saddest news, and poor Maud is heartbroken – you should see the letter—'

'But my dear, what are you saying? What letter? What have you heard?' asked Kat in some bewilderment. 'The Abbot says he's tired and half-starving, and much troubled in his mind, but he's returned, he's been spared to us – oh, Cecily, whatever's the matter?'

For Cecily stood staring at her mother in disbelief. 'Who has been spared, Mother? What do you mean? Do you speak of . . . of Friar Valerian?' she said, almost under her breath.

'Who else, my Daughter? He's at the Abbey. I thought you must have heard.' Kat glanced at Edgar. 'Haven't you?'

'No, Lady Wynstede,' he said gravely. 'We bring ill news from Waldham. My sister, Mistress Keepence, has again miscarried.'

'Again? Oh, sweet heavens! The Lord giveth, and the Lord hath taken away,' said Katrine, crossing herself. 'But my news is of the good friar, restored to us from the war.'

'Have you seen him, Mother?' asked Cecily, making an effort to control her voice.

'No, my dear, he's being cared for at the Abbey, but we shall see him when the Abbot thinks he's ready to meet people. But poor Maud – such a disappointment to happen again!'

With tears still wet on her cheeks from mourning her friend's loss, Cecily's heart leaped, and her tears turned to joy. Her daily prayers for Valerian had been answered, and he was at the Abbey and he was safe, thanks be to God!

'When may I see him, Mother?'

'When the Abbot allows us, Cecily, and not before. By what Abbot Athelstan says, he needs to rest. Now, do tell me about your sister-in-law. Did you say that Meribel wrote the letter? I suppose poor Maud was too grief-stricken. What a tragedy!'

So Cecily had to restrain her joy, and hide her emotional turmoil under her sorrow for Maud, while the hot summer days passed without a further word or sign. Did he not want to see her, married as she was to a kind husband, and mother of two young children? Had his year in France changed him? Was his face badly scarred, and was that the reason for his non-appearance? When the Blagges and the Wynstedes attended Mass at the Abbey, there was no sign of Valerian, but in her heart Cecily believed that his love continued, and that she must go on waiting patiently.

At the Abbey Friar Valerian attended the daily offices and spent hours kneeling in silent prayer; he ate frugally at mealtimes in the refectory, taking advantage of the Benedictine rule of silence. During the afternoon recreation hour he walked alone in the demesne of the Abbey, not seeking the company of the brothers. After a week the Abbot decided to talk to him, not by a summons to the Abbot's parlour, but by falling into step beside him in the gardens.

'Are you ready yet to speak of your experiences in France as chaplain to the King's army, Friar?' he asked kindly, and added, 'Do you need to make confession? If you do, I advise you to make it soon, or it will become an increasingly heavy burden, unless you take advantage of the Blessed Sacrament. I am available to you at any hour, my son.'

'Some things are beyond description,' muttered Valerian, shaking his head. 'My tongue refuses to name them.'

'My good Friar, you will not tell me anything I haven't heard before. Come back with me to the Abbey now, confess and be forgiven.'

So kneeling to the Abbot and the wooden Crucifix above him in the Lady Chapel, Valerian began to speak of what he had seen and heard, the horrors of the *chevauchée* through Normandy, the wounding of men and raping of women, the plundering of property; he spoke of the sacking of Caen and the vengeance carried out on its citizens.

'I know that war can never be gentle,' said the Abbot, 'and acts of violence that would be punished in peacetime become acceptable when committed in warfare. How did our King and his young son the Black Prince conduct themselves?'

'King Edward is a greedy monster, thinking only of extending his lands and power in France. And his son shows every sign of becoming as warlike and merciless as his father.'

'Hush, my son, these are treasonable words, and could land you and all the community of this Abbey in danger of our lives!' gasped the Abbot, truly shocked by this unreserved condemnation of the King.

'Either I make a true confession to you, Father Abbot, or I do not. Do you know, the French peasantry say that the English are so cruel that they cannot be properly human – and have tails! Which must be the six-foot lances that hang down from their belts at the back, even when on horseback. And after that bloody battle at Crécy, the King went straight on to lay siege to Calais, blockading it by land and sea until its citizens either capitulated or starved to death – and it's still going on, nearly a year later. The King got his men to build wooden huts to shelter them through the winter, and supplied them – us, I should say, with food brought over in small boats, though no boats could get through the blockade of Calais.'

'And King Philip VI of France, was he a more moderate leader?' asked the Abbot.

'Inept and cowardly,' replied the Friar contemptuously. 'The only hope for those poor people of Calais was to be rescued by a French army of liberation, yet the siege had lasted ten months before Philip rode up with his soldiers to the cliff at Sangatte to break it and you should have heard the grateful shouts from the citizens who could see them up on the hill.

'They were weeping for joy – until King Philip saw the English encampment and took fright. Within sight and sound of Calais, we actually saw Philip order his men to retreat. My God! I hope the lamentations of his starving people will ring in his ears, as they certainly do in mine. That's when I could no longer stay, but got on one of the small supply boats on its return to Dover. I came home, shamed above all to be a part of so much evil. And still the siege goes on.'

There was silence for a moment, and the Abbot put out a hand to touch Valerian's shoulder. 'Thank you, Friar,' he said. 'After hearing you, I too feel a sort of shame at the behaviour of my countrymen. You did well to stay as long as you did, but let me remind you never to utter a word that could bring a charge of treason against you, punishable by death.' He paused and then quietly enquired, 'Is there anything else you wish to confess, my son?'

There was no reply, and the Abbot continued, 'Was it your faith which sustained you through all this trouble?'

'Yes, Father Abbot, it was my faith in God which helped me and comforted me in keeping the blessed St Cecilia always in my mind, and she who is the embodiment of Cecilia upon earth to me.' Valerian's voice shook, and he covered his face with his hands.

'Ah, yes,' said the Abbot. 'You still have this . . . this attachment to Mistress Blagge?'

'Forever, Father Abbot. As long as I live and beyond.' He was scarcely audible.

'And you have no lust for her body, no unlawful obsession with a virtuous married woman and a mother?'

'None whatever, Father Abbot, as God sees and knows – but the vision of her sweet face sustained me throughout the horrors of the past year – literally kept me alive.'

'Very well, my son. Now make an act of contrition, and by the authority vested in me by the Church, I shall absolve you from your sins.'

At last there came a morning when Dan Widget brought an invitation to Master and Mistress Edgar Blagge to attend at the Abbey on the following afternoon.

'Your mother, too, and young Ethelreda and Wulfstan; he's asked 'em all, and wants ye to bring little Kitty and the baby, to receive a blessing from the Friar,' said Dan, happy to bring her good news, though the Abbot was clearly taking no chances; this was to be no private tête-à-tête.

Edgar asked his wife to make his apologies to the Abbot, having no desire to spend an afternoon in the company of the young Wynstedes, chasing each other round the monastery gardens, nor of his mother-in-law and her incessant chatter.

'And I'd leave baby John Aelfric at home with Janet if I were you, Cecily,' he advised. 'Heaven help the Friar if he's feeling as exhausted as the Abbot says! And tell Widget to bring you home at once if you feel tired.'

Cecily nodded and thanked him for his concern, but said she would prefer to take baby Aelfric John with her. 'I like to be within reach of him at all times while he is yet so small.'

'As you wish, Cecily, but keep him on your lap for his safety,' he warned, thinking of the young Wynstedes and their mother's lack of control over them.

When the ladies arrived they were shown into the sunny cloistered courtyard adjoining the chapter house. Refreshments were provided on a table in the shade, and there were seats enough for Lady Wynstede and Kitty, Mistress Blagge who held her baby son on her lap, Ethelreda and Wulfstan and the Abbot. Friar Valerian sat on a stone seat in a carved alcove, a favoured place out of the sun's glare. Lady Wynstede immediately exclaimed her welcome, her pleasure at seeing him again; she knelt to kiss his hand, and there were smiles and compliments on every side.

When Valerian rose to greet the lady of Ebbasterne Hall and her daughter and grandchildren, one glance between him and Cecily Blagge was enough to reassure them both. The war, the months of hardship at Calais and the pitiless ferocity of the King against its citizens had taken their toll, and the Friar had aged. At thirty-one his hair was mostly grey, and the livid raised scar down the right side of his face had not healed well; the edges of the skin overlapped and pulled down the outer corner of the eye. Even so, to Cecily he had not changed; he was the prince among men that she remembered, the valiant knight of her imaginings before they had ever met. And to him, this young matron holding her baby son in her arms appeared even more beautiful than his memory of her, his bright Saint Cecilia in human form, his fair Lady. And in one single glance, a lightning flash between their eyes, all this was conveyed, the one to the other in happy recognition.

Lady Wynstede proudly brought forward her granddaughter, little Katrine who had been christened by the Friar eighteen months ago.

'You were there in the birthchamber, Friar, and named this dear child,' she said. 'You also saved my daughter's life. It is a day I shall never forget, and likewise all your lawyer's skill that saved me and my family from ruin – we mustn't speak ill of the dead, but I don't think there are many who mourn for that man.' She crossed herself. 'When we heard from Abbot Athelstan that you were back in England, we offered up thanks for the answer to our prayers – for as the weeks went by and the months went by, our hopes began to fade.'

Her mother's torrent of words gave Cecily a brief breathing-space during which she could compose herself. She sat with downcast eyes, holding her baby close.

Presently Valerian smiled and put out a hand towards Kitty who gave him one of her happy looks and trotted towards him on sturdy little legs.

'She's only just begun to walk,' said Kat Wynstede, slightly apprehensive about how the little girl would react to the Friar's scar. She need not have worried, for as soon as the child reached his knees she held up her arms to be lifted up, which he did, and sat her on his lap, where she smiled round at them all, as if to say, Look at me!

'She's quite fearless,' went on the proud grandmother, unaware that her words could be taken as meaning that the Friar's scarred face might make him frightening to a child. On the contrary, Kitty nestled close in the circle of his arm, laying her rosy face upon the rough weave of his grey habit. This tenderness sent a message to Cecily which had no need for words. All the anxiety and uncertainty of the past week – all the past year, in fact, dissolved in the July sunshine like a vapour. A great peace and thankfulness filled her heart, and she rose with Aelfric John in her arms to receive his blessing on both her children as he placed a hand on each head in turn. Inevitably Kat Wynstede wanted a blessing on Ethelreda and Wulfstan, and the Abbot could not but be touched by the sweetness of the scene, the innocent children gathered round the Friar's knee with their mothers. And he thought of the starving children of Calais who would haunt Valerian for years.

When the visitors had left, the Friar turned to the Abbot. 'See to it that this congregation of brothers prays daily for God's forgiveness upon our nation, and humbly ask Him to turn away His wrath in the evil day.'

Abbot Athelstan took a quick, sideways glance at his guest. The good Friar was clearly feeling the effects of the past year's horrors, and needed to rest more.

Sixteen

War-weariness had set in. After the fall of Calais a steady stream of tired English soldiers sailed for home, and there were many stories of how the siege had been broken, of King Edward's refusal to agree to any peace proposals that did not admit his title to the French crown. In desperation, it was said, six courageous burghers of the town, men of respectability and standing, came out under a flag of truce, and wearing only their shirts, to offer their lives in return for their town to be spared. The story went that the King had ordered them to be beheaded forthwith, but for the intervention of his Queen who went down on her knees to him, imploring him to spare their lives. This he did, and while he did not sack the town and kill its inhabitants as at Caen, he nevertheless turned its citizens from their homes, replacing them with English colonists, securing it as crown territory, a convenient seaport for trading and future invasion. Edward III was now hailed as the victor of Sluys, Crécy and Calais.

In Hyam St Ebba the daily round continued as the year declined. On the land there was the reaping and gathering, the threshing and grinding of corn into flour; in the kitchens the salting down of beef and pork, the preserving of fruit in sugar; in the dairies the churning of milk into butter and cheese, the brewing and the winemaking. In the Abbey the division of each day by the eight offices went on as it had done for uncounted years, observing the feast days of the Church. Friar Valerian worked with the brothers in the fields and kitchen gardens, feeling the sun upon his face, and his sinews strengthened by hard, healthy labour. Abbot Athelstan asked him to stay through the winter before returning to the harsh, uncertain life of a mendicant friar, and sometimes at the Masses the people attended, his eyes would meet Mistress Blagge's in silent mutual understanding.

'Thank heaven that dreadful war's over, and we can return to

our workaday lives again,' said Lady Wynstede, echoing the
thoughts of many, but nobody knew that while England rejoiced,
an enemy of greater power was marching inexorably through
Europe, leaving devastation in its wake, and soon to cross the
Narrow Sea.

When the Feast of the Nativity came round, a High Mass was
held on Christmas Eve at the Abbey, and afterwards when wine
and cake were shared with the congregation, the Friar quietly
took the opportunity to say farewell to Cecily.

'Soon I shall be on the open road again, Mistress Blagge, a
beggar for the Lord, and you will be out of sight but never out
of my mind,' he told her, taking her right hand and raising it
to his lips. 'We're strangers and sojourners in this world, but we
travel as pilgrims towards the same end. Wherever I am, you are
closer to me than the air I breathe, and I ask only for your
prayers.'

'You have no need to ask, good Friar,' she said in a low voice.
'I shall be with you in prayer day by day.' And taking his right
hand, she returned his kiss.

When Valerian took leave of the Abbot and his brothers, he set
off towards London where later that year he had been invited to
attend a Convocation of Bishops at Westminster, to discuss the
growing unrest among peasant farmers and labourers, half of whose
wages went in rents to their overlords, while the Church demanded
a tenth of what remained as tithes to maintain the most powerful
force in the country, next to the Crown. The Bishop of London
had asked Valerian to join the gathering because of his legal
knowledge and first-hand experience with the unlearned peasants
who had no redress against influential landowners. Until the
Convocation was called, he would live as a mendicant friar among
the townspeople.

Master Blagge was interested in finding new markets in Europe
now that the war was over.

'With Calais in English hands, we can go straight across the
Narrow Sea from Dover, and then in any direction we choose,'
he said, rubbing his hands together in anticipation. 'Trade with
the Continent is going to get better and better!'

He sent Edgar on a longer journey than usual, to find markets in the city states of Italy – Milan, Florence and Venice – for the much-coveted English broadcloth. Edgar carried a new order book, and set off on a cold, bright day in early spring. He returned two weeks later with few entries in the book, much to his father's fury.

'What's this? A couple o' traders that are already on our books, and one from the Flemish border? We *know* there are merchants in Milan on the lookout for English wool cloth – so why didn't ye go straight to 'em?'

Edgar looked embarrassed. 'I'm sorry, Father, but few travellers are taking that road at present, for there are rumours of the plague ravaging the city states, especially Venice – they're all in the grip of it, with great loss of life.' He glanced uneasily at Cecily who sat in a corner with her sewing.

'God's bones, there's always plague *somewhere* in Europe, one city or another, and rumours get stirred up by merchants to frighten off their rivals,' his father raged. 'It could've been a chance for you to seize the advantage, instead o' comin' home with next to nothin'!'

But Edgar for once was ready to stand his ground. 'This is worse than other outbreaks, Father. In Venice they've been throwing hundreds of cadavers into the lagoon, and they say that the stink rising up from the water is enough to kill the rest. I kept away for the sake of my family. How would it be if I brought the contagion home to the children? No, Father, if you want to trade with Italy, you can take your order book there yourself!'

Cecily waited for Jack's anger to explode, but after one initial gasp of disbelief, he clapped Edgar on the shoulder.

'Hah! So you'll answer your father face-to-face now, will ye? Did ye hear that, Cecily? Keep it up, my son, and we'll make a Blagge out o' ye yet!'

He gave a bark of laughter, which strengthened Cecily's belief that her husband would gain more respect if he stood up to his father's bullying. She smiled at him, but he looked grave and shook his head, and she realized that he was genuinely alarmed by the rumours he had heard of the virulent outbreak of 'black plague' in Europe, so-called because of the dark swellings that appeared on the bodies of its victims.

It was inevitable. At midsummer a ship from Gascony disembarked in the bay of Weymouth in Dorset, and sailors came ashore bringing the fleas that lived on the rats which infested most ships, and whose bites transmitted the deadly infection which spread rapidly among those who had contact with it.

Friar Valerian in his rough grey robe and tonsured head drew mixed surprise and amusement from some of the Bishops and Abbots from many rich and powerful monasteries gathered in Westminster Hall under the leadership of the Bishop of London. Their minds changed, however, when he was called upon to give a legal opinion, and stood up to speak without fear or favour, his words grounded in good sense and compassion. He was at once regarded with new respect, and one churchman in particular stepped forward to shake his hand.

'Friar Valerian! How good it is to see you again – and to hear you!' cried Abbot Athelstan, greeting him with evident pleasure. 'Mine was a late acceptance because of the rheumatics in my knee joints, but I'm very glad I made the effort. Tell me, how have you fared since you left the Abbey?'

Valerian gave a good account of his life among townspeople, and the Friary at Newgate where he was currently lodging. He refrained from asking for news of Hyam St Ebba, but the Abbot guessed his thòughts, and remarked casually that Lady Wynstede and her family were all well, and that Master Edgar and Mistress Blagge were happily devoted to their two children. This satisfied the friar's unspoken questions while discouraging him from dreaming of the woman he loved; he nodded, grateful for this sympathetic tact.

'Have there been any cases of this "black plague" in Hyam St Ebba?' he asked.

'None to my knowledge, thank God, but it's rumoured to be spreading quickly, and may strike at any time, anywhere,' replied Athelstan, 'so we must be vigilant.'

His words proved to be prophetic, for on the following day they heard that one of the servants waiting on their Lordships had been taken ill in the night, and that it might be the dreaded plague. The Convocation ended prematurely, before any definite conclusions had been reached; each delegate speedily set out for home, anxious to get out of the town.

Valerian was surprised when Athelstan asked him to ride back with him, both for his company and for better safety from outlaws; Hyam St Ebba was the very place he had once been told to leave to avoid temptation; but now he readily agreed, secretly admitting to himself that he would be near to *her* again.

They said very little as they journeyed, and Valerian glanced frequently at his companion who admitted to being very tired, and sat with drooping shoulders on his steed. A terrible suspicion seized Valerian, and when they reached the Abbey he jumped down from his horse, just in time to catch the Abbot as he fell from his horse in a swoon. The gatekeeper rushed forward to help him carry the Abbot to his cell and lay him on the narrow bed; there Valerian removed the Abbot's cloak, pulled up his shirt, and saw that his fears were confirmed; the dreaded black 'buboes' were already present in the armpits and groins. Valerian thought quickly, and sent the gatekeeper to fetch the Prior who had been deputizing in the Abbot's absence, and told him that he would have to continue to deputize, because their Abbot had the plague, and their first consideration must be to stop the contagion from spreading. The brothers must be told, and nobody allowed to enter or leave the Abbey. There could be no gatherings in the chapel, and the daily offices would have to be recited by the monks in their cells. He then offered to care for the Abbot himself, with no assistance, and to submit himself to the Lord's will, whether he lived or died.

Whatever reports there had been about the virulence of the plague, the reality passed all imagining. Nowhere was safe; towns and villages were struck down, and people collapsed in the street; death intervened within two to four days or less, the victim sweating and shivering and coughing up blood. The King ordered prayers to be said in all the churches, and the Archbishop of Canterbury led a procession of penitents dressed in sackcloth and with ashes on their heads, to pray for forgiveness for the sins of the nation which, it was believed, had called down the wrath of God.

At Hyam St Ebba the de Lusignans offered to make their castle home a sanctuary from the 'black plague' for their friends. As yet there had been no cases in the town, and the Count and Countess called their friends to come to the castle and remain there until the scourge had passed. Lady Wynstede, Sir Oswald, Ethelreda and

Wulfstan were invited, and the Blagge family. Then the gates
would be closed, the drawbridge pulled up, and nobody would
be allowed in or out. Jack Blagge refused to go, and influenced
Edgar also to decline the offer, though Edgar insisted that Janet
and the two young children should lodge at the castle, and that
Cecily should follow them a day later, when she had baked bread
and brewed ale enough to sustain the men at Blagge House for
a time, and these included Dan Widget who had moved to Blagge
House when the Wynstedes had gone to the castle. There had
been no word from Waldham, and Cecily wondered how Maud
was faring, when a messenger from the Mill House rode into the
yard, bearing a sad letter from Maud with the news of a third
miscarriage. Edgar went out to see the messenger and offer him
refreshment, but the man was clearly unwell and slithered off his
horse to fall to the ground. Cecily watched as Edgar knelt beside
him in the yard, and unbuttoned his tunic; she saw the utter
dismay on her husband's face.

'Cecily, this messenger has the plague,' he said. 'You must go
at once to the Castle de Lusignan and tell them to close it to
any further comers.'

Cecily stared. She knew he was right, for they could not risk
taking the infection into the sanctuary of the Castle.

'I'll wrap this poor fellow in a blanket and leave him here in
the open air,' Edgar told her. 'But Cecily, there's still time for you
to escape if you go up to the Castle *now*.'

'No, Edgar, thanks be to God that Kitty and Aelfric are safe
with my mother and brothers and sister, and Janet. I will stay
with you and father. Dan must ride to the castle and shout out
to them to close it at once, but he must not enter.'

Jack Blagge raged furiously at what he called the carelessness
and sheer blind stupidity of his daughter Maud Keepence for
writing about her wretched miscarriage and sending it to carry
the plague to Hyam St Ebba.

'And that fool of a messenger must have *known* he was harbouring
the plague when he set out with that damned letter! Why couldn't
he have stopped and hidden himself in some deserted spot to die
and save others from dying? You're not to touch him, Edgar – don't
go near him. If he's as bad as you say, he won't last long, and when
he's gone, nobody's to touch the body. We'll all stay here in the

house, and live on such vittles as Edda can prepare for us. Anybody who disobeys will be thrown out and not allowed back in.'

Early the following morning the plague victim was found to be dead. Edgar and Dan buried him in a makeshift grave they dug in the grassy area beyond the wall surrounding Blagge House and Edgar hardly bothered to defend himself to his father.

'If the corpse were to lie there in this summer heat, the stink would be unbearable, and the danger of plague all the greater,' he said with a shrug, and Cecily shivered, thankful beyond words that her children were safely shut away in the castle.

On the following day Cecily woke in the summer dawn, and Edgar was not beside her. She got out of bed, sensing something amiss, and went out into the corridor: there was no sign of him, and she ran down the stairs in her night shift and bare feet. All was silent; there was no sign of Edgar in the parlour or his father's counting-house. The kitchen was empty, but the door was not on the latch, and she ventured out into the yard, then stopped in horror, for there before her, almost at the gate, Edgar was lying on the ground in his nightshirt. He was shivering and sweating, and his teeth chattered as she leaned over him.

'Edgar – husband, what's the matter? Why are you out in the dew at this hour?'

His eyelids fluttered as he tried to speak: his voice was low and harsh.

'Don't come near, Cecily. I . . . I have got the plague.' He groaned and tried to speak further. 'Let Dan wrap me in a . . . a sheet, and carry . . . carry me far from the house, I beg—'

'No, Edgar, no, I will care for you!' she cried.

'Then you . . . you will court certain death. Do . . . do as I say.' He gasped, and phlegm rattled in his throat. 'Save yourself, Cecily. Come not near, come not—'

His eyes closed, and his jaw grew slack as he sunk into unconsciousness. Cecily looked wildly around her, then straightened herself up and ran to the stable where Dan slept. Standing there beside the black stallion that Edgar used, she softly called up to him, and immediately he came down the ladder and quickly took in the situation.

'Go back indoors, Mistress, and I will deal with him.' He picked up a horse blanket from the floor.

'Boil some water, Mistress, and find me a couple of towels. I won't set foot in the house, neither must ye come to the stable. I'll look after him for as long as he needs, and ye can pray, for his end is near.'

'Thank you, Dan, and may God reward you,' was all that she could say.

By now the household was waking up, and she heard footsteps overhead. Edda came into the kitchen looking frightened, and Jack Blagge clumped down the stairs asking what the damned hubbub was all about. When he heard from Cecily that Edgar had the plague and was being cared for in a stable by Dan Widget, he turned pale and spoke with a quiet deliberation that was more threatening than a roar of rage.

'So that damned daughter of mine and that old fool Keepence have sent us to our deaths. If I survive this filthy pox, I'll be revenged on 'em. May they rot in hell.'

When he saw Cecily filling a basin with hot water and taking a towel over her arm, he grabbed them from her.

'Devil take ye, girl, ye'll not go near. Give 'em to me, and I'll take 'em – and see my son.' His voice broke on the last word.

'And don't go back to that bed,' he warned. 'Tell Bet and Mab to strip it off and burn the lot, for it'll be full o' the plague after Edgar's slept in it. Ye'll be the next to fall, most likely.' He covered his eyes for a moment. 'Edgar – oh, Edgar, my son. My son.'

Slowly the hours of that day dragged by. Dan faithfully carried out his care for Edgar while Jack watched, and when Cecily ventured to the stable door, Jack ordered her back indoors. Edgar never recovered consciousness, and by mid-afternoon his life had departed. Cecily watched from the kitchen doorway as Dan took the spade and dug a hole near to the one where the messenger lay; he and Jack Blagge dragged the body in the blanket across the yard and beyond the gate, where he tipped it into the grave with the blanket, heaped soil over it and trod it down. Edgar Blagge had gone from them, and Cecily wept for the husband who had always treated her kindly, and was the father of her two beloved children.

From then on, they stayed in the house, Cecily and her father-in-law and the three domestics. Dan continued to live apart in the stable, and Mab took him food and water, being told to keep her distance, for he would surely be the next victim. On the second day after Edgar's death, Mab tearfully reported that Dan was nowhere to be seen, and when by midday he had not reappeared, Cecily sorrowfully concluded that he must have developed symptoms of the plague, and had fled to avoid infecting them. After losing her husband she had now lost the most faithful manservant – no, not a servant but a dear, good friend who had faithfully guarded her at risk to his own life. Now she could only pray that he had found somewhere peaceful where he could lie down and commend his spirit to God.

'You and me, Cecily, we're the only ones left here now with the maids, and all likely to fall sick,' said Jack Blagge as they sat at table eating bread with a thin potato soup, the best that Edda could now provide.

'Yes, Father,' she replied, feeling uncomfortable alone with Jack Blagge. 'Shouldn't we ask the maids to sit at table with us? As time may be short for us all, we ought surely to be equal in life as we'll be in death.'

'They'd prefer to stay in the kitchen where they belong,' he answered, eyeing her narrowly as if trying to divine her thoughts. 'And *I* prefer to eat such food as there is left with what family *I* have left, Cecily.'

There was an emphasis on the last word which put her on her guard; she remembered what had happened on the night of Maud's wedding, and though she had tried to push the memory out of her mind because he had been drunk at the time, she decided to lock her door that night.

'Oh, come on, girl, there's good wine in the cellar, and not much time left to drink it,' he said with assumed joviality. 'No sense in going to waste, eh? Come on, little Cecily, stop moping and be merry while we can!'

'No, Father, I'm sorry, I can't be *merry* at a time like this,' she told him, getting up from her chair. 'I have to speak with Mab, so excuse me.'

And without asking permission she left the room, leaving him staring after her. She went outside and stood in the kitchen garden, breathing in the mild air and looking up at the clear sky where high, fleecy clouds stretched like lace across the firmament of heaven. Was God going to let them all die of this terrible plague? Oh, Valerian, Valerian, if only you were here to explain it all to me!

What happened next was so sudden that she was totally unprepared for it. Hands roughly seized her from behind and threw her to the ground. Her body was turned over so that she was lying on her back, and a hand was clamped firmly over her mouth. Another hand pulled up her kirtle and pushed her legs apart. A man breathed heavily on her face, and his voice grated hoarsely in her ear.

'Playing the fine lady with me, eh, ye little madam? Prefer to be out in the fresh air, eh? Well, ye're going to get what I've been wanting to give ye for years – hah! We'll be dead tomorrow, but today we're going to ride a cock horse – *now* – aah! Oh, God—'

His words became incoherent as he entered her, and her body was flattened under his weight. She could not have shouted for help – and what help was there? – and she gasped with pain as he thrust into her again and again.

'Better 'n Edgar, eh? Never had it like this before, eh? And better'n that cantin' monk, eh? I never did trust ye with that one!' His words turned to groans as he approached a climax and she felt a rib crack as he lay heavily on top of her, panting and muttering oaths while he gradually regained his breath.

The pain, the soreness, the weight of Jack Blagge upon her and within her, the sky above, the hard ground beneath, and her sense of utter helplessness brought her to a realization of where she was and what had happened. She had been ravished, shamed, and degraded – and she hoped that she would die of the plague. Even the thought of Friar Valerian was no longer a comfort, for what would a holy friar have to do with a dishonoured woman?

She became aware of Blagge, sitting up beside her and regarding her sheepishly.

'Ye're all right, girl, there's no harm done, and I'm sorry if I was a bit rough. The truth is that I've wanted ye since I first set eyes on ye, when I asked your father about ye marrying Edgar. I was married then, but – after I lost my wife I always felt – oh, look here, Cecily, don't turn your face away, I'll marry ye next week if we're not dead o' the plague. I'm sorry, I wasn't myself, losing Edgar – come on, let me take ye indoors.'

She turned her face upon him, and stared straight into his eyes. Her voice was low and surprisingly level as she answered him.

'I hope I will die of the plague. I'll never return to your house. Don't touch me!' she said, shrinking away from his outstretched hand.

'But ye can't stay out here, girl, it'll soon be dark. Come home to rest, and ye'll feel better in the morning. I'm sorry, but I'll marry ye, Cecily.' His voice had taken on a note of pleading. 'Please come home, dear.'

'Never. I'll do like Dan, and go to find myself a place to die in.'

He realized that he could hardly force her to return to Blagge House, and decided to go and tell Edda to fetch Mistress Cecily home. Turning on his heel, he walked out of the kitchen garden, back to the house and in through the kitchen door.

'Edda!' he called. 'Er, I need ye to fetch Mistress Cecily home. Bring one o' the other girls if ye like. She's in the kitchen garden. I'll explain later, don't worry, she's all right, she's just had a bit of a shock, that's all.'

Edda noted his red face and apologetic manner, so unlike his usual brusqueness. She called to Bet. 'The master wants us to go and fetch Mistress Cecily.'

'It'd be better with just the two o' ye,' he said. 'Just tell her there's nothing to worry about, and bring her back.'

The two women raised their eyebrows at each other. Edda had her suspicions that the Master had behaved badly towards his daughter-in-law, perhaps by trying to kiss or fondle her, and his son scarcely dead of the plague. They reached the kitchen garden and looked all around.

'Mistress Cecily! Mistress Cecily!' called Edda. 'It's Edda and Bet, we've come to take you home, Mistress Cecily!'

'It's no good, Edda, she's gone and she won't be coming back,' said Bet with a knowing shake of her head. 'She's run away.'

Bruised and shaking, Cecily had indeed run away from Blagge House and its master. Where could she go, seeing that she might be carrying the seeds of the plague? The bailiff Will Goode, at present in charge at Ebbasterne Hall, would probably let her in, but how could she risk endangering him and the household staff? Could she stay out all night, and rest in a field or in woodland?

It was one thing to wish for death, but not so easy to lie down and wait for it. And she must not risk passing on the plague to anybody. Stumbling on up through Hyam St Ebba, she was heartened by the sight of the Abbey tower, and the thought occurred to her that she might go there, and without crossing the threshold, beg to spend the night in a shed or outhouse of some kind. She decided to try.

That same evening, Valerian went down to the front entrance to see the elderly lay brother at the gate. Before he reached the entrance hall with its holy picture and statue of the Virgin and Child, he heard voices: the man was refusing entrance to somebody.

'Ye can't come here, mistress, we have the plague.'

'But by God's mercy, Brother, I have fled from a house of plague. Can you let me sleep out of doors in an outhouse or . . . or stable?'

Valerian gasped, and his heart leaped. He knew that voice, now tearfully pleading. 'Please, good Brother, I ask only for a place to lie my head on the ground.'

'I can't let you in, woman.' The man made a movement to close the door, but Valerian dashed to intervene.

'She can sleep in an empty stable,' he began, but stopped speaking and stood and stared at Cecily, her clothes torn and grass-stained, her hair dishevelled, her eyes full of shame and terror. Valerian gasped in horrified amazement, for he had seen too many women in that state while he was abroad; it meant they had been ravished by the soldiery. She swayed, and he dashed to her side, catching her in his arms.

'I'll take her to Nutbrown's stable,' he said to the old lay brother.

'But she says she's come from a house with the *plague*, Friar,' warned the man, thoroughly bemused.

'Then I shall care for her until she dies or recovers,' answered Valerian, lifting her up and carrying her out of the door and round the building to the stables.

'We'll die together if need be, my Cecily,' he murmured under his breath.

Seventeen

1348

It seemed to Cecily that she was floating up to the surface of deep water to find herself in a safe, dry place; there was a bed of straw on which she lay between sheets of bleached linen. A warm, familiar smell of horses filled her nostrils, and strong, sensitive hands were wiping her face with a towel dipped in cool water scented with lavender; it was an exquisite sensation. Was she dreaming? Had she died of the plague and was waiting now at heaven's gate? But then pain intervened, and she ached from her bruises, and felt a sharp stab on the right side of her chest. And a soreness of her woman's parts brought back to mind what had happened, and she moaned feebly at the memory.

Somebody was wringing out a cloth, and water trickled into a basin; fingers as gentle as a woman's smoothed back the damp strands of hair from her face, and a comb was passed through, freeing it from tangles and spreading it out on the sheet. She opened her eyes, and a man's voice murmured, 'Ah, she stirs and wakes,' as if talking to himself. Was this real? Could it possibly be true? She touched the little wooden Crucifix round her neck, and a hand was laid over hers.

'You are safe now, Mistress Cecily,' said the voice, and she knew it was no dream, though the sharp stabbing from a cracked rib was real enough, and so was the soreness below.

'Friar Valerian?' she whispered, and opened her eyes to see that indeed it was he. But what sort of place was this? A stable?

As if he had heard her thoughts, he said softly, 'A stable was a place where our Lord chose to be born, Cecily, and this one is at St Ebba's Abbey. You are safe here.'

Avoiding his eyes she said in a low voice, 'I can never go back to Blagge House. My husband is dead of the plague, and . . . and my father-in-law says he'll marry me.'

There was a pause, and then he asked, 'And was it he who ravished you, my Cecily?'

She could not for shame say the word 'yes,' but answered indirectly, 'I told him I'd die of the plague rather than stay with him.'

She heard him give a sharp intake of breath. 'You are innocent, dear Cecily, as innocent as that man is guilty. Don't be afraid, you're safe here, and you'll stay here until you've recovered, for you haven't got the plague. Now, I shall leave this basin of water and a towel for you to bathe your body, and here's a clean shift to put on. I'll come back within an hour with syrup of valerian to help you to sleep, and arnica to heal your bruises.'

He then left her alone and she managed to remove her tainted clothes, then held the wet, lavender-scented towel to the inflamed, swollen flesh between her legs. She put on the plain white shift, and when he returned, she took the syrup he brought her, and applied the unguent of arnica to the visible bruises. When he placed his right hand on her head, and said the blessing of the Trinity over her, she crossed herself and responded with 'Amen.' She felt washed clean of the outrage her body had suffered, and fell into an untroubled sleep; when she woke the next morning she felt refreshed, the bruises were healing, and she gave thanks for escaping the plague.

But the Abbey had not, as she soon discovered. Friar Valerian came to her in the early light of the summer dawn, bringing her a breakfast of bread and butter, with fruit cordial. He also brought a Benedictine monk's habit, newly laundered, with rope to tie it round her waist, having folded it to make it shorter; he also had a white linen scarf to tie over her head.

'I burned the clothes you wore yesterday, Cecily,' he said quietly, 'and hope you will be able to make do with these for the time being. How do you feel this morning?'

'Much better, good Friar, and I thank the Lord for your care of me,' she replied with a shy smile at the remembrance of such intimacies as washing her face and combing her hair. 'But how came you to be here? I thought you'd gone to London.'

'Yes, I've been in London, but the Lord in His mercy brought me here with Abbot Athelstan who had the plague.'

'The Abbot has the *plague*?' she repeated in dismay. 'How is he? May I see him?'

'He died in the night, Cecily, and my hope is to prevent the contagion from spreading through the Abbey.'

'Oh, may Christ receive his soul, dear Abbot Athelstan,' she said. 'But what of *you*, Friar Valerian – and the danger of the plague?'

'My life is in the Lord's hands, Cecily,' he said gently, 'and He brought me back to this Abbey to serve my brothers, whether I live or die.'

He looked thoughtful as he recalled the Abbot's wax-pale features in death, and his last whispered words. 'Do not touch her, my son' – and his clear reply, 'Never, Father Abbot, I never will, I swear by God's Name.'

He left Cecily to dress. She put on the habit and tied the rope round it, then covered her hair with the scarf, folding it like a nun's wimple, then pulled up the monk's hood to cover her head. When Valerian returned to tell her that one of the monks was showing signs of the plague, she felt destined to assist him in his care of the brothers in their distress, and nothing he could say would change her resolve. And so she entered the Abbey.

The Abbot's body had been removed and buried as soon as possible. Two monks had been detailed to perform this service, and the grave had already been dug. At midday yet another brother was said to be seriously ill, and for the rest of the day plans were made for coping with the possibility of many deaths. One of the choir monks, Brother Damian, was willing to share the Friar's duties in caring for the stricken, and in the kitchen a rota was drawn up for monks to fetch water from the Abbey well, and to bake bread and cook such vegetables as could be gathered.

On the following morning a visitor with a familiar face arrived at the Abbey, one who refused to be turned away. Cecily was called for, and when she saw the young man she almost shouted for joy, and would have embraced him but for the restrictions of the plague.

'*Dan! Dan Widget!* You're *alive!* Oh, praise the Lord's mercy in sparing you and sending you to us! Where have you been?'

'I was sure I had the plague, Mistress Cecily, so I went away so's not to give it to ye. I wandered around, and called at Ebbasterne Hall from outside, and Will Goode gave me bread and meat, keeping his distance.'

'Oh, Dan, what news is there from Castle de Lusignan?' cried Cecily, though in fear of what answer there might be.

'Will said there'd been no news o' the plague or anything else from the Castle, and by then I knew I must be well clear o' the plague, so went back to Blagge House. Edda told me ye'd run away, and the two maids had gone back to their families. I got one look at old Master Blagge, all unshaven and calling down curses on his own family, or that's what it sounded like. So I came here, and ah! Mistress Cecily, I thank God for the sight o' ye. Let me stay!'

Friar Valerian agreed that Dan would make a very welcome extra pair of hands, but warned him that he might well fall victim to the plague. Dan answered without hesitation.

'I'd sooner serve Mistress Cecily in a plague house than in a clean one without her.'

His first task was to dig a large, wide communal grave at some distance from the Abbey, because a high death toll was expected.

Thus began a strange twilight existence for Cecily. In the weeks that followed, she worked harder than ever before in her life. She was at the bedside of plague victims at all hours, wiping faces and hands, giving sips of water to drink, and comforting their final hours. Friar Valerian was always among them, giving Absolution and administering the Last Rites to those close to death. Brother Damian shared his duties in caring for the stricken, and Dan Widget too attended to their intimate needs, doing what a man can do for another *in extremis*, just as comrades in arms do for their wounded fellow soldiers. Monks who were unaffected helped with the care of those who succumbed to plague, and set about making winding-sheets for the dead who had to be carried out of the Abbey and buried in the communal grave. There was scarcely time for them to eat; days blurred into nights and back into days again. Time was suspended, and they hardly knew what day it was; the sour-sweet smell of sickness hung over the Abbey like a miasma, turning it into a charnel house, a place of death.

As Valerian prayed with the victims, and Cecily worked at his side with Brother Damian and Dan, they were all aware that any day might be their last. She slept in the stable when she could snatch an hour, and Valerian slept on straw in a corner of the parlour, the room where they rested briefly during the day, and took such refreshment as there was. There was little time to talk, and Valerian secretly wondered if *any* of them would be left alive, or was this

the end of humankind, visited upon them by a vengeful God? If
so, he was thankful to be doing his duty in these last days, and by
the side of her whom he loved.

He stole a look at Cecily, breaking a crust of barley bread with
cheese before returning to the sick and dying. They had become
so close during these last critical weeks, and he could hardly admit,
even to himself, that he had known great happiness in this shared
sojourn in the valley of the shadow of death, about which the
Psalmist had sung. And there was something else: his feelings towards
her had subtly changed. She was no longer a married woman, but
a widow with two children, and he did not want her to marry
any other man. Temptation, surely sent by the devil, told him that
if he renounced his monastic vows he would be free to marry her
and take care of her and the children. Hitherto she had been the
embodiment of chaste St Cecilia, but now he had come to look
upon her as a beautiful, desirable woman. And this in the midst of
a terrible plague when any day might be their last.

Cecily turned her face away, but she had seen his look. Here
they were, uncertain as to the future, if any, serving the stricken
brothers of the Abbey, and here was she imagining a situation in
which he would take her lawfully and she would be willing. Valerian
would never behave as Jack Blagge had, but – might he desire her?
And if such temptation came to him, and he yielded to it, how
would she respond? Would she conspire with him to break his
solemn monastic vows? Oh, shame, shame upon her for ever
imagining that he, a holy friar, a man of God . . . she must pray
for forgiveness for harbouring such thoughts, and was thankful that
he would never know.

What was she thinking, Valerian silently asked himself, troubled
by a vivid dream he'd had as he slept on the straw. In it, she had
willingly lain in his arms, and he had taken her. She had clung
to him, and he had woken up crying out, his heart thudding,
overwhelmed with relief that it had been only a dream. He
remembered once being told that a hundred dreams and a hundred
fantasies do not add up to one single sin – who had said that?
It was Brother Paulus at Netley, who had in fact yielded to
temptation in a way that Valerian never would. And so the devil's
whisperings were banished, and he gave heartfelt thanks that she
would never know of such gross imaginings.

Eventually there came a day in September when there were no fresh cases of the plague, and Valerian, Cecily and Dan were left with Brothers Damian and Matthias and seven other monks, three of whom were lay brothers. The death toll, including the Abbot and Prior, was seventeen, out of twenty-five brothers.

'Why should we be spared when so many have gone?' asked Brother Matthias, genuinely mystified. 'We've all had close contact with the victims, and shared the same air.'

'I've found that sometimes a man or woman comes in contact with the plague but instead of succumbing, they gain a kind of protection from it,' said Valerian. 'It has been the Lord's wish that we few have survived, and He must have His reasons.'

Brother Matthias looked earnestly at Cecily. 'Surely, Mistress, the Lord sent you to this house. You came in time to comfort the dying and raise the spirits of the rest of us.'

Valerian and the rest echoed his words, but she lowered her eyes and did not answer, sure that she would be dead had it not been for the Friar's intervention.

By mid-October the Black Death, as it had come to be called, finally left the Abbey, and though it went on to strike other towns and villages all over England, at Hyam St Ebba it was time to give thanks for deliverance, to open the doors and let the healthful air blow through. Cecily longed to see her family and friends, especially her children, all held like prisoners in the Castle de Lusignan for their own safety. There had been no word of them, for there were no messengers to ride from one house to another.

'Shall we send Dan to the Castle to find out what news there is?' she asked Valerian. 'It will surely be safe now.'

He looked at her eager face, paler and thinner than before their shared ordeal.

'It may be that your mother has returned to Ebbasterne Hall,' he said. 'We'll send Dan there tomorrow to see what he can find out.'

But in fact a note arrived by messenger the very next day from Lady Wynstede to say that the family was indeed back at Ebbasterne Hall. Valerian shared her joy while at the same time feeling a pang of regret that they would have to part again, continuing on their separate pilgrimages through life. She would return to Ebbasterne Hall, and live with her mother, her siblings and her two young children. And no doubt at some time a suitable son of the gentry would come along and lay claim to this young widow and take her children as his own. And then – but Friar Valerian gave himself an impatient shake; he had long renounced the world that she lived in, the world of marriage and family ties, to embrace a higher calling.

Overjoyed as she was at the thought of seeing her children again, Cecily felt a deep sadness in saying farewell to Valerian; she longed to throw her arms around him in love and gratitude, but had to be content with a handshake and a blessing from him.

Escorted by Dan on her short journey home, Cecily saw few people about in Hyam St Ebba, which had a melancholy air; it was possible to see which homes that had suffered deaths, by their silence and neglected appearance, though the crops had been harvested, and the chickens and geese who had lost their owners had obviously found new ones.

Ebbasterne Hall looked the same, for Will Goode had clearly managed the demesne well as bailiff in sole charge, rewarding himself with the sale of farm produce, just as Ned the groom had rented out horses. But now the family was back, and came out to meet Cecily and Dan with great jubilation. Lady Wynstede had visibly aged during the three months' incarceration at the Castle, and used a stick for walking. Kitty, who would be three in January, seemed a little shy at first, and Aelfric John was taking his first few tentative steps; he had no objection to being picked up and hugged by his mother.

'We've survived, Cecily, and must always be obliged to Hélène de Lusignan,' said Katrine Wynstede, 'though we're *so* thankful to be home again. That dear girl Janet Blagge has gone back to her father, but she'll find things sadly changed. Mab and Bet the maidservants foolishly returned to their parents' homes, and took the plague with them. Bet and her parents are dead, and Mab has survived, though her poor little brothers and sisters succumbed. Anyway, dear, I know that Janet wants you to join her at Blagge House, though of course I'd rather you stayed here with me.'

Cecily's mouth hardened. 'You need have no worries on that score, Mother. I shall never return to that house, and I do not wish to talk about it any more. Now, how's Oswald?'

'Oh, the dear boy has completely changed, and is taking life much more seriously now. It's such a relief to know that he'll be here to manage the estate when—' She broke off, and gave a little sigh. Cecily was worried, and said as much to Oswald when they got a chance to talk. He agreed that their mother was looking frailer.

'She's been a valiant woman since our father's death, and I haven't been much help to her, but from now on I'm going to work alongside Will Goode, and learn to be a proper master,' he told her.

'That makes me so happy, dear Brother!' said Cecily with unfeigned admiration, ready to forgive his past incompetence. The war and the Black Death had had *some* useful consequences, she thought wryly.

Her mother seemed determined to return to the subject of Blagge House.

'Have you some reason, Cecily, for avoiding your father-in-law?'

Cecily did not want to shock her mother with an account of her ravishment, but said merely, 'Master Blagge asked me to marry him, Mother, and I—'

'*Marry* you? Oh, Cecily, that's a very good offer, and shows just how much he knows your worth!' said Kat Wynstede in amazed delight. 'He may not be the youngest or the handsomest of men, nor the most refined, but he's a very successful merchant, and our family has greatly benefited from your marriage to poor Edgar. I hope you'll think it over, at least.'

'Mother, I'd be obliged if you would say no more on the matter. I know that I could guarantee a good legacy for Kitty and Aelfric by such a marriage, but I cannot consider it.'

'Very well, Cecily, I'll say no more about it,' replied Kat, and then proceeded to go back to it. 'I can give you another very good reason for living at Blagge House. Your great friend and sister-in-law Maud Keepence will be returning there soon, a childless widow.'

'*What*? Good God, has Master Keepence died?' cried Cecily.

'Yes, of the plague, more sad news among so much other trouble. And it seems that no sooner was poor Keepence dead, than his eldest son, Maud's stepson, came to lay claim to Mill House and his father's business. And yet I can't help being pleased that she'll be returning to Hyam St Ebba and her childhood home. Just think how much she'll enjoy having the children around her!'

Cecily was deeply dismayed at hearing this. Her dear friend Maud, widowed like herself, but without the consolation of children – how on earth could she explain to Maud the reason why she could never again enter the house which had been her matrimonial home?

She was not comforted when Oswald took her aside to confide a secret of his own.

'Being marooned up at that Castle has had a happy outcome for *me*, Cecily, for I found myself drawn to a young lady, a sweet girl I could talk to – Mistress Janet Blagge.' He paused when Cecily gave a sharp intake of breath. 'Yes, I suppose it's a bit of a surprise, and she is but fourteen, but time passes, and I know how it would please our mother, and presumably old Jack Blagge as well. How do you feel about it, Cecily? Do you think me good enough for her? Because if you give me your approval, I'll go to old Blagge and ask for at least a promise of a betrothal, and I know that Janet will not object. It would be another happy uniting of our two families.'

Cecily's heart sank even lower. She could not, she *would* not go back to that disgusting old man – but here were her mother and brother Oswald clearly expecting her to do so, as if in fact it was her duty, a convenient marriage in every way. Her heart was given to a consecrated man of the Church, one she could never marry; and now this sacrifice was being demanded of her for the benefit of her family and friends.

O Lord, show me what I must do, she prayed. *Teach me, show me the way that I must take, the path I must follow.*

And an answer came. No sooner had Cecily settled into her childhood home, reunited with Kitty and Aelfric John, than a visitor rode purposefully up to Ebbasterne Hall, sent his compliments to Lady Wynstede, and politely requested a few minutes of her Ladyship's time.

'Good heavens, it's Master Blagge come to see me!' cried Katrine, rising from her chair. 'And I think I can guess the reason,' she added, giving Cecily a significant look. 'Send him in to me!'

At which Cecily dropped her needlework and practically ran from the room and up to her bedroom where she bolted the door. Katrine Wynstede sighed heavily, but put on a smile for her visitor, and invited him to take wine with her.

'I thank your Ladyship for your kind reception,' he said, bowing and taking her proffered hand which he raised to his lips. 'We've come through a very difficult time, and by God's grace survived it. Now it's time to put the past behind us, and I've come on a happy mission – or at least I hope it may be so. My daughter Janet is home with me again, and of course I'm much obliged to Lady de Lusignan for giving her refuge – as I say, it's time to put the past behind us.' He smiled again at an astonished Kat Wynstede, unable to believe that this address was from the same rough-edged Master Blagge she'd known.

'My poor daughter Maud is also on her way back to her old father,' he went on, 'and knowing how close she is to my daughter-in-law Cecily, I know they'll live together in harmony, and Maud will share the upbringing of my grandchildren and yours.

'Your daughter Cecily was a very good wife to my son Edgar, as you know, your Ladyship, and bore him two healthy children. Now, I want to bequeath the bulk of my fortune to Kitty and John, and the rest to my older grandchildren. This may not please the family, but there is a way of ensuring that my wishes are carried out.' He looked Katrine straight in the eyes and thought he saw encouragement there. 'And that would be to take Cecily as my wife.'

He stopped and realized that he was sweating slightly, and was conscious of blushing, which infuriated him, though in fact it added to his appeal to Lady Wynstede.

'Your directness does you credit, Master Blagge, and of course I shall always be deeply obliged to you for your help at a difficult time in my life,' she said pleasantly. 'However, my daughter is a grown woman and a mother, so I think you had better approach *her* with your offer. She is . . . er, not here at the moment, but there should be an opportunity soon, and when you speak to her, you may say that you have my consent.'

'God bless you, Lady Wynstede,' he replied with relief, and clearing his throat, he went on, 'Perhaps I should mention that there was a little misunderstanding between Cecily and myself the last time we met, that was, er, nearly four months ago. I must take the blame for that, and freely admit that it happened at a bad time when my son Edgar had died of the plague – one of the first to succumb in Hyam St Ebba, and it was very upsetting. I obviously offended Cecily, for which I'm sincerely sorry.' He broke off, looking somewhat sheepish.

'Well, may I suggest a little delay before you approach her again,' Katrine continued. 'Let's say until Mistress Maud has returned to Blagge House – and on my part, Master Blagge, I wish you success. It's up to you now to apologize for any want of discretion on your part, and we'll hope for a happier outcome.'

He bowed, thanked her and bowed again, overcome with relief, and took his leave. Only when she saw from the window his departure from the Hall did Cecily come downstairs. Her mother greeted her warmly.

'Now, Cecily dear, Master Blagge has made you a fair and generous offer, and I think you should accept him.'

'*What?*' Cecily stared in blank disbelief. 'Are you telling me to *marry* him, Mother?'

'My dear girl, it would solve a lot of problems, and what possible objection could there be? He has great respect and regard for you, and you will have the children with you – they are his grandchildren after all – and the company of Maud and Janet.'

'Did . . . did he tell you what he *did* to me, Mother, after Edgar died?'

'He said there had been a misunderstanding, for which he was very sorry. I can just imagine the grief and turmoil you were all in, and as he has told me, here in this room, he takes all the blame for it, so surely it should be forgotten?'

'*Forgotten?* Did he tell you that he *ravished* me, knocked me down in the garden and *ravished* me that same evening? It was the worst experience of my life, and you say I should forgive him?'

Kat Wynstede was taken aback by this, and sympathized, but she still thought Cecily should forgive the repentant Jack Blagge.

Cecily felt trapped and betrayed. She had half a mind to run back to the Abbey and tell Valerian, but some instinct deep in her heart prevented her. It would place the Friar's vocation in danger if they were to declare their love, for he would have to choose between breaking his solemn, lifelong vows to God in order to marry her – or remaining faithful to those vows, a holy priest of the Church, consecrated to God for ever.

In silent and solitary agony of spirit, unadvised and uncomforted, Cecily made her decision; she chose *not* to go to Valerian and lead him into possible temptation; and following on from that, after a few days of prayerful consideration, she told her mother that she would accept Jack Blagge in marriage.

'Oh, well done, my Cecily, my own dear daughter!' cried Kat Wynstede, embracing her. 'Well done, you've chosen rightly, and I know you'll be rewarded. You must know by now, dear, that most marriages have little to do with romantic love, but affection grows as the years go by and children arrive – and you'll have the satisfaction of having done your duty. By marrying Master Blagge you'll be doing what is best for you, your children and all of us.'

By hanging on to Blagge's moneybags, thought Cecily bitterly, but she never said it aloud.

She was not surprised when Oswald congratulated her with uncharacteristic brotherly affection, and told her frankly that her betrothal to Jack Blagge was a perfect opportunity for him to ask for Janet's hand, and suggest a betrothal of two years, until 1350 when she would be seventeen. Oswald's visit to Blagge House was very successful, being good news for Blagge in the present circumstances. Katrine Wynstede also wished the young couple joy, and was about to commend Cecily's decision again when something about the expression in her daughter's usually soft brown eyes warned her to keep silent.

Mistress Maud Keepence duly arrived at Blagge House, accompanied by the faithful Meribel who had seen her through so much disappointment, and Cecily braced herself to visit her with the children. The first overnight frosts had sent the last leaves scattering to earth, and Cecily felt that the threshold of winter reflected the bleak chill in her heart that even Maud's welcome failed to melt entirely. Fortunately Kitty and little John Aelfric provided a useful distraction, and Maud's unfeigned delight in them was good to see, though Meribel thought how unfair it was that Mistress Blagge had what Maud had not. Janet was radiant with her own happy betrothal, and Cecily sat holding little John on her lap, silently praying for the strength to await her fate. It came with the arrival of Jack Blagge into the room, full of fatherly and grandfatherly good humour.

'Ah, we have a fine picture here,' he said, beaming round the room. 'Three handsome daughters and two pretty children!' He went straight to Cecily and held out his hand. 'And we have a happy announcement to make, haven't we, Mistress Blagge?'

'You had better tell it, Master – Jack,' she said, almost inaudibly.

And so the news that had been private became public, and Maud and Janet were all smiles, kissing her and little John Aelfric, and wanting to know if a date had been fixed.

Jack Blagge told them that the wedding would be a quiet family affair in the week before Christmas, and the ceremony would be in the Lady Chapel of the Abbey.

Maud clasped her hands together in delight – but suddenly thought of Friar Valerian. Cecily went to find Dan Widget. He had heard the news, but did not insult her with congratulations.

'I want you to go up to the Abbey, Dan, and take a note for Friar Valerian. It will give him a chance to avoid the marriage ceremony.'

'I'll do it today, Mistress Cecily, whatever you bid me, and I shan't put it into any hands but his.'

At the Abbey Brother Damian had taken charge, and a visit from the Bishop of Winchester was expected to confirm his status as the new Abbot. He had asked Friar Valerian to stay over until the new year, when two new novice monks were arriving to start building up their depleted numbers. Valerian had agreed until he received the note that Dan Widget put into his hand. When he had read Cecily's farewell and the news of her coming marriage to the man who had ravished her, he went into the Abbey and knelt before a statue of the Virgin and Child in the Lady Chapel. There he prayed in bitterness of heart, imploring the help of God and the intercession of St Cecilia. Then he went to Brother Damian, and said that he must go: he must leave the Abbey and leave the country.

On the following day he left the Abbey and Hyam St Ebba, to beg his way as a mendicant friar to Portchester, and from there he sailed across the Narrow Sea to Le Havre from where he travelled on foot to the Benedictine Abbey at Berlay in Normandy.

* * *

The wedding took place on a blustery December day, and the marriage ceremony was performed by Brother Damian, soon to be the Abbot. Lady Wynstede could not kneel, and leaned upon her stick during the prayers, praying earnestly for Cecily's happiness. Oswald and Janet stood together as a betrothed couple, Ethelreda was unusually solemn and nine-year-old Wulfstan dreamed of a future as a knight serving in the King's army. No de Lusignans had been invited. Everything went well; the bride made her vows in a low voice and held out her hand for Blagge to put his ring above the one that had been Edgar's.

Back at Blagge House a wedding breakfast had been prepared by Edda and Meribel, assisted by a sad-faced Mab who had returned to her employers after the death of her parents and siblings. Maud took charge of Kitty and John, reassuring Kitty that this was a happy day, and that her mother was not going away again. The bridegroom himself poured the wine, and a determined effort was made to be festive, so close to Christmas.

That night in the matrimonial bed where Blagge had lain with his first wife, Cecily yielded her body to her new husband who approached her with carefulness, completely unlike that horrendous former occasion, and awkwardly thanked her for receiving him. Afterwards, as she lay awake in the cold of a winter bedroom, she reflected that the act of marital union was hardly different from the way it had been with this man's son.

And remembered an old saying, that all cats are grey in the dark.

Eighteen

1349–1350

That winter set in with unrelenting frosts and falls of snow. Lady Wynstede felt it in her old bones more acutely than in previous years, and having been chilled to the marrow in the Abbey at Cecily's wedding, her deep, rattling cough could be heard all over Ebbasterne Hall. Cecily made her up a linctus of pine and honey which brought only temporary relief, and Ethelreda, now fourteen, looked after her mother as well as she could, earning Cecily's praise; the girl had been inclined to mope since the family's return from Castle de Lusignan. Cecily visited daily, leaving the children in Maud's care, and was worried at her mother's lack of improvement as the bitter January and February days went by. With the coming of March and the lengthening of the hours of daylight, Kat Wynstede seemed to be a little better, and then one afternoon she had a visitor who lifted her spirits more than any medicine: Lady Hélène de Lusignan came to see her, accompanied by her daughter Alys, and bringing two bottles of good French wine. Katrine was sitting in the parlour, and Hélène told her not to rise, but sat down with Alys on a bench seat.

'If your husband Sir Aelfric were yet alive, Katrine, my husband the Count would have come to consult with him,' the lady began, crossing herself at the mention of Sir Aelfric. 'However, in the present circumstances he has sent me to give you some notice of a plan he hopes will be agreeable to you.'

Kat was intrigued, and nodded towards Ethelreda who sat on a stone ledge beneath the window. 'You had better leave us, dear, while Lady Hélène and I talk privately.'

'No, please don't send the girl – the young lady away, said the Countess, smiling. 'What I have to say will affect her, too, and I hope she will . . . er . . . be happy to hear it.'

This was interesting indeed, and Katrine's thin face became animated as she pointed Ethelreda back to the window seat.

'Please feel free to continue, Hélène – your Ladyship,' she said eagerly.

'My son Charles will be his father's heir to the Castle and the title which would have passed to Piers,' she said, crossing herself again. 'At twenty-five he is a sensible man, conscious of his obligation to his family and to the estate. He says he has had his fill of warfare, and the wholesale slaughter of the best men in the kingdom.' Her voice shook a little, and she paused for just long enough for Kat and Ethelreda to exchange incredulous looks, having caught her Ladyship's direction, and hardly daring to draw breath. Kat put a finger to her lips to bid her daughter to keep silence until formally addressed.

'Charles has been spared, thanks be to God,' the Countess went on, 'and he has told his father that he has no wish to travel far to seek a wife. In fact he has requested that we give our consent for his betrothal to . . . to a young lady of his choice, which, er, happens to be Mistress Ethelreda Wynstede.' She stopped speaking when she saw that both Lady Wynstede and her younger daughter were weeping – for joy, as it turned out.

'Oh, Hélène!' Katrine said shakily. 'We are honoured by this request, and gladly accept – with what happiness—' She was unable to continue, and was overcome by a fit of coughing, with no kerchief at hand to wipe her eyes on.

Ethelreda was almost beside herself. She and Charles had sought each other's company during the Wynstedes' sojourn at the Castle, and she had not shared her family's relief at leaving it. She had been looking out for a message from him, but none had arrived – and now *this!* A formal request for her hand from Charles's mother! It seemed too wonderful to be true, and words deserted her.

This was the tearful scene that greeted Cecily's astonished eyes when she arrived on her daily visit to her mother, and she went straight to her mother's side.

'What's this, what's this?' she demanded, forgetting the respectful bow due to the Countess. 'Mother, are you not well? Ethelreda, fetch Mother a cup of hot cordial.' She glanced from one to the other, and when the Countess briefly explained her errand, Cecily too felt tears pricking her eyes, but quickly blinked them away. Ethelreda was but fourteen, and her mother would need to consult the Count and draw up a contract of betrothal.

'We are indeed honoured at the proposal,' she said courteously, 'though of course it's a surprise – a happy surprise.' When Ethelreda returned with the cordial, Cecily held it to her mother's lips. It was good news, of course: Ethelreda was early spoken for, and the parents' choice happily accorded with the young couple's own wishes; the arrangement would please everybody, she thought, unlike her own two experiences of matrimony. Marriage into the de Lusignan family would ensure financial security for the Wynstedes – so perhaps she need not have been so easily persuaded to marry Jack Blagge. Yet even as these thoughts flashed through her mind, she accused herself of envy, and was determined to rejoice at her sister's good fortune and her mother's pride in this match. Lady Hélène and Alys were smiling, somewhat taken aback by the emotional response to their message. Cecily could imagine what Jack Blagge would say if he could witness such open, unashamed gratitude to the de Lusignans. He had recently been laid low with a severe head-cold and high fever, and had to engage a clerk to keep the books in order, something that Edgar had always done regularly and efficiently; too late, thought Cecily, the father had come to appreciate his son's steady reliability. Jack expected her to fuss over him and make him possets of warm milk and honey; the first flush of pleasure in his second marriage had dimmed over, and Cecily had to bear patiently with his fretfulness; and she privately thought the less said at Blagge House about the coming matrimonial link between the Castle de Lusignan and Ebbasterne Hall, the better.

She thought of Friar Valerian, and a feeling of emptiness swept over her. Dan Widget had told her that the friar had left England, and Abbot Damian, because of his knowledge of her and the service she had given when the Abbey had been struck down by the plague, had gently answered her enquiry after Mass one Sunday, that Friar Valerian had been received as a brother into the Benedictine Abbey at Bernay in Normandy.

So far away – and not only by distance but also by his detachment from all worldly hopes, wishes and disappointments, in a life of contemplation. Just as she had prayed for strength to follow the path of duty by marrying Jack Blagge, *he* had deliberately left England, left Hyam St Ebba, and had left her, Cecily, for ever. They would never meet again on earth.

On hearing the Abbot's words, her face had showed such desolation that he, who had heard the Friar's confession before he left the Abbey, spoke kindly to her.

'You must direct your life towards maintaining your marriage, Mistress Blagge, and to bring up your children to be followers of Christ. Pray for them and turn to Mary, the Virgin Mother of Christ and of us all, and imitate her example.'

The Black Death continued to ravage England; having reaped the southern counties, it now struck at London and the east midlands with devastating results. Terrible stories were told of villages completely deserted and bodies piled into mass graves without a priest to absolve them from their sins and give the Last Rites. Some monasteries had been decimated as at Bury St Edmunds and St Ebba's, although the town of Hyam St Ebba had been but lightly touched by comparison with many rural areas where scythes and sickles rusted in scenes of ruin and neglect, where sheep and cattle wandered unattended in unharvested fields, and cows were swollen and lowing for want of being milked. In London it was said that men and women dropped dead in the street, felled by the hand of Death.

Yet life still had to go on for the living, and the seasons came and went as they had always done. The strong winds of March gave way to April's sunshine and showers, and Hyam St Ebba was once again bedecked with daffodils.

Lady Wynstede looked out of her window one bright morning, and remembered another such day when she and Aelfric had gone out riding with the children, he with Wulfstan sitting up in front of him, and she with Ethelreda. Was that only seven years ago? It seemed like another world. Yet that same pretty Ethelreda would one day be the Countess de Lusignan, and Kat glowed at the thought. Looking out at the demesne, she thought of her son, Sir Oswald, soon to be married to Mistress Janet Blagge who would become Lady Wynstede, the chatelaine of the Hall. Kat smiled to herself, and then thought of her daughter Cecily, Mistress Blagge twice over, the mother of two beautiful children and no doubt there would be more, sired by Edgar Blagge's father.

Kat Wynstede gave a long sigh, and the smile faded; she swayed, and fell to the floor. Cecily, on her daily visit, entered the room and rushed to her mother's side, calling for help. A maidservant came running in, and together they carried her to the bed and laid her upon it. Kat opened her eyes and looked straight at Cecily.

'Forgive me, Cecily,' she whispered. 'Please forgive me.'

Those were the last words she ever spoke.

Following the death of their mother, Cecily and Oswald decided that his marriage to Janet should take place that same year, instead of waiting the two years the betrothal contract had decreed. Other girls had married and become mothers at sixteen, though Oswald privately assured Jack Blagge that he did not intend to get Janet with child for another two years; Jack had laughed in frank disbelief, but was pleased to see his daughter married, and his own influence at Ebbasterne Hall thereby confirmed. He had not yet been told of the other marriage in the offing.

The June wedding of Sir Oswald Wynstede to Mistress Janet Blagge was a quiet family affair, coming so soon after the death of Lady Wynstede. The ceremony took place in the Lady Chapel of the Abbey, followed by a feast, not at the Hall but at Blagge House, which seemed more fitting in the circumstances. Jack Blagge's elder son came from Ebbchester with his family, but his elder daughter and her lawyer husband would not travel for fear of the plague. The de Lusignans had not been invited, but Abbot Damian who conducted the ceremony was there, and young Mistress Blagge introduced him to her husband, children, sister-in-law Maud Keepence and her pretty younger sister Ethelreda; she looked round for Wulfstan, but he was nowhere to be seen.

Edda and Mab prepared a good table, for Jack Blagge had spared no expense; there were game pies and quails' eggs, suckling piglet and eels in aspic, and good French wine flowed. It was a sunny day, so guests wandered in and out of the garden, and it was in a shady corner behind a hedge that Cecily found eleven-year-old Wulfstan, sitting on a tree stump. From the house came the sound of laughter and merrymaking, but the boy turned his head away from his sister.

'What's the matter, little Brother?' she asked quietly.

'Don't chase after me, Cecily, I'm not in the mood for feasting and silly talk,' he mumbled, shrugging off her hand. Her heart ached for him.

'Dear Wulfstan, I know you're sad, but it really is better this way, you know. Janet will help Oswald to look after the Hall, and you'll like her when you know her better.'

'But she'll be Lady Wynstede, and I can only think of *one*, and that's our mother!' he burst out, wiping his sleeve across his eyes and not looking at her. 'If *you* could come and be Lady Wynstede, I wouldn't mind so much!' he continued with all the tactless honesty of a grieving boy. 'But you *can't*, because you've married that horrible old man!'

'Now, Wulfstan, you mustn't say that.'

'But it's *true*, Cecily. I didn't mind you being married to Edgar, but not that old man!'

There was a long silence while she held his unresponsive shoulder. 'I'm so sorry, Wulfstan, but one day you'll understand that we can't always have what we want, and have to do what's best for others,' she said seriously. 'I do understand how you feel at present, but it will get better as time goes on. And you'll be able to come and see me at Blagge House – you can ride over on that new horse that Ned helped you choose – what's his name? Troilus?'

'I wish I could join the army.'

'Oh, Wulfstan! Look, I'll have to go back in the house now, but please try to be happy and helpful when Janet speaks to you.' She could think of nothing more to say that would comfort him, so she leaned forward and kissed him on the cheek.

Seated at a supper of leftovers that evening with Maud, Cecily's thoughts were with her young brother. Jack Blagge had retired early in a cheerfully bibulous haze, and Cecily had no wish to join him in the matrimonial bed until he was sound asleep.

'We're going to miss Janet,' remarked Maud. 'It seems strange not to have her at table with us – and for young Ethelreda and Wulfstan, to see her there with Oswald, in your mother's place. Wulfstan was so miserable at the wedding, and I don't think a crumb of the feast passed his lips.'

'He'll just have to get used to the new routine, poor lad,' replied Cecily, shaking her head. She was reproaching herself for not realizing how much the boy had suffered on the death of his mother; Ethelreda had been equally bereaved, of course, but her mourning had been lessened by her betrothal to Sir Charles, an event that had gladdened her mother's last days. How the Black Death had changed their lives, thought Cecily, claiming Edgar Blagge and August Keepence, precipitating her into marriage with her father-in-law, and bringing about the marriage of Oswald and Janet.

And Valerian was so far away. Daily she prayed for him and his life at the Abbey of Bernay. There were times when she felt that he no longer thought of her, but there were also moments that came to her like a faint whisper on the still evening air, gone before she could realize it, but which gave her hope that he still prayed to the blessed St Cecilia for her. But so far away.

In August Cecily realized that she was with child again, which delighted Jack Blagge, but in early October she miscarried the unformed child, much to Jack's angry disappointment.

'That's because of all this traipsin' back and forth to Ebbasterne Hall! Your mother isn't there any more, and your place is here with your husband and children. Ye leave them too much with Maud. My God, ye look as white as a ghost. Lucky we've got nursemaids enough in this house, with Maud and – that maid What's-her-name to fuss and feed ye soup. Ye'd better keep to your couch until ye get some colour – damned nuisance.'

Cecily had no choice but to keep to her bed. She had lost a great deal of blood, followed by a profuse and unpleasant-smelling discharge which continued as the days went by, and she became seriously ill. Maud nursed her devotedly, and she alone heard Cecily's feverish mutterings of the name *Valerian*. When she sent for an apothecary to see her, he looked grave and shook his head, saying that Cecily's condition was like childbed fever after the miscarriage, and that she might not recover.

'Where are my children? What will happen to my poor little Kitty and Aelfric?' Cecily asked fretfully, and Maud promised that the children would always be safe with her in the event of a tragedy that she could not name, but which they both knew might happen.

'I love Kitty and Aelfric John as if they were my very own,' she said, and Cecily blessed her sister-in-law and became calmer in her mind; from about the middle of November, she slowly began to improve. Jack Blagge forbade visitors, but towards the end of the month Lady Janet Wynstede called, and was taken aback by Cecily's appearance.

'We must get you built up again before the winter,' she said. 'I'll send over a cask of barley wine.'

'I feel so useless lying here,' sighed Cecily. 'Tell me, how's my brother – my young brother Wulfstan? Is he settling down to the changes?'

Janet pursed her mouth. 'Not really. He's so surly when he can't have his own way. Of course he's only a boy as yet, but I'm quite tired of hearing his plans to join the army.'

'What does Oswald do to help him?' asked Cecily. 'Do they go out riding together?'

'The only time Wulfstan brightens up is when Ethelreda takes him on a visit to Sir Charles. I think he should go to live at the Castle and be trained as a squire.'

'Oh, but he's so *young!*' said Cecily.

'He may be young, but he has no parents to keep him in check,' said Janet, frowning. 'Oswald isn't strict enough with him.' She was clearly irritated by her young brother-in-law.

'When I get over this illness I'll speak with the Countess and see if an arrangement can be made,' promised Cecily. 'Leave it to me, I'll get my young brother to the Castle, for I don't like to think of him being unhappy.'

It was not until December that Cecily was strong enough to ride to Ebbasterne Hall where she had invited the Countess to meet her. When the subject of Wulfstan was raised, Hélène was open to the suggestion that the boy might spend a few years as a groom to Sir Charles and whatever other duties he could perform.

'Of course, I shall have to speak to the Count,' she said, 'and he'll want to see the boy and find out his inclinations. May we send for Wulfstan now, and ask him what he thinks?'

Wulfstan's unmistakable joy at hearing of the proposal was almost comical, but Cecily warned him that everything now depended on the impression he would make when presented to the Count by his elder brother.

Which was how Wulfstan Wynstede came to be groom, manservant and messenger boy to Sir Charles de Lusignan for a three-month trial period. Cecily was greatly relieved, and grateful to Hélène for her influence with the Count.

As expected, Jack Blagge was furious.

'Why wasn't I told? Why do you keep everything from me, wife? Why am I always the last to know?' he thundered.

'Because I knew you'd be angry, Jack, so I kept it from you as long as possible,' said Cecily wearily. 'And now if you'll permit me, husband, I will go to rest in bed.'

Since the miscarriage she had slept apart from her husband because of her continuing weakness and the tiredness that accompanied the lightest household task. She was more than ever thankful for Maud's kindness and smooth running of the household.

1350

Brother Valerian had lived the life of a monk in the Abbey at Bernay for fourteen months. It had been built some three hundred years ago, and compared to the Abbeys of Hyam St Ebba and Netley, was enormous. It stood on low ground where two rivers met, and on winter mornings was often shrouded in thick fog. The coughing of the brothers disturbed the chanting in the Abbey and the silence of the refectory, but troubled Valerian far less than his spiritual problems.

For to this solid, Romanesque house of God had he fled to escape temptation, to avoid living near to Mistress Blagge, married to that detestable man who had ravished her. He thought of her subjected to Blagge, bearing him children, losing the fresh beauty of her youth, and the agony of it did not decrease, but rather grew worse.

And he found he could *not* escape. He could *not* forget. Whether he knelt before the altar, or recited the eight Offices of the Church or walked alone in the stone cloisters open to the air – or whether he worked with the lay brothers attending to the poor who came to the Abbey for help, food, refuge in sickness – whatever he did, he could never forget her.

The Abbot, whose iron-grey hair and stern features reflected his nature, showed Valerian little sympathy at Confession, when they spoke in Latin.

'You are old enough to overcome this unlawful attachment to a woman, and a married woman at that, Brother Valerian. Her choice of a husband is no concern of yours, and you must pray to be delivered from this unholy fancy.'

'I pray daily, morning, noon and night, Father Abbot.'

'Then pray harder. Do not allow these idle dreams to possess you, for they are of the devil, and will ruin your vocation as a man of God. Discipline yourself in prayer and fasting, wear a hair shirt under your habit for a week – and serve God in acts of Christian charity such as we dispense here to the poor.'

'I can but try, Father Abbot.'

'Do not try in your own feeble strength, but give this burden over to God, my son, and listen to the voice of conscience. Now bow your head and make your act of contrition, and by the power of God vested in me, I will absolve you from your sins of the heart.'

Sins of the heart! Was it a sin to remember Cecily? To live again through those confused nights and days working beside her among the sick and dying in the Abbey of Hyam St Ebba? And now to imagine her under the domination of Jack Blagge . . .

In the silence of his cell, Valerian groaned aloud. *'Cecilia!'*

Wulfstan's three-month trial period was over, and Cecily had slowly regained strength; she felt years older, but tried to count her blessings. Oswald and Janet were happily settled, and there was no news as yet of an expected event, so Oswald must be keeping his promise. Ethelreda, who was coming up to fifteen, made no secret of the fact that she longed to be married and live at the Castle.

'That will happen all in good time, little sister, don't be impatient, but enjoy these years of youth and freedom,' Cecily counselled her earnestly. 'Once you're married you'll belong to your husband and his family.' She little knew how Ethelreda pitied her, married to that old man and having a miscarriage. Life would be so different with Charles!

When the message came from Count de Lusignan requesting that Sir Oswald Wynstede and Mistress Cecily Blagge attend on him to talk of Wulfstan's future, they rode up to the Castle on a spring day, the signs of the awakening earth all around them.

'I think I know what he'll say, Oswald. He'll compliment Wulfstan on his progress!'

Oswald fervently hoped she was right, because if his young brother was sent back to Ebbasterne Hall, Janet would have something to say. She had never got on with the boy.

They need not have worried; on arrival they were shown into a sunny parlour where the Count put them at their ease, and offered them wine. Having exchanged greetings and praised the fine weather, the Count said that Wulfstan had been an exemplary pupil, but that he needed more experience than Sir Charles could give him.

'The trouble is that since the loss of my elder son, Piers, my younger son has declared an aversion to warfare, inflicting death and injury on people who have no blame,' said the Count rather awkwardly, lowering his voice when he mentioned Piers. 'Young Wulfstan has become an excellent horseman and groom, but Charles refuses to teach him swordsmanship or the use of the longbow.'

Oswald and Cecily nodded, wondering where this was leading: Wulfstan was but twelve years old.

'My suggestion is that he be sent to an acquaintance of mine who lives at Lisieux in Normandy,' the Count continued. 'Monseigneur Duclair is highly accomplished, and would be happy to take on a promising pupil such as Wulfstan, on my recommendation.'

He smiled and waited for a response.

'We are in your hands, Sir Robert,' said Oswald, much relieved. 'We'll follow whatever advice you give us.'

'I agree with Oswald,' said Cecily, 'though he is young to travel so far.'

'Excellent! Let us send for the boy and see what he says.'

Wulfstan strode into the room. Taller and more confident than he'd been three months ago, he bowed to Sir Robert, kissed his sister and shook hands with his brother.

'Have you heard the plan?' he asked eagerly. 'Next month I'm off to a military training school at Lisieux, and they'll make a soldier of me!'

They exchanged smiles, for there was clearly no need for a discussion here.

'And can Dan Widget escort me, Cecily? He's the best of all the grooms we've got.'

'Yes, certainly,' she replied, remembering the journey to Waldham and Dan's fearless protection of her. 'In fact,' she added slowly, 'I could wish I was coming, too.'

The Count, pleased that his suggestion had been so readily taken up, advised them about the journey. 'It would be best to sail from Portchester to Honfleur, not as busy as Le Havre on the opposite bank of the Seine. Then the road runs due south, some thirty miles to Lisieux. It's dominated by the Cathédrale St Pierre, and the Hotel Duclair is not far from it.'

Wulfstan turned bright eyes on his sister. 'And you'll really let me go, Cecily?'

There was a slight pause, and then Cecily replied. 'Yes, Wulfstan, Oswald and I will let you go. But I will come to Normandy with you and Dan, and see this Hotel Duclair.'

'Splendid!' said the Count. 'The Monseigneur will gladly accept you as an overnight guest – and he has an English wife, so no trouble with the language!'

Cecily now had two pieces of unwelcome news to break to her husband: the first was that her brother Wulfstan was being sent for military training in Lisieux on the Count's recommendation, and the second, likely to infuriate Blagge even more she guessed, was that she intended to accompany him on this journey. She guessed rightly.

'Christ's blood! Will ye spend the rest o' your life in the shadow o' them Normans! First ye send your brother, scarcely out o' the nursery, to live in that bloody castle, and now ye say ye're going with him into God knows what foreign mischief and you hardly up from a sickbed. Well, ye're not going – I absolutely forbid it!'

Cecily regarded him with a clear, cool gaze, and he saw that she was not afraid of him.

'And I say that I *am* going, Jack. I stand in place of a mother to that boy, and I need to know where he is and what sort of people are with him. There's no more to be said.'

'*What*? There bloody well *is*, a lot more! You leave your own children to go fussing over a brother – it's not right or natural. What sort of a mother are you? What sort of a wife?'

Cecily closed her eyes, refusing to argue about a matter on which she had made up her mind. He saw that she would not submit to him, and glared at her. 'I made a mistake in marrying you,' he muttered, and turned away. Those few bitter words reached her heart in a way that his anger had not, for it was true. She had married him as a family duty, and that too had been a mistake, one that could not be undone.

She turned her thoughts to Wulfstan. When would he journey to France with herself and Dan Widget? Next month, which was May? There seemed to be no good reason for delay, and the sooner he could begin his training under this Monseigneur Duclair, the better.

But then came a bolt from the blue that upset her plans. Ethelreda came to Blagge House to see her elder sister and make a confession: that at not quite fifteen years old, she had twice missed her monthly flux, and was with child. She had not felt able to confide in her brother and sister-in-law, and had turned to Cecily.

'I thought you'd know best what to do, Cecily. Are you happy for me? It means that Charles and I will have our wedding *soon,* and I'll go to live at the Castle!'

Cecily closed her eyes and shook her head slightly, trying to take in this latest news.

'Oh, Ethelreda, what do you expect me to say? There are so many people who will have to be told before we can start planning a wedding. Does Sir Charles know?'

'Er . . . no, I haven't told him yet,' answered the girl, her excitement turning to dismay at the expression on her sister's face.

'Then he must be told at once, and he will have to tell his parents, and I hope they will reprimand him severely, a man of his age. He hasn't shown the self-discipline that Oswald has shown with *his* young wife. They will have to be told, and Maud and my husband, and *he'll* have plenty to say, and I shall have to listen. And as for your brother Wulfstan – his journey to France will have to be postponed, poor boy – he won't thank you.'

'Oh, Cecily, I didn't know it would cause such a lot of bother!'

'No, you and Charles have been thoroughly selfish, not giving a thought to all the inconvenience to others,' said Cecily with

some bitterness. 'Peasants and humble folk may shrug off something
like this, but not a family like the de Lusignans or even the
Wynstedes. You'd better go and tell Charles today, and then Oswald
and Janet, while I face the Blagges.'

Maud was sympathetic, agreeing that Sir Charles shouldered
the greater fault, being some ten years older than Ethelreda.

'But no great harm has been done, Cecily. Betrothals are often
looked upon almost as marriages these days,' she said, 'and I'm
sure the Countess will see that Charles carries out his duty towards
Ethelreda who has no mother to guide her.'

If Maud was comforting, Blagge was predictably scornful.

'Hah! No sooner do ye get your feet under the table at the
Castle – big match, big wedding, big feast – than it turn's out
the bride's with child! Hah, what a joke! Them Normans'll say
that the bridegroom's been cuckolded already, and they'll want
him to wait and see who the child looks like before he puts his
head in the noose, ha, ha, hah!'

Cecily did not reply, for she too feared the de Lusignans might
not take such a charitable view as Maud, and if the hasty wedding
did not take place, the dishonour to her family would be doubled.
What would then happen to Ethelreda and her child? She sighed
and felt unutterably weary. Was there to be no end to trouble?

But young Sir Charles de Lusignan surprised her and everybody.
He accepted his parents' censure and rode to Hyam St Ebba to
admit his fault to Oswald and Cecily, saying how deeply he
regretted the situation – and what endeared him more to Cecily,
he swore on the Bible that he loved Ethelreda above all women,
and wanted only to make her his wife.

The Countess too was kind, and having lost her eldest son,
looked forward to a grandson who would be named Piers. She
recommended a simpler wedding than at first planned, with a
short ceremony at the Abbey, followed by a modest wedding
breakfast at Ebbasterne Hall rather than at the Castle, to which
Charles would take his pretty young bride at the start of their
married life.

It was a beautiful May morning for the wedding, and the sun
shone down on a happy family gathering, with smiles on every
face except for Jack Blagge who had been invited but couldn't

face such joyful celebrations among people he despised, so stayed away.

'There now, dear Cecily, hasn't everything turned out well after all?' smiled Maud. 'I think your sister Ethelreda will have an indulgent husband!'

'Yes, he has acted honourably, and I'm grateful,' replied Cecily. 'And now with this wedding happily accomplished, I'm ready to take my brother Wulfstan to France!'

'Yes, dear Sister, and I shall care for Kitty and little Aelfric John, for I love them as my own.'

Cecily's only answer was to hold Maud in a close embrace.

Nineteen

1350

It was time. Cecily had accompanied her young brother to Lisieux, and handed him over to Monseigneur and Madame Duclair. At the last moment he had flung his arms around her and gruffly tried to thank her, perilously close to tears. Cecily had to hide her own emotion as she returned his embrace, told him that she would pray for him, and with a sisterly smile left him to begin his new life.

Dan Widget was waiting for her, standing at the crossroads where the road back to Honfleur joined the one that led further south-east, towards Bernay. She looked at Dan, and neither of them spoke, but simply turned their horses' heads southwards. Little was said as they rode through the green and golden orchards, the rich pasture where cows grazed, the fields and farmhouses. Cecily noticed the half-smile on the face of her escort, and silently blessed him for understanding.

When the Abbey of Bernay came in sight, Cecily reined in her horse and Dan did likewise. It was time for her to speak honestly to him, though her voice trembled.

'Dan, I only ask to see him for a minute or two, and speak to him if it's allowed, just to be near him, just for this day. If . . . if he's told that I'm so near, and if he's allowed to have a visitor, could he – would he speak to me – just for one last time?'

'I hear ye, Mistress Cecily. I'll go over and see the gatekeeper or whoever it is, and ask what the rules are. Wait here for me.'

So Dan rode to the Abbey's entrance while she waited, seated astride her horse. When he returned after a very few minutes, his face gravely sympathetic, she felt afraid.

'Good God, Dan, what news? Is he there? Is he . . . alive?'

'Dear Mistress Cecily, I have to disappoint ye. He's not there, not now.'

'Then where—?'

'The monk on the gate didn't want to tell me anything – but I gather that Friar Valerian, also known as Brother Ralph, left the Abbey a week or two back, to return to the world, so this man said, and they don't ever mention his name now.'

'Oh, Dan! I shouldn't have dragged you all this way for nothing!' she wailed, bursting into tears. 'I'm a fool, I know, but I was so hoping—'

'Never say so, Mistress Cecily. Ye've done what ye came to do for your brother, and nobody'll ever know about today.'

'How good you are, Dan,' she said, wiping her eyes. 'I'm grateful.'

They rode back in silence along the way that they had come, arriving at Honfleur as evening shadows were falling. There were a few boats getting ready to sail on the night tide, and when Dan had returned the hired horses, he looked for one of the flat-bottomed, high-sided cogs with their single square sails, carrying cargo and passengers back and forth across the Narrow Sea. The owner and captain of the *Dido*, carrying casks of French wine, said he could take a few more passengers, and Dan helped Cecily down from the landing-stage and settled her on a narrow bench seat that circled most of the deck; then went to look for some refreshment to take on board.

Left with her sorrowful thoughts, Cecily pulled her cloak around her and closed her eyes in utter weariness of body and mind. Two men were playing cards and three younger men constantly teased each other and roared with laughter. The weatherbeaten captain and his cheery mate boasted openly of the two illicit extra casks they had hauled down to the hold, to be smuggled into a small, quiet bay after leaving their legitimate cargo at Southampton.

Cecily supposed she should pray for forgiveness for trying to contrive a secret meeting with Valerian; the chance to travel to Normandy with Wulfstan had seemed like a God-given opportunity, but today's bitter disappointment was surely her punishment for foolishly chasing after a forbidden dream.

Searching among the quayside booths frequented by the boat crews, Dan found a woman selling newly baked bread from a wood-fired oven. The small loaves had thick crusts and a soft, smoky texture inside, and there were earthenware pots containing meat juices and fat dripped beneath a roasting spit. The smell was appetizing, and Dan joined an eager circle of French-speaking mariners.

And that was when he heard his name called: 'Dan! *Dan Widget!*'

He spun round to see a man in a grey habit and black cloak. For a few moments he stared back before recognizing Friar Valerian, an older, thinner Friar Valerian with eyes shadowed by suffering. Almost bereft of speech, Dan could only gabble excitedly. 'We looked for ye today at Bernay, Friar, and now by God's grace ye're here – and she's waitin' for ye!'

The Friar's eyes widened in disbelief at what he was hearing. 'Do you speak of Cecily? Where is she, Dan? Here in Honfleur?'

'She's waiting on a cog called the *Dido*, to sail on the night tide—' Dan began, but the Friar seized his shoulder, his voice rough with urgency.

'Take me to her, Dan, I must see her – come, show me where she is,' he demanded, and the two of them literally ran along the quayside to the *Dido,* gently rocking at anchor. Valerian jumped down to the landing-stage, took one look around the deck – and there he saw her, drooping half asleep on the hard wooden bench.

'Don't upset her, Friar, she's been ill,' warned Dan, a little alarmed by Valerian's almost frantic behaviour, but the Friar turned to him and shook his head.

'I won't hurt her, Dan, but please stand back while I go to her.'

Dan watched him walk quietly across the deck, and sit down at her side. She woke from a light and uncomfortable doze.

'Dan,' she whispered, not raising her head. He leaned close to her and whispered her name. '*Cecilia.*'

She straightened up with a sharp indrawing of breath. 'What? Who's there? Dan?'

He laid his hand on hers, and incredulously she turned to face him. '*Valerian!*'

'Cecilia – oh, my Cecily, yes, it is I, Valerian.' And there indeed he was, alive and real and speaking to her! And his wide blue eyes were full of the love she remembered.

Her pale features lit up with pure joy, and her voice shook. 'We looked for you at Bernay, but you'd gone. Oh, Valerian! I never thought to see you again in this world.'

With a sound that was almost a sob, he put his arms around her and she nestled against him like a child, her face buried in the folds of his habit. He wrapped his cloak around them both, oblivious of their surroundings. 'Dan told me that you're to sail overnight for Southampton. And so will I, my Cecily, so will I, and wish myself nowhere else on earth.'

Dan stood aside, watching their reunion without envy, only thankful that he had been the means of bringing it about. He saw Valerian gently remove her arms from around his neck, and hold her at arm's length to look into her face.

'Cecily! Are you not well?'

'I was very ill after I miscarried my husband's child. They thought I was going to die, and little I cared, but my sister-in-law looked after me and I got better. My young brother Wulfstan – I've brought him to Lisieux to learn to be a knight in the King's army – and Dan took me on to Bernay – and oh, Valerian, you weren't there!'

'*No*, dearest Cecily, I left, because I too have pined for you and couldn't forget you. The Abbot advised me to pray and fast and wear a hair shirt.' He laughed softly. 'How gladly would I wear one *now*, for sheer thankfulness at finding you again! I left the Abbey and went back to being a mendicant friar in France – but no, it was too far away from you, so I decided to return to Hyam St Ebba where I can be near to you without causing harm to your family and now I believe it was God who called me, because today He led me to the same bakehouse as Dan Widget! Oh, my Cecily, I—' And for the first time he kissed her mouth, and she responded, her lips as sweet as honey.

'You'll know that I'm there in the Abbey, Cecily, if you ever need my help.'

Dan Widget on the opposite side of the deck saw Cecily encircled in the friar's arms, and could not wish it otherwise; he had been able to give them these last few hours together, for which he was wistfully thankful. The morning would come and then they would have to part again, but the hours of this night were theirs.

It was time to sail; the anchor was drawn up and the square sail billowed out; they left the harbour and were out on the open sea, making good speed.

'Calm as a millpond, and a following wind,' said the captain with satisfaction, adjusting the rudder to the direction they were taking. 'These casks are a bit heavier than the wool we brought out, eh? Good job we got that carpenter to check her bottom!'

The three young men guffawed, but Cecily and Valerian only had eyes and ears for each other. He held her head upon his shoulder, and she drifted into a light doze from which she surfaced at intervals, rejoicing to find herself still in his arms. She forgot the past, and would not think of the future; the only time was *now*, the only place was *here*, sailing beneath the stars with this man she loved. Valerian stayed awake, so as not to waste a moment of this enchanted night, clasping her body in the shelter of his cloak, kissing the top of her head.

'I've loved you from the first day I saw you, Cecily, at that tournament.'

She smiled, for she too at that moment had known he was the prince of her youthful dreams, her valiant knight, the love of her life.

He kissed her again and refused to think of having to let her go.

It was shortly before dawn when the *Dido* began to roll strangely in a relatively calm sea. The captain gave a shout and yelled for his mate, which woke the passengers, and Valerian tightened his arms around her. Uttering a curse, the captain ran down the short ladder to the hold.

'Christ, it's them casks – that bloody carpenter can't have sealed the caulk, 'cause it's comin' in – *pourin'* in, oh my God!'

An insufficiently sealed crack in the *Dido's* flat-bottomed hold had been unable to bear the weight of the extra casks, and had widened to a serious leak; the sea gushed in rapidly, filling the hold, while the weight of the wine casks pulled the boat down. The passengers were shouting, running hither and thither, demanding to know what was going on.

'Christ's bones, it's a torrent!' bawled the captain. 'For God's sake get a bucket and get 'em all balin' out!'

But the *Dido's* too-heavy cargo made any kind of baling out impossible, and she sank very quickly. Darkness and confusion reigned, and oaths gave way to cries of fear.

'Don't be afraid, my Cecily, we shall go together,' whispered

Valerian, seeing this calamity as the end of all their troubles on earth; but he also remembered that he was a man of God, and had responsibility for all of the doomed crew. He rose to his feet, drawing her up beside him and praying as loudly as he could above the yelling and cursing of men's voices.

'Into thy merciful hands, O Lord, we commend the souls of all on board! Help us in our extremity, receive us into the light of thy presence! Holy Mother of Christ, pray for us in our last hour!' He added under his breath, *Hail, bright Cecilia, intercede for us.*

There were cries of 'Amen, Amen!' and 'Lord, have mercy upon us!'

The water had risen up to the deck, and swirled around their feet, rapidly rising as the *Dido* was drawn downwards; in minutes their bodies were submerged, and heart to heart, with their arms clasped around each other, Valerian and Cecily sank down into the deep.

The sun was up and the morning was clear. There was very little wreckage of the *Dido* which had been pulled down to the seabed by her cargo, but Valerian felt strong arms around him, heaving him up on to a substantial fragment of the side of the boat, now being used as a makeshift raft. He lay face down on it while a hand slapped his back; he coughed and shuddered, vomiting salt water, gasping between retches. He had not breath to speak.

'That's right, Friar, fetch it up – that's better,' said a man's voice, and slowly, very slowly did Valerian understand that he was alive and floating on a roughly rectangular wooden part of the *Dido,* wrenched from her side as she went down.

Still coughing and retching, he was unable to speak, and his eyes implored Dan to answer him.

'Cecily's gone to her rest, good Friar,' came the gentle answer. 'She's finished with the troubles of her life. We're the only survivors, yeself and me, though I don't know where we are or whether we'll see land.'

Valerian groaned. *Where are you, my Cecily?* He thought he felt her clinging arms around him, and saw them falling limply from his shoulders and her body floating away, while he had risen to the surface. *Why have you left me here?*

Something bright and dazzling caught the corner of his eye,

and he looked up to see a brilliant white bird ascending into the blueness of the sky.

There goes her soul up to heaven. He watched it flying higher and higher, until it seemed that it flew straight into the risen sun, a light too strong for his human eyes to bear.

Dan was lowering his head and squinting. 'I think . . . I *think* that's a boat o' some sort, Friar, that little grey dot on the horizon, see?'

Valerian groaned and could not raise his head, but Dan could see it getting bigger and closer, taking shape as a sailing boat. He waved frantically, taking off his wet shirt and using it as a flag while he shouted at the top of his voice, 'Help! Help us, for the love of God!'

When it came within hailing distance, they were seen by the crew who threw down a rope ladder. Drenched to the skin and stiff in every joint, Dan climbed aboard, and then with the help of another man, he hauled Valerian up on to the deck of a fishing smack manned by an English crew.

'We've been spared to see Hyam St Ebba again, Friar,' said Dan solemnly, but Valerian lay sprawled on the deck, only slowly recovering his senses. *Would to God I had gone with thee, my Cecilia. Why have you left me alone?*

Dan was overwhelmed with thankfulness. Hyam St Ebba! Friar Valerian would return to the land of the living, and they would tell their news at Blagge House where Jack Blagge would curse and Mistress Maud would hide her grief from the children she adored and whose mother she would now become. Oswald and Ethelreda would mourn for their sister, and poor Mab the maidservant would shed tears of joy for his deliverance . . .

Life would go on.

Epilogue

Summer, 1361

Abbot Damian had noted the absence of the Infirmarian from the Chapel, and found that the Infirmary had been left in the care of a choir monk, Brother Bernard, dour but dependable. He had shrugged and told the Abbot that the friar had taken his horse and gone out to visit two sick children and a woman in Hyam St Ebba, and had put Bernard in charge until his return.

'He spends more time in people's houses than here, Father Abbot,' observed the monk with an aggrieved air. 'And there's always somebody or other coming up to see him – old men, young men, women and their children, all sorts of rabble, shouldn't be allowed in.'

'It's fortunate that he can depend on you to deputize for him, Brother,' smiled the Abbot soothingly. 'We must remember that he's a *friar*, accustomed to travelling miles from one place to another, from shire to shire, unlike the rest of us here. He's used to entering the homes of rich and poor alike, wherever there's sickness, including birthchambers. We are blessed in having such a man as Infirmarian, seeing that he can no longer travel as he did.'

Brother Bernard briefly rolled his eyes but could not argue with his superior, nor could he deny the friar's extraordinary gifts as a healer and physician; it was just that the man seemed to be a law unto himself, above the monks who spent their lives praying and toiling.

'Unless he's back by Vespers, I'll have to miss that too, Father Abbot,' he said flatly.

'I shall understand, Brother,' Abbot Damian assured him, and went to stroll in the nearby herb-garden, breathing in its fragrance on a hot summer afternoon. There was rosemary and lavender in abundance, dominated by a row of stately foxgloves with pink and purple trumpets, their soft, wrinkled, poisonous leaves used by the friar to strengthen the heart. Bees were busily at work on the blooms of the borage, taking nectar back to the three Abbey hives adjacent to the garden, and pollinating the plants in the process. The Abbot smiled; if the friar had not dedicated his life to God, he thought, he would surely have been a highly successful apothecary – and as if he had been summoned, the friar himself appeared, having ridden up from the front entrance.

'God save you, Friar Valerian, and who have you seen today?' asked the Abbot with pretended sternness. 'What kept you from the Offices of Sext and None?'

The Friar slipped down from his placid little mare, his leather bag strapped over his right shoulder. 'Good Father Abbot, I'll be in the Chapel for Compline, praying for all the sick I've seen today – and especially a poor woman who has a foul canker eating at her breast. There was nothing I could do but pray beside her bed and leave a posy of rosemary and lavender to sweeten the room.'

'And who came with you into her room, Friar?' asked the Abbot curiously.

'A maidservant only, Father, devoted to her mistress and willing to bear the stink from the lesion. What a fate for a good woman to endure – I pray that she be taken soon.'

The Abbot nodded in sympathy. 'And who else did you see?'

'The little twins at Ebbasterne Hall who have hacking, whooping coughs. I gave their Lady mother the usual advice – keep them warm, let them sleep and give them plenty of clean water to drink. I took them a bottle of pine and honey syrup, for they're young as yet to be given infusion of yarrow. They're well cared for, and that's their best hope.' He sighed. 'I called on Mistress Keepence and her charges – we met in the garden to avoid that man. Katrine's a sweet girl with a look of her mother, and already fourteen, so I suppose *he'll* be looking out for a husband for her. John Aelfric or Aelfric John's thirteen, and his grandfather's pride by all accounts.'

'You still don't enter Blagge House, then?'

'No, and never shall. I couldn't trust myself to face that man,' answered Valerian quickly. 'He holds the moneybags to enable Mistress Keepence to run the household and care for her – her children without extravagance – another good woman, if ever there was. Ah, there's the bell for Vespers. I must take over the Infirmary from good Brother Bernard.'

'Peace be with you, Friar,' said the Abbot, noticing again how years of living as a mendicant friar in all weathers had taken their toll of Valerian who looked older than his forty-five years. He was rake-thin, the auburn hair had faded to grey, and his face was deeply lined, with the scar still showing as a raised ridge down the right side. The Abbot knew that at times his heart fluttered and he treated himself with foxglove. Valerian might be considered a law unto himself, but Damian's memories of the black plague that had nearly wiped out the community of brothers some dozen years ago were such that he could never forget Valerian's devotion, equalled by that of the widowed Mistress Blagge and the excellent Master Widget, now bailiff to Sir Oswald at Ebbasterne Hall. It had been a time of death, and fear of death – but it had also been a time of shining courage, of spiritual awareness that drew them all together, the living and those who had died. Friar Valerian had blessed their last hours, and Mistress Blagge had eased their bodily discomforts, given them water to drink and bathed their faces. Abbot Damian sighed as he remembered what had happened afterwards, when Mistress Blagge had been coerced into marrying her father-in-law, and Valerian had wept bitterly in the Abbot's parlour before leaving the country and entering the monastery at Bernay where, Damian now knew, he had been unable to forget her. And then they had met again – only for him to lose her within hours in a shipwreck on the Narrow Sea.

Yes, thought the Abbot, I spoke the truth to Brother Bernard: we are indeed blessed in having such a man as Infirmarian.

The summer weather continued, and Valerian was much occupied with the Abbey beehives, securing the new mated queens when a swarm filled the air with their humming, and then settling them into a new colony. He was engaged on this work when a messenger rode up to the Abbey, and when one of the brothers came to summon him to attend in the Abbot's parlour he surmised he was being called to visit a home where there was sickness. He removed the veil and gloves which he wore when attending to the hives, and hurried to the parlour where the Abbot and the messenger stood. The look on Damian's face warned Valerian of trouble, and he almost dreaded what he would hear, before a word was spoken.

'Ah, Friar Valerian,' said the Abbot gravely. 'We have a message from Mistress Keepence of Blagge House. Her father Master Blagge has been ill for some time with a stone that causes him pain when he voids his bladder, and he has now taken to his bed. She says he is very distressed, and has asked for you to give him the Last Rites.'

Valerian's heart fluttered as he listened, and his throat was so dry that he could not speak. That detestable man who had so abused his daughter-in-law and added insult to injury by marrying her and getting her with a child that had miscarried and ruined her health – *no*, he would not so much as touch the man. There were holy brothers enough in this community, including the Abbot himself; it was a duty that could be done by any of them.

'Master Blagge has asked for *you,* Friar Valerian,' said the Abbot quietly, as if reading his thoughts, and glanced at the manservant who nodded and added, 'That's right, Father Abbot, he's in bad pain with the blockage, and wants only the Friar.'

Valerian took a deep breath. 'I cannot go to that man, Father Abbot,' he declared. 'It's impossible, I cannot forgive him. I can't do it.'

Abbot Damian spoke very kindly. 'If you cannot do this duty in your own strength, good Friar, then do it in the strength of Christ your Saviour who has forgiven your sins. Go back with this messenger, and take what is needful for Last Rites.'

Valerian stood still as he struggled inwardly. A voice seemed to come to him out of the air, speaking in his inward ear, and he answered as silently, *Blessed St Cecilia, intercede for me.*

He swallowed, moistened his lips, and replied to the Abbot. 'Very well, Father, I will go to him.'

Abbot Damian nodded and bowed as to a superior, making the sign of the Cross over him. 'Go in peace, my son, with God's blessing.'

Mistress Keepence herself answered the door to him, pale-faced and with tears on her cheeks.

'Thank you, good Friar,' she said. 'My father's been calling for you, over and over again, like a soul in torment. If you can bring him peace before he departs—'

'Lead me to him, Mistress Maud,' he said, and followed her up the stairs he remembered from years before, when he had arrived after little Kitty's birth. He was shown into the room where

Cecily had laid then, pale as death, but had lived. Now Jack Blagge lay as pale as she had been, his bald head glistening with sweat, his beard matted, his eyes red and sunken; a soul in torment indeed. At the sight of Valerian he tried to rear up, but sank back on his pillow. Valerian was repelled by the sight of him, but spoke quietly as to a stranger.

'Peace be with you, Master Blagge. I have come in obedience to your wishes.'

Blagge's voice was hoarse and rasping. 'I'm dying, Friar, but I want ye to give me your hand before I go, and tell me I'm forgiven.' He held out his right hand, and Valerian reluctantly took it in his.

'First tell me that you repent, Master Blagge.'

'I've been a selfish old brute. I've made my family fear me. I've been a blasphemer. I've worshipped money instead of God.' The words came out jerkily. 'Nobody loves me. I'm old and alone. I'm in pain. Have pity on me, Friar, give me the holy oil and . . . and bless me.' Keeping hold of the friar's hand, he looked up pleadingly.

Valerian had to say it. 'You have more to confess, Blagge.'

The old man's eyes filled with fear. 'There's nothing worse than what I've said.'

Valerian drew a deep breath and trying to stay calm, said merely, 'Cecily.'

'Cecily? Oh, yes, my daughter-in-law and then my wife, she never loved me but I did my best for her, she was never short of money, I tried, I really tried,' he gabbled, but stopped when he saw the hate on Valerian's face, who now spoke through clenched teeth.

'You ravished her, Blagge. You took her by force, you hurt and humiliated her, she whose name you're not fit to utter, don't you remember?' Valerian's voice rose almost to a shout, and his anger triggered a response in Jack Blagge, who still gripped his hand.

'Yes, all right, *yes*, I *did* ravish her on the day my son died, I wasn't in my right mind, and wanted to punish her – God knows I've regretted it, and never more than now.' Blagge wept as he spoke, and threw Valerian's hand aside.

'You wanted to *punish* her? In God's name, why? What harm did that angel ever do to you?' Valerian's breathing was harsh, and his heart fluttered like a captive bird in his chest.

'Why, because she only wanted *you*,' said Blagge with a groan.

'She never loved me, nor my son Edgar, because she wanted *you*. I knew it right from the start, it was only *you* – you stole her from both of us, treacherous friar! I saved the Wynstedes from being thrown out o' the Hall, but you got all the thanks. And the child I got upon her miscarried and nearly killed her – and then she went and drowned in the Narrow Sea because she thought more o' that young brother than her husband. Oh, God knows how she hated me!'

There was silence in the room for a long minute. Both men were exhausted by their furious outbursts, and as Valerian looked upon the face of the man he had hated, he knew himself to be equally in need of forgiveness. He sat down on the wooden framed bed.

'Master Blagge, we are soon to stand before our Maker, from whom nothing can be hidden.' He paused, and took the man's hand again, looking straight into his eyes. 'Yes, I *did* have Mistress Cecily's heart, though I never possessed her body, she was never unfaithful to you; yet you could say that I stole her love from you and your son. Now *I* must confess and be forgiven, and then we shall make peace with one another, if we wish for God's mercy.'

Considering that Valerian had vowed never to forgive Blagge, or to enter his house again, the mutual pardoning of wrongs done in the past was surprisingly easy; both men had admitted their grievous faults, and so opened the gate to mercy. After receiving the holy oil on his forehead and mouth, Jack Blagge sunk into sleep while still holding the friar's hand, and after offering up prayers for both their souls, Valerian quietly got up and left the bedchamber, telling Mistress Maud that though her father might soon die, his soul was at peace with God.

That evening while awaiting the night Office of Compline, Friar Valerian sat on the wooden bench overlooking the herb-garden. His heart was fluttering, but without pain, and a pleasing drowsiness came over him. The air was cool after the heat of the day, and a light breeze wafted fragrances from the garden over his face; the murmurous humming from the beehives faded slowly into silence. He closed his eyes in thankfulness, at peace with God and man.

Hail, bright Cecilia . . .